Iced

A Matthew Paine Mystery

Matthew Paine Mystery Series

Pre Kill (prequel short story)

Dead Spots

Prefer Death

MIA

Christmas Punch

Iced

Relics (coming fall 2023)

Iced

A Matthew Paine Mystery

Lee Clark

**Cypress
River
Media
LLC**

Burlington

This book is a work of fiction. Names, characters, and incidents are the product of the author's imagination or are used fictitiously. Any resemblance to actual events or persons, living or deceased, is coincidental.

Copyright © 2023 by Leesa K.C. Payne.

All rights reserved. In accordance with the US Copyright Act of 1976, no portion of this book may be reproduced, stored in a retrieval system, or transmitted in any form by any means – electronic, mechanical, photocopy, recording, or any other – except for brief quotations in printed reviews, without the prior permission of the author. To use the material from the book (other than for review purposes), prior written permission must be obtained by contacting the author at Lee.Clark@cypressrivermedia.com.

Cypress River Media, LLC
Burlington, NC 27215
CypressRiverMedia.com

First Edition: May 2023

The publisher is not responsible for websites (or their content) that are not owned by the publisher.

Clark, Lee.
    Iced / Lee Clark. – First edition.
        Pages ; cm. – (A Matthew Paine mystery)
        ISBN 979-8-9864074-5-6 (hardcover) – ISBN 979-8-9864074-4-9 (paperback) – ISBN 979-8-9864074-3-2 (e-book) 1. Paine, Matthew (Fictitious character)

Dedication

Transparency. Sometimes that word is hard when what it really means is "vulnerability." I'm about to show both.

Iced is dedicated to Jesus, my Lord and savior. That might turn some people off but I hope it encourages others because without him, I wouldn't have been able to write the first book, much less the fifth!

Acknowledgments

I try diligently to be accurate and factual with events that could occur as well as in their proper context. To that end, I'd like to thank Dr. Jerri McLemore, medical examiner and forensic pathologist at Wake Forest Baptist Health in Winston-Salem, North Carolina, for her advice on the unlikelihood of the state of the first body in the story. Matthew's postulation was Dr. McLemore's that she so graciously provided for him to borrow.

My thanks also to Michelle Wise, gemologist at Wade's Jeweler's in Gibsonville, North Carolina for her overview of black diamonds, how they differ from white, how they're evaluated, facets, inscriptions, and confirmation of the GIA process.

Very special thanks to Rachael Payne, who designed the art on the cover from my description and to Austin Guthrie, whose artwork inspired the design. I can describe a scene with words but I'm useless with graphics and therefore so thankful for helpful friends and family who can translate descriptions into pictures!

As always, I'm thankful for the editors who provide their expertise to put these books through multiple levels of review and critique prior to making them available to readers. Special thanks to Genie Clark, my most trusted content editor, and Elizabeth McConnon of <u>Proof, Read, Repeat</u> for proofreading the first bit.

Contents

1 ~ Quick thaw		1
2 ~ A girl's best friend		9
3 ~ Bleakest winter		15
4 ~ A rose by any other name		25
5 ~ Invitation to snoop		33
6 ~ Quips and questions		41
7 ~ Crimson feathers		49
8 ~ Tearful		55
9 ~ Never a dull moment		65
10 ~ Everybody and nobody		73
11 ~ What was that?		79
12 ~ Going, going, and going		89
13 ~ Enter help		97
14 ~ Empathy and patience		105
15 ~ Trust test		117
16 ~ Blew by you		125
17 ~ Turnabout		135
18 ~ Long man standing		143
19 ~ Developments		153
20 ~ When inspiration strikes		159
21 ~ Next steps		167
22 ~ A few more things		175
23 ~ Got a line		183
24 ~ Solid things		189
25 ~ Crazy days		195
26 ~ Sightings		203
27 ~ Saddest story ever		211
28 ~ Restless for a reason		217

29 ~ Fully invested	225
30 ~ Which cat?	237
31 ~ On the offensive	249
32 ~ Black ice	257
33 ~ Wake up, Doc	265
34 ~ Connections	273
35 ~ Professional assessment	281
36 ~ That's a new one	295
37 ~ Stinging	303
38 ~ Stung	313
39 ~ Blinding blur	323
40 ~ Coming to terms	331
41 ~ Pulling threads	339
42 ~ Knot unraveling	353
43 ~ Golden bow	363
44 ~ Hope reigns	373
Epilogue ~ A week later	381

1 ~ Quick Thaw

"Hey, Doc," Matthew heard Danbury say as he clicked to answer the incoming call on his car system. "Where are you?"

"I just dropped Cici at the airport, and I'm headed home," Matthew replied dully.

"Are you still consulting?" asked Danbury. "Or was that last one because you were involved?"

Having resigned from his role as a medical consultant with the police department the previous summer, Matthew had recently been pulled back into that capacity. Helping with a murder investigation the month before was just temporary, or so he'd thought.

Sighing deeply, Matthew answered slowly, "I guess I'm still consulting. I'll need something to do over the next four months to keep my mind off Cici."

"Good to hear. I need you up here. We've got a body. Frozen in an outdoor pool. I'll drop you a pin."

Before Matthew could agree, question it, object, or even think about it, Danbury had disconnected in his usual abrupt manner. "Here we go again," said Matthew aloud as he saw the text come in and clicked to get the routing information. "Déjà vu."

Checking the rearview mirror, Matthew hit the gas and slid his Corvette over into the left lane of I-40. Passing a clump of cars, he slid back to the right to reverse direction at the next interchange.

"Frozen?" he muttered to himself. "How could a body be frozen in a pool now? It is January, but temperatures haven't gotten down to freezing for a while, even overnight." Winter temperatures in North Carolina were unpredictable, at best, but there had been nothing more than a light frost for well over a week.

Matthew shot up an exit ramp, over the bridge, and down the other side. Raleigh roads were lightly populated with traffic this Sunday evening. Relieved to have a task, somewhere he was needed, he thought it odd to be happy to have been summoned to a murder scene. If Danbury was already there and there was a body, it was a murder investigation. Matthew welcomed the respite from his own depressing thoughts – as strange as that seemed.

The thirty-year-old general practitioner in a family practice had worked alongside homicide detective Warren Danbury on several murder cases, ostensibly as a medical consultant. The tall broad Nordic-looking detective – who nobody but his girlfriend Penn called by his first name – had become a friend.

Matthew had shared far more than his medical knowledge in helping Danbury with murder investigations. Though he'd never admit it, Danbury had come to rely on Matthew's ability to notice details and connect seemingly unrelated dots of information.

Following the map on his phone from the pin that Danbury had dropped for him, Matthew saw that he was heading up to the edge of Durham. Purposefully trying to turn his attention from Cici as he passed back by the exits for the RDU airport, Matthew pondered what Danbury had just told him. It made no sense at all.

Tearing up the exit ramp, he headed north on Florida Boulevard and passed through the edge of Research Triangle Park. The area was populated mostly with industrial buildings and office complexes, the majority being technical and pharmaceutical companies. The businesses became smaller and the area more suburban as he approached a gas station on the right and turned onto Laurel Road behind it.

Passing a couple of driveways on his left, he noticed that the houses were set well back from the road, and only outdoor lighting was visible. He passed a church and followed the map to make a quick left turn onto Arbor Avenue and a quicker right onto Ashley Place.

It was obvious to Matthew that he had arrived when he saw the night sky illuminated brightly behind the house to his left. It looked like Times Square, with the dark night lit up like daylight.

Like the others he'd just passed on the way in, the house was set back off the road. Turning into the long driveway, Matthew made his way carefully down the uneven pavement that had buckled in places. The driveway, he soon saw, wound behind the house and he found the sources of light there.

The U-shaped two-story house wrapped around a back courtyard to his right, but the focus was on the other side of the driveway, on what looked to be a mother-in-law suite behind the house to his left. As he pulled in and located a spot that was somewhat out of the way to park his Corvette, Matthew texted a simple "Here" to Danbury.

As Matthew slid out of his car, Danbury rounded the corner of the smaller building on the left. Clad in a white jumpsuit, latex gloves, shoe covers, and a bouffant hair cap, Danbury had a mask dangling from a cord around his neck. He looked like a massive marshmallow. The man had little fat on him, but the suit hung from his huge shoulders in a big lump nearly to his knees.

"Hey, Doc. Thanks for coming."

Matthew felt his jaw drop. Danbury had just thanked him.

That was unusual, Matthew thought, though he didn't take much time to ponder the nuance. He attributed it to Danbury's girlfriend, Penn Lingle, and her efforts to morph Danbury into a less abrupt and abrasive version of himself. Matthew pulled a small medical bag from the Corvette as he greeted Danbury.

"What's going on? Why am I here?"

"We have a body. Just pulled from the pool. Stiff. But not from rigor mortis. Looks to have been frozen."

"In the pool? Nothing has frozen in over a week. How is that possible?"

"You tell me, Doc," said Danbury with a shrug. "That's why you're here."

"Where's your medical examiner?"

"Our ME is detained. Working another case. Across town. And her backup is away. On a family emergency."

"What do you need me to do?"

"An initial exam. The usual. Potential cause of death. That sort of thing. You don't have a rape kit, do you?"

"Ah, a female body," said Matthew, eyebrows raised in concentration as he ran his long, tapered fingers through his soft, wavy brown hair. "I don't. I carry medical supplies to treat injuries and stabilize patients," he added, indicating the medical bag he'd just retrieved. "But nothing like that. I'm not sure how much help I can be, but I can take a look. You know I'm not an ME. I'm not even trained as a coroner."

"Yeah, but you're a doctor. And a GP is the next best thing. You see it all. Treat it all. I hope you can tell me something. Here, suit up," Danbury instructed, handing over a bundled white jumpsuit, cap, and shoe covers that matched the set he was wearing.

Matthew refrained from making any of the sarcastic comments that were running rampant through his mind. He would have looked more dubiously at the jumpsuit had he not seen Danbury, who was a good inch taller than Matthew's six-foot-three, broad-shouldered frame, already clad in one.

"She's over here. Behind the pool house," said Danbury, motioning for Matthew to follow him and leading the way after he had donned the jumpsuit and annoying accessories.

The building was a pool house and not a mother-in-law suite, noted Matthew as he glanced around at several other buildings. One seemed to be an older but large detached garage, and the other was potentially a potting shed or storage for gardening tools of some sort.

A tent had been erected on the cement slab between the pool house and what looked to be a partially covered large Z-shaped pool. Portable industrial lighting shone down in and around what Matthew discovered was a tent without a top. Danbury held the flap of the makeshift tent back, and Matthew stepped through.

As he approached the body of the deceased woman, Matthew took a deep breath. Danbury pulled a recording device from somewhere and turned it on. Since his medical program, Matthew hadn't worked with the dead much, and he purposefully shifted into his detached healthcare professional mode. She was just like the cadavers he'd dissected and studied back in medical school, he told himself. Except that she wasn't, and he knew it. This woman hadn't volunteered herself for any such purpose, either pedagogical or research.

The prone figure was slender but voluptuous in all the right places. Her matted hair had been streaked blonde, though it showed several shades darker at the roots. The woman was lying on a tarp, slightly on her side, with her left knee pulled up. Her left arm was draped across her chest, but both her right arm and leg were flung wide. Her skin was exceedingly pale in death. *She must have been quite beautiful in life*, thought Matthew sadly.

Pulling latex gloves on, Matthew knelt carefully beside the prone figure and began to gingerly examine her. There were huge heat lamps above him, he presumed to thaw the body, and he could feel himself heating up under the layers of protective gear that he wore.

Two things immediately stood out. First, she was scantily clad in a bright-royal-blue negligee, with one stiletto heel still stubbornly clinging to her left foot. And her eyes, wide open and staring up at him with a look of surprise, were the same vibrant blue as the negligee. He wasn't sure how that could be possible.

Sharing his thoughts with Danbury for the recording and to be studied further by the ME during the autopsy, he noted, "Unless she was quickly frozen with her eyes closed and they popped open after she was dumped into the pool, her eyes shouldn't still be that vibrant royal-blue color. Even then, she couldn't have been in the pool long, or they'd have become much more opaque."

"Duly noted," said Danbury, and Matthew moved on.

"I don't see a gunshot wound, at least not on this side. And no bruising. I don't see blood pooling here, either, so she was likely on her back when she died," said Matthew. "There's no petechial hemorrhage in the eyes. I don't see any ligature marks on her neck. I don't think she was strangled, though this is odd," he said, pointing.

"What is it?" asked Danbury, leaning in.

"It looks like two small puncture wounds on the left side of her neck. They're too big to be needle marks, but they were made by something relatively narrow. They look like the vampire bites you see in movies. Obviously, that isn't it, so maybe something like an ice pick stabbed her twice here," he said, pointing and holding her hair back for Danbury to lean in.

Snapping some pictures of her neck, Danbury nodded his agreement.

"There don't appear to be any bloodstains on her clothing, what there is of it. At least not that I can see," said Matthew. "It could have been washed off in the pool if she was dumped straight in. I'm not sure how likely that is, given that she had to have been frozen first. I see no abrasions, and no bumps or knots that I can feel on the back of her head, but that doesn't mean she wasn't struck with something. I don't see any obvious needle marks to indicate that she was a drug user. There might be cuts or hematomas on her back that we won't know about until we can roll her over."

Matthew examined her hands and continued, "I see no signs of a struggle or physical altercation, no defensive wounds on her hands or arms. The pads of her fingertips look odd, though."

"Very. What do you make of that?"

"She wasn't maimed. The tissue wasn't sliced off."

"Her fingerprints were removed," replied Danbury.

"What?" asked Matthew, shining the potent penlight on her fingertips. "Was the tissue frozen off?"

"That would be my guess. That's why we can't ID her yet. Can you scrape under her fingernails? To be sure there was no struggle? We can send the sample to the lab. To test for trace evidence. Her swim won't have helped that."

"Yeah, we can do that," said Matthew.

"Can you get a DNA sample?"

"I can try. Get an evidence bag ready." After Danbury complied, Matthew added, handing Danbury the penlight, "And hold this."

Pulling a scalpel and a swab from his medical bag, Matthew gently pried the woman's mouth open, thankful that the heat lamps had begun to do their job. At least something had, he thought. She had thawed enough that he could open her mouth. He scraped and swabbed the inside of her cheek, handing the sample to Danbury to bag and tag it.

As Matthew shone the penlight down her throat, he said, "I don't see swelling in her mouth or throat. Wait. What is that?"

"What's what?" asked Danbury, leaning in.

Matthew reached into his medical bag and retrieved a long pair of forceps. "Can you angle the light over to this side of her mouth?" he asked Danbury, pointing.

"Sure, Doc."

Carefully, Matthew poked and prodded, wiggled and jiggled, until the object was freed from her back right molar. Finally able to retrieve the dark object that he'd seen catch the light, then reflect and redistribute pinpoints of it throughout the inside her mouth, he pulled it carefully out with the forceps.

"Where's that evidence bag?" Matthew asked Danbury as he held up the object in his forceps.

"Right here," said Danbury. "What is that?"

2 ~ A GIRL'S BEST FRIEND

As Matthew dropped the object into the evidence bag, Danbury held it up to the light.

"It looks like a black diamond," said Matthew.

"Yeah, to me too," said Danbury, turning the bag above his head to inspect it in the lights that were blazing down on them. "A diamond. In her tooth. It was stuck there?"

"It was solidly embedded. I wonder if it's real."

"No idea."

"Why would it be there?" asked Matthew. "Maybe she was trying to hide it."

"We'll send it to the lab. Hopefully, they can tell us more."

"I can think of better places to hide a black diamond if that was the goal," said Matthew, still pondering their discovery. "I wonder if she was killed for it. Maybe somebody was looking for it and didn't find it."

"Could be," said Danbury, nodding pensively.

"Unless it's a serial killer's calling card," said Matthew, only half jokingly. "Have there been any cases like this that you know of?"

"None that I know of. But we'll check. As usual."

"It'd be really annoying, though," added Matthew. "She couldn't have closed her mouth all the way. She couldn't have bitten down."

"Yeah, true," said Danbury with a shrug. "We can roll her over. If you're finished with this side."

Matthew agreed, and they gently and carefully rolled her to the left, the side where her limbs were tucked and not flung wide. After finding nothing more than the blood pooling that he'd expected to see on her back, they rolled her over again. Matthew scraped under her fingernails while Danbury held the evidence bag beneath her hands. Then he carefully took hair samples with follicles and bagged those, just to be thorough.

"Anything else we need to do here?" asked Matthew.

"Nothing I know of. Body temp wouldn't have helped. And you don't have a rape kit. I think you're done, Doc."

Matthew gathered his supplies, zipping the instruments he'd used into a plastic bag to sterilize later. Stepping out of the tent, he removed the latex gloves and pulled them fully inside out as Danbury reached for them. While Danbury disposed of the gloves, Matthew slathered his hands in sanitizer, wringing them carefully together until they dried. He was thankful to be able to pull off the mask and hair covering and step out of the jumpsuit.

It was ten forty-seven, Matthew noted as he checked his watch, and the evening had gotten noticeably cooler. Danbury handed the evidence bags off to a uniformed officer to deliver to the lab in north Raleigh for testing.

"How'd you find her?" asked Matthew as they walked toward his car. "Did she live here?"

"Apparently not. The owners are out of the country. So the pool guy says. He's here regularly. The guy contracted to service the pool. He found her. Doesn't recognize her. Says he's never seen her before."

"OK, so she doesn't live here," said Matthew, well familiar with Danbury's staccato speech patterns and abrupt, stoic manner. "Could she have been house-sitting, maybe, while the owners are away?"

"I guess it's possible. The pool guy was here Tuesday. He said nobody was here then. He wasn't due back yet. Not until the week after next. But he got an alert. On an app on his phone. It monitors the pool. Constantly. It showed that the filter was clogged. He thought it was an error. He'd just cleaned it Tuesday. And he knew it was covered. But he came back to check it anyway."

"Huh," said Matthew, eyebrow raised and foot tapping in concentration. "When was that?"

"About four thirty this afternoon. He rolled back the cover. And found the source of the clog. Her hair."

"Oh!" said Matthew. "The pool was covered, and she was under the cover of the pool?"

"Right. She didn't get there by herself. Not likely that she drowned. Unless she was frozen afterward. And then put back in the pool. She didn't do that herself. Either way."

"I don't think she drowned at all, here or elsewhere, before being frozen. But an autopsy will tell you for certain. That the body was frozen is odd. I guess the intent was to obscure the time of death. An assessment of rigor mortis isn't possible. Neither is an internal temperature. That might not have been helpful anyway, depending on how long she's been deceased."

"She probably wasn't meant to be found yet. We might not have detected that she'd been frozen. If the body had thawed. And begun to decompose."

"The pool is heated?"

"Yeah, the owners use it year-round. The pool guy keeps it ready for them."

"How long have they been gone?"

"Two weeks. They're due back in another two."

"That's according to the pool guy?"

"He and the next neighbors down. They don't have a sight line. Not from their house. The trees obscure the view. Nobody saw anything from that side. And there's construction on the other side. A new neighborhood is going in. On the other side of those trees," said Danbury, pointing beyond the house.

"This is a short road, isn't it?" asked Matthew, nodding to Ashley Place, the street in front of the house.

"It is. But it's well connected. There are at least five ways in."

"Really? It looks so isolated."

"Not at all." Danbury gestured to the roads around them and explained the myriad ways to come and go to either Highway 70 to the north, I-40 to the south, or back to the airport to the east. The new neighborhood going in beyond the house provided several more ways to enter and exit.

"Wow. This little road that looks almost rural is nowhere near as isolated as it seems, then."

"It's not at all isolated. Too many ways in. And out. Limited visibility into this property. Somebody had to know the owners were away. And would be for a while. If the motive was obscuring the time of death. For dumping her here. It was either planned. Or somebody got lucky."

"That makes sense. If the body wasn't found for another two weeks when the owners or the pool guy returned, it would have thawed and been heated by the pool. The time of death would have been impossible to determine."

"An exact time is probably impossible. If we can figure out who she is. When she was last seen. That'll narrow it down."

"I hope you get a quick match on the DNA, then," said Matthew as he replaced his medical bag in the trunk of his Corvette.

"We need a comparison sample. Something to compare it to."

"Yeah, true," agreed Matthew. "Aren't there any security cameras around the house? I'm sure you looked."

"There are. Or there were. On the house. And around the pool house. All disabled. Busted and dangling from the wiring. We're contacting the homeowners. To see if anything was recorded. Maybe we got a look. While they were being disabled."

"If the cameras and equipment were operational when the homeowners left, surely they were recording. Otherwise, what's the point? I mean, maybe they can log in remotely and look things over periodically, but that would just be spot-checking without it set to record. Can you get inside the house to look around more thoroughly?"

"The neighbors have a key. They provided the owners' cell numbers. We've tried to contact them. To get permission. Without a warrant. We'll keep trying. The inside looks undisturbed. What we can see of it. Through the windows. The pool house is what we want to see."

"As the potential murder scene?"

"Maybe. It doesn't look likely. It appears to be undisturbed. Like the house. But we won't overlook it."

"Sounds like you've got it all under control."

"As much as it can be. It's still early. Maybe we'll catch a break. At least identify her. And see where that leads."

"Are you going to transport her now?"

"Yeah, it's all been photographed. And we have the evidence you gathered. I don't think we can do much else here. At least not with the body. Thanks, Doc," said Danbury as Matthew slid into his car.

Trying to keep his jaw from dropping at having been thanked by Danbury again, he quickly replied, "Sure. Glad I could help, at least with an initial assessment. Keep me posted on what you find out? And let me know if I can help with anything else. As much as I hate it for the woman and her family, and as sick as this sounds, the diversion was good."

"Good to know," Danbury said with a chuckle. "I'll keep you posted."

Matthew fired up the Corvette and waved as he pulled away, heading down the bumpy driveway and back out the way he'd come in. His mind was consumed with thoughts of the woman he'd just examined, and he felt a sudden sadness wash over him.

He'd managed to stay detached to perform the examination. It was still difficult for him to shift into that mode, separating the anatomy from the person who had previously inhabited it. He was unused to seeing murdered bodies—until he'd gotten pulled into an investigation the spring before and then befriended Danbury. He was also unused to staying in that detached mode for very long.

Cici's flight would have already left, and she'd be over the Atlantic and well on her way back to London by now, he thought as he tried to distract himself.

Their relationship, his and Cici's, was complicated. They had met in college when Cici was a junior in her undergraduate prelaw program and Matthew was in his second year of medical school. After dating for over five years, they called it quits due to what seemed at the time to be disparately irreconcilable differences—namely, that Matthew wanted a family of his own and Cici had said she never wanted children. They were painfully apart for over a year.

Reconnecting the spring before when both were pulled, quite unintentionally, into a murder investigation after Cici was abducted, they decided that maybe their life goals weren't quite as polarized as they'd thought. After her ordeal, Cici declared that she needed a change of scenery. She accepted a role assisting clients—important ones—of her prestigious law firm for a year in London.

Since then, Matthew had seen subtle changes in Cici. She had begun to entertain the idea of children in the future just "not right now."

He knew he'd never loved another woman like he loved Cici. That much, he was certain of. As he thought of their past and longed for their future, Matthew realized he needed something cheerful to think about. Dividing his attention between two sad and depressing things wasn't helping in the shorter, darker days of winter, but he couldn't seem to divert his mind from those thoughts.

What must her life have been like? he wondered about the pretty young woman he'd just examined in death. *And what must her death have been like?* That thought caused a shiver to run down his spine as he turned off I-40 and onto the US-1 and US-64 exit, headed for his home just outside of Peak.

3 ~ Bleakest Winter

Monday morning dawned dark and dreary as Matthew trudged to the kitchen to pour himself a cup of coffee. He had set his coffee maker up the night before with a timer to grind and brew it fresh this morning. Rinsing and refilling the food and water bowls for Max, he placed them back under the desk in his kitchen. The large gray tabby cat dove in; he always seemed to be hungry. His sister, Monica, had foisted Max off on Matthew as a kitten after she learned that her husband was highly allergic. Max had been tiny with huge ears, which he'd then proceeded to grow into.

Max was Matthew's faithful furry companion, a compatible friend. Often, Matthew woke up in the mornings with Max curled around his head. His morning "hair by Max" was an ongoing joke with Cici and his family.

While Max happily munched on his breakfast, Matthew trundled back down the hallway, coffee in hand, to his bedroom. His morning routine of showering and shaving was well underway when Max joined him in the bathroom, jumping up onto the tiled ledge of the shower, and proceeded to bathe himself.

Pulling on a long-sleeved button-up shirt, warm sweater, and gray pants, Matthew declared himself ready for the day.

Matthew chose to drive his Honda Element the short distance to work because the weather forecast promised misty rain and chilly temperatures. After setting the alarm system and locking up, he slid into the Element, and it started easily. He was thankful that it continued to be the champion it had always been, even after having the back end wrecked the month before when a miscreant for hire had slammed into him and run him off the road.

Having just gotten it from the body shop that had repaired it the week before, he was happy to have it back in time for the worst of the winter months yet to come. He habitually chose to drive it instead of the Corvette when the weather was less than stellar.

His mind raced with the events of the previous evening as he left his condominium community, carefully chosen for its quiet location at the end of a dead-end street. Seeing no other cars on Chester Road as he drove the mile length of it, he cranked up his eclectic playlist and turned left onto Highway 20, heading for his office in Peak. He wondered what new discoveries Danbury had made after he'd left the night before.

Crossing the railroad tracks with the historic train depot that was being repurposed as office space by the town of Peak on his left, Matthew jigged right onto Winston Avenue, then quickly left again beside the cultural arts center. Peak Family Practice, which Matthew had joined after he finished his medical program and boards, was behind the arts center, a block off the main street in the historic downtown area.

Matthew parked the Element in his usual spot, grabbed his satchel and travel mug with what was left of his coffee, and slid out. He'd just entered through the back side door that was closest to his office, fumbling with his keys, when he felt his phone vibrate in his pocket. Letting himself into his office, he stashed his satchel, switched his leather bomber jacket for a lab coat, and picked up his tablet. Thinking he'd quickly check his phone before starting his morning round of patients, he paused in the doorway.

He had two new messages. The first, from Cici. She told him she'd arrived safely at her flat in London, planned to sleep for a couple of hours, and she would check in with him later. The second, from Danbury, was brief and to the point, as always.

"Might have an ID. Missing person report. Matches description. Peak Eats for lunch?"

That was fast, Matthew thought, as he checked his watch and then his tablet to see his schedule for the morning.

"Eleven-thirty?" he texted back. Peak Eats, a combination diner, café, and soda shop, was just down the main street in town, and it was a favorite meeting spot. It had begun its existence as an apothecary. At some point, a soda fountain and ice cream counter were added. More recently, the business had been transformed altogether into what some people in town called a diner and others called a café or soda shop. What remained through it all was the ever-popular soda fountain and ice cream counter.

"See you then," was Danbury's texted reply.

If they'd identified the woman whose body he'd examined the night before, thought Matthew, that would get them off to a good start on figuring it all out. At least he hoped that it would. Just when he thought he'd seen it all, a frozen body with a black diamond in a molar and vampire marks on her neck was dumped into a heated pool. That was the craziest thing he'd heard in a while.

As he stepped out into the hallway, closing the office door behind him, Gladys appeared from the stairwell, coddling a cup of coffee in her hands. Matthew marveled at how her coffee with cream always perfectly matched her lovely mocha complexion.

"Good morning, Dr. Paine," she said formally, looking around her to see if anyone was listening. His most trusted nurse, Gladys tended to treat him with all the respect due to him in front of staff and patients, but she was more like a mother hen who had added one more chick to her already-overflowing brood when nobody else was around.

"We've got the Steinmans next this morning," she said. "They're in with their granddaughter for a checkup and shots. Good of them to take care of her while her mama's away for her Army Reserve training." Gladys lowered her voice. It was now barely audible as she added, "But they are pieces of work! Both of them. It's always interesting when they bring that baby in."

"It'll be fine. Besides, you're the one who has to do the shots," Matthew teased her, grinning.

She shook her head at him, muttering, "Mmm, mmm, mmm, what are we gonna do with you?" as she waddled down the hallway toward the nurses' station. Short and stout, Gladys was the antithesis of tall, slender, broad-shouldered Matthew.

Knowing he needed coffee too, he headed for the stairwell and up to the break room on the second floor above his office. It was small, with a balcony that hung over the back side entrance to the building that Matthew usually used. In nicer weather, the café chairs and tables on the balcony provided additional seating.

This morning, Matthew had no time to linger. He quickly poured his coffee into one of the disposable cups. Adding cream, he was relieved that Gladys wasn't there to reprimand him for his generous use of sugar. He thought she'd have given up the effort by now. Surely, she knew that he wasn't going to change that habit.

After finishing his coffee, Matthew washed his hands and joined Gladys in the exam room. As he greeted the Steinmans, he was relieved to see that their infant granddaughter was only whimpering in her grandmother's arms. Gladys had obviously already administered the booster shots, and the tears were still fresh on the little girl's cheeks.

"How is Elizabeth doing?" asked Matthew, smiling down at the baby and beginning to gently examine her.

"She's six months old and still colicky every night," answered Mrs. Steinman.

Checking the chart that Gladys handed him, Matthew said, "Her weight, height, and fine motor skill development all look great. We can talk about introducing some solid foods now, and that might help with the colic. You'll get a list of foods that you can introduce with your paperwork when you check out today. The order to introduce them in will be listed, but do follow the instructions and try them one at a time and in the recommended order. If she seems to have any sort of allergic reaction to any of them, remove them from her diet and call our office."

Mrs. Steinman nodded in agreement but then said, "Except, I don't think it's just colic."

"Tell me about your concerns," said Matthew, gently rubbing the baby's chubby arm with his finger and smiling down at her. She had begun to hiccup rhythmically.

"I think she has an ear infection," she replied.

"Has she been pulling at her ear?" asked Matthew as he reached for an otoscope from a tray on the counter behind him and rolled the stool he had been perched on back for a closer look.

"Not that I've noticed," said Mr. Steinman.

"Ah, it is red," said Matthew as he cooed at the baby and checked both of her ears. "Particularly the right one. It does look infected. I can give you an antibiotic for it."

"Bah!" said the older man. "We don't use antibiotics!"

"No?" asked Matthew.

"No. The natural ways are best. You put oil on cotton balls in her ears for the ear infection. Chamomile tea with honey in a dropper for the colic. It worked for our daughter. Just ask Gwen," he motioned to his wife. "I'll take the baby and get her in the car seat while you check us out," he said to Mrs. Steinman as he scooped Elizabeth up and left the exam room.

Matthew could hear his retreating footsteps. His voice softly crooning to the baby grew fainter as Gwen Steinman gathered her purse and jacket. She leaned over and said conspiratorially, "Except I didn't do that with our daughter."

"Oh? What did you do?"

"Gave her Benadryl."

"An infant? You gave your daughter Benadryl as a baby?"

"Yep. Put her right to sleep. No more screaming baby."

"You know, you really shouldn't . . ." began Matthew.

"She'll be fine," Mrs. Steinman cut him off with a wave of her hand. Matthew stared after her as she sashayed out of the exam room to follow her husband out to the lobby.

"Didn't I tell you they're both some pieces of work?" asked Gladys, quietly chuckling and obviously working hard not to laugh aloud.

"You did," agreed Matthew.

*****

The rest of the morning was spent treating the usual seasonal winter ailments, including several infections that had developed from lingering colds and flu. Matthew was surprised to see that it was shortly after eleven when he finished up with his last morning patient. Letting himself back in his office, he swapped the lab coat for his jacket and put the tablet on his desk. Even in the worst weather, he usually opted to walk to Peak Eats. It was just a block forward on Winston Avenue and a couple of blocks down from Matthew's office.

When he arrived, he heard the bell jingle over the door, and he saw Danbury motion to him from the booth in the back corner where they habitually sat.

"Hey, Doc. I just got the pictures. Of the missing woman. I think it's a match. See what you think."

Matthew hung his jacket on the peg at the end of the booth and slid in across from Danbury. Taking the phone that Danbury held out to him, Matthew saw Danbury peering over it expectantly, awaiting his opinion. Matthew studied a close-up picture of the missing woman's face.

"I think it's her," he agreed. The pretty blonde woman seemed to sparkle in the picture. "Those bright-blue eyes are very distinctive, and they were still blue last night. That caught my attention because it shouldn't have been possible. On a body that had been frozen and then dumped in a pool, the corneas should have been cloudy and opaque. Like I said last night, if her eyes were closed when she was frozen and then popped open later, maybe it's possible. I'd love to know what your medical examiner makes of that. I'm thinking she hadn't been deceased or in the pool for very long."

"Not long. If this is her," said Danbury. "Reported missing four days ago. She was on a trip out of town. But didn't come back. If she ever left. She didn't come back to work. We're tracking her movements backward."

"Who reported her missing?" asked Matthew. "I'm guessing it wasn't her family if you know that it was her job that she didn't come back to."

"No, not her family. A coworker did. A hostess at a nightclub. She won't identify the body. Flatly refused. We're getting a warrant. To check the apartment. Of the missing woman. That'll tell us if it's her. We'll find DNA to compare. And maybe other evidence. Should have the warrant this afternoon."

"Did you get a warrant to search the house where the body was found?"

"Didn't have to. The owners gave permission. The neighbors gave us the key."

"And the pool house?"

"It's been searched. Both came up clean. No signs of forced entry. Or habitation. Or anything out of place. We fingerprinted both. The main house and the pool house. Just to be sure."

"Do you have the owners' fingerprints to compare and potentially rule out?"

"Not yet. They went to the US embassy. And provided them. The prints will be in the system soon. They're cooperating fully. They're pretty upset. That it happened at their house. We sent that close-up picture. Electronically. Of the missing woman. The one you just saw. The homeowners don't recognize her. She's no one they know."

"Yeah, I can see why they would be upset. It's almost like having your house firebombed, I bet. You feel violated."

"Probably so," said Danbury, stashing his phone and picking up a menu. Putting it back down again, he said, "The specials today include chili. And a beef stew. I might get one of each."

"The beef stew sounds good," said Matthew. "On a chilly day, it always is."

Mallory, the dimpled ex-cheerleader server, sidled up to their table, all smiles. The two tall handsome men were, at least on this visit, unencumbered by women. She seemed to be taking full advantage of that.

"Hi, guys, you know I'm Mallory, and I'll be your server today. I'll be happy to get you whatever your hearts desire," she said in a honied southern drawl. It sounded to Matthew to be a bit exaggerated as she turned to him and asked, "Can I get you something other than the water to drink?"

"That coffee looks good." Matthew pointed to Danbury's cup. "I'll have one too."

Knowing exactly what they wanted, they quickly gave her their food orders before settling in to discuss the events of the previous evening and the outcome so far.

"The ME started work this morning," said Danbury. "I don't have an update yet."

"I will be interested to know how that diamond was mounted in her tooth and how deep the puncture marks on her neck are."

"Yeah, me too," said Danbury, sipping his coffee.

They had gone over the details of the previous evening, everything they'd seen and could infer from that information, when their meals arrived. Matthew bowed his head for a quick, silent blessing and then dug in. The beef stew was some of the best he'd tasted, he thought, and he was enjoying the last of it when he heard Danbury's phone ding. Looking up, he realized that Danbury had once again already finished double the amount of food in half the time.

"We got the warrant. To search the victim's home," said Danbury, tapping his phone. "I'm going there next. Decent apartments. On the edge of town. Not the best area of Durham. Not the worst either."

"I hope you can identify her. I mean, on the one hand, I hope it isn't her. But she was somebody's friend, girlfriend, wife, daughter, or sister who was found last night, regardless."

"I know," said Danbury. "I hate telling the family. Or close friends. Of any victim."

"Me too," said Matthew, having just helped to do that the month before.

"Can you stop by later? After work? What time are you done today?"

Matthew pulled out his phone and tapped it to access a group calendar app that everyone in his office had just installed. With the addition of a physician's assistant and a resident the spring before, it had become more difficult to know who was in the office and when. Shuffling patients between physicians had also become more complex. The new calendar app had so far proven effective. Their young and energetic office manager, Trina, had researched and recommended the app.

"I should be done by five," he said. "Maybe a little before, if there aren't many walk-ins this afternoon."

"OK, text me when you're done. I'll drop you a pin. If I'm still there. Depends on what we find," Danbury added.

They paid their checks, declined refills of coffee to go, and stepped out of Peak Eats, which had grown exponentially more crowded and noisier since they arrived.

After a quick, "Later, Doc," from Danbury, they went in opposite directions. Pulling the collar of his bomber jacket up against the chill of a slight breeze, Matthew headed for his office.

*****

Following a full afternoon of patients who had scheduled appointments and several walk-ins with small children, Matthew was tired but felt a sense of accomplishment. He hoped his patients had all left better off than they had been when they'd arrived.

Cici had texted during the barrage of Matthew's early afternoon patients to say that she had gotten up from a few hours of sleep and checked in with the office but was exhausted after her travels and would FaceTime with Matthew in the morning. He'd been too busy at the time to be disappointed, but as he headed down the hallway toward his office, he felt a weight drop into his stomach.

Matthew had known that it would be hard to have her leave for London again after she was home for the holidays, particularly for four more months. The winter felt bleaker, somehow, with her gone. He was also a little concerned about her because she was normally a boundless ball of energy – even if she was of a tiny five-foot-nothing stature. When she'd left for London the first time the previous spring, she went to the office after she arrived and worked the full day with no sleep, except the naps she'd managed on the plane. That was classic Cici, Matthew thought.

As he unlocked his office door, he realized that it was already after five thirty, and he'd done no patient charting at all that afternoon. It had been far too hectic to manage any. He still had that ahead of him this evening, he knew. He also saw what he could only conclude was a jubilant text from Danbury. That conclusion was based on Danbury's actual use of punctuation. The message simply said, "It's her! Text for address."

Matthew responded, "Just finished up. You at her apartment?"

As he was packing his satchel with his computer and tablet, Matthew heard the ding of his cell phone and looked to see Danbury's response, "No. Meet you there." That was followed by an address in Durham.

"Leaving now," Matthew texted back as he donned his coat and locked his office door. He climbed into his Element, clipped his cell phone into the holder on the dash, plugged in the charging cord, tapped to open a map for the address Danbury had texted, and set off.

Traffic was heavy through Raleigh and into Durham at this time of the evening on a weeknight, as Matthew had expected it to be. It was already mostly dark, and there was a slight drizzle falling, which made it more arduous. Still, he thought that he'd made decent time when he pulled into a parking spot in front of an older four-story brick apartment building.

"Her apartment has been processed. I wanted you to have a look," said Danbury by way of greeting as he approached Matthew, who was just sliding out of his car. "You might notice something. You see details," Danbury added.

Joining Danbury on the sidewalk, Matthew followed him up a set of outdoor metal and cement steps to a landing. They turned and were climbing the final steps to the second floor when Danbury froze in his tracks. Handing the tablet he was holding behind him to Matthew, Danbury drew his weapon from the holster at his waist. Motioning for Matthew to stay behind him, Danbury moved over to the wall and edged along it up the remaining stairs.

4 ~ A Rose by Any Other Name

Matthew took the tablet from Danbury as they silently reached the top of the stairs on the second floor of the apartment building. Police tape dangled on either side of the door to the apartment they were approaching – which was ajar. Danbury nudged the door open with his foot and then quickly peeked around the door frame, jerking his head back out again. Identifying himself as a detective, Danbury stepped into the doorway, gun drawn.

"Don't shoot! I ain't done nothing! Don't shoot me!" Matthew heard a male voice yelling, and he peered in to see a wiry guy with his hands in the air jump backward and nearly trip over a glass coffee table.

"Who are you?" asked Danbury calmly, still aiming his gun at the chest of the lanky guy.

"Name's Preston Priestly," said the guy. He had mousy brown hair that looked like it had been styled to stick out at odd angles and huge eyes the color of pond scum.

"Do you have any identification, Mr. Priestly?"

"In these things?" asked Priestly, looking down at the tight faux-leather pants he wore. "Naw, my ID's out in my truck."

Moving over to him, Danbury lowered his gun, the Beretta M9 he always carried, and said, "Stand still," as he quickly patted the squirming guy down. "What are you doing here?"

"I have a key."

"Doesn't answer my question. You removed police tape. Why?"

"I came to get cat food."

"Cat food?" Danbury repeated dubiously.

"I've been takin' care of Misty's cat for her. But I ran out of food."

"How do you know Ms. Blue?" asked Danbury.

"We work together."

"Where?"

"At Silver Silhouette."

"The strip club? In downtown Durham?"

"It's an entertainment club," said the guy, sounding almost offended. "But yeah, it's in downtown Durham. Can I put my hands down now?"

"Nobody told you to keep them up," said Danbury as the guy dropped his hands to his side, looking annoyed. Danbury holstered his weapon. "But we need to talk. You've entered a crime scene. That's serious. Have a seat."

Danbury reached his hand out as he perched on the edge of an overstuffed chair, and Matthew handed him the tablet. "You're a stripper?" he asked as the guy sunk sulkily back into an adjacent sofa.

"Yeah, sometimes. But mostly I'm in the movies."

"Silver Silhouette makes movies?"

"Yeah."

"What sort?" asked Danbury, though Matthew figured he already knew the answer to that question.

"The sort you wouldn't want your kiddos to see," said Priestly, his brown-green eyes wide and his head nodding meaningfully. That was amusing because the guy didn't look much like a stripper or a porn star. He was medium height, maybe five-eleven, but shy of a medium build.

"Were you and Ms. Blue together? In any of the, ah, productions?" asked Danbury.

"Naaaaw. Not Misty. She mostly sang and danced at the club. She didn't do no movies."

"And stripped?"

"Yeah, she had real talent. She was goin' places. She was my friend, and that's all, I swear."

"You're saying 'was.' You're aware that she's deceased?"

"Yeah, it's all over the club. After you asked Cara to ID the body, she got real freaked out, and she was crying and carrying on. Everybody who was at the club this afternoon knows Misty died."

There seemed to be a lot Danbury had learned but hadn't yet had the chance to share. Cara must be the coworker who had reported the woman – whose name must be Misty Blue – missing from a strip club called Silver Silhouette. Danbury had said a coworker was asked to ID the body, but she'd vehemently refused. That, Matthew understood well enough. It was still difficult for him to see the bodies of people who had met with a violent end.

After Danbury tapped his tablet, he looked up and asked pointedly, "Why can't I find you, Mr. Priestly? You're nowhere in the system. I need to see some ID."

"Changing your name ain't a crime!" said the guy defensively.

"Maybe not," answered Danbury. "Unless you're concealing something. A record of past crimes?"

"Hey! I don't got none!"

"Maybe underaged girls? Dark-web porn with children?"

"Naw, man. I don't know nothin' about the girls. They bring 'em. I bang 'em. That's it."

Matthew tried to keep his face neutral, not wanting to ostracize the guy and interrupt the conversation, but he felt his face heat in anger. He stood, arms folded and foot tapping with the effort to stay calm, behind the chair that Danbury occupied. He was pushing down the fury that he felt rising like a tidal wave against this guy, flexing and unflexing his fist under his arm.

Having encountered the result of sex trafficking the summer before, Matthew had no patience with or tolerance for anyone involved in it, and he really wanted to punch the guy squarely in the face. He took a few deep breaths and tried to regain control.

The guy had admitted to not knowing or caring if there were underage and potentially sex-trafficked girls involved in the videos he was shooting. Maybe they weren't giving their consent to being violated, but this guy didn't care. Taking a few more quiet deep breaths, Matthew continued to try to calm himself.

"Who brings them?" asked Danbury calmly.

"My producer. You can ask her where she finds 'em. I got no clue. It's not like we sit around and sing 'Kumbaya.' We don't have no small-talk conversations or nothing. It's all business."

"I will ask her," said Danbury. "I need her name. And contact information."

"Charlene O'Connell," Priestly answered, and he reeled off her phone number as Danbury tapped the tablet he was holding.

"The owner of Silver Silhouette?" asked Danbury.

Priestly nodded.

"OK, let's have it," said Danbury. "Your legal name."

"I got nothing to hide," said the guy, squirming in his seat. "It's just that my birth name ain't right for a stage name, that's all."

"Names mean very little. Right, Doc?" Danbury asked with a smirk over his shoulder to Matthew.

"What's your name?" asked the guy, looking up at Matthew, clearly trying to dodge the question. Procrastination and diversion were just prolonging the inevitable. Danbury would not let the guy leave without thoroughly checking him out.

"My name is Matthew Paine," he answered and waited. The guy's blank expression told him that this was like a joke grenade. Matthew and Danbury had pulled the pin and tossed it, but it was taking some time to explode in the guy's mind.

After an embarrassingly long pause, the guy's face finally lit up with understanding and he said, "Doc? You mean like Dr. Pain?" and he guffawed.

Normally, when Matthew's name and occupation were combined, people at least tried to stifle the laugh. His standard response had become to tell the snickerer to give it their best shot. He'd heard them all before, all the jokes about his name and profession, and he could use some new material.

"It's not that funny," said Matthew instead, thinking that nobody had laughed that hard at his last name since probably middle school. And that was before he'd added the title to precede it.

"And I own it," added Matthew. "That's my name, and I'm not changing it, despite my profession. Your turn."

The guy squirmed uncomfortably in his seat. "Shamus," he finally mumbled. "Shamus Jones."

"Thank you, Mr. Jones," said Danbury, tapping the tablet. After a moment, he added, "I see two parking tickets. In the last six months. Both unpaid."

"Yeah, I ain't got around to that yet. But there ain't nothing else. I swear!"

"I don't see anything else. The picture looks like you. But let's be sure. I'm going to escort you to your truck. To get your ID. And I'll need your fingerprints. I don't see them on file."

"My fingerprints? What for?" asked the guy in alarm, jumping up from the sofa.

"To compare to any we found here. You said it yourself. You have a key. You've been here before. How recently?"

"Not lately," said the guy. "Misty brought Fluffykins to me."

"Fluffykins?" asked Matthew and Danbury in unison.

"That's the cat. I know, I know, no self-respecting man would have a cat, much less one named Fluffykins. But I can't just throw her out, now, can I? Misty loved her. Maybe Cara will take her. But I just need to get some more food for her right now."

Matthew raised an eyebrow in amusement but refrained from mentioning that he had a cat. As a self-respecting male, he just didn't feel the need. Danbury donned a pair of latex gloves.

"Stay right there," said Danbury. "I'll get the food. Then escort you out. Check your ID. Get your fingerprints. And get your contact information. Then you can be on your way. Where is it?"

"Why do you need to contact me?" asked the gangly guy, who had inched his way toward the door.

Matthew stepped between the guy and the door as Danbury answered, "You might have information we need. To find out what happened to Ms. Blue."

"Oh," said the guy. "It's in the kitchen cabinet left of the sink. It's in a blue plastic bin with a sparkly lid." The guy eyed Matthew and shifted uncomfortably while Danbury rummaged in the kitchen.

Returning with the bin of cat food, Danbury pulled a large clear-plastic evidence bag from his pocket and proceeded to carefully pour the bag of cat food into it. He watched closely until all the food had been transferred, sealed the bag, and handed it to the guy.

"What'd you do that for?" asked the guy.

"Stranger things have happened," answered Danbury. "Already on this case. I'm not taking chances."

"On what?"

"On transporting anything. In cat food."

"Oh," said the guy. "I never thought of that."

That was probably true. There were likely lots of things this guy hadn't ever thought of. Somehow, the head on his shoulders didn't strike Matthew as the primary one driving this guy's actions. Preston Priestly was anything but. Without a doubt, the guy was sleazy, but could he also be guilty of murder? Did his vulpine smile belie true cunning or merely triple-X-rated filth? Matthew wondered.

Unless it was all an act, Preston Priestly couldn't be the murderer. He wasn't capable of planning and carrying out what seemed to be an elaborate attempt at concealing the details of the murder. Danbury, Matthew thought, must have arrived at the same conclusion because he was allowing the guy to leave.

"Do you want me to look around?" Matthew asked.

"Have at it. It's why you're here," said Danbury. Handing Matthew a pair of latex gloves, he added, "You know the drill."

Matthew did indeed know the drill, though he wasn't looking forward to going through the belongings of a dead woman. Feeling a bit of dread, he snapped on the gloves and turned to explore the apartment while Danbury escorted Preston Priestly out into the damp, dark night.

5 ~ Invitation to Snoop

While Mathew appreciated Danbury's confidence in his ability to notice details, he wasn't sure what he could possibly find that the police team would have missed earlier in the day. He chose to have a look around anyway.

Much of the apartment was decorated in what he was coming to understand as the deceased woman's iconic color of blue. It was the color of the negligee she'd been found in, which matched the vibrant blue of her eyes. The apartment was plushily furnished, but it looked cheap in Matthew's untrained mind.

He pulled out his phone and snapped some pictures of the boudoir, which was clearly what her bedroom was intended to be, and sent them to Cici, asking her to confirm his thoughts on the room. Not that she'd see it immediately in the middle of the night in London, but if anybody would know expensive from cheap at a glance, it would be Cici.

Against the right wall was a dressing table with a little seat that had a blue faux-fur cushion. The bed looked to be queen size and had a bolster with pillows propped up at the head of the bed, three deep. They were in various shades of cream and blues, from pale to the now-familiar vibrant blue and all the way to a deep navy. A faux-fur throw rug beside the bed matched the seat on the dressing table.

In the far corner was a rounded chair. It was upholstered in a fabric that looked like abstract art, with various colors of blue splattered, splashed, and swirled around. Beside it was a little writing table in the same cream color as the dressing table. Above the bed hung a huge mirror in a blue and cream frame.

Matthew flipped the light switch on in a large closet and found an array of clothing hanging neatly by color palette and purpose. Most of it was blue, too, he noticed. Or at least most of a certain type of it was blue. Boas, slinky sequined dresses, stiletto heels, and the like were mostly shades of blue. In another section, he saw jeans, shirts, and sweaters in various colors hanging together. In another still, he saw what he'd consider more professional clothes that were better suited to an office setting—blouses, skirts, slacks, and blazers. At the far end of the closet, a full-length mirror leaned against the wall. Two identical tall, narrow, cream-colored chests of drawers stood like sentinels on either side of it.

There were shoes in abundance. Shoes were paired in pockets down hanging racks, on slotted rails that ran the length of both sides of the closet floor, and some looked like their owner had merely kicked them off in passing.

Matthew carefully took stock of the shoes. There wasn't a match to the one they'd found clinging to the victim's left foot. There were several similar pairs, but each one had its mate.

As he made his way into the bathroom, Matthew couldn't help but feel like he was snooping. Of course, he had permission to be there, he chided himself. He'd been asked to assess. There was still something creepy about being alone in the personal space of the recently deceased, he decided.

The medicine cabinet was of particular interest to him, so he pulled bottles from it and read the labels. The woman apparently had trouble falling asleep, he noted, as he put the bottle of trazodone pills back. That prescription was current. She had experienced some issues with depression in the past. She might have, once or twice, had cold symptoms that she'd treated. Probably an upset stomach and a headache or two. Those medications were in over-the-counter boxed pop-out foil pouches and pill bottles.

There was nothing out of the ordinary, he concluded, returning the medications to the cabinet and moving on. As he poked through the drawers and shelves beneath the sink and then through a slim linen closet in the bathroom, he found all of the usual necessities. Tissues, toilet paper, towels, soaps, lotions, gels, hair accessories, and makeup. Those, he found in vast quantities. But what he didn't find surprised him.

Venturing back into the bedroom, he went through all the drawers there. There were lots more makeup palettes and hair products scattered about. In her bedside table drawer, he found a nearly empty box of condoms and a couple of other items that made his face heat. Snooping into someone else's personal life was becoming increasingly uncomfortable.

Looking under the bed, Matthew found bins that he slid out to examine. They mostly contained sweaters. One had an assortment of photo albums and smaller boxes of notes and cards. She saved things from friends and family, Matthew guessed. There were no envelopes to identify the senders, and there was still no matching shoe.

Just as he was concluding that there were things missing, Danbury returned. "Hey, Doc. Finding anything?"

"It's what I'm not finding that makes me curious. Did you ever find her other shoe?"

"No. It isn't here. It wasn't in the pool. We didn't find it in daylight. Nowhere on the property. It wasn't where the body was found."

"Do you have the report back from the ME yet?"

"I have a partial report. She doesn't like to provide that. But I insisted. Why?"

"I guess you'll get the usual things like the last meal that she ate, but will the ME look for things missing? Like, would she notice if the victim had an appendectomy? Or maybe a hysterectomy?"

"She'd note the scars. From an appendectomy. And missing organs, in general. Maybe she'd notice a hysterectomy. From the rape kit. I'm not sure. Why?"

"If she doesn't report on that, would you ask her? I don't know if it matters, but the one thing that I'm not finding is all of the, ah . . ." Matthew left the sentence dangling. "You know, the feminine products. Women usually have lots of them in every bathroom. And I'm wondering why she didn't. Why wouldn't she have those female supplies? Maybe because she didn't need them for some reason. It would be odd for a woman so young to have had a hysterectomy, but it's one possible answer and that might be helpful to know, somehow."

"Interesting," said Danbury. "I'll ask."

"I found condoms in the bedside table. That could be to prevent the spread of disease. At least, that's my guess," added Matthew. "I found a few, uh, interesting personal items in her bedside table too. Probably nothing you could fingerprint, though."

Danbury chuckled, nodding his understanding, obviously having seen the same items. "OK. Anything else?"

"Not really," said Matthew. "There's a current prescription for a sleep aid and an older one that's usually for depression or anxiety in the medicine cabinet. Otherwise, it's just the usual assortment of over-the-counter medications for colds, scrapes and cuts, and upset stomach."

"Good to know."

"I guess you checked for hiding places? If she had excessive amounts of money or drugs or anything she'd want to hide?"

"Yeah, the usual places. In the toilet tank. No floorboards to get under. No carpet pulled up."

"You checked the kitchen?"

"Yeah, did you?"

"Not yet. I came back here first. I was looking for the mate to the shoe she had on. That's why I wondered if it had been found."

"No. She must have lost it somewhere else. There was something odd. With the shoe that was still on."

"What was that?"

"It was glued. Onto her foot."

"Glued? Not just stuck when she was frozen?"

"That's what our medical examiner said. She was hesitant. With that information. She called it spirit gum. I didn't know what that was. Until I looked it up. It's used in the theater."

"Huh, if she worked in a strip club, would she glue anything on?"

"Pasties, maybe?"

"I guess that makes sense. Did your ME find glue on her right foot too?"

"Good question. I didn't ask."

"Maybe they were both glued on, and the right one came off. Or maybe there was a reason to glue only the left one on. Have you talked to her coworkers yet?"

"Just the one. This afternoon. There were a few people around. It picks up about eight. Thought maybe we'd get something to eat. And then go talk to them."

"We? You want me to go to the strip club?" Matthew asked, eyebrow raised.

"Hey, I need an alibi. If I tell Penn I was at a strip club."

At that, Matthew just laughed.

"Seriously, Doc. I might need your opinion. Medically."

Matthew couldn't imagine how that would ever be the case, but he shrugged and agreed. "I haven't looked at the kitchen. There wasn't anything in the sitting area?"

"No. They tossed it pretty good. Nothing under cushions. Or in table drawers. That room was clean. No pictures. No knick-knacks."

"Huh, meaning nothing personal."

"Right."

Matthew checked the hall coat closet on the way to the kitchen. Predictably, it held coats. A top shelf had boxes of odds and ends, things collected over the years, but nothing to identify the collector and therefore nothing of interest. The coat pockets held lipsticks and lotions and one odd ticket stub with nothing but a number on it. "I guess you saw this?" he asked Danbury.

"Yeah, nothing identifying the location. Where it came from. Could be a ticket for a coat check. Or for a prize drawing. No way to know."

After a perusal of the kitchen turned up nothing of further interest, they discussed where to have dinner, locked up with a key that Danbury had procured from the building management, and headed out.

They'd decided on a Mexican restaurant not far from the address of the strip club.

*****

Over dinner, they discussed what they hoped to learn from Misty Blue's coworkers and what Danbury's team had learned about the woman herself so far.

"Misty Blue isn't her real name," said Danbury. "Not the one she was born with. It can't be. Unlike Priestly, she changed it. Legally. We're having trouble finding her birth name. Misty Blue showed up about six years ago. Who she was before that"—he shrugged—"it's an enigma. At least so far. We've got our team working on it."

"Huh," said Matthew. "So there's no way to know if she was running away from something or someone or just running to something else."

"Not yet," said Danbury. "We don't know where she came from. Not originally. She was in Ohio. And then North Carolina. Under the Misty Blue name."

"She could have come *back* to North Carolina," said Matthew. "And not just to North Carolina. Did you check the cards and photo albums in the bin under her bed?"

"We did. Took pictures of some. Looking at the backgrounds in the pictures. Other people. Things like that. So far, nothing. The cards had no envelopes. I guess you saw that. No addresses."

"Yeah, I did notice that. Some of the pictures that I saw looked like her at younger ages, but I didn't see labels on those either. Maybe she didn't want anybody to know where she came from. Maybe she was running from something—or somebody. An abusive ex-husband or ex-boyfriend, maybe?"

"Both possible. Could be anything. We'll keep digging."

"If that's it, then maybe they found her. But why kill her, freeze her, and dump her in a pool? And then there's the diamond in her tooth. Do you know if it's real?"

"It looks to be. We'll have a jeweler examine it in the morning. There's something called a GIA report. It can confirm a diamond's value. Whether it was laboratory-grown. And its origin if it wasn't. It can give a geographic location. But it has to be sent off. To do that analysis. At a special lab."

"I didn't know you could do that," said Matthew, who intended to do some research on diamonds himself. "I mean, I knew you could tell a fake from a real one well enough. But the origin, that's interesting."

"I didn't know it either. Until the jeweler explained it."

He needed a crash course on diamonds, Matthew thought, because he was contemplating having one for Cici when she returned home from her final four months in London. There were still a few kinks to work out in their relationship, but they'd come a long way in the past eight months.

He'd watched Cici become more like the young woman he'd met all those years ago in college. Cici had always been intense, but she had also been compassionate and fun-loving. Those characteristics had started to wane after she graduated from law school and went to work at the prestigious law firm in downtown Raleigh. Matthew was elated to see that part of her personality reemerging lately.

"There are some well-known diamond mines," said Danbury, interrupting Matthew's thoughts. "One in Russia. It's the biggest. And one in Botswana. It's the most valuable. I guess in terms of diamonds. What gets mined from it. Then there's Canada."

Matthew nodded as he was finishing his steak burritos and looked over to see that Danbury had long since finished off double the quantity that Matthew had ordered. How did the guy eat so much so quickly? Matthew figured he would never understand. Having been a marine played a big role in how Danbury did everything. Sleeping when he could—anywhere at any time—and eating mass quantities at lightning speed had probably both been important abilities from the Corp that had carried over.

They paid their bills and stepped back out into the chilly, dark evening. Glancing up at the night sky, Matthew saw a large moon, not yet full, glowing brightly through the haze around it.

Pausing, they briefly discussed their approach to the staff at the club. As usual, Matthew would play the "good cop" to Danbury's brusque, abrupt manner if he thought it would garner information from any of the deceased woman's former coworkers. He'd previously objected to this role in favor of "not a cop," but he had signed up to work with Danbury again. So, good cop it would be.

This wasn't technically a medical role, but he would watch those being questioned closely and draw his usual conclusions about them to share with Danbury later. He had learned to read people well, both their verbal and non-verbal responses. It was part of what made him successful at assessing the conditions and needs of his patients.

Matthew had mixed feelings about going to the strip club. He'd only ever been in one once, when he was in his undergraduate program and a friend who was getting married had a stag party. He'd been the designated driver that evening, and his main source of entertainment had been watching his drunken friends do ridiculous things that they'd never consider doing otherwise.

Drawing a deep breath of the cool night air, he climbed into the Element and started it up. A strip club wasn't a place Matthew would choose to hang out on a chilly January night, or any other night of the year, for that matter. He wasn't looking forward to the adventure.

6 ~ Quips and Questions

As they entered the Silver Silhouette, Danbury flashed his badge because the club wasn't open for business yet. A young woman admitted them and went in search of the owners. Apparently, this was not the woman who had reported Misty missing. She showed no recognition of Danbury.

The main room, in which they stood, was well lit, but a haze seemed to hover over it. Matthew took in the glass, wood, and steel tables and counters. High stools lined a long oval-shaped bar area to the right. Glancing up, he saw a high ceiling with wooden rafters and exposed ventilation ducts.

A guy was on a catwalk above the room, moving what looked like lighting canisters around on long bars. Matthew was surprised by this because he had assumed that would be an automated process these days. The guy paid no attention to the two men standing below and continued carefully down the catwalk, as if he had done it hundreds of times and could do it in his sleep.

A door to the right beyond the bar and beside the main stage area opened, and a woman stepped purposefully through it. If he had to guess, Matthew would place her in her early fifties. The cigarette that dangled from her lips might mean that she was younger than she looked, though. She was an attractive woman. When she spoke, it was in a hoarse and gravelly voice.

"How can I help you gentlemen?" she asked as she approached.

"Are you Charlene O'Connell?" asked Danbury. Flipping his badge open when she nodded, he introduced himself. "Homicide detective Warren Danbury. And medical consultant Matthew Paine," he added, indicating Matthew and replacing his badge. She nodded in greeting through a plume of smoke.

"You're the proprietor here?" asked Danbury.

"I'm the owner," she responded, taking a final puff of her dwindling cigarette and blowing it toward the ceiling in a practiced manner. She stubbed it out in an ashtray she'd retrieved from behind the bar. By North Carolina law, most places that served food and drink were smoke-free, Matthew thought. But maybe if you owned the place, you could smoke as you pleased when it wasn't open for business.

"Half owner," corrected a balding older man who had waddled out behind her. If Matthew were asked to describe the man in one word, he knew what it would be. *Round.* The guy's face was flushed and resembled a ripe tomato. His body was similarly shaped.

"I'm the other half," the guy added, sticking his hand out for Danbury and Matthew to shake. "Phillip O'Connell."

Rolling her eyes, Charlene O'Connell answered, "In name only. I run the place. How can I help you?" she asked again.

"We need to talk to you. And your staff. About one of your performers. Misty Blue."

"I don't know how much I can tell you. She kept to herself," said Charlene, perching on a stool in front of the bar and lighting up another cigarette. Through a cloud of smoke, she added, "Shame to hear that she died."

"A shame because you care that she was killed or because you hate to lose your star performer?" asked Phillip pointedly, perching on a stool just out of her reach.

"Well, both, of course!" she retorted, her tone sounding annoyed.

"Your relationship," began Danbury. "Husband and wife?"

"Nooooo!" exclaimed Charlene, dragging the word out to multiple syllables for emphasis.

As Phillip was simultaneously saying, "It's complicated."

"I'd have opened a can of whoop-ass on him years ago if I'd been married to him," said Charlene.

That, thought Matthew, was an expression he hadn't heard before.

"If I had married her, I'd just have gotten out of prison for doing twenty-five to life! 'Cause I'd have killed her years ago!" added Phillip vehemently, and then he paused. These seemed to be very practiced jabs at each other, and the man was clearly waiting for a response.

Matthew stifled a laugh, not because he would normally have found the comment funny. Instead, because it was something he wouldn't ever have said in front of a homicide detective, particularly one actively conducting a murder investigation. Glancing over at Danbury, he noted that the big detective was not amused. At least not outwardly. His face remained impassively unreadable, even to Matthew, who thought he knew the guy about as well as anybody except for his girlfriend, Penn.

Instead of acknowledging the quip, Danbury tapped the tablet he'd brought in and started firing questions. "When was the last time you saw Misty Blue?"

Charlene screwed her face up before responding. "Nearly a week ago now."

"When, exactly?"

"It was New Year's Eve. She wanted the night off, but she's our star performer. Or, she was," Charlene corrected herself.

"What did you tell her?"

"I told her absolutely not. It's in her contract that she performs for the holidays and special events. I told her to take a few days afterward if she wanted time off, but we needed her New Year's Eve more than any other night of the year."

"She performed?"

"Yeah, she did."

"What did that entail?"

"She sang and danced and stripped down to nearly nothing, of course. She was the one performer who got to keep a little more than her stiletto heels on. And only because she was talented and drew crowds. Her voice was the draw. It had a honied but rough quality, all at the same time. She had top billing. She was usually the last to perform in each set."

"What time was that? Her last performance?"

"It was after midnight," chimed in Phillip. "We have the last bar call at two a.m."

"That's standard." Charlene rolled her eyes at him. "Misty did a set just before midnight. The cast members were all on stage to do the countdown. Misty sang 'Auld Lang Syne' just after midnight. That was her last set of the night. We had more exotic dancers follow until nearly two."

"Did you see her afterward? After midnight on Tuesday?" Danbury asked, taking them both in with his glance.

"I didn't," said Phillip. "I was working behind the bar that night. I didn't get out from behind it much."

"I didn't either," said Charlene. "I was backstage most of the night, keeping the sets in order and running."

"Do you have security cameras? To see when she left. And if she was alone."

The O'Connells just looked at each other, and they seemed to agree on one thing, at least, in their response. They both laughed at him.

Charlene said, "No way! With our clientele? We wouldn't have half of them if we had cameras around and word got out about that."

Returning to the earlier line of questioning, Danbury asked, "Why did she want the night off? Did she say?"

"Not that I can remember," answered Charlene, expelling another puff of smoke ceilingward.

"How did she seem? That night. And in the previous week. Was she acting normally?"

"She was upset when she asked off for New Year's Eve, now that you mention it," answered Charlene pensively.

"Do you know why?"

"No, and I didn't ask."

"Does she have family here? Anybody she's close to?"

"If she does, she never mentioned them to me. Like I said, she kept to herself. Some of the girls might know. They were mostly jealous of her, so I don't know if she'd have confided in any of them. If she had, it'd likely have been Ruby. I saw them talking together sometimes. Her dressing room was beside Ruby's. Ruby brings in crowds too. She's a pole dancer. And a good one."

"No boyfriend?"

"Men sent her flowers and candy and even jewelry, I think. I never asked if there was a special one. So I really don't know. Maybe Ruby does."

"When was she due back?" asked Danbury.

"Saturday," said Charlene. "I told her she could have four days off, but we'd need her here for the weekend, at least for Saturday night."

"They argued over Friday," interjected Phillip. "And Misty hated to argue. But of course, Misty won."

"Of course?" asked Danbury.

"Misty was the draw. She was really that good. Our regulars knew it, and she was constantly drawing in larger and larger crowds. Even from outside of this area."

"How do you know that?" asked Danbury.

"They don't talk like they're from here," said Phillip. "Come to think of it, neither did Misty."

"Where was she from?"

"You got me," said Phillip with a shrug.

"When talent that good walks in and auditions, you don't ask too many questions," added Charlene. "You just hire 'em. She was the whole package. And she had experience."

"Did she give you references? A résumé?"

"No, but she had all of her own costumes, and she was ready to get right to work. I hired her, and she performed that night."

"When was that?"

"Almost a year ago," said Phillip.

"That's pretty specific," said Danbury.

"She had a year contract," said Phillip. "It was just about up."

"Was she signing back up?" asked Danbury.

"Of course she was," answered Charlene defensively before Phillip had the chance to respond. "Why wouldn't she? We treated her well. She got a raise after three months."

"Because she doubled the weekend business," said Phillip. "And it was a tiny raise. I didn't see her signing on again. Not without some major negotiation. And Misty wasn't into confrontation like some of the others. She stayed in the background, except when she was on stage."

"But you didn't report her missing?" asked Danbury.

"No," said Charlene, looking uncomfortable.

"Why not?"

"Because I thought that she'd just decided to take the time she'd asked for off anyway and that she'd come back, tail between her legs, this week, begging for her job back."

"Her job back?" asked Danbury.

"She was in breach of contract," answered Charlene. "She had no job to come back to if she didn't show up Saturday night."

"Silver Silhouette makes movies?" asked Danbury, changing the subject entirely.

"Where'd you hear that?"

"From Preston Priestly."

Her face contorted at the mention of his name and she responded simply, "Yeah, we do."

"Tell me about that. When did that start?"

"About five years ago," said Charlene.

"Why did you start making them?"

"We had a few challenges, financially. It helped keep us afloat."

"You've worked with Preston Priestly?"

Charlene rolled her eyes, looking pained. "Yeah, he owes me money. I loaned him some to get his truck fixed. I haven't seen him since."

"He doesn't work here? At the club?" asked Danbury.

"As a performer?" asked Charlene. At this, both she and Phillip laughed long and hard.

"Hardly," said Charlene after she'd recovered. "There's only one thing that little weasel is good for, and it isn't dancing or stripping at the club," she responded, curtly as she crushed out her cigarette. "Now are we about done here? I've got things to do to get ready for the show tonight."

"One more thing. The, uh, 'actresses.' The women in your films," clarified Danbury. "Where do you find them?"

"Same as I find the men," she said. "They answer ads, they apply, they audition, and we hire or we don't. Same as the club."

"None of them are underage? Or imported?"

"What are you saying? That you think I've got a slave trade going?" she asked angrily.

"I'm not implying anything. Just asking."

"They have IDs and Social Security numbers," she retorted.

"They give us numbers anyway. They do get paid creatively," goaded Phillip.

"Meaning?" asked Danbury.

"Meaning under the table. In cash. No taxes taken out. We don't file anything with the information they give us."

"That's because they sign on as contractors," interjected Charlene. "They're responsible for their own taxes. We just pay them a flat rate, per hour, in cash."

"OK," said Danbury. "That's it for now. I might have more questions later. I need to talk to Ruby. Where can I find her?"

"Through that door," said Charlene, pointing to the door to the right of the stage that both she and Phillip had come through. "Then up the stairs. Last dressing room on the left."

"It was Misty's," added Phillip. "Ruby just moved in. When we found out that Misty wasn't coming back."

Matthew raised an eyebrow at that. Maybe Ruby had something to do with it. If she had second billing and the second-best dressing room, there was something to be gained there. But looking around, he couldn't imagine that someone in this environment had gone to the trouble to disguise the time of death and set up the body quite so elaborately to gain a dressing room and top billing.

Having watched the whole exchange with the O'Connells, Matthew turned back and asked Charlene, "Did you argue about anything else? Other than the time off that she wanted?"

"No," said Charlene. "Why would you ask that?"

"Just curious," said Matthew as he followed Danbury through the door to the right of the stage and up the steep steps of the narrow stairwell.

"What are you thinking?" Danbury asked quietly.

"That Phillip seemed to want us to know that Misty was going to be leaving soon and that Charlene wasn't happy about it. If they're not married, they don't look much like siblings. What's that relationship?"

"A question I want answered," said Danbury. "Scuttlebutt should tell us."

"I bet this place runs rampant with rumors and gossip," said Matthew.

"I'm counting on it," replied Danbury as they turned at the top of the landing and made their way down to the last dressing room on the left to meet Ruby.

The door was open just a crack. They both peered in to see a very red woman. Everything about her was red, from her hair, which was dyed an unnatural color of red, to the lipstick on her full mouth. She sported a velour warm-up suit, minus one red track shoe. From between the toes of her left foot, she pulled a needle recently injected there.

7 ~ CRIMSON FEATHERS

Danbury tapped gently on the dressing room door and the woman looked up, apparently unfazed by having been caught injecting drugs. The room was drab, Matthew thought, except that there were bits of red clothing strewn all over it, hanging from pegs and over two dingy chairs in the corner. A red feather boa hung from the mirror over a shabby wooden dressing table in front of which the woman sat. She had one shoeless foot propped on the edge of the table and the syringe still in her hand as she withdrew it from between her toes.

"We don't go on until ten," she said, looking up at them. "And no visitors are allowed back here. It's not that kind of club," she added in a bored tone, as if the statement was rehearsed and she'd said it hundreds of times.

"Warren Danbury, homicide detective," said Danbury, flashing his badge. "And Matthew Paine, medical consultant. Ms., ah . . ."

"Ruby. It's just plain Ruby. And I guess I know what this is about," she said. "It's about Misty, isn't it?"

"It is," confirmed Danbury. "Were you friends?"

"She wasn't the friendly type," the woman said with a shrug.

"You weren't friends?"

"She wasn't mean. I just don't know much about her."

"Did you talk to her?"

"We talked some. But it wasn't nothing important. Maybe about some men we were talking to. Or about changing things about our acts. We never did nothing together. Not outside of here. I talked more to her than she did to me. I guess she did know a lot about me, now that I think about it."

"What can you tell us about her?" asked Danbury, tablet poised in his hand.

The woman looked suspiciously up at him. He towered over her, even after she replaced the shoe and stood. Matthew stepped forward, interjecting, "Ruby, we want to find out what happened to Misty. Anything you can tell us might help, any little detail. It might not seem important, but you never know what might help us find her killer."

"So, she was murdered? I thought so."

"Why? Why did you think that?" asked Matthew softly as Danbury stepped aside and let him take the lead in questioning.

"Because something wasn't right. Right before she left. She was jumpy. I walked in here on Monday. This was her dressing room, you know," she said. Matthew nodded without interrupting, and she continued, "I tapped on the door. She had her back to it, and she just about jumped out of her skin. Like I wasn't who she was expecting. She laughed when she saw it was me and tried to play it off. But it was a nervous laugh, you know? Something else had spooked her, and I knew it."

"Do you have any idea what that might have been?"

"I didn't think much of it at the time," said Ruby pensively. "But I don't know what it woulda been. She was the star here. She got all the attention. Sometimes it was too much for her, though. She didn't like it. She loved performing, and she lit up on stage. But she didn't want all of the attention that goes with it. If that makes any sense."

"She was shy?" asked Matthew, seeking some clarification.

"Not really shy. She could belt out songs and dance on stage like nobody I've known before. She was just closed off when she wasn't on stage."

"Were you surprised that she didn't come back for the performance on Saturday?" Matthew asked.

The woman seemed to consider this deeply. Either that or the drugs she'd just injected were kicking in. Finally, she answered, "Sort of. I mean, I knew she wanted to take off longer than Charlene would give her. When she didn't come back, I thought maybe she'd found another job somewhere else. Like, somewhere better. Maybe found an agent and decided to really sing for real."

"Do you know why she wanted the time off?"

"I overheard her on the phone saying something about putting tires on her car for a trip somewhere out of town. With the new tires, I figured it was a long one, but she didn't tell me about it."

Checking his notes, Danbury stepped forward. "She drove a Toyota?"

"Yeah, it was older. A Camry. Never gave her any trouble, so she liked it. She'd had it awhile."

"Do you know where it is?" asked Danbury.

"I guess she drove it wherever she went," said Ruby. "Like I said, brand-new tires on it. I figured that's why she put 'em on there. To drive it on her trip."

Danbury rubbed his chin with his thumb and looked frustrated. They weren't learning much new information from Ruby.

"Were you surprised to find out that she'd died?" asked Matthew, changing the line of questioning.

"Yeah, I guess I was. I mean, men were her kryptonite. Drugs are mine. I thought mine would kill me first, if ya know what I'm sayin'?"

"Did Misty do drugs?" asked Danbury.

"No. Not that I ever saw. If she did, it wasn't here. But I'd have known about it if she did. I can spot 'em miles away, drugs and users. I was in here a lot when it was her dressing room. I shared one with two other girls. I had no privacy like she had. She helped me with my makeup and hair sometimes. Stuff like that. I never saw her high."

"Did she leave anything behind? Here in the dressing room?" asked Danbury.

"Just that box over there." Ruby flipped her hand at a cardboard box in the corner. "It's mostly old makeup and junk stuff, but I guess you can have it. I doubt anybody else wants it."

"Were there any particular men in her life? Any that you know of?"

asked Matthew as Danbury retrieved the box, donned gloves, and began poking through it.

"There were a couple of regulars who'd come see her after her sets at the end of the night. Not overlapping or anything. One-at-a-time regulars. None that stuck around too long. And some who wanted to. Like Preston Priestly. He followed her around like a sad little puppy dog. But she was too good for the likes of him. Way too good. She was nice to everybody, so I guess he must have thought he still had a chance. They were friends, I guess. She left her cat with him to take care of while she was gone. I didn't think that was the best choice, but I'm allergic."

"Do you know who the men were?" asked Matthew. "Or who the most recent one was?"

"Hmmm..." said Ruby, leaning back in her chair, her mood mellowing by the moment. "I know one was named Adam. I don't know his last name, never did. Or maybe that was his last name?" She shrugged. "I think he was the one who proposed to her. But he wasn't the last one. The last one was. . ." She paused, creasing her brow in thought.

Matthew wondered how old she was. She looked like someone who should be carefree, living a young life. Instead, she'd likely had a difficult one and had graduated from the school of hard knocks. Still, if she was a pole dancer, she had to be in decent shape physically, drugs and all.

"Keith. Or Kent. Kevin, maybe. Something like that." She waved her hand dismissively.

Matthew assumed that Danbury was thinking the same thing he was. They weren't going to get much more out of Ruby. At least not on this visit. Before they left, though, the physician in Matthew took over, and he decided to give her his public service announcement.

"You know there are fentanyl test strips available to make sure the opioids are clean, right?" He pulled his business card from his wallet, picked up a pen from the dressing table, and jotted the samhsa.gov web address and the 800-662-HELP number on the back. He had memorized that information the summer before when he was in Miami searching for a missing young woman. Holding out the card to her, he told her how to find the substance use disorder resources on the website.

"Who do you think you are?" she asked indignantly. He'd obviously ruffled her crimson feathers. He knew it was a possibility, which is why he'd chosen to do it after they'd interviewed her.

"I'm a medical doctor," replied Matthew simply, deciding to forego the more detailed description of how osteopathic medicine treats the whole person, not just an isolated condition or a specific symptom.

"You don't know nothin' about me, all high-and-mighty doctor! I got stuck on this mess from a doctor. He gave me pain pills when I threw my back out. Just so I could keep dancing. And I like 'em. So, you can take yourself and your help right on out of here."

"I actually care about my patients. They're not numbers to me; they're people. All of them. Here. If you change your mind. Or if you need medical help," said Matthew, laying the pen and his card on the dressing table. Danbury thanked Ruby for her time, added his business card to Matthew's on the dressing table, and asked her to contact him if she thought of anything that might be helpful.

Danbury gave Matthew a sidelong glance as they made their way out of the dressing room, but he said nothing. They went along the hallway, tapping on doors and asking questions of any and all of the women who were primping in mirrors, mostly three to a dressing room. None of the other women had much to say about Misty, one way or another. It was as if neither her presence nor her absence was of any consequence or concern to them.

Matthew led the way back down the steep, narrow staircase and through the door into the main room, which was bustling with activity. Boxes were being hauled behind the bar and glasses stacked and hung; pieces of sets and cables were moving around on the stage with the crew members. It was a much bigger production than he'd realized.

Danbury approached the bar and asked if Cara Mason would be in soon.

"Not tonight," said Phillip as he connected hoses to a drink machine. "She has the night off."

"Where can we find her? Do you have an address?" asked Danbury.

"I thought you already talked to her," said Phillip. "After she reported Misty missing."

"I did," admitted Danbury. "By phone. But I'd like to meet her. I have more questions."

"Tell you what," said Phillip. "Let me finish this up and I'll look up her information. I'll call her, and if she agrees, then I'll give you what you're asking for."

"That's OK," said Danbury. "I'll call her." Handing Phillip one of his business cards, he added, "Call me at any time. If you think of anything else. Anything could be important."

"Yeah, sure," said Phillip, taking the card and placing it by the cash register.

Matthew and Danbury stepped out into the cool night, and Danbury made the call. Cara Mason agreed to talk to them and gave Danbury the address.

"You want to follow?" asked Danbury. "It's on the way to Raleigh."

"All right," agreed Matthew. "Text me the address, though, just in case."

"Yeah, OK," said Danbury tapping his phone.

8 ~ Tearful

Matthew followed Danbury to a quiet neighborhood north and slightly east of Durham, not far from where the body was found. They pulled up in front of a small but neat bungalow house and parked at the curb. Silently, Matthew followed Danbury up onto a small porch. Danbury pushed the doorbell button, and they waited.

From within the house, Matthew heard a screechy voice yell, "Cara, dear, get the door, please!"

"Coming, Grandma!" answered a younger voice from somewhere else within. The door opened, and a tiny young woman stood, backlit, in jeans and an oversize sweatshirt that said "Duke University" across the front.

"Cara Mason?" asked Danbury, introducing himself and Matthew as he flipped his badge open to show her.

"Yes, that's me," she answered, choking on the words. Like Ruby had, Cara obviously knew why they were there. Unlike Ruby, Cara seemed to care.

"Thanks for agreeing to talk to us," said Danbury in a tone that Matthew thought was approaching friendly—at least, it was less gruff and abrasive. "Can we come in?"

"Sure," she said, stepping back from the door and holding it open to them as she brushed a tear from her cheek.

"My grandmother is in there with the TV turned up," said Cara, pointing to the front room off to the left. "Let's go to the kitchen so that we can hear."

"Who is it, dear?" called the older voice from the sitting room.

"It's the police, Grandma. We're going to the kitchen to talk," she said as she quickly rushed them by the doorway before the older woman, whom Matthew glimpsed ensconced in a recliner with a quilt pulled up to her chin, had a chance to object.

"Oh my!" the older woman exclaimed.

"My grandmother doesn't approve of me working at Silver Silhouette," said Cara by way of explanation.

As they entered the tiny kitchen, Cara leaned against a counter, and Danbury filled most of the rest of the room. Matthew was nearly as tall, with broad shoulders, but Danbury was just broad. He looked like a misplaced Viking in the small space.

"I work during the day, and I have evening classes at the community college. I can work extra night shifts there, and the pay is pretty good for a hostess. I guess it's hazard pay," she tried to joke, but it fell flat, and she continued on. "I want to transfer to Duke next year. I've applied for scholarships and financial aid. I'm waiting to hear. It's the only way I'll ever get to go. But I'll still have expenses. Books, clothes, gas, and stuff."

Matthew didn't think that Duke University – a massive and highly selective private university with a renowned medical program and attached hospital – took transfer students from community colleges. He refrained from commenting on the lofty goal, but maybe the young woman knew something he didn't. He hoped so. She seemed like a nice person, not jaded like the others he'd met so far during this investigation.

"I'm sorry. I guess I'm just postponing the inevitable. You didn't come to hear about me. You want to know about Misty," Cara said, and another tear slid down her cheek, unchecked this time.

"That's right," said Danbury. "You reported her missing. Nobody else did. Do you know why?"

"I did because she was my friend. She encouraged me to pursue my dreams and achieve them. She believed that I could. I knew something was wrong when she wasn't back Saturday night. She gave her word and agreed to be back. She didn't have much, but her word was important to her. She was always dependable, both at her job and as a friend. I don't know why Charlene didn't know that and report her missing. She certainly should have!"

Cara was the first person to call her a friend whom Matthew actually believed when she said it. If you didn't include Preston Priestly, she was the only person so far to say that. And that guy didn't come across as reliable.

Holding the tablet up and tapping it, Danbury began asking questions in a soft voice. Matthew was impressed that he had found that tone.

"When did you last see her?" he asked.

"Tuesday night. It was New Year's Eve, and she'd wanted to take off, but Charlene basically guilted her into working. And Misty was still under a contract for another month or so. So she stayed. And that's the same reason I knew she'd come back if she could. If she were going to leave, she'd have just done it then."

"Did you notice anything unusual? With her behavior? Or her attitude? Anything odd? Off in any way?"

Cara pondered this a moment before responding, "She did seem edgy. Like, nervous, I mean. I'm not sure what was bothering her, but now that you ask, something definitely was."

"Did she tell you that she was going on a trip?"

Cara nodded.

"Do you know where she was going?"

"No, and now I wish I'd asked her. There are so many things I wish I'd asked her," said Cara, breaking down and reaching for a paper towel from a holder by the sink. Giving in to the tears momentarily, she didn't bother trying to finish her thought. She just cried. Matthew wished there were a female officer with them. Maybe it would help. But then again, maybe it wouldn't matter at all.

"Do you know if she put new tires on her car? Did she mention that to you?" asked Danbury as the sobbing began to subside.

"Yeah," Cara said with a sniffle. "She said she was replacing them for her trip. She said she'd worn the last set down to nothing and needed new ones anyway."

After a pause while Cara composed herself, she added, "She asked me to take Fluffykins. That's her cat. She loves that cat. I mean, loved. She loved her." More tears followed before she blew her nose loudly.

Clearing her throat, she said, "I'm sorry. I want to help you, I do. I just don't know what to tell you. I wish I'd taken Fluffykins, but I knew my grandmother wouldn't allow any animals in the house. And Fluffykins is an indoor cat. She's never been outside, and she wouldn't be safe. The roads are dangerous enough for people with the crazy drivers around here."

She hesitated a moment before continuing. "Preston Priestly, that slimeball, was hanging around her dressing room when Misty asked me to take her, and he volunteered. I don't think she wanted him to take Fluffykins, but I guess she couldn't take her wherever she was going, and she didn't have a choice. Does he still have her?"

"As far as we know," said Danbury. "Priestly said maybe you could take her."

"I'll try," said Cara. "I really will try to convince my grandmother. She wants nothing to do with the club, though, or anyone who worked there. And she's not a fan of cats. So it'll be tricky, but it's the least I can do for Misty. She'd want me to have Fluffykins."

"How long had you known Misty?"

"I started working at the club about six months ago. Misty was already there. She'd been there a few months already. Some of the men were harassing me one night, and she stepped in and put them in their place. She taught me how to do that, to tell them off and make them leave me alone. She did it nicely but firmly. I wasn't very good at it at first. But I wouldn't have lasted there a week if she hadn't helped me. She was like a big sister. I'm an only child, but I can guess what it would be like to have one. And she'd be it."

"Did she ever mention family? Or close friends? Anyone like that?"

"Not directly. From what she did say, it sounded like she wasn't in touch with them and that she wasn't sorry about that."

"What did she say?" asked Danbury.

Cara pursed her lips, and a crease formed between her eyebrows. "I wish I could remember exactly what she said, but it's fuzzy. Something like not all parents were created equally and some you're better off without. Something like that. She knew that my parents died when I was little, and that's why I live with my grandmother. I thought maybe she was just trying to make me feel better. But it was probably more about her own parents, now that I think about it."

After a pause to give her time to consider the earlier conversation with Misty, and after which she said nothing further, Danbury asked, "What about boyfriends? Men? Dates?"

"What about them?" she asked, as if startled.

"Ruby told us that she had several, a string of them, one after another," said Matthew. "What can you tell us about them?"

"Not much. She did like guys' attention. A lot. Men were always after her. But I wouldn't listen to what Ruby says. She's not always in touch with reality. She's a nice enough person, I think, but she was always mooching off Misty. Makeup, stage jewelry, a few bucks here and there. I never saw her give any of it back, and I never heard Misty complain about it."

"The guys?" asked Danbury, redirecting her to the question at hand. "Who, in particular?"

"You know, she'd been proposed to three times while she was working there," said Cara.

"Ruby mentioned one of those," said Matthew. "But she couldn't tell us anything about any of the boyfriends. Do you know names or anything that'll help us to locate any of them?"

"Umm, I think the last one to propose was Adam. But he wasn't the latest boyfriend. She broke it off with him when he proposed. I think he was pushy about it. Misty wasn't going to be pushed into anything. At least nothing important like marriage. She let Charlene push her around sometimes, but not the guys."

"Let's come back to Charlene," said Danbury gently. "But first, do you know Adam's last name?"

"Wilson, I think," said Cara.

"Adam Wilson," clarified Danbury. "When did they break up?"

"It was before Christmas because he wanted to take her home to meet his family for the holidays, engaged. And she refused. That's probably why she broke it off, now that I think about it. She didn't want to meet his family or go home with him for the holidays. He was nice enough, but he was pushy about all of that."

"Is this him?" asked Danbury, showing her a picture from a driver's license on his tablet after he'd tapped it and pulled up the DMV record.

"Yeah, that looks like him."

"Did you meet him? What can you tell us about him?"

"I met him once, but I can't really tell you much about him."

"Who was the next one? After Adam Wilson?"

"That one didn't last a week," she said. "I think his name was Jonathan, maybe? Something like that. I'm not sure what she didn't like about him, but she only went out with him a couple of times and then broke it off with him too."

"Do you know his last name?"

"I might if I heard it. I don't know, though. I'm not sure I ever heard his last name. I didn't actually meet him. I just saw her leaving with him a couple of times after her sets. He had some sort of souped-up car. Really fancy. I think it was a Corvette."

Matthew stifled a smile that she thought a Corvette was really fancy. "Anything specific about it that you can remember?" he asked instead.

"It was silver and really loud. It had huge pipes sticking out of the back of it. A lot of them."

Danbury glanced at Matthew and smirked over her head.

"So he had a silver Corvette with quad exhaust," summarized Matthew. "Anything else?"

"Oh yeah, the license plate was funny. I had forgotten that. It was something like 2F@ST4U."

"Who was the next one? Her next boyfriend?" asked Danbury, tapping his tablet. He was taking notes about everything she was telling them.

"His name I know because it rhymed and we laughed about it. I did meet him a couple of times. The first time was only for a minute when Misty was on her way out with him. His name is Trent Kent. Misty thought it was funny and wanted to know why his parents would do that to him. She really did have an issue with parents, didn't she?" she asked, looking up. "I hadn't put that together until now."

"Trent Kent," repeated Danbury. "Was he the last one?"

"Yeah, she was still dating him, as far as I know."

Tapping his tablet to retrieve the driver's license picture and blow it up, Danbury asked, as he held it up for Cara to see, "Is this him?"

"Yup. That looks like TK. He went by that, I think. Or at least that's what Misty called him. She really liked him. Maybe she'd finally found the right one, and then," said Cara, choking up again.

"You're doing great, Cara," said Matthew encouragingly. "You've given us more helpful information than anyone else so far."

"Did she have other friends?" asked Danbury. "Ever mention any?"

"Nobody outside of the club," said Cara. "She did say something about women being catty everywhere she'd been, but she didn't mention any names."

"Did she say where? Where she was before here?" asked Danbury.

"Not specifically. I think she'd worked in other places like Silver Silhouette, from the sound of it. But I don't know where."

"What can you tell us about Charlene?" asked Danbury. "And Phillip. With the same last name. But not married. They aren't siblings. Are they?"

Cara laughed at that. "They do have a strange relationship, don't they? It's like they hate each other, but they really don't. What I heard was that Charlene had been married to Phillip's younger brother. And she was head-over-heels in love with him. They opened a bar together, and they were struggling to get it going when he died. He was killed in a motorcycle accident, or so I heard, a long time ago. Like, maybe fifteen years ago or so."

After blowing her nose profusely and tossing the paper towel into the nearby trash bin, she continued, "Phillip stepped in to help. I know he helped finance it, but then they turned the bar into a strip club together. I'm not sure whose idea that was. Or who owns what. But they really don't hate each other. I'm not sure why they pretend that they do all the time."

"Just one more thing," said Danbury. "Have you ever been to Misty's apartment?"

"Yeah, a couple of times. It's not too far from here."

"Was anybody else there?"

"Just TK the last time I was there. And Preston Priestly invited himself over and followed her home once. That would have annoyed me, but Misty was nice to him. Unless he got too crude, and then she'd call him on it. He's really sleazy, but she mostly ignored that and talked to him like anybody else. She had that way about her. She could really see people, the good inside them, I mean."

"Thank you, Cara," said Danbury as he handed her a business card. "You have been very helpful," he said, reiterating Matthew's words. "Contact me. If you think of anything else. It might not seem important. But anything might help."

"Sure. I will. I want to know what happened to Misty. She was wonderful, and she didn't deserve to die."

Matthew and Danbury said their goodbyes to Cara and stepped back out into the cold night air.

"That's it for the night, right?" asked Matthew meaningfully as he checked his watch. It was nearly eleven, and he hadn't fed Max, he hadn't done his charting for the day, and he still had a half-hour drive to get home.

"Yeah, that's it. We're getting warrants for information. Like Misty's phone records. Her phone is still missing. Just like her car," said Danbury. "Maybe we can get a location. On both. And a previous address. From the DMV. I can pull up current records. But I had to request past records."

"What about the diamond?" asked Matthew. "Did that lead anywhere?"

"Not yet. A jeweler is evaluating it. A certified gemologist, actually.

She was quick to point that out. She's newly vetted. By the Raleigh department. She's proving herself, I guess. The guy we used for years just retired. Anyway, she had a quick look. With something she called a loupe. It's a handheld device. But she wants a better look. Under her microscope in her office. She signed it out. Through all the protocols. Maintaining chain of custody. All of that. She'll tell us what she can. There is one anomaly she noticed, though. Round traditional diamonds are cut with fifty-eight facets. This one has an extra facet."

"Huh," said Matthew. "Meaning what?"

"No idea. Maybe nothing."

"OK, keep me posted." Matthew chuckled, thinking that Danbury was becoming quite the expert on diamond assessment.

"Will do," answered Danbury as they climbed into their vehicles to go their separate ways.

Matthew pondered the conversations they'd had with the various people all the way home. Nobody had many nice things to say about any of the others, except for Misty. Either nobody was speaking ill of the dead, or the woman had really been a nice person, and nobody had anything bad to say about her. He was betting on the latter, but he was intrigued by this investigation and curious to know more, despite his earlier intention to stop consulting for the police department.

9 ~ Never a Dull Moment

Matthew awoke to an annoying noise that he initially couldn't place. It wasn't his alarm, he thought, as he slid Max from his usual spot around his head. It was coming from his phone, though, he realized, rolling over and picking it up.

"Good morning, sleepyhead," he heard Cici's chipper voice say as he clicked to accept the incoming FaceTime request from her. "Oh, wow, love the hair by Max," she added, laughing.

"What time is it?" Matthew muttered, trying to shake the cobwebs from his tired brain.

"Six fifteen, your time," she responded confidently. "I waited until just before your alarm was about to go off. I didn't want to wake you early or interfere with your morning routine."

That was thoughtful, Matthew had to admit, and he muttered something to that effect.

"Did you stay up too late last night or something? You're usually not quite this out of it in the morning."

"Yeah, I was out pretty late. And then I had patient charting to do when I got home last night. It was a late night. I think I got about five hours of sleep," he added on a yawn. "Maybe less."

"You were out that late on a Monday night?" she asked incredulously. "Out with your friends from your childhood neighborhood?"

"Nope. At a strip club," he answered with a lop-sided smile.

"Excuse me, I thought I just heard you say you were at a strip club."

She laughed. "But this is you I'm talking to. And you're an old soul, Matthew Paine. So I can't have heard that right."

"Yeah, I said strip club." He thought he'd have some fun with that and not explain right away, so he paused and waited.

"O . . . K . . ." she said slowly. "What's going on?"

It was Matthew's turn to laugh at her. Of course she knew he had no interest in strip clubs, so he quickly explained about the woman who'd been murdered and how she'd been a performer at an "entertainment club."

"It was her bedroom I sent the pictures of," added Matthew.

"I see," said Cici, looking concerned. "You're getting yourself mixed up in another of Danbury's murder investigations." She didn't look particularly happy with this development. If Matthew had to categorize her responses, she was more bothered by this information than she'd been about him having been at a strip club.

"About the pictures, cheap stuff, right?"

"Mostly," said Cici. "Except maybe some of the clothes in the closet. But they might be knockoffs. It's hard to say from the pictures. Does it matter?"

"It's too soon to tell what matters and what doesn't yet. I was just trying to understand the woman who was killed, her lifestyle, at least."

After a momentary silence, she said, "Matthew, please be careful. I'll be back in three months, twenty days, and a few hours. Please try not to get killed in the interim."

Chuckling, he knew that she was trying to make light of the situation, but there was genuine concern behind her words. After reassuring her as best he could about his safety, he asked about her flight and readjusting to the London flat and her life there.

She'd been home to the States for nearly a month over the Christmas and New Year holidays after being in London, working with clients, for the seven months prior. When she had initially agreed to work in the London office, she had committed to her law firm to be there for a year. She was working alongside them to transition major operations to the US. At the time, it had seemed the right choice to her, but Matthew knew she'd had serious apprehension about going back for the remaining months after the holidays.

"It was easier the first time," she said. "It was all this shiny new adventure then. And it was spring. Now it's dreary winter here, too, and the novelty has definitely worn off. I didn't have jet lag the first time I did this trip. I thought I could sleep for days when I arrived this time."

"I know the feeling." Matthew yawned. "I don't think the short days and dreariness are helping me any either."

After they chatted for a bit, they said their goodbyes and I love yous and made plans to talk later, just as Matthew's alarm was going off silently on his phone. He clicked to end both the call and the alarm. Climbing out of bed, he trudged down the hall. After caring for Max, he fixed a cup of the steaming coffee that he'd set up to brew the night before. Then, he went to get ready for his Tuesday morning and to make the short drive into Peak.

Traffic along Highway 20 heading to his office was heavy, like usual, as he drove in at eight that morning. He was happy not to live any farther away than he did. His condominium community, of which his house was the last on the end on the right, was off Highway 20, east of Peak, just past the King's Country Club. The location was ideal, as far as Matthew was concerned. It was close enough for convenience but not in town. That gave him some space and the breathing room that he enjoyed, the best of both worlds.

After a full morning with patients, Matthew grabbed a quick lunch in his office. He'd had tacos ordered through Trina, his office manager. The lunch-train initiative was a program she'd started as a perk for the staff. Each day, she ordered from a different restaurant for any of the staff who wanted to participate. Trina's program was wildly successful, and large quantities of lunch were brought in daily from the local restaurants.

Grabbing a napkin, he was relieved to see that his fingers were reasonably clean as he pulled his ringing phone from his pocket. The display showed that it was his father, so he answered it.

"Hey, Dad. It's not Wednesday yet," he joked because his father usually checked in with him in the middle of the week.

"I know, but I was just checking to see how you were doing with

Cici back in London."

Well, that's new, Matthew thought. His parents hadn't been fond of Cici after they broke up nearly two years ago, and they'd been pretty vocal about it.

"Thanks, Dad," said Matthew meaningfully. "I really appreciate that. I've been busy since she flew out Sunday. Purposefully busy, but it's gotten a little crazier than I'd intended."

Matthew explained how Danbury had called before he'd even gotten home from the airport Sunday night and that he'd been out late the night before helping with the investigation.

Like Cici, his father sounded concerned as he, too, told Matthew to be careful. He made his father the same promises that he had made Cici.

Cici, Matthew thought with a smile that warmed him from the inside out. Checking the time, he decided to quickly FaceTime her. She answered but sounded distracted.

"Hey, Matthew, how're things on your side of the puddle?"

"Going pretty well," he answered. "My dad just called to check in to see how I was doing with you so far away again."

"What did you tell him?" she asked, and he could see the playful smile and hear the warmth in her voice. She seemed pleased as he recounted the conversation to her.

As they were ending the call, Matthew's phone dinged before he could put it down, and he saw a text from Danbury.

"Hey, Doc. You free for dinner? Penn's cooking. Six thirty. Her house."

Matthew texted back, "Sure. Tell Penn thanks for the invite. What can I bring?"

"She likes that red wine. The one you brought before."

"Got it," texted Matthew, knowing exactly the cabernet that Danbury was referencing. "See you at six thirty."

He was amazed that Penn had time to cook. She loved to cook, he knew, but with the new business she'd just opened, he wondered how she'd managed to take an evening off. Lingle Wellness was a combination gym and spa. The one she'd just opened in Peak replicated one she'd opened in Denver. She'd rebranded both locations to include her brother Leo in the venture when she'd moved home to Peak the previous spring.

*****

After a full afternoon, Matthew managed to leave the office at five to get home, feed Max, and change into jeans and a warm, soft flannel shirt. He pulled up his patient records on his laptop and began reviewing their charts. It was just after six when he put his computer aside and grabbed his jacket from the end of the soft leather sofa, where he habitually piled it with his work satchel. He had time to get by a grocery store on the edge of Peak to pick up the bottle of wine, then get to the Lingle Plantation—which was what the locals called the old historic family home of Penn and Leo Lingle.

When Matthew arrived, he was warmly greeted by both Penn and Leo, who was holding his kitten. Leo, who looked only slightly like his sister, with lighter brown hair but the same vibrant blue eyes, was of medium height and build.

Leo had gotten the kitten after caring for Max while Matthew was away in Miami the summer before. She was a gray tabby like Max, and he'd named her Maxine in his honor. She was happily purring as he stroked her soft fur. Matthew reached over and scratched behind her ears the way Max liked, and she purred louder.

Penn was dressed, as usual, in workout clothes. Her slender, muscular form was clad in spandex pants, a long-sleeved quick-dry T-shirt, and running shoes. She had some of the bluest eyes Matthew had ever seen. They reminded him of the murdered woman's eyes. Unlike the victim's, Penn's blue eyes were in stark contrast to her dark hair, which she'd pulled back in a ponytail. Matthew shook the unwelcome comparison from his mind as she motioned them down the center hallway and into the kitchen, from which a wonderful aroma emanated.

"Thanks for the wine," she told Matthew, taking it from him and handing the bottle to Danbury. "Will you do the honors, Warren?"

Danbury nodded in response and went to retrieve a cork-screw and glasses from the cabinets behind him.

"It's a pot roast with all the trimmings," said Penn, pulling on oven mitts and opening the oven, filling the room more completely with the wonderful aroma. "And it should be ready now."

"How can I help?" asked Matthew.

"Just have a seat," said Penn. "Leo already set the table. I'll get it served up and we'll be ready."

Danbury handed Matthew a glass of wine and then helped Penn separate the roast from the potatoes, carrots, and onions, placing the roast on a platter and the vegetables in a bowl. The roast, Matthew noted, was huge. But then, Penn was probably well used to feeding Danbury by now, he thought.

As they put the bowl and platter on the table and added dinner rolls, Penn said, "Let the feasting begin! Oh, but Matthew would you say a blessing first?"

Matthew readily agreed, and they settled down to a wonderful meal with lots of conversation and laughter. "I have an apple pie for dessert," Penn announced just as Danbury's cell phone sounded. "Ugh!" she groaned as she watched him pull it from his pocket and then disappear into the next room to answer it.

"That must be hard," said Matthew as he rose and began to help clear the table. "He's always on call, isn't he?"

"He always *puts* himself on call," she replied, taking the dishes as he handed them to her. "There's never a dull moment with Warren around, that's for sure." Then Penn added, "When he's in the middle of an investigation, he's always on call. He doesn't know how not to be. And I just choose my battles. I've been coaching him to be less abrupt and abrasive."

"It's working," Matthew said, laughing. "He actually thanked me the other night for going to the crime scene and helping out. Twice. And I think you're smart to choose your battles," added Matthew as Danbury rushed back into the room, the look on his face readable.

"I've got the dishes," said Penn. "And the pie will wait. Go."

"I'll help," said Leo. Getting up from the table and moving to the sink, he began rinsing the dishes that Penn was still stacking there, and he added with a boyish grin, "But there might be less pie when you get back."

"You coming, Doc?" asked Danbury. "They found the victim's car. By the VIN number. Or vehicle identification number. It's a match."

Matthew nodded. As a self-confessed motor head, he knew full well what a VIN number was. Raising an eyebrow, he wondered how his medical expertise could possibly be needed. Realizing that Danbury more often treated him like a partner on the police force than truly a medical consultant, Matthew asked, "Where to?" as he retrieved his coat.

"RTP. Want to ride?"

"No," said Matthew definitively. "I'll follow you. I need to get home at a decent time tonight. I think I'm on five hours of sleep from last night, and it's catching up with me."

"Yeah, I got three," said Danbury, turning to kiss Penn. Danbury was fully functional on three hours of sleep. It defied logic, but Matthew knew it was true. Danbury's credo was to sleep when you could and eat when you could because you never knew when you'd be able to do either one again. It seemed to work for the guy.

"Are you coming back here tonight?" Penn asked.

"Depends on the time," Danbury said. "When is too late?"

"It's never too late," she said, winking at him. "You have a key."

With that, Matthew followed Danbury out to make the trek west of Raleigh to Research Triangle Park and see what there was to be learned from the vehicle of a murdered woman.

10 ~ Everybody and Nobody

Matthew left the interstate at the Florida Boulevard exit and tracked behind Danbury to turn right beside one of the hotels. The hotels in this area were frequented by travelers from the echelons of corporate America, by which they were surrounded. Circling in front of the Home Away Hotel building, they followed the road beyond it. There was a sign indicating a dead-end street. The narrow road seemed to parallel the interstate, from what Matthew could tell.

There were mattresses, shopping carts, and other detritus, suggesting either the presence of a homeless population or an area that had recently been vacated by them. The flashing lights of the police vehicles on the scene that were lighting up the night sky probably had everything to do with that vacating, Matthew thought.

Danbury's big black SUV pulled off the edge of the road behind a white-paneled van that was labeled as belonging to the North Carolina Crime Lab. Matthew pulled in behind the SUV and climbed out of the Element, following Danbury down the road and onto the scene. There was a car, a silver sedan, sitting low on the edge of the road ahead.

The license plate was missing, and it was sitting on the rotors. All four tires, including the rims, were entirely gone. Rough neighborhood, Matthew thought, but then he remembered that Misty had just replaced the tires for her road trip. They'd been brand-new tires. Ruby had told them that, and then Cara—a more reliable source—had confirmed it.

As they approached, Danbury started asking questions about when the car had been located and by whom.

"Young couple," said one of the uniformed officers who was

already on the scene. "They came down to, ah, well, it's not exactly lover's lane, is it? Anyway, they knew it wasn't here the last time they were, and the girl got spooked and made the guy call and report it."

"Where are they?" asked Danbury.

"They were questioned and released to go home," said the older officer. "They couldn't tell us much. Just that it wasn't here two weeks ago when they last were. But we knew that much after we ran the VIN number and matched it to your victim. The car wasn't missing until a week ago, right?"

"That's right. Could they tell you anything else? About this area? Anything new? Different?"

"Not really. They said they figured that there was a homeless camp down farther in the woods there. They'd heard voices down that way before. But they said they'd never seen anybody out here."

"They just now got spooked? By an abandoned car?" asked Danbury, and Matthew, too, appreciated the irony.

"Yeah, go figure," said the other officer. "But you know how it is. Teenage hormones and all."

"Yeah, I guess so." Danbury shrugged. "Has Forensics gone over it?"

"They just finished the interior. They're bagging and tagging before they start on the trunk. They're not hopeful, though. With a derelict population so close by and the tires and plates missing, well, anybody's prints could be on it. Everybody's and nobody's. Lots of prints we can't identify from the homeless population down here, and none that we would need to be able to identify someone other than the owner. Probably the killer. Likely the same story with hair and fibers. Evidence in and around the car has been compromised. We'll send it all to the lab and do what we can with it anyway."

"Right," said Danbury. "Are there cameras? Around the hotel?" he asked, motioning to the Home Away Hotel.

"Haven't checked that yet," replied the officer before turning to yell to another officer, sending him to the hotel to ask.

They watched from across the street as two guys in white suits like those that Matthew and Danbury had donned the night the body had been found approached the trunk. A few jerks of a crowbar later and the trunk was popped open. What happened next Matthew experienced first as if in slow motion and then so much faster than he could process to later recall.

"Bomb!" yelled one of the guys in the white suits as both of them ran and then dove into the nearby ditch. Meanwhile, Danbury, Matthew, and the officer they'd been talking to turned, ran a few steps, and dove into the ditch behind one of the police cruisers on their side of the street.

A fireball lit up the night sky above them, and the noise was louder than anything Matthew remembered ever having heard. Even when he'd been in a rock band in high school and in his undergraduate program in college, the noise level didn't compare. He covered his head with his arms, but the explosion rocked the ground, and he couldn't block out either the light or the sound, despite attempting to.

After the initial shock, Matthew lifted his head slightly to see Danbury and the police officer in the ditch beside him also lifting their heads and looking around. Before Matthew could react, Danbury was out of the ditch, across the street, behind the inferno that the car had become, and into the other ditch line, checking on the forensics team.

The air was already acrid. It smelled of burning plastic and rubber. There was something else more sweetly repugnant, Matthew thought as he pulled his shirt up over his mouth and nose.

After a moment, he realized that the police officer in the ditch beside him had been injured. The guy's mouth was moving as if he were shouting, but the roar in Matthew's ears prevented him from hearing what the officer was saying. Half crawling and half walking over, Matthew could see a gash on the officer's head and another down his left hand. The bottom portion of his right leg was under him at an odd angle.

Before he moved farther, Matthew assessed himself. He'd been behind both Danbury and the officer on the street, which put him first into the ditch. All of them had managed to get mostly behind a police cruiser, the windows of which had blown out, so there was glass all over the ground around them. The officer was just barely behind the front end of the cruiser, and he'd been hit by some sort of flying shrapnel, Matthew assumed. Finding no bodily injuries beyond some bruises and scrapes on himself, Matthew checked the police officer over.

The officer's calf, Matthew realized, would need to be set. The compound fracture would require traction and was certainly extremely painful. The bleeding took precedence, though. After checking and being satisfied with the officer's vitals, Matthew pulled out and wadded up the guy's sleeve. Motioning to show him to hold pressure on the hand with the sleeve while pressed to his head, the objective was to staunch the bleeding of both simultaneously.

Pulling his jacket off, Matthew covered the officer with it. Going into shock from severe injury was always a possibility, even for the tough guys who literally put their lives on the line every day they left their homes for work. He held up a finger to indicate that he'd be right back, then stumbled out of the ditch behind the police cruiser, heading for his Element. He always carried a medical bag in each of his cars, and he was thankful that he'd remembered to put it back after the Honda had been repaired. The medical bag, however, would remain momentarily unretrieved.

As Matthew limped across the street, he realized that he'd twisted his left ankle somehow in the confusion and it was painful. Looking up, he saw Danbury waving one arm wildly from the ditch line on the other side of the road. Danbury pulled off his stiff leather jacket, tossing it aside, and then pulled his shirt off over his head. Simultaneously, the officer who'd been sent to check for cameras was running toward them from the other direction.

"Call an ambulance!" Matthew tried to yell to the running officer, but he wasn't sure if any sound was coming from his throat. Pivoting, he limped over to Danbury as quickly as he could. Matthew couldn't hear what he was saying but Danbury's motions showed that a member of the forensics team had been hit by a bigger piece of shrapnel, and the guy had a chest wound. Dropping to his knees beside him, Matthew helped Danbury to pull away the clothing and then used Danbury's shirt to wad up and try to slow the bleeding. He checked the wound and the guy's vitals. It wasn't looking good, but without a bag of blood to go in, the best they could do was to prevent mass quantities of it from coming out.

While Danbury held heavy pressure on that wound, Matthew

quickly assessed the other member of the forensics team. He had cuts and abrasions. Matthew had been moving back and forth across the street between the two men with the worst injuries for what felt like an eternity, when the welcome flashing red lights from rescue vehicles came into sight. Two fire trucks rushed past them to the burning car while a fire-and-rescue ambulance from a little town north on Florida Boulevard came to a stop alongside him.

Matthew was yelling, or at least he thought he was yelling, to them. He asked if the two guys who had disembarked could hear him, and they both nodded as they ran, one toward the rear of the vehicle and one toward Matthew. Quickly identifying himself as a doctor, Matthew pointed, telling the guy that he'd done the initial triage and where to go first as a result. They hauled the stretcher toward the still-burning vehicle and off to the edge of the road to reach the guy from the forensics team with the chest wound.

Matthew followed, helping Danbury to hold pressure on the wound while the paramedics worked to put on a neck brace and carefully lift the injured man onto the stretcher. Matthew had been barking out information while they moved, and he told them they'd need at least one more transport unit. One of the guys nodded. Reading his lips, Matthew thought he'd said, "They're on the way." He couldn't be sure, and maybe that was wishful thinking on his part, but he hoped he was right.

Danbury moved to the remaining guy from the forensics team while Matthew limped back across the street to check on the officer with the compound fracture. The officer's face was ashen, even in the flashing lights, and Matthew was concerned about shock from the pain. Just then, lights from two more ambulances arrived, and Matthew hobbled over to meet them. Yelling to identify himself and then sending them to the police officer, he quicky summarized the injuries they'd find there. He worked alongside them, hobbling along at a frenzied pace, to secure and load the injured officer for transport.

When the lights from those ambulances had finally faded from sight, only one remained. Two EMTs were motioning him over to it, and he joined Danbury and the remaining forensics guy, who were perched on the back. He wasn't sure how much time had passed, but his hearing was starting to recover slightly. A loud buzzing still filled his ears, but he was able to make out voices around him. They sounded very far away, but he was thankful to at least be able to hear them.

"My ankle," he responded to one of the EMTs who was asking about his injuries. "I think it's just sprained. I've been on it since the explosion."

"Let's have a look," said one of the guys, sounding like he was underwater.

Danbury, who was still bare from the waist up, stood and crossed the street, in search of his leather jacket. Matthew propped his foot up on the edge of the ambulance in the spot Danbury had abandoned and rolled the leg of his jeans up.

His swollen ankle was already turning interesting colors. The EMT wrapped a warming blanket around him, for which Matthew was thankful because his jacket had just ridden off in an ambulance with the injured police officer. The EMT poked and prodded and then broke open an ice pack, wrapping it around the ankle with a brace and securing it all with Velcro straps.

Matthew was only half paying attention to the treatment of his ankle as he replayed the series of events of the explosion in his mind. It had happened after the trunk of the car had been pried open—but not immediately afterward. That, he thought, was strange. Was somebody watching and detonated an explosive device remotely? Matthew shivered as he looked, searchingly, at the darkened tree line down the right side of the road.

11 ~ What was that?

"You know the drill, Doctor," said the EMT. "Ice it and elevate it."

Matthew nodded to indicate that he'd heard the guy, despite the loud buzzing that was still ringing in his ears. Police and emergency vehicles were lining both sides of the dead-end road. The fire had been mostly extinguished, but it was difficult to tell that the smoldering lump that remained had once been a car. Pieces of the vehicle had been flung in a wide arc, and they were hanging in the trees along the road.

As Danbury returned to the ambulance with his jacket, the guy from the investigative forensics team, who was still perched on the other end of the back of the ambulance from Matthew, stood up. "Warren Danbury, right?" he yelled.

Danbury nodded.

"Homicide detective?"

Again, Danbury nodded.

"Ross Dresden," shouted the guy, holding out his hand, which Danbury took and shook. "We need to talk about what was in that trunk."

"OK," Danbury yelled back, looking around. "Let's go sit in the SUV."

As they wandered in that direction, Danbury looked over his shoulder and called out, "You coming, Doc?"

The EMT nodded his dismissal and Matthew thanked him before sliding gingerly from the back of the ambulance. Hobbling behind Danbury and the guy who had introduced himself as Dresden, he felt like he was a kid pretending to be an injured superhero. The warming blanket was flowing behind him, and the ice wrap strapped in place around his ankle made him swagger. Climbing into the back seat through the door on the driver's side, Matthew figured he'd give law enforcement the front of the vehicle to talk. Having been included in the discussion, he didn't want to intrude on it.

"What did you see?" Danbury yelled, turning to Dresden.

"A package of C-4 with a timer. A small package. There wasn't that much of it. A cell phone, a computer, and a body," Dresden yelled back.

Matthew wiggled his fingers in his ears for what felt like the hundredth time since the blast, though he wasn't sure it was helping at all to clear his hearing. He was pretty sure, despite the continued buzzing, that he'd just heard the guy say that there was a body in the trunk of the car. The car that had been identified by the VIN number as belonging to Misty Blue.

"Tell me," said Danbury.

"It was so fast," said the guy. "I got an impression, not really a good look. But the body was male. Not a big guy. Slender build. He had to be, anyway, right? That trunk wasn't huge. I didn't see his face. He was shoved in facing the front of the car. By his head was a computer and a cell phone. Sandwiched in front of his mid-section was a package of C-4 with a timer that I think we tripped when we forced the trunk open. The timer showed fifteen seconds, and I saw it flash to fourteen when I yelled and started running."

That explained why Dresden was the farthest from the blast when it went off even though the other guy had been behind him. He'd been the first to see and recognize the C-4 and timer. He'd been the one to yell and alert everyone else to get away and down.

"Are you sure he was dead?" asked Danbury.

"Um, well, I thought so. He wasn't moving, but like I said, I didn't see his face," said Dresden.

"Close your eyes," said Danbury.

"What?" yelled Dresden.

"Close your eyes."

After Dresden complied, Danbury continued, "Take a deep breath. Blow it out slowly. Now focus. You're back at the trunk. You pop it open. You can see inside. The body. A small man. What else do you see?" After a few seconds, Danbury added, "No, don't open your eyes. Concentrate."

The car was quiet, and then, slowly, the guy said, "His hands were tied behind his back with some sort of cord. Like a phone charger cable or something. I think his feet were too. His feet were bare. He had brown hair, I think. Not dark but not blond. Brown or dirty shirt and pants."

"Good," said Danbury. "Now the phone. What color was it? How big? Was it in a case?"

"Yes," said the guy, slowly contemplating. "It was in a sparkly blue case."

"And the computer?" asked Danbury. "Anything distinctive about it?"

"No." The guy slowly shook his head. "Just a laptop, black case, smallish, so probably fairly new."

"Anything else? Was there anything else in the trunk?"

"There was," said the guy. "Down by his feet. A briefcase or messenger bag. Something like that. It was dark. I'm not sure what color. Dark brown, maybe?"

"Did you smell anything? When you opened the trunk?"

"The guy was definitely dead!" exclaimed Dresden. "There was a smell, not strong, but there was a smell of decomposing flesh."

After another moment of silence, Danbury said, "Open your eyes, Dresden. Good job. You did well. You only had a second. Your recall was great."

"I've been trained to notice things after the fact," said Dresden, who seemed pleased with himself, particularly in light of Danbury's praise. "To look closely for trace evidence. But I've never had to recall details of a scene beforehand."

"He didn't mean to kill anyone else. The bomber. Otherwise, why add a timer? Why not explode it instantly? When the trunk was opened."

"Maybe they thought the homeless population would be the ones to open the trunk," yelled Matthew.

"Interesting," said Danbury, rubbing the stubble on his chin with his thumb. "We need a profiler. If that's true. It's possible. And we need to tell them." Danbury motioned to the state police and detectives who had arrived on the scene after the blast. "We're looking for DNA. In the rubble. We'll need to set up lights. Call in a K-9 unit. But we need to keep this under wraps. The details. Nobody outside of this car hears about the body."

"Why do we tell them that we're looking for the DNA, then?" Dresden yelled back.

"Leave that to me," said Danbury. "I'll handle it. We don't want any press. Not about the body. The blast, we can't prevent that. It'll be news before morning," said Danbury, pointing to two local news vans that had arrived on the scene and were being corded off with the yellow crime-scene tape by a fresh reinforcement of police officers.

"Doc, do you want to stay?" Danbury yelled, turning to Matthew.

"No," Matthew yelled back definitively. "Not even a little bit."

"Are you OK to drive? With that ankle?"

"I'll be fine. It's my left ankle," yelled Matthew dismissively as he opened the door and slid out, landing gently on his right foot. "I'd say let me know if you need anything else. But somehow, I don't think that'll be a problem."

Danbury just smirked at the snide remark and yelled, "G'night, Doc."

As Matthew drove home, he checked the time to see that it was after midnight. He couldn't account for the time of most of the evening. It was such a blur. As he drove, thankful that it was his left ankle that throbbed and not his right one, and grateful that he didn't have a manual transmission on either of his cars, requiring him to use his left foot on a clutch pedal, he replayed what had transpired. He couldn't get the exact order of events straight in his mind, which was frustrating. What had just happened, and why had it happened?

With his ears still ringing and his ankle throbbing, he vehemently wished he hadn't gone with Danbury to see the car that evening. But then he thought about the injured men, particularly the severely injured one. Though he had been unable to do much to help the guy, he was glad he was there, monitoring the situation and handing it off professionally to the paramedics. They had hauled him off efficiently to what would surely be an immediate operating room.

He was, Matthew admitted to himself, miffed with the situation. He had a job, a career, one that helped people, after all. And he was less than fully effective doing it on so little sleep multiple nights in a row. He fumed most of the way home until, turning onto the end of his street, he felt the peace and tranquility of the carefully chosen location wash over him.

Happy to be home, he punched the button on the garage door opener and pulled the Element into its spot inside. He turned the car off, and as the garage door closed behind him, he leaned over the steering wheel and took a deep breath before climbing out. His life felt out of control in this new year. Cici was back in London. A murderer was running unchecked through the Durham area, toying with the police and blowing up cars. Thoroughly exhausted, Matthew knew he was facing another long day treating patients with an ankle that there'd be no time to prop up and ice.

After schlepping into the house and, turning off and resetting the alarm, Matthew set everything up for his morning routine and pulled a fresh ice pack from his freezer. He grabbed a bottle of water from his refrigerator and from the cabinet above his microwave, he pulled out a bottle of naproxen sodium to help with the pain and swelling. Limping back to the bedroom with his supplies, Matthew swallowed two of the pills and downed the water bottle.

He washed up for the night and rearranged the pillows on his bed to prop the injured ankle up. Setting the morning alarm on his phone, he turned the volume up to be sure to hear it above the buzzing noise in his ears. After replacing the ice pack in the ankle wrap with the fresh one and strapping it back in place, he climbed into bed. Thinking that he might have trouble getting the ankle comfortable enough to be able to get to sleep was the last thought he had as Max curled up beside him and he fell deeply asleep.

"What *is* that?" Matthew muttered when the annoying sound woke him up seemingly a few minutes later. Rolling over to retrieve his phone, he realized that it was Cici on FaceTime, and the volume was excessively loud. That was a relief, he thought, that his hearing was much better this morning. The ringing in his ears was mostly gone as he propped himself up on the one pillow that wasn't under his ankle and tapped the phone to accept the incoming FaceTime request.

"Good morning . . ." began Cici. She stopped before finishing the sentence and asked with concern, "Are you OK? Don't take this the wrong way, but you look awful."

"Thanks, Cees," said Matthew, reverting to the name that only he called her. "I've been better, but I'm sure I've also been worse."

"What on earth happened?" she asked pointedly.

He raised an eyebrow as he observed her concern turn to something akin to an accusing annoyance as he began to tell her the story of the night before.

"Why did you leave Penn and Leo's with him?" asked Cici, rolling her eyes at him.

"Yeah, my ankle is fine," he said tersely. He was still cranky about it all himself, and he didn't need her to tell him that he should have gone home instead.

"I'm sorry, Matthew." She amended, "How is your ankle? And your hearing?"

"The ankle is throbbing this morning," he said. "My hearing is much better. The roar is just a dull one now, but my head hurts."

"Can you get your colleagues to cover for you and just rest today?" asked Cici, the concern returning to the lovely features that Matthew adored. He had always been drawn to her big brown eyes and her pert little nose. A fresh wave of missing her washed over him.

"I wish I could," he said. "But Dr. Rob is off on a winter-semester trip with his daughter, Ariel, and it's cold and flu season. Not to mention a rash of a nasty stomach bug we've seen lately. We had to send one teenager to the hospital yesterday for fluids to get rehydrated. It's just that time of year."

"I wish I were there to help."

"Me too," he said simply. "I'll get through the day and try, again, to get home and in bed early tonight, Danbury or no Danbury."

"I hear you, but promise me something?"

"Anything, Cees."

"Promise me that you'll take care of yourself as well as you do your patients. Your hearing and your ankle—both need time to heal. And you need to take care of yourself so that they will."

Taking a deep breath and blowing it out, he said, "I promise to do my best."

She grimaced at him, but she seemed to accept that answer. After their usual proclamations of how much they loved and missed each other, they said goodbye, and Matthew turned the alarm on his phone off. It was due to sound in another two minutes. He wanted to pull the covers over his head and make the day start in another three or four hours, at least, but Max was headbutting his arm.

"Yeah, big guy, I know, you're hungry," said Matthew, scratching the big cat on the head, between his ears and down the side of his face. Max lifted his chin to have it scratched under and purred loudly. Then, abruptly, Max jumped down and headed down the hallway to the kitchen.

Matthew carefully swung his legs over the edge of the bed and sat up fully, stretching. Gingerly, he put some weight on both feet to stand and then winced as pain shot through his left ankle. Determinedly, he made his way down the hallway to the kitchen to get his usual cup of coffee before going, albeit much more slowly, about his morning routine. With that accomplished, he replaced the ice pack in the ankle wrap and took more naproxen sodium.

Grabbing his satchel from the end of the sofa, he realized that his favorite leather bomber jacket wasn't with it and had gone to the hospital the night before. He limped down the hall and dug through his closet for another one. After checking that he had everything, he pulled the key from the hanger beside the door to the garage, locked up, and reset the alarm.

Despite the unpredictable winter weather and his somewhat limited mobility, he had chosen the key fob for the Corvette. Needing something racy and exciting in his life this morning, he backed carefully out of his garage and clicked to close the door behind him. As he started down the street, Mrs. Drewer was out walking her yappy little Pomeranian, Oscar, and she waved a gloved hand at him. Neither the neighbor nor the dog had liked him initially, but he'd befriended both, so he stopped to greet them.

"Good morning, Mrs. Drewer," he said, lowering his window and trying to lower the volume of his voice as well.

"Good morning, Matthew," she said after scooping Oscar up. "It's a chilly one. I've been in North Carolina too long." She laughed. "When I first moved here, I loved brisk mornings like this, and I didn't think they were cold at all. But now," she added, leaving the statement hanging as she pulled her parka closer around her chin with the hand that wasn't holding the small fluffy dog.

"It is pretty chilly, I agree, but we've had worse in January. Hi, Oscar," said Matthew, holding his hand out to have it licked by the darting little pink tongue. That was the invitation he wanted before scratching Oscar's head for a moment.

"I haven't seen much of you this week," said Cordelia Drewer. Before they'd become friends, her tone would have been accusatory, and Matthew would have known that the comment was both a dig and a request for him to tell her where he'd been. A retired schoolteacher who had moved south, Cordelia Drewer was on the neighborhood watch committee. It was a responsibility she took quite seriously, and she missed nothing that was going on around her.

Feeling no judgment from her now, Matthew explained that he'd been helping Danbury with an investigation since Cici had flown out Sunday night.

"Which you can't talk about," finished Mrs. Drewer for him. "I understand. Oh, did you see the paper this morning? Of course not," she said, answering her own question. "You don't take the paper, do you?"

Matthew shook his head no.

"There was a big explosion up on the edge of Durham in Research Triangle Park last night. They're still trying to figure out exactly what happened, but it sounds like it was a car bomb, and two police officers were injured, one critically," she added.

"Only injured?" Matthew inquired, lifting an eyebrow. "Nobody was killed, I hope?"

"Not at the time the paper was printed," she said. "It said the officer in critical condition was undergoing surgery. The other sustained severe injuries but was stable."

"Good to know," said Matthew, relieved that the forensics guy had at least made it to the hospital and into surgery. "I've got a busy day ahead, so I need to get going. It's cold and flu season, you know. Stay well, and have a great day, Mrs. Drewer."

"You too, Matthew," she said, waving a gloved hand at him as he drove off.

Ordinarily, he'd relish cranking up his playlist and enjoying some of his classic rock music on the way to work. This morning, though, he thought he'd spare his ears further assault and chose to drive to work in silence. He paused for a moment to pray for the injured officers and the safety of the others involved in the investigation. It had taken an ugly turn last night, and Matthew was concerned for them. Danbury hadn't seemed to think the police force was the target of the bomb, but Matthew was certain that there was no way to know that yet.

12 ~ Going, going, and going

When he arrived at his office, Matthew dreaded the inevitable confrontation with Gladys. He knew she'd pepper him with questions about his injury and lecture him like a mother hen when nobody else was around. Hoping to get it over with, he limped awkwardly in and down to the front desk to place his order with Trina for the daily lunch train. Today, the order would come from Peak Eats, and Matthew loved most everything on their menu.

To his surprise, he hadn't run into Gladys. Letting himself into his office, he swapped his heavy jacket for his lab coat and pulled his tablet from his satchel, stashing the latter under his desk. His usual morning routine included climbing the stairs outside his office door to the break room above and getting one more cup of coffee before beginning to see patients.

Just as he was contemplating whether the strain on his ankle to get up and down the stairs was worth getting the caffeine into his overly tired body, the stairwell door opened and Gladys waddled out, coffee in hand.

"Well, good morning," she said to him, looking him up and down, as if she was trying to figure out what was different about him. "You look tired," she finally concluded.

"I am tired, Gladys. And I sprained my ankle last night. So I was just trying to decide if it's worth it to make the trek upstairs for coffee. I need the coffee, but the ankle doesn't need the stairs."

"You know there is a perfectly good elevator at the other end of this hallway, and I hear it works real well," she said, smiling up at him mischievously, obviously enjoying his dilemma. She didn't understand half of the severity of it, or she'd derive no pleasure from teasing him.

"Yeah, I know. I've only used it a handful of times since I've been here, but I guess today is a good day for it, huh? I'll see you in exam room two in about fifteen," he said as he limped away as quickly as he could.

"Hold up!" she ordered. "You sure that's just a sprain?" When he turned to look at her over his shoulder, one hand was on her hip, and her head was tilted accusingly at him.

"I'm sure, Gladys. It's just a really bad sprain."

"You need to get off that thing. And you a doctor. You know this."

"I do, Gladys, but with Dr. Rob away, we're stretched thin. If I'd thought I could have stayed home and kept it propped up all day, believe me, I'd have done it." Before she could object further, he stiffly shuffled as quickly as he could for the elevator, pushed the button, and limped in. If she'd really been concerned, she could have offered to get his coffee for him, he thought irritably. He knew he would have to be careful not to voice any of the cranky thoughts that were in his mind today.

Lack of sleep and the ankle pain were causing his normally positive attitude to slide to the negative side and he didn't like it at all. Besides which, Gladys would never get enough sugar in his coffee for his taste. Once off the elevator, he shuffled to do it himself.

*****

After a full morning of patients, Matthew washed up carefully. He retrieved his lunch from the front desk and a fresh ice pack from the freezer in the nurses' station behind it. Hobbling down to his office, he propped up his foot and replaced the ice pack before diving into his lunch. He was just starting on the first bite when he felt his phone vibrate in his pocket.

He put the meatloaf sandwich down long enough to pull out the phone and see that he had an incoming text from Danbury. Most of him wanted to put the phone back in his pocket and ignore the text. That was just the tired and irritable part of his brain talking to him, he knew, so he clicked to open the text.

Danbury wanted to talk to him and asked if he could meet at Peak

Eats to grab a late lunch. Matthew quickly texted back, "Eating now. In my office. Join me if you want. I can't get away today." Satisfied that he'd answered honestly, he returned his phone to his pocket and picked up his sandwich, determined to enjoy the rest of it in peace.

He'd finished his lunch and was sipping the last of the hot apple cider on his desk, making updates to his patient charts, when he was startled by a knock at the door.

"Come in," he called, determined not to get up on the ankle to go and open the door.

The door opened abruptly, and Danbury stepped through. "Hey, Doc," said Danbury, closing the door behind him. "I need your help."

Pushing back every ill thought that was fighting to break the surface of his mind and then come out of his mouth, Matthew leaned back in his chair. "Come on in and have a seat. I'm not sure I can be of much help to anyone," he said, motioning to his foot propped on the chair beside his desk.

"How bad is it?" asked Danbury, pulling up the chair opposite Matthew's desk and sitting heavily in it.

"I should be at home with it propped up and iced," admitted Matthew, who was feeling entirely mortal at the moment. "But we're short-staffed, and I'm needed here."

"I see," said Danbury, who was hedging about something. That was unusual for the man, Matthew thought. He usually came bursting in like a bull with whatever requests he had of Matthew or anyone else.

"What do you need?" Matthew finally asked, knowing that he'd regret it as he templed his fingers, elbows on the desk in front of him.

Danbury took a breath and then dove in. "I need you to talk to some people."

"What people?"

"Homeless ones. In the camp. At the end of Defender Drive."

"The homeless people we didn't see down that dead-end road last night?"

"Yeah," said Danbury. "Those people."

"Why me?" asked Matthew simply.

"Several reasons. You're not a cop. You are a doctor. They disappear. When they see us coming. Two uniformed officers went this morning. Then I tried. They've been there. You can tell they just left. But they won't talk to us. They hide. I need somebody who isn't a cop. Maybe somebody who can offer help. Like medical attention."

Matthew didn't reply immediately. As he had done for a good bit of the day so far, he was fighting with himself, and the internal battle was heated.

"You can drive in. Almost all the way in," added Danbury, into the silence. "You won't have to walk far."

"I have the Corvette here today," said Matthew. "I'm not going off-roading out there in that."

When Matthew didn't offer to swap cars, Danbury shifted uncomfortably in his chair. "Doc, I wouldn't ask if I didn't need you. I know you've been out all week. Every night. Late. And last night was rough."

"Really rough," Matthew emphasized, but then he remembered the homeless population he'd encountered living under the bridges when he was in Miami. The homeless children he'd helped rose to the forefront of his mind as thoughts of his own physical comfort faded into the background. He had a strange knowing that there would be children involved again, young ones who needed his help. Unsure how he knew, he realized that he just knew.

"Yeah, OK," Matthew said after a moment. "Are there children down there? Or just adults? Do you know? What do they need? Blankets or coats or medications?"

"No idea," said Danbury, grinning triumphantly. "Ask them when you find them. Then ask what they saw. They likely saw something. They probably watch all that goes on. Everything down that road. Maybe they saw who left the car. Or how the body got in it. No telling. But they'll talk to you. Everybody always does. You put them at ease."

Matthew initially felt like the biggest pushover on the planet. But then thoughts of helping homeless people, particularly children, treating medical conditions and providing some hope, took over. It was why he'd gone to medical school to begin with. He'd wanted to help people, and here was a chance to reach the unreachable, those who would never grace his office door.

"OK, Danbury. You can stop with the sales pitch. I'm going. I won't finish up with patients until nearly four today. But I need to go while it's still light out. I'll ask my office manager to shift some of my patients and see what I can do to get out earlier," Matthew pondered aloud. "I need to swap out my car, though. I really can't take the Corvette down there, even if I wanted to. It's too low to the ground."

"Keys," said Danbury, sticking his hand out. "And security code for the kitchen door. I know you have it set."

"I do." Matthew sighed. "You're going to swap my car out?"

"It's the least I can do," said Danbury, grinning as he rose from the chair.

Danbury thought he'd just won a major battle, but it wasn't the war, so Matthew figured he'd just let him think that. He could cash in the favor later. With a smirk at that thought, he reached down for his satchel and handed over the keys to the Corvette. He rattled off the security code and asked Danbury if he needed to write it down.

"Nope. I got it. I'll bring your Element back. In a half hour. Maybe less."

"I'll be with patients. Just drop the keys with Maddie or Trina at the front desk."

"OK. Oh, and Doc." Danbury paused in the doorway. "Thanks. I appreciate it."

Before he could recover from the shock and respond, Danbury was gone, leaving Matthew alone again in his office. Penn's work on Danbury was obvious. Danbury had probably succeeded and perhaps even survived by his quick wits in the military, and the result was abrupt mannerisms. It was ingrained.

Matthew wondered, briefly, what Danbury's quick wit had enabled him to survive. Likely more than he could probably even imagine. As he gathered his lunch trash and began to prepare for his next round of patients, he figured he wouldn't have a chance to ask. That wasn't a question for casual conversation, and Danbury was an extremely private person.

Remembering his promise, he called the front desk and asked Trina if she could shift his final two patients of the day, explaining that he was needed across town to treat a group of homeless people. He knew Trina would move heaven and earth to help him if she knew that detail. She readily agreed to try.

After Matthew limped through exam rooms to treat his next three patients, he made his way to the front desk. Maddie, the young receptionist, had finally overcome most of her shyness around him and looked up, grinning at him adoringly.

"Dr. Paine, I have your keys here," she said, retrieving them from a drawer beneath the desk and handing them to him. "Your detective friend dropped them off. Trina transferred your last couple of patients to Megan, so you only have one left to see today."

Megan Sims, a physician's assistant, had joined the practice back in June and brought a resident, Sadie Peterson, with her. The last two patients were women, Matthew remembered, and he thought that should work out well.

"With Dr. Garner's blessing, Trina put together some supplies for you. I hope this helps," added Maddie as she handed him a bag. Matthew peered inside. There was a vial of insulin and syringes; two injectable epinephrine pens for severe allergic reactions; naloxone to treat a drug overdose in both spray and injectable forms; and a host of tablets and syrups to treat fever, cold symptoms and upset stomach. There were also topical treatments, bandages, and wraps.

"It does help, Maddie. Thank you," he responded. Smiling his sincere thanks, he winked at her and turned carefully on the injured ankle. Hobbling, he made his way back through the double doors and down the hallway.

*****

Driving in RTP after four in the afternoon wasn't fun on the best of days, so Matthew was happy to manage to get to Florida Boulevard by three thirty. He'd changed his ice pack and added a sturdier ankle brace just before he left. He had also added the supplies Trina had gathered to the medical bag in his car and moved it to the front seat within easy reach.

Danbury, whom Matthew had called from the car as he was leaving his office, told him there'd be backup stationed in the hotel parking lot, ready, watching, and waiting, in case Matthew ran into difficulty with the people living in the camp and needed help. He hadn't considered that possibility, but he was grateful that Danbury had.

Matthew was replaying the events of the evening before as he retraced the route he'd taken. A male body locked in the trunk, one that smelled only after opening the trunk. The forensics team had worn masks, and he assumed they'd had them on when they were working on the inside of the car. But still, a dead body in a warm trunk wouldn't take long to begin to decompose and emit nauseating odors. The days had been warm, so the trunk would have had to have been hot too. It was parked under the edge of the trees in the shade, so what would the temperature have reached within the trunk? He wasn't sure.

As he pondered this, another thought struck him. How long had Ruby said Misty had owned the older car? Had she said? Did she know? Would Cara know? And how long ago had she legally become Misty Blue? He couldn't remember what Danbury had said about that either, but he figured he'd ask the first chance he got.

Circling in front of the hotel and heading down the dead-end road beyond, Matthew felt both elation at the opportunity to help people and foreboding as he considered what it might take to convince them to let him help. The road had been cleared of debris from the evening before, the remains of the car hauled off somehow.

Matthew pulled off the end of the roadbed and through a low, grassy area. The clearing was wide enough and the undergrowth low enough for him to traverse in the Element, though he hoped there were no sharp objects hiding in the tall grass. On his right, he could see a path worn through the brush. Not one made by a car but by foot traffic from the end of the road. Where it went was the question. He came to an abrupt stop in front of a large oak tree because the wide path ended. On either side were saplings and larger trees. It was literally the end of the road for the Element, so he slid gingerly out, bringing his medical bag with him, and looked around.

The footpath that he had seen on the right seemed to go around the huge oak. He hobbled along to follow it. Watching the ground closely for holes that could turn his ankle again or roots that could pose a tripping hazard, he made his way into a grove of trees beyond the oak. Each tree beyond it, it seemed, had a teepee-like structure leaning against it. Anything that could be used had been: boards, tree limbs, tarps, boxes, and some crinkled metal that looked like sheeting of some sort.

The slight clearing in the middle of the trees had been recently occupied. A fire smoldered inside a ring of rocks that formed a makeshift firepit, and a grate straddled the rocks. Crude seating surrounded the fire, upturned logs, rocks, and piles of debris arranged at seat height. Looking around him, Matthew called out, "Hello?"

He wasn't really expecting an answer to that, so he added, "I'm Matthew. I'm a doctor. I came to see if anyone down here needs any medical attention. Anyone sick or injured? Anyone need help?"

He paused, listening to the silence. He could hear traffic from the nearby I-40 interstate that would only get louder over the next couple of hours. It was what he didn't hear that made him think the people who had recently vacated the area weren't far away. There were no forest sounds. No squirrels or birds, both of which were plentiful in any wooded areas of North Carolina, rustled in the bushes or the underbrush. That would be because the people were there, watching him, waiting for him to leave.

Leaving wasn't what he intended to do, so he sat down on one of the logs by the smoldering fire and said, "I can wait. I just want to help you. Anyone who needs medical attention can come on out. I'm here to help, really."

After another moment of silence, Matthew was initially startled by a barking sound that he realized he knew well. He sat still, silently waiting for the source of the sound to be revealed, knowing that it would be soon.

13 ~ Enter help

At the far edge of the clearing, a woman materialized from the underbrush. She was carrying a well-wrapped bundle in her arms.

"Help?" she said. "Doctor? Help?"

"Yes," Matthew said without standing up and startling her. His ankle was happier with him sitting down anyway. "I'm a doctor. I help sick people."

"My son," she said, unable to finish the statement, if she'd intended to, because the child she held was racked with another coughing fit. It was the noise Matthew had heard as he waited in the clearing, a barking cough, not a low, wet one. From the sound, he assumed it was croup and not respiratory syncytial virus, or RSV. The two were related in that RSV could have been the virus that caused the croup, so he was eager to examine the coughing child.

The mother held the small boy upright and patted his back vigorously. When the coughing subsided enough for her to continue, she slid the child up to her shoulder. "He does this days," she said haltingly, holding up five fingers behind the child's back. "Is more bad."

"How old is he?" asked Matthew.

Holding up two fingers from behind the bundle of the child, she said, "He has two years."

"May I see him?" asked Matthew, still not standing up but motioning for the woman to bring the child to him. Matthew knew that his six-foot-three-inch height could be intimidating to children and probably also to diminutive parents who were clearly not born in

America. The tiny woman had dark hair, brown skin, and penetrating dark eyes that were darting all around as she slowly approached.

Nervously, she held out her child for Matthew to see. Before he could do much, the child was again racked with a barking cough, and the fit lasted longer this time.

"I need to check for fever," said Matthew. Reaching into his bag and pulling out a forehead reader that he used with small children, he held it aloft for her to see. He was certain that the boy would have a fever. The thermometer proved him right, and he tried not to show the alarm that he felt when he read it. Without the ability to do an x-ray, run a blood test, or check the oxygen level of the boy's blood out here in the woods, he couldn't verify his initial diagnosis, but he could at least partially treat the symptoms.

"Is he allergic to anything?" asked Matthew.

"Al-er-git?" the mother tried to repeat what Matthew had said. "*No sé*," she said, shaking her head.

Unsure if it was the allergic reaction or his question that the woman didn't know, he reached back into his bag and withdrew a bottle of children's liquid ibuprofen. "Medicine," he said, holding it up for her inspection. "To bring down the fever. He is too hot."

The woman nodded, wide-eyed. She looked scared but determined to help her son.

Shaking the bottle, Matthew removed the protective wrap and unscrewed the lid. He guessed at the child's weight, based on the size of the bundle the woman held, as somewhat below average for his age and suctioned up some of the purple liquid. He wished he could be more precise with all of it, but maybe he could convince her to get additional help.

"Sit down here"—Matthew indicated the upturned log beside him—"and hold his head up." The child drooped in the woman's arms. "He needs to drink this," he instructed.

She complied. Matthew slipped the dropper between the dry lips, and the child didn't object as he swallowed and the liquid slid down. That was the first step, but the coughing fit that immediately followed made Matthew wonder if the medication had stayed down. Needing to quickly address the next issue, the cough, he examined the child as well as he could in the little clearing, sitting on upturned logs.

He'd learned, in Miami, that the homeless Latina population of illegal immigrants was terrified of anyone and anything that looked official. Police officers, definitely, but hospitals also topped the list. He asked her if they could take the child to the hospital, and he got exactly the reaction he thought he'd get.

She withdrew the child, shaking her head violently. She jumped to her feet and was preparing to run when Matthew held out his hand to her. "It's OK," he said. "No hospital. But we need more medicine. I don't have any, but I can get what he needs. Will you wait for me to get it?"

She looked unsure initially, then glanced down at her son and nodded her agreement.

"OK, will you sit here with me and wait?"

Again, she nodded and dropped back onto the log beside him.

Matthew pulled his phone out of his jacket pocket. He knew he could call his office and ask Trina to get Dr. Garner to call in a breathing treatment to whatever pharmacy was closest to where he was. The problem was that he needed some patient information first to submit the prescription. And he wasn't sure how he was going to get it. He could get an over-the-counter inhaler, if it came to that. He knew that an albuterol nebulizer would be more effective, both in terms of getting it in the child properly and of it working effectively.

They had stocked up his medical bag for lots of eventualities, but not this one.

"What is the child's name?" he asked.

"Joseph, like father," she said.

"When was he born?"

"*Noviembre?*" she said.

Matthew nodded. "November," he repeated. "What day?"

"*Dieciocho.*" This one, Matthew didn't know. He had no idea how to spell it to look it up. But then he had another thought.

"Just a minute," he said, searching his mind for the Spanish. Finally, he came up with, "*Uno momento, por favor.*" That got him a weak smile from the small woman. He tapped his phone to pull up Dr. Rob's number. He hated to disturb his colleague on the trip with his daughter, but it was she who could help just now, and Matthew knew that Ariel would want to. Ariel had decided to go into the medical profession specifically to help underserved populations, and she was fluent in Spanish.

To Matthew's relief, he heard, "Dr. Rob here," on a fuzzy connection after the third ring.

Matthew quickly explained the situation and what it was that he needed. Dr. Rob put Ariel on the phone.

"Hey, Uncle Matt!" he heard her young, exuberant voice say. Though they weren't technically related, Ariel had started calling him that after he'd helped to find and rescue her in Miami the summer before. "Dad says you need a translator. You know I'm happy to help."

"I do. Thank you, Ariel. I'm going to put you on speaker so that you can talk to Joseph's mom for me, OK?"

"OK, sure."

After tapping the phone, he said, "OK, Ariel, can you tell her who you are and that you'll explain what we need to do to treat her son and get him well?"

"Of course," she said and then spouted off something, most of which entirely eluded Matthew. The mother just said, "*Sí, gracias,*" which Matthew did understand.

"Tell her I need his name and birth date so that we can get a prescription for him, a breathing treatment, to help him to stop coughing and be able to breathe better."

Again, Ariel quickly said something that Matthew didn't understand. The woman said, "Joseph Velázquez." After another quick question, she said, "Mira Velázquez."

Ariel asked her something else, and she responded again with *Noviembre* and then a string of words that went entirely by Matthew without the least bit of understanding.

"Ariel, can you explain to her how the breathing treatment will work? We'll be using a nebulizer, and he might not like it, but she'll have to keep him still for it to work. I'll need to get it delivered from a pharmacy and brought here, so she'll have to wait, unless you can convince her to come with me. We also need to get them to some place warm, out of the cold night air."

"OK, got it," said Ariel, and then she let loose with a fast string of words, none of which Matthew understood.

The woman responded in a rush of words that Matthew didn't comprehend, either, but she was becoming more distressed as she spoke until Ariel calmly said something to her. Matthew heard his name. Whatever else Ariel said, along with the soothing tone in which she said it, seemed to work.

"Matthew?" said Ariel.

"Yeah, I'm here."

"Take me off speaker?" she asked, and he tapped the phone and held it up to his ear.

"I can text you the information you need for Joseph, but she's scared, so I gave her all the reasons not to run. I promised her you'd take care of her and Joseph. She's afraid they'll deport her and her son like they did her husband. She's pretty sure he's been deported, or at least detained for deportation, and she doesn't know where he is. Her name is Mira; the son and husband are both Joseph. Their last name is Velázquez. She has a married daughter who was living in Durham. She was trying to find her, but she has no transportation, she ran out of money, and she isn't sure where to look. The daughter's name is Maria; her married name is Álvarez. Maria's husband's name is Alfonso. Promise me you'll take care of Mira and Joseph?"

"I'll do my best, Ariel. Thank you."

"No problem. I know you will. And you know this is my passion, so I'm glad you called me. Let me know if you need more help. You can call or text my cell directly, anytime. Take care, Uncle Matt!"

Matthew heard the ding on his phone a few minutes later and saw the promised text with the information Mira had given Ariel. Calling his office, he asked for Trina and explained what he needed. As he had known she would, Trina readily agreed to help. She looked up the pharmacies near him and provided the address of the closest one, where she'd have the prescription sent. Matthew thanked her and forwarded the patient information that Ariel had texted for the prescription. Then he called Danbury.

"Hey, Doc. How's it going?"

"I've got a sick child here, and I need to get a prescription picked up for him."

"Any word? On seeing the car?"

"I haven't asked about that yet. I'm treating the child first. I'll get to that, but I need *your* help right now," said Matthew, stressing the statement that Danbury had made earlier to talk him into being here. The battle that Danbury thought he'd won earlier that day to get Matthew to agree to help wasn't the war, and a turnabout on the next battle was fair play.

"What's that?" asked Danbury, sounding impatient.

"A couple of things. First, go to the pharmacy and pick up a prescription for Joseph Velázquez, birth date eleven, twenty-seventeen, eighteen. Got that?"

"I got it."

"And Pedialyte liquid in the little bottles, PediaSure, and chicken broth, in whatever form you can find them. That's the most urgent. Then, run down the last known address for Alfonso and Maria Álvarez. They are supposed to be in Durham, so that should narrow it down. And then see what you can find out about Joseph Álvarez being detained for deportation or having been deported."

"That's three," pointed out Danbury. "Or four. What's the prescription?"

"A breathing treatment, a nebulizer, which is basically a souped-up inhaler for little children. He needs it as fast as possible. My office is calling it in, and the sooner I get it and get his breathing stabilized, the sooner I can ask questions and get answers," prodded Matthew.

"OK, Doc. I'll go get it. Text me the address."

"Yeah, will do. Just let me know when you're here and I'll come get it. Don't come back here. I've got this," said Matthew, disconnecting this time before Danbury could and quickly texting the address Trina had given him.

"Mira," said Matthew, turning to the woman. "I think you can understand what I say better than you can tell me what you want to say. Right?"

She nodded uncertainly.

"So I'm going to explain this to you in English. We need to get your son out of the cold for the night. He is very sick. We want him to get better, not worse. Joseph needs a warm bed and medications. He needs soups and broths to get rehydrated. Drink," he added, making the motion of drinking from a glass when she looked confused.

She nodded, but the anguish on her face was more than Matthew could stand.

"I'll check you into the Home Away Hotel up the road for a week. Just you and Joseph," he clarified, wanting to put her at ease. "Until we can find your husband or your daughter. I can bring you some groceries. I think the rooms at the hotel have little kitchens so you can prepare meals. You can stay there and care for Joseph to get him well while we search for your husband and your daughter, OK?"

She looked scared, but she nodded her agreement. Caring for her son clearly took precedence over her fear of American authority figures.

Just then, a rustling in the underbrush startled Matthew. He turned to see a man clad from head to toe in camouflaged military fatigues, boots, and a matching beret. He carried no weapon that Matthew could see, but his face wasn't friendly.

"Gerard!" said Mira, and then she rattled off something that Matthew didn't understand.

The camouflaged man merely nodded and said, "*Sí*, Mira." That was followed by a string of other words that Matthew didn't understand, but the guy nodded accusingly at him twice during the course of his dialogue. Then, to Matthew, the guy said, in perfect English "You are not welcome here. Please leave."

"I can't do that," said Matthew. "Not until I get Joseph taken care of."

"Mira made a mistake talking to you. I know what you want, and we will not get involved. We take care of our own. She is staying here; she is one of us," he added, waving his hand at the woman, who was now cowering, head bowed over her son's tiny, coughing form.

"Mira," said Matthew. "Come with me to the hotel where you can care for Joseph. I will not stay, but I will get you checked in."

"Mira," said the camouflaged man, and then another stream of indistinguishable words flowed from his mouth that seemed to very much upset her. She broke down in sobs, which were only drowned out by her son's next coughing fit.

Standing and placing himself between the camouflaged man, whom Mira had called Gerard, and Mira, Matthew took her arm gently and began to lead her. Hobbling along, he guided her toward the massive oak. Out of the clearing and toward his car, he directed her. When he looked back over his shoulder, the man was gone. Noiselessly, he'd disappeared back into the brush that surrounded the clearing and camp.

"Come," said Matthew, motioning to his car. "We'll get Joseph well."

He got them settled in the Element, turned the heat on, and texted Danbury, "Change of plan. Meet me at the hotel. Checking them in. Text when you get there."

Slowly, Matthew drove around to the front of the hotel, parked, and helped Mira out, with Joseph still in her arms. As they entered the lobby, Matthew approached the desk. Mira cowered behind him. A woman behind the desk looked up in alarm, picked up a desk phone, and cupped her hand around the mouthpiece as she spoke quietly into it. Then, she turned on her heel and left the desk.

"Excuse me," said Matthew. "We need a room."

"No, sir. Not here," said a male voice behind them. Turning, Matthew looked down on a man dressed in khaki slacks and a blue blazer with a crest on the pocket. "We will not allow those people to stay here."

Matthew could feel the heat rising in his face in anger as the guy said "those people."

14 ~ Empathy and patience

"Why would you not allow a paying guest to stay in this hotel?" asked Matthew while he enjoyed the difference in height as he towered over the guy. Normally, it wasn't something that he thought much about or chose to use to his advantage, but there were times when it was incredibly helpful. This topped the list of those situations.

"Because they come in, use the public restroom in the lobby, and make a mess of it. They are most unwelcome," replied the man.

"Sir, do you have a family? Children?"

"Well, yes, but what does that have to do with—"

"Everything!" said Matthew forcefully. "We have a sick child here who needs medical care and attention. Dr. Matthew Paine," he said, thrusting his hand out.

Dubiously, the guy shook it. "Ronald Aiken, general manager," said the man.

"If your children were sick, Mr. Aiken, and they needed care, would you want to be literally left out in the cold, incapable of caring for them? Or would you appreciate someone providing them a warm bed and proper care to get them well? What wouldn't you do to get your children well, Mr. Aiken?"

The man just stared at Matthew, speechless.

"That's what I thought," said Matthew. "This 'person,'" he seethed with barely controlled anger, indicating Mira, who was still cowering behind him, "she is a mother. A parent, just like you. But she is the parent of a sick child. Now, I can take her somewhere else that will allow me to pay for her to spend the next week, or you can open your heart, your mind, and your hotel to allow them to stay here and try to help little Joseph get well."

"I ... guess ... maybe," stammered the man. "It's just the one woman, right? And the child?"

"Yes," said Matthew. "I'll be checking on them over the next few days, bringing food and medication, but it'll just be the two of them staying in the suite."

"OK, I guess we can do that," said Aiken, somewhat reluctantly, and the woman who had walked away suddenly returned to the counter and started tapping keys on the computer.

"Name?" she said.

"Matthew Paine, and the credit card is mine. Mira Velázquez will be occupying the room."

"Credit card," the woman said tersely, obviously not impressed with the decision to allow a homeless woman access to the hotel under any circumstances, paid or otherwise.

As Matthew was signing the paperwork, he heard a familiar voice behind him. "Got it, Doc," said Danbury. "The prescription. And the fluids." Matthew saw, over his shoulder, that Danbury carried two bags, one in each hand, as he walked into the hotel lobby.

Before Matthew could respond, the woman behind the desk, whose face had suddenly gone from puckered in disapproval to lighting up like a Christmas tree, said, "Detective Danbury! How can we help you?" She was clearly flirting with him. Matthew raised an eyebrow but said nothing about the guy having a serious girlfriend.

"You just did. If you checked them in," replied Danbury.

"You're with the police? Why didn't you say so?" asked the manager, handing Matthew a paper packet containing two plastic key cards with the room number scribbled on the front.

"Shhhh," hissed Matthew as he watched Mira prepare to make a run for it.

"Witness protection?" the hotel manager misinterpreted and whispered to them. "Ohhhhh, you're undercover, right?" he added, conspiratorially, as if he'd just been admitted to the secret club. Matthew didn't contradict him directly, nor did Danbury.

"*Policía?*" Mira asked, looking up at Matthew, the panic obvious in her eyes.

"No, Mira. I'm a doctor. And it's OK. He's with me," he told her quietly as he gestured toward Danbury. "He's a friend. He wants to help."

Holding her elbow gently and steering her toward the elevator, Matthew added, "Let's get you and Joseph upstairs and settled in for the night. I can have food delivered for you and bring you groceries later."

Matthew reached behind him and took the bags that Danbury handed over and then held a hand up behind his back to keep Danbury from following. Over his shoulder, he said, "I'll be right back. Give me about twenty minutes."

"OK, Doc. I'll wait here."

He didn't look back, but Matthew was sure that the woman behind the desk was delighted to hear this news.

After getting Mira and Joseph settled and managing to get the breathing treatment into the small boy, Matthew gave instructions, as best he could, for giving the child another treatment before he went to bed for the night. Three a day, he told her. Maybe they'd need more, he thought, but they would start there. Checking Joseph's temperature again, Matthew was relieved to see that it had dropped to a less concerning level. He was thankful to see it coming down.

Carefully, speaking as slowly and clearly as he could, Matthew instructed Mira to look at the clock, and he explained the medication schedule. Writing it down on a hotel note pad, he told her when to give the ibuprofen again, and he showed her how much. He explained the liquids to get into Joseph and why those were important.

Showing her the peephole in the door, he told her to answer for a pizza delivery and said that he'd come back later that evening to bring more groceries and supplies. He showed her how to flip the security lock behind him. There were tears in her eyes as she thanked him, and he slipped out quietly, closing the door behind him. Hearing the security bar click into place, he headed back downstairs.

In the lobby, Danbury was waiting by the front door, and the woman behind the desk looked annoyed by this development. Matthew stifled a smile as he walked by her.

"All set?" asked Danbury.

"For a while. I got the meds in Joseph, and I'll order a pizza for Mira. If we're getting something to eat, I'll take her some groceries and maybe a change of clothes later. She didn't bring any with her. Maybe she left some belongings down in the camp. I didn't think to ask."

"What did she say?"

"About the car? Nothing yet. I haven't asked her."

Danbury shot Matthew a hard look, then sighed. "OK, Doc. I trust you. And your timing."

"Good. She's scared, and I need her to trust me before I start asking her questions. She needs to know that I genuinely care about her and her son. It's not just about police work. She needs empathy, and you need patience. I'll talk to her when I take the groceries and clothes."

Then, changing the subject entirely, Matthew added, "Now, about dinner. Are we ready to get some?"

"Yeah, I'm hungry," said Danbury.

Matthew refrained from mentioning that the big detective was always hungry and tapped his phone to see what was nearby. "There's a sports bar and grill just on the other side of the interstate from here. Rubrios. According to the app, it has Italian and American fare at reasonable prices and a good rating. How does that sound?"

"Close, good, and reasonable. Rubrios it is."

"First left on the other side of the interstate, then just down on the left. You can probably see it from Florida Boulevard."

"OK, meet you there."

Matthew shuffled slowly out into the evening, already dark and chilly. Though he liked the cooler weather, he wasn't overly fond of the shortened days and early nightfall of winter. Climbing into his

Element, he started it up and navigated out onto the bridge over I-40.

As he looked down over the interstate, he saw cars tightly packed along multiple lanes in both directions and lots of brake lights. He was thankful not to be sitting in that traffic jam. Why did people call it rush hour when nobody was ever able to rush anywhere? Snails could rush faster than the traffic he saw backed up out of sight in both directions. He crossed over the interstate and turned left.

When they'd reconvened on the other side of the interstate at the restaurant moments later, they were shown to a table, but Danbury asked for a booth in the back corner instead. The hostess led them to a dark far-right corner booth.

Matthew realized that he was feeling jittery and jumpy. His knee bounced and foot tapped anxiously, but he wasn't sure why. Maybe dinner would help. At least, he hoped so.

After they'd gotten settled and placed their drink orders, he looked around and said, "I have so many questions."

Danbury said, "Yeah? Me too. And only some answers. Let's order first. Then we can talk shop."

Nodding, Matthew asked the waiter who had appeared at his elbow, "Do you deliver?"

"Within a five-mile radius," the guy answered. "That's mostly hotels, with a few private residences."

"That's exactly what I need," said Matthew and placed an order to send to Mira before placing his own. After Matthew ordered a small calzone and a side salad for himself, Danbury doubled Matthew's order with a large calzone and a large salad.

When the waiter had walked away, Danbury leaned back into the corner of the booth and said, "OK, Doc, shoot."

"I'm not sure where to start. The box of Misty's things that you took from the strip club. Let's start there. Did it contain anything useful?"

"Not really. There were notes from admirers. And notes about performance times. A few receipts. One we're running down. The tire store. Where she had her tires replaced. Maybe she mentioned where she was going. To someone at that store. It's a long shot. Charlene and Ruby both said she was private. Even Cara didn't know where she was going. But we're checking. Running down all leads."

"Did you get Misty's phone records? Was it her phone Dresden saw in her trunk? And was that the last location it was active?"

"Yes, likely so, and no," said Danbury, with a half smile at Matthew's barrage of questions. "I contacted Cara. She said Misty had a sparkly blue phone case. Like the one in the trunk of the car. It was probably Misty's. We found her cellular service provider. From bills in her apartment. We got the phone records. From the cellular company. After we got the request approved. The phone's last known location was north of Durham. Last Thursday. Not where the car was found."

"That just gives us a general location, though, right? It's a cell tower and not a specific spot?"

"Right."

"Huh," said Matthew, his foot tapping and knee bouncing under the table in concentration as his eyebrow rose in thought. "That doesn't really tell us anything, though, does it? Misty might have already been dead, and somebody else used her phone. Could you see who that last call was made to?"

"Yeah. We're working that angle. It was her latest boyfriend. Trent Kent."

"Which makes it sound more likely that she made the call."

"Could be," said Danbury. "We're trying to find him. To ask him."

"Trying?"

"He hasn't been at work. Not this week. He's not answering his phone. Or his door. And his neighbors haven't seen him. Not for several days. We're working on a search warrant."

"Interesting." Matthew nodded. "Were you able to find any DNA from the car explosion?"

"They're working on that too. Testing the debris. Anything that didn't completely burn up. Though that doesn't look promising. Why? What are you thinking?" Danbury asked perceptively.

"Maybe it was Misty's boyfriend, Kent, in the trunk. Maybe that's why he wasn't looking for her, why he didn't go to the police and file a missing persons report."

"Yeah, I thought of that too. Maybe it was. I hope they'll find some trace DNA. It's not looking good."

"Either Kent wasn't worried about where she was because he thought he knew," said Matthew, "or he wasn't around to look for her. Or maybe they broke up already. Everyone we've talked to about her said she went through men regularly."

"All valid theories."

"What if it was Kent in the trunk, and the killer wanted us to know he was dead?" asked Matthew. "Or at least, that whoever was in the trunk was dead. Why else was there a timer on the explosives? Why weren't they set to detonate immediately, as soon as the trunk was pried open? It's like the killer wanted whoever opened the trunk to be able to walk away and talk about what they saw."

"They didn't leave evidence. Nothing left behind. Of the killer. Or the person in the trunk."

"Did you get Misty's autopsy results back yet?"

"Yeah. There are some oddities. With those results," said Danbury.

"More odd than a diamond in her tooth and vampire marks on her neck?"

Danbury chuckled. "OK, maybe not. There were needle marks. Barely noticeable. Between the first two toes. On her left foot. The one the shoe was glued on."

"If Misty wasn't a drug user, maybe that's why the shoe was glued on. To prevent notice of the needle mark and whatever was injected."

"That's what the ME thinks. The victim was injected. The shoe was glued on to hide it. I think we found the body early. Sooner than the murderer anticipated. Or intended."

"That makes sense. If she'd been in the pool longer, that needle mark would have been obscured in shriveled, decomposing skin," concluded Matthew.

"But we found it. She was injected with a sedative. Used to subdue her. At least. Possibly enough to kill her."

"What about the marks on her neck?"

"Not surface wounds. Made with something long and sharp. Maybe an ice pick. Like you suggested. Severed an artery. The other possible cause of death."

"Puncture wounds that were deep enough to sever the carotid artery," muttered Matthew.

"Right."

"She would have bled out quickly if that was the cause of death. If that wound were inflicted postmortem, the bleeding would have been slower with no pumping heart."

"The killer likely injected first. Drugged to subdue her. Then stabbed her."

They sat in silence for a moment before Matthew began to summarize. "She was given a sedative, the quantity of which is unknown. The marks that looked like a vampire bite went deeper and severed an artery. Her fingerprints were removed from her frozen body, which was then put in a heated pool. The killer went to a lot of trouble to obscure the time and method of death, as well as the identity of the victim."

Danbury waited while Matthew pondered, his foot tapping loudly under the table in concentration before he added, "And the eye color being so vibrantly blue instead of the cornea being cloudy and opaque, did your ME come to any conclusion about why that was?"

"The corneas were cloudier. When the ME got the body. She did remark on the pictures. Those taken at the scene. She said your theory is as good as any."

"That the eyes were closed when the body was frozen and then popped open in the pool?"

"Right.

"What about the diamond? How was it attached to her molar?"

"It wasn't."

"It was just lodged in there?"

"As far as the ME could tell. She found no residue. Nothing to indicate it was attached."

"What did the gemologist say about the diamond? Anything useful?"

"Black diamonds are harder to classify. Gemologists report on cut and carat. But they can't comment on color and clarity. Because black diamonds are opaque. She thinks it came from the Central African Republic. Or CAR."

"So maybe they're blood diamonds?"

"Apparently, not technically. If she's right about the origin. Being a black diamond narrows it down. At least a little bit. According to the gemologist. There's a village there. In CAR. Sam Ouandja. It's near the border of Sudan."

"She can get that specific?"

"Not yet. CAR and Sam Ouandja are a guess. An educated one, apparently. We're securely transporting the diamond to a GIA lab. That's the Gemological Institute of America. They can tell us more. Like the origin. We'll get a full report. It's getting rushed."

"Huh," said Matthew, pondering this. "But otherwise, nothing distinctive about it?"

"What? You wanted a coded message? Etched into the diamond? A full confession from the killer?" asked Danbury when Matthew looked disappointed.

"That would have been nice," said Matthew, chuckling at Danbury.

"They can do that. Etch tiny characters on diamonds."

"Really?" asked Matthew.

"Apparently. But mostly on white diamonds. Those are usually more valuable. The GIA lab can put an identifying mark. On the girdle of the diamond. That certifies their valuation. That's usually only on the most valuable diamonds."

"Huh," said Matthew, taking it all in. "There is one other thing."

Danbury held up his hand in warning as the waiter approached from behind Matthew to deliver their meals. After he'd left, Danbury said, "What's that?"

"Misty's car title," said Matthew. "Ruby said it was an older Camry but that it was reliable, so Misty loved it."

"Yeah?"

"How long did you say she'd legally been using the name Misty Blue?"

"Almost six years."

"What year model was the car? And how long had Misty Blue's name been on the title?"

"It was a 2004. She'd owned it almost six years. I see what you're getting at. Maybe she was the previous owner."

"Exactly. Maybe Misty Blue was the owner before that but under her former name."

"Great idea," said Danbury. "And worth checking out."

They ate in silence, Danbury finishing twice as much food in half the time as it took Matthew to eat his meal. Matthew appreciated the irony. Penn had coauthored a book called *Mindful Dining*. It was all about slowing down and enjoying each bite of food, being present in the moment so as not to over-eat. She was seriously dating a guy who consistently inhaled his food in mass quantities so fast that it would put cyclones to shame.

Leaning back from the table, Danbury interrupted Matthew's thoughts. "You're going to ask? About the car. When you take her supplies."

"I am," said Matthew. "I might have to call Ariel again to get her to translate, but I'm going to ask and see what she says."

The checks arrived. After credit cards were tapped on a portable reader and the waiter had left the table, Danbury said, "Think I'll stick around. To see if she can tell you anything."

"OK, suit yourself," said Matthew. "Right now, though, I need to go get some groceries—and clothing, I guess. I don't know what size. Women's clothing baffles me."

"I think it baffles them too," said Danbury astutely. "Penn says sizes vary a lot. In women's clothing."

"Great," said Matthew, tapping his phone to try to locate both a grocery store and a clothing store. "There are no grocery stores really close by. It's all at least four miles away. The bulk store that I have a membership to is up in the Thorny Branch area. I guess I'll go up there. They have clothing. Maybe a sweat suit. I can't go wrong with that. It's pretty adjustable, right?"

Danbury just shrugged, having no more clue about women's clothing than Matthew did.

15 ~ Trust Test

"Mira, it's Matthew Paine," he said as he tapped on the door to the hotel room. He waited, with his hands full of bags of groceries and clothing, hoping that she was still there. At last, the door opened a crack, and then Mira, wrapped in the hotel's huge terry-cloth robe with her hair up in a towel, stepped back to allow Matthew to enter.

"How's Joseph?" he asked immediately.

"*Dormido*," she said, then thought for a moment. "Sleeps."

"That's great! He needs lots of rest," said Matthew. "The cough is better?"

"Better," she answered, nodding her head.

"I brought you some groceries—milk, eggs, and cereal and bread, cheese, and meats for sandwiches. I'll put them in the refrigerator. But first, here—this is for you." He handed her a bag with a warmup suit, size small, and some women's underwear, also in a small. A second bag contained diapers and sleepwear for Joseph, warm one-piece zip-up pajamas with feet in them.

"*Gracias, señor*," she said, after peeking inside. "Doctor," she amended before taking the bag into the bathroom, from which steam was still emanating.

"*De nada*," he replied, thinking he probably knew just enough Spanish to be dangerous with it.

Matthew set the groceries on the counter and then put the perishables in the small refrigerator. It wasn't tiny, by hotel room standards, but neither was it a full-size refrigerator.

Everything in the suite was sized just right. There were two queen-size beds in a bedroom that Matthew had seen earlier. The door was now closed on the sleeping Joseph. A sitting area with a pull-out sleeper sofa provided more-than-ample sleeping accommodations. It was into this area that Matthew wandered to wait for Mira Velázquez and attempt to have the hard conversation.

When she emerged from the bathroom, she was clad in the sweat suit, which was nearly too big for her, even in the small size. She was trying to tell him something, and she was struggling with the words.

"*Uno momento*," said Matthew, holding a finger up and pulling out his phone. Tapping it, he managed to call Ariel, and as he knew she would, she readily agreed to translate. He updated her on the whole situation—that Mira and Joseph were in the hotel, Joseph was already improving, and he'd brought in food and clothing. Ariel sounded delighted.

"But there's one other thing," said Matthew. "I found Mira because Danbury sent me to try to talk to people living in a homeless camp. There was an incident involving a car, and we need to know if any of them saw who dropped the car off and when."

"What incident?" asked Ariel.

"It's part of a murder investigation that I'm helping Danbury with," said Matthew simply.

"OK, so what do you need me to do?"

"First of all, ask her what she was trying to tell me just now. And then ask her if she saw who dropped the car off, the one that exploded, and if she knows when it was dropped off."

"It exploded?"

"Yeah, long story. But I figure if you mention that, she'll know what car I'm talking about. That will make it obvious."

"OK, sure. Put me on speaker."

Matthew obliged, and Ariel chatted with Mira. The conversation was small talk, from what Matthew could gather, but then Mira's face got serious. After a few minutes, Ariel said, "Matthew, she wants to thank you for taking care of Joseph and her. And she's embarrassed to ask for anything else, but she wants to know if you're making any progress on finding her husband and her daughter. She had a little money and got as far as Durham to search for her daughter before she ran out."

"Tell her that Danbury, the police officer she met in the lobby, is already looking for both her husband and her daughter. Be sure she understands that our purpose is to reunite them, not to deport anyone. I gave Danbury the information that she gave me to try to find them. If she can think of any other details that might help him locate them, ask her to tell you."

After a few more back-and-forth bits of conversation, Ariel said, in English, "Mira says that she last saw her husband at the train station in Raleigh. They'd come up from Florida, and he was detained when they got off the train. Some officials separated them and pulled her husband aside. The last she heard from him was him telling her to run. So she did. She picked up her son and ran."

"Raleigh is good. Danbury has jurisdiction and contacts here. What about clothing? Does she have any?"

After another quick discussion, Ariel said, "No, she left their bags at the train station when her husband told her to run."

"Tell her I'll get her a few more things to get them through the week. And we'll go from there." He waited while Ariel imparted this information, and Mira thanked him again, both in English and Spanish.

"Now for the hard part," he told Ariel. "I need to know if she saw who dropped the car off at the end of the dead-end road and when."

"OK," said Ariel and then began what sounded like a description that ended in a question. Mira answered that one, and Ariel seemed to be asking others.

Then, to Matthew, Ariel said, "She said that Gerard told them not to talk about it and not to get involved, so she's scared. Gerard kind of runs the camp where you found her. She says he took her in and was sharing food and blankets with her and Joseph, so she feels like she owes him something. She didn't see anything, but she overheard Gerard say that the car showed up on Friday afternoon. A guy got out of it and walked back toward the hotel where you are now. It's another reason that she's scared, because then the car blew up, and she's afraid of the man who left it there."

"Did he say what the guy looked like? Did she hear him say anything about that?"

After more exchanges that Matthew didn't understand, Ariel said, "She said that Gerard didn't see him up close but that he was a long man. Whatever that means. I'm not sure, and she couldn't clarify it for me."

"Thanks, Ariel. Can you just remind her to give Joseph one more breathing treatment before she goes to bed? And if he wakes up in the night, he can have more ibuprofen. She knows how much and how to give both medications to him. Tell her I won't be able to come back to check on her again until tomorrow evening, but I'll leave my card with my phone number on it. She can call from the phone here in the hotel room if she needs anything before then."

"Got it," said Ariel, then started spieling off information to Mira again.

Matthew thanked Ariel again and said goodnight to both of them. Motioning on his way out, he reminded Mira to be sure to flip the extra lock on the door when he left. She agreed, and he heard it click into place behind him. Satisfied that they were safe and cared for as well as they could be for the night, Matthew hobbled back down the hallway to the elevator and met Danbury, who was waiting for him in the lobby.

"What did she say, Doc?"

"She didn't see anything herself, but she overheard Gerard say that he saw the car get dropped off late Friday afternoon. Gerard would be the guy who unofficially runs the camp down there. He took her in to care for her and Joseph. That's the guy who told me to get lost."

"OK, so what did he see?"

"He saw 'a long man' drop the car and then leave, on foot, headed back this way toward the hotel."

"A long man?"

"That's what Mira told Ariel, and she couldn't explain what that meant. Did your officer learn anything about security cameras around this area last night? I know he was headed up here to ask when the car blew up. I saw him come running back."

"Yeah, he asked. They have security cameras. Aimed around the parking area. The road runs around the perimeter. Outside the camera range. So they're not much help. Unless the guy had a ride out. If it was waiting in the parking lot for him. And he had to come onto the property. Then maybe we could see him. At least now we know when to look. A time frame," said Danbury.

"Mira said Gerard saw it all from a distance, so it sounds like he didn't get a good look. Maybe that does give us a timeline, though not much more."

"Unless we can get something more. From Gerard."

"Be my guest," said Matthew. "That one's yours. He was dressed in camouflage fatigues, so you can talk military service with him to connect."

Danbury just grunted in response.

"I'm heading home," said Matthew. "I'm hoping to get in bed before midnight tonight," he said, checking his watch. It was already after nine, but the drive should be much easier at this time of the evening on a weeknight.

As he'd predicted, the drive home was uneventful and took only a half hour. Traffic was light, and what there was of it was moving well.

When he arrived home, Max met him at the door and complained loudly of not having been fed yet. Matthew locked up and turned on the security alarm before plopping his coat and satchel on the end of the sofa in their usual spot. After rinsing and refilling the big cat's food and water bowls, he set up the coffee maker for the next morning and changed into his flannel sleep pants and a soft T-shirt.

Replacing the ice pack in the ankle brace, he pulled a kitchen chair in beside the desk in his living room and propped his foot up. Settling in at the desk, he began to go through his patient records. He'd considered a bottle of beer that he'd gotten from a Raleigh microbrewery or a glass of wine while he did so but thought either would put him immediately to sleep.

Just as he was finishing up with the records and relieved to be able to get to bed, he got a text from Danbury.

"Doc, you still up?"

"For the next five minutes," Matthew texted back, thinking to stave off anything else that night.

He sighed when he saw the call come through from Danbury. Clearly, that strategy hadn't worked.

"Hey, Doc. I talked to Gerard."

"Oh," said Matthew, surprised. "How'd that go?"

"He's former military. Army, probably. PTSD, definitely. He gave a description. Of the guy who dropped off the car. He saw the guy from a distance. Long wiry frame. Brown messy hair. The description fits Priestly."

"Yeah, it does."

"I checked Priestly's address. What's on his license isn't current. I'm searching for the correct one. I checked with Charlene O'Connell. She hasn't seen him at the club. Not since Misty died. She doesn't have an address for him. Just a phone number. She texts him. Then pays him in cash. For the movies. She has no records on him. I called the number. Straight to voice mail. And that's full."

"Huh," said Matthew pensively. "Maybe it's all an act, then, his general cluelessness. If it is, he's a much better actor than I gave him credit for."

"I agree. It seemed genuine. His general lack of common sense."

"I can't believe he's behind this, but maybe it is all an act and that's part of his game. Making us think that he hasn't got any sense while he's masterminding the elaborate murder game. I guess it's possible."

"I've seen stranger."

"Yeah, me too," agreed Matthew. "You're going to find Priestly and question him again?"

"That's the plan."

"Keep me posted."

"I just did."

"Touché." Matthew chuckled. "G'night, Danbury."

"G'night, Doc."

After organizing everything for the next morning and checking the ice pack on his ankle, Matthew fell into bed and propped his left foot on a pillow. Thinking he'd be out like the light he switched off on his bedside table, he snuggled in. Max jumped up beside him and settled in to bathe.

Though Matthew was truly exhausted, sleep was initially elusive. Tossing and turning as carefully as possible around his propped foot, he replayed the events of the past two days. He was thankful that his hearing had returned and his ankle was a bit less painful and somewhat less swollen.

When he finally dropped into a fitful sleep, he was awakened by a disturbing dream. Startled, he checked his phone on the nightstand and saw that it was only two a.m. It must all be getting to him, he reasoned, the senseless murders, the elusive murderers. But why wouldn't it? He'd been trained to help heal people, and sometimes their injuries were inflicted by other people. But those weren't the patients he usually dealt with.

In his medical practice, patient issues were more likely a result of disease and sometimes of neglect. One of the reasons he hadn't pursued his initial career goal as an emergency department physician was because of the violence and abuse he'd encountered during his rotation in the ED. Wishing he could turn his mind off and go back to sleep easily, he tossed, turned, and finally got up to get a glass of water.

While he was up and in the kitchen, he switched out his ice pack and got a naproxen sodium. He'd twisted his ankle oddly in his sleep, he realized, and the pain from it was likely what had awakened him.

After getting resettled in bed, the next thing he heard was the sound of his phone from his bedside table. Groggily unsure of his place in time and space, he finally concluded that it had to be Thursday morning. He wondered how that was possible as he rolled over to silence his phone. Only then did he realize that it was Cici on FaceTime and not yet his alarm.

Cici, he thought, wishing with the now-familiar ache he couldn't have begun to describe that she were there with him. Instead, he bemoaned, she was on a video connection from the other side of an ocean. He clicked to see her, however remotely.

16 ~ Blew By You

The morning had gone by in a blur, and it was late afternoon before Matthew stopped to catch his breath. The scheduled patients would have provided a full day without several he'd treated who had walked in without appointments. He'd hastily eaten a sub sandwich ordered through Trina's lunch-train program and downed a bottle of water standing in the break room. As he unlocked the door to his office that afternoon, he realized that he hadn't been in his office at all since his arrival that morning.

Pulling off his lab coat and hanging it behind the door, he settled in at his desk. Propping his foot up on the chair beside the desk, he switched out the ice pack on his ankle for one he'd just retrieved from the nurses' station. Having only switched it once during the day and not having had the chance to prop it up at all, his ankle felt as if it was staging a full protest over that lack of care. It throbbed, and Matthew grimaced as he saw that it was badly swollen again.

Grabbing an ibuprofen from his desk drawer, he realized he had nothing to swallow it with except the remains of the now-cold coffee in the travel mug on his desk from that morning. Getting back up at this exact moment wasn't an option. Shrugging, he gulped it down stoically, cold, stale coffee and all. He had just accessed the patient charts on his computer when his phone sounded. Tempted to ignore the ding, he reluctantly pulled the phone from his pocket. Danbury had texted, "Can you talk?"

"Yeah, what's up?" Matthew texted back.

"I need your help, Doc," said Danbury when Matthew answered the incoming call. "Priestly won't talk to me."

"And you think he'll talk to me?" asked Matthew.

"I don't know. But he'll talk to Cara. If she's picking up Fluffykins. If you just happen to take her. When she goes to pick up the cat."

"She can take Fluffykins?"

"That's the other part," answered Danbury.

"What other part?" asked Matthew suspiciously.

"She's still working on it. With her grandmother. But Priestly is impatient. Ready to be rid of the cat. He's threatening to take her to the pound. Cara's upset."

"Sounds like you're getting yourself a cat, at least temporarily," answered Matthew smugly.

"I can't," said Danbury. "I can't have pets. Not where I live."

Matthew realized that he'd never seen Danbury's residence and had no idea where that was, except that it was somewhere in or near Peak.

"You have a landlord?" he asked aloud.

"Yeah. No pets allowed. I'm good with that. I'm never home. Never intended to have any."

"So who's actually taking Fluffykins?" asked Matthew.

"I hope Leo will," said Danbury. "He has Maxine. But he's away. Until next week. He's in Denver. Working with the business there."

"And Penn?" asked Matthew.

"Says she can't handle it. Not right now. She's at the new business. All the time. Trying to get it up and running. Busy time for a gym. And a spa. New Year's resolutions. Christmas gift cards. All of that."

Matthew took a deep breath and blew it out loudly, stating the obvious, "You want me to take the cat."

"Just temporarily."

"I have no idea how Max will react. Does this cat have all of her shots? And no fleas or parasites?"

"I'll ask Cara."

"If she's clean, I'll try this. Just until Leo gets back. If she isn't, you can board her at the vet and get all of that done first."

"Fair enough," agreed Danbury. "And you'll talk to Priestly?"

"What do you need from Priestly?" asked Matthew, thinking there were few things in life he'd less like to do right now. Priestly was so vile that Matthew felt his skin crawl in the guy's presence. The way he talked about women as objects, all of them except Misty, apparently, made Matthew more than a little angry. It made his blood boil.

"A couple of things. Get a reaction. About the car being dropped off. See if he knows about it. And he said Misty's boyfriend was gone. Wouldn't be coming back. He meant Kent. The latest one. Cara overheard him. New Year's Eve. Just before Misty left. He knew something about that. Or thought that he did."

"Why would he say that?"

"No idea. That's why you're asking him."

That, thought Matthew, was probably a foregone conclusion in Danbury's mind.

"Unless he was commenting on Misty's notoriously bad track record with men. Or maybe it was wishful thinking on his part. Did Cara tell you the context? Who he was talking to or under what circumstances?"

"At the Silver Silhouette. Just after Misty performed. New Year's Eve. He told a guy at the bar. And Cara heard him."

Taking a deep breath, Matthew blew it out and agreed, "Yeah, I'll talk to Priestly."

"How fast can you get here?"

"Get where? I need to check on Mira and Joseph."

"They're fine."

"How do you know?"

"I dropped off some clothes. At lunch today. Penn sent them. She gets lots. From vendors at her business. Salespeople. Wanting her to order from them. And add her logo. Mira met me in the lobby. She said Joseph is better."

"I'm happy to hear that, but I need to go see him myself. And they're likely running out of the children's ibuprofen, so I need to get more of that to her."

"OK, Doc. Can you get to Cara's house? Right after that?"

"Yeah, OK," said Matthew reluctantly as he saw another quick dinner grabbed on the run in his future.

"Thanks, Doc," said Danbury. "Text me when you're on the way." And then he was gone again.

Matthew tapped his phone and ordered a large pizza and salad from Franco's, his and Cici's favorite Italian restaurant that was between Peak and Quarry, where she lived. It was more or less on the way to Durham where he was headed and it would keep him off the interstate for a little while longer if he went that way. Mira might be sick of pizza. But he didn't know what else she liked and it was so easy. *And who didn't like pizza?* he rationalized.

He packed his satchel, locked up, and stopped by the nurses' station on his way out to grab another bottle of the children's ibuprofen for Joseph before leaving to pick up the pizza.

The drive to Durham wasn't as bad as he had thought it would be. After sharing the salad and pizza with Mira and checking on Joseph's progress, he texted Danbury and headed to Cara's house. Danbury's big black SUV was parked in front of the house, and Cara and Danbury were standing on the front walk under a bright streetlight. Cara had her arms folded in front of her, looking defensive, when Matthew limped up.

"Hey, Doc," said Danbury in greeting. Cara just turned to wave sweetly to him with her hand under her crossed arms but said nothing. Then, turning back to Danbury, she said, "I'm not wearing that thing, and that's final."

"What thing?" asked Matthew.

"He wants me to wear a wire to talk to Preston Priestly, and I refused. No way am I wearing that thing."

"Hey, Danbury, I'll wear it if you really need the recording," said Matthew appeasingly. If he had to talk to the guy anyway, why not?

"Always the peacemaker, huh, Doc?" asked Danbury, grinning at him. "I really need the recording. I need his voice. And speech patterns. We've requested a profiler for the case. A psychiatrist. She's highly acclaimed. And this is important."

"Sure. Wire me up. And then let's get going," said Matthew. "Did you get the vet records, or are you boarding her tonight?"

"Boarding. Can't get the records tonight. It'll be tomorrow. But they'll take the cat."

After he was appropriately wired and knew how to activate the recording device, Matthew reiterated the understanding that the cat would be taken, by Danbury, directly to the vet for the night when they returned with her. She would be checked out thoroughly before Matthew exposed Max to her. Danbury agreed, and Matthew drove Cara to pick up Fluffykins.

Pulling up in front of a duplex that was marginally maintained, Matthew wondered what the guy's income was like from the movie business and if he was supplementing it with anything else. The front yard, which was a misnomer, was small, and the house was close to the road. A sidewalk interrupted what there was of the bare dirt yard, at least what he could see of it from the feeble glow of a nearby streetlight. One of the lights beside the door on the front porch was lit, and the other was missing the bulb entirely.

Flipping on the recording device in his pocket, Matthew was about to knock when he paused with his hand in midair. He and Cara looked at each other, startled. From inside, they heard a warbling voice attempting to sing what sounded like "Blue Bayou." The lyrics weren't quite right, and Matthew wasn't sure he was hearing it clearly through the door anyway. Maybe the guy could act, but singing wasn't his forte.

"Oh, that was one of Misty's songs," whispered Cara. "At least, I think that's what he's trying to sing. It's hard to tell."

Attempting to stop the horrible noise from within as much as anything else, Matthew knocked soundly on the door. The caterwauling stopped, and the door creaked open to reveal Preston Priestly, standing in boxers and a sleeveless T-shirt. Matthew shivered partially from the cold but also from seeing far more of Priestly in the chill than he'd ever have wanted to.

"Preston! Put some clothes on," said Cara. "You knew we were coming to get Fluffykins. Why aren't you dressed?"

"I am dressed," he answered. Seeing Cara's glare at him, he added, "Come on in. I'll be right back."

Matthew and Cara went in through the creaking door and closed it behind them, waiting impatiently. The house smelled of stale food and Matthew was afraid to guess what else. The croaking voice started up again from somewhere off to the right, the direction in which Priestly had disappeared. Just as Matthew was thinking the cat yowling would be preferable, a fluffy calico peered at them from around the corner, rubbing up against the door frame.

"Fluffykins!" said Cara, rushing over to scoop the cat up. She wasn't overweight, Matthew thought as he assessed her. As her name implied, the feline was just extremely fluffy. She seemed content in Cara's arms, so Matthew took two strides to cross the tiny living space and held his hand out for her to sniff. After the initial introduction, cat style, she rubbed her head against Matthew's hand, welcoming him to pet her.

"OK, is this better, missy?" asked Priestly, returning in a shiny but badly picked dressing gown that he probably thought was a smoking jacket. His spindly legs still stuck out beneath it, and his feet were clad in socks that might have once been white.

"Somewhat," said Cara. "Why were you singing Misty's song?"

"I was singing it to the cat. Because Fluffykins got what Misty called the zoomies. She loves running up and down this here hallway. She blows by you, so I was singing her song, the 'Blew by You' song," added Priestly as Matthew worked hard to stifle a laugh. "I guess Misty musta sung 'Blew by You' to her when she got the zoomies because she seems to like it. I just don't know all the words, so I kinda make it up as I go along. But I bet she likes the song."

"I would bet not," said Matthew, trying not to laugh at the guy he'd previously wanted to punch. Rewriting song lyrics, he completely understood that—he did it all the time. Music was his favorite relaxation method, though he'd had no time lately to play any of his instruments. Musically talented, if Matthew could get his hands on an instrument, he could play it. He had several guitars, an electric keyboard, a drum set, and a ukulele. Habitually, he entertained himself by comically rewriting song lyrics in his head to fit the situation. Rarely did he share them.

"I know not," said Cara, giving Priestly a hard stare. "Where are her things? Her bed and bowls and food. And her litter box. Didn't Misty send a couple of toys with Fluffykins?"

"Yeah, yeah, I found most of it. Lemme go get it."

Matthew was wondering how to talk to Priestly about Misty's car when Priestly brought it up himself. "Here you go." Priestly handed Matthew a thick, soft, fuzzy blue bed. In it was a familiar clear-plastic bag partially filled with hard cat food, two dark-blue bowls, and a little fuzzy mouse with a blue feather on it. "I'll get the litter box. I think there was another couple of toys. Misty said she couldn't find one of them and thought it came out of the bag in her car."

"She brought Fluffykins?" remembered Matthew aloud. Then he clarified, "In her own car?"

"Yep."

"Was she alone? Was anyone with her?"

"Yep and nope. Didn't see nobody else in the car," clarified Priestly. "'Cept for the cat."

"Does she have a carrier?" asked Matthew.

"A what?"

"A cat carrier. Did Misty bring her to you in a cat carrier?"

"Naw, she brought her to me in her lap, near as I could tell."

"Did you go get her out of the car?"

"No way. Misty brought her inside. I ain't carrying no cat around outside."

"So you weren't in Misty's car?"

"Naw, why would I be?" asked Priestly defensively.

"I was just curious if you saw a cat carrier," said Matthew, providing half of the reason he was asking. The other half was trying to determine if there would be a valid reason that anything the techs managed to salvage from the front of the car before it blew up could have Priestley's DNA or prints on it.

"Danbury is taking her to the vet for the night, and they'll want her to arrive in one," added Matthew by way of explanation.

"Oh," said Priestly, appeased. "Naw, I walked out to the car and saw the brand-new tires she'd just put on it, but I didn't touch the cat until Misty brought her in the house. And then it took her a while to warm up to me. Know what I'm sayin'? Cats are funny like that."

Matthew thought this one seemed to be a pretty good judge of character. She had allowed Cara to scoop her up and Matthew to pet her immediately.

"You saw the new tires on the car?" asked Matthew. "Sounds like she must have been going on a long trip if she replaced the tires. Do you have any idea where she was going? Did she say anything to you about it?"

"Naw. Misty was a hard nut to crack. She didn't want to tell nobody nothing that she didn't have to about her personal life. Ya know? What happens to those tires now, anyway?" asked Priestly. "I could use a new set on my truck if they'd fit."

"I think they've already been, ah, redistributed," replied Matthew. "One more thing, about Misty's latest boyfriend. You were overheard saying that he wouldn't be coming back after New Year's. What made you say that?"

"Don't none of 'em come back after the first few weeks. I don't know how or why, but she chases 'em all away. Every one of 'em. Don't none of 'em last long," said Priestly. "And she was actin' that way with him, that way that she does just before they're gone for good. I've seen her act that same way over and over."

"And that's what you meant by that remark?"

"Yepper. Don't know who I said it to or when, but if I said it, that's what I'd have meant by it. Why? Did he kill her?" Priestly asked, his eyes widening.

"Why would you ask that?"

"No particular reason. But somebody did."

"It's too early to know much," replied Matthew noncommittally as he turned and carried the bed containing the bowls, food, and cat toy out to the car. Cara held the cat, leaving Priestly to retrieve and bring the litter box.

Either Priestly was a practiced liar and a great actor, or he truly knew nothing about the car blowing up or about Misty's boyfriend disappearing. Matthew was betting on the latter. He knew he had it all on tape for Danbury to assess later, so they loaded the cat's belongings and climbed into the Element.

After Priestly retreated back inside, Matthew retrieved the recording device from his pocket and turned it off. Reaching up under his shirt, he removed the wire and microphone, wrapping it around the device and plopping it into the cup holder of the console between Cara and himself.

Matthew pulled his phone out and texted Danbury, "Got the cat and the recording. Where are you?"

In typical Danbury style, there was no actual response, just a pin dropped to get Matthew to his location.

"He's at Misty's apartment," said Cara as she looked at the phone Matthew had clipped to the dash to navigate by. "I wonder why he's there?"

"Let's go find out," said Matthew as he turned from the end of Priestly's street and followed the directions to Danbury's dot.

17 ~ Turnabout

"I really don't want to go in there," Cara said, handing Fluffykins to Matthew at the door of Misty's apartment. "It's just too awful with her gone."

"You can wait in the SUV," said Danbury, who had opened the door for them. "Give me just a minute. Then we can take her to the vet."

Cara nodded sullenly and turned toward the vehicle as Danbury clicked to unlock the big black SUV remotely. After watching to be sure she was in it safely, Matthew closed Misty's apartment door and said, "Priestly can't be our killer."

Putting Fluffykins down, Mathew pulled the wired device from his pocket and handed it to Danbury.

"Based on what?" asked Danbury.

Raising an eyebrow, Matthew contemplated this question. "I don't think he's smart enough to plan all of it and be that deceptive. I mean, Misty's fingerprints were removed, and a diamond was stuck in her molar postmortem, or she wouldn't have been able to fully close her mouth. Why do any of that?"

After bolting down the hallway to the bedroom, the fluffy cat wandered back through the apartment, as if searching for Misty and returning sadly alone. She rubbed up against Matthew's leg until he scooped her up again and scratched behind her ears.

Danbury nodded pensively as Matthew continued, "And he would have had to plan ahead for disposal of the body so that the time of death was obscured, first by freezing it in something other than a deep freezer. It wasn't fully thawed, and the body was in a natural position, not compacted like it had come out of a deep freezer. And then the killer left it under the cover in a heated pool at a house where nobody was home and wouldn't be for another couple of weeks."

Continuing to scratch behind the cat's ears as she purred in his arms, Matthew added, "Either after or during all of that, the killer put a body in the trunk of Misty's car. The body might have been that of her latest boyfriend, Trent Kent, because he's also missing."

Danbury nodded.

"The killer left the car rigged with explosives on a timer so that whoever opened the trunk had just enough time to escape the blast but still see the body. Does that sum it up?"

"Yeah, that's about it."

"That took some intelligence. I don't think the head on Priestley's shoulders is his strongest attribute. Either the guy is an accomplished actor and his talents are being wasted on triple-X-rated movies because he's extreme genius." Matthew paused. "Or he's exactly what he appears to be and not capable of beginning to plan any of that."

Danbury rubbed the scruffy growth on his chin with his thumb as Matthew asked, "What? You don't agree?"

"Oh, I agree. I just wanted to hear you lay it all out. Sometimes it helps. To have somebody else do that."

"Happy to help," said Matthew sarcastically, scratching the cat one last time before handing her to Danbury and opening the door to the apartment. "Let me know what the vet says and if you can get Penn to take her. If not, she's pretty sweet. We'll see what Max thinks of her."

"Thanks, Doc," said Danbury, following him out and locking the door behind them. After they'd transferred the cat's belongings to Danbury's car, he added, "Good night, Doc. I really do appreciate it."

Miracles never ceased, thought Matthew as he waved to Cara and climbed into the Element to drive home. Max, he knew, would greet him accusingly when he got home late and the big cat hadn't been fed. Adding insult to injury would be that Matthew would now smell like another cat.

The drive was easy, and Matthew soon arrived home, locked up, fed Max, and settled in with his favorite beer. He switched out the ice pack on his ankle, then checked and updated his online patient records from the little desk in his living room. After laying out and organizing everything for the next morning, Matthew climbed into bed, hoping that sleep wouldn't be elusive and that he could get through the night without the interruption of weird dreams.

*****

Matthew awoke with a start and wasn't sure why he was awake. Then he realized that his cell phone was sounding, and he rolled over to snatch it off his bedside table. The display showed an unidentified number and the time was four a.m. He was definitely annoyed with that development. Though he wasn't on call this week, he answered it anyway, just to be sure it wasn't a patient needing help.

"Dr. Paine?" he heard a tenuous female voice ask on the other end.

"Yes, this is Matthew Paine," he responded groggily.

"I, uh, I need to talk to you," said the voice.

"Are you a patient? I'm not on call this week, but if it's a quick question, I can answer it," he said, trying to be polite but so completely exhausted that he wasn't sure what he was saying.

"No. I'm, uh, I'm a friend of Mira's."

Pushing himself abruptly upright in bed, Matthew was immediately awake. "Is she OK? Is Joseph OK?"

"Yeah, they fine," she said. "But I gotta talk to you. A big guy came down to the end of the road tonight and he axed Gerard about that car. Gerard, he say tell him to go away—t'ain't none of his business. But the big guy, he say something that makes Gerard start spilling his guts. I ain't never seen him do that before. He say he saw the guy but not up close. Gerard don't know I'm here."

"Where? Where are you, and why did you call me?"

"I'm in the hotel here with Mira. They don't want to let me up here, but I told 'em I'd pitch an unholy fit like they ain't never seen the likes of if they don't call her and let me up here. They say they gonna call the cops, and I tell 'em, 'Go ahead, I want to talk to them anyway.'"

"Why?"

"Because I was worried about us. Her and me. I did see the guy, and

I thought she did too. She say she didn't. But I did."

"You saw the guy who dropped the car off on Friday?"

"Yeah, I saw him. Pretty close up. And I don't think he saw me seein' him, but I ain't sure. We was in the edge of the trees, me an' Mira. But she say she didn't see him. I guess she had her back to him 'cause she was looking at me. But I saw him. Plain as day."

"OK, can you describe him? For a police sketch artist?"

"I ain't talkin' to no police!" she said vehemently, contradicting her previous statement that she wanted to talk to them. "I didn't wanna call you, but Mira, she say you can help. Whoever that man was, I don't want him wanderin' around, blowin' up no more cars. I mean, Dewayne could've got blown sky high takin' those tires."

"Yes, I can help you," said Matthew, running fingers through hair that he knew was by Max because he'd disturbed the big cat from around his head when he'd rolled over to answer the phone. Amused, despite it being four in the morning, that she had just confessed to knowing who had stolen the tires, too, Matthew said, "You're right. The biggest help would be to find this guy. If you can give a good enough description to create a picture, it'll help the police know who they're looking for. If they can find him, then you can stop worrying about what he did or didn't see."

There was a long pause, and he could hear the phone being muffled. Then, he heard the voice again. "OK. Mira say if you come, too, you won't let nobody take her or Joseph away. Or me neither."

"I won't let them near Mira or Joseph," said Matthew, wondering how Mira had communicated all of that and knowing that he had some leverage to keep his promise of protection by his association with Danbury. "If you're not wanted by the police for anything, you don't have any reason to worry."

"Naw sir!" she said, "They don't want me for nothing 'cept some vagrancy. I say it ain't no crime to just hang out in places. But they don't always agree."

Matthew stifled both a yawn and a chuckle at her expressiveness in the middle of the night. Climbing out of bed, he limped down the hallway to turn off the timer on the coffee maker and manually start it brewing. Obviously, eight hours of sleep were just not to be had in succession this week.

His ankle was less sore, but it was stiff. Habitually tapping his foot anyway in both thought and impatience with the coffee maker, he said, "Can you stay there with Mira until I get there? I can request a sketch artist and meet you in an hour. Maybe a little more."

"I reckon I can. Ain't got no place particular to be."

"Thank you for deciding to do the right thing and agreeing to help. With a sketch, the police can begin to track him down. I'll see you in about an hour."

He realized that he hadn't asked for a name, though he wasn't sure he'd get one anyway, and he had to admit to being curious about this oddly expressive woman who had called him at four in the morning. What might she be able to tell them about the guy who was likely a stone-cold killer and who liked to play games? And would it be enough to locate him?

Max seemed to always be hungry in the winter months and not at all upset about getting his breakfast a little early. Calling Danbury in the process of his morning routine, which he rushed through to make good on his promise to be there in an hour, Matthew explained the situation. When he requested the sketch artist, he heard, "At four thirty in the morning?"

"Hey, they've asked me to be there with anyone from the police department, sketch artist included. I told them I would be. If you want to find this guy, we need to know what this witness saw. For that, we need a sketch artist at that hotel this morning. It's best if she's a woman. I have patients to see in a few hours, so it's all I've got."

Matthew wasn't usually so direct or demanding outside of medical emergency situations, but his patients needed him back in Peak this morning by nine at the very latest, so he had little choice. Besides which, he reasoned, Danbury had pulled him into this case to help, not the other way around. And he was doing just that.

"Who is this new witness?"

"I didn't ask for a name. She's extremely hesitant to talk to us, so I'm not sure she'd have told me anyway."

"OK, Doc," said Danbury. "I'll call in some favors. And meet you there." After a momentary pause, Matthew heard a quick intake of breath. "Thanks for setting it up," Danbury added, and then he was gone. Matthew chuckled, thinking that Danbury was no less abrupt, just a bit more polite. But still, progress was progress, and Penn would be proud.

As he drove across town in the early-morning darkness, Matthew was relieved to find that traffic was much lighter at this time of day. Except for the truckers, who were out in force, he had the interstate mostly to himself. He cranked up the eclectic playlist from his phone to help keep him awake. That, his travel mug of coffee, and his window cracked to let a stream of chilly air in to blow on his face was an effective combination of stimulants.

When he pulled into the well-lit hotel parking lot, it was half-full of cars but totally devoid of people. He waved slightly at the startled front-desk night clerk as he entered the lobby but headed straight for the bank of elevators without engaging in any more conversation than a hasty "good morning."

Tapping lightly on the hotel room door, he said, "Mira? It's Matthew Paine." He didn't know who else he'd find inside, and he didn't know her name to call it as he tapped softly again.

After a moment, Mira opened the door a crack and peeked out. Then, opening the door wide, she stepped aside to admit him. "Hi, Doctor," she said shyly.

Matthew stepped in to see a slender woman with dark skin and huge brown eyes, slouched and lounging on the sofa. "Hi, I'm Matthew Paine," he said to her.

She neither rose from the sofa nor looked all that impressed with his presence. Nodding, she looked him up and down. Apparently deciding that he was worthy of a response, she said, "You can call me Sherwanda."

"OK, Sherwanda. Thank you for calling and for being willing to help find the guy who left the car. I've asked for a female sketch artist. I'm not sure when she'll arrive, but she and only she will be joining us up here."

"Good, 'cause I don't wanna talk to no cops!" said Sherwanda. "If they come, I go. You don't look like a cop, so I guess you're OK," she added grudgingly.

"Would you be willing to let me record just your voice telling me what you saw Friday afternoon? I can send the recording to the police as your official statement. They might ask you to sign a printed copy of it, but that's all you'd have to do. And maybe not even that."

Sherwanda gave Matthew a hard sidelong look before she pulled a toothpick out of her jacket pocket, stuck it between the gap in her top front teeth, and finally said, "Yeah, OK. I guess I can't see no harm in that."

Matthew pulled his phone out, but before he set it to record, he texted Danbury, "Here at the hotel. With Mira and Sherwanda, the witness. Recording her statement. Text me when the sketch artist gets here."

Just as he was about to tap to record, he saw a text flash in from Danbury that contained a single symbol, a thumbs-up.

"OK, I'm recording this conversation, ma'am. Today is Friday, January tenth, twenty twenty. Please state your name and then tell me what you saw last Friday afternoon." Even as he said it, Matthew thought that it was unbelievable that only a week had passed since all of this had been set in motion.

"My name's Sherwanda Raynor," said the woman. "I don't have to give my Social Security or address or nothing, right?"

"No ma'am. Just tell me about last Friday afternoon and what you saw."

Matthew leaned back in the chair he'd taken across from where Sherwanda perched on the sofa and hoped he could keep from yawning as she hesitated. If he'd been worried about falling asleep on the story, though, that would have been impossible after she began.

18 ~ Long Man Standing

After a few throat clearings and encouraging nods from Matthew, Sherwanda finally began to speak.

"So it was last Friday afternoon. Later in the day, but not dark yet. Maybe about four or so, right, Mira?" she asked, looking above Matthew's head to where Mira hovered behind him.

Matthew turned to see Mira nod her agreement.

"We was walking back down to the camp from up here on the corner where we'd been, ah, asking for donations to our cause. Mira was carrying Joseph, and he was asleep. He wasn't coughing like crazy then. There's a path through the trees off the other side of the road, and we were on that when I saw this car pull up.

"You can see the road there, but can't nobody on the road see you through them big ole trees. 'Least I don't think they can. But that's what's got me worried, see? If I saw him, I don't know for sure that he didn't see me seeing him."

"OK, tell me exactly what you saw. What did he look like? What did he do? Tell me everything that you can remember."

"He drove by, looking all around. Then he parked up in front of where we was walking and got out of the car. He looked back one time, and then he put on a hat and sunglasses and just walked away, through the woods up toward this way. He didn't do nothing else. He didn't lock the car or nothing."

"When he looked back, you saw his face?"

"Yeah, but when he drove by, I seen it good then. He was looking all around. He was farther away when he parked and got out. So I didn't see his face so good then. And when he stood up out of the car and he was walking away, it was funny. Not ha-ha funny. But weird funny."

"Weird funny how?" prompted Matthew after she got quiet for a minute.

"He had long legs. I mean really long legs. And arms too. Itty-bitty body and long legs. Like one a them granddaddy longlegs spiders. Them things creep me out!" She shivered as she said this.

"Well, not itty-bitty around," she amended. "But his body just wasn't long enough for his legs. I thought maybe I'd seen wrong and he was a she. He had some hips and a belly, I think. But that didn't make no sense. He was a he. I saw his face."

"Got it. He had disproportionately long arms and legs. Can you describe his face?"

"Yeah, I can."

"The sketch artist is going to want more detail, and she'll ask specific questions about the size and shape of each part of his face. Let's just start with a general description."

"OK, I can do that. He had a long face too. Like his legs and arms. But not as bad. He had brown hair. Medium-brown hair, a little bit lighter than yours," she said, looking up at Matthew's soft, wavy brown hair. "I didn't see his eye color, so I don't know about that. I think he had hair on his chin. Just a little bit. He didn't have no full beard."

"Like a goatee?" asked Matthew.

"It wasn't even that much. Like a kid starting to grow face hair, but he wasn't no kid. That was a grown man."

"Tell me about his face. Was it long and squared off at the jaw? Or more rounded?"

"He looked like Mr. Sticks. You know, that pretzel guy?"

Matthew knew the cartoon advertisement she was referring to, and that was a pretty good visual, he thought. "Did his face look like that too?"

"Nah, that pretzel guy has a happy face. Friendly, like. This guy's face, it wasn't friendly at all. He had little rat eyes peeking out of eyebrows that were low. And his forehead stuck up too high for those low eyebrows."

Matthew figured the artist was about to have a fun time with Sherwanda, and just as he had the thought, the text popped in from Danbury saying that she was there.

"Send her up. I'll meet her at the elevator," he texted back after clicking to end the recording.

"The sketch artist is here, and she can do a much better job asking for these details than I can. She's coming up alone, and I'll go meet her at the elevator and bring her in."

Both women looked alarmed, and he continued, "I'll come back with her and stay while she's here. She'll get the sketch, and then I'll take her back downstairs. That's all."

"It's OK," he reassured Mira. "I'll be right back." Standing, he shuffled stiffly out and flipped the swinging brass lock behind him to keep the door from closing all the way and locking.

When he arrived at the elevator, the doors were opening. And a slender woman stepped through. She was of medium height and older than he was, but he wasn't sure by how much. Very unremarkable and also not at all intimidating would describe her well. She'd be perfect for talking to the women, Matthew thought, and for that, he was very thankful. She looked up at him with gray eyes in a serious but not unkind face and said, "Matthew Paine?"

"Yes. Hi," he said, shaking her hand. "Nice to meet you."

After their introductions were completed, he said, "I'm sure Danbury briefed you on the situation."

"He did. And the importance of getting this right."

"And the potential difficulty in working with the witness?"

"Yes, that too."

"She's been very cooperative in providing me with a description, which I recorded. I'm going to airdrop it to Danbury when we go back downstairs. If you want a copy too," he began.

"Thanks, but no," she said. "I need to hear it all myself and sketch as I listen. I can read the speaker's face and gauge her reactions to the sketch as I develop it. Then I'll ask her specific questions based on her responses and reactions."

"OK, they're this way," said Matthew, leading the way back down the hallway and into the hotel suite he'd just vacated. As he entered, he could hear Joseph whimpering from the next room, and he didn't have to ask where Mira was. He introduced the artist to Sherwanda and took a seat on a barstool that was in front of the pass-through counter from the tiny kitchenette.

The artist perched on the edge of the chair adjacent to the end of the sofa where Sherwanda lounged, briefly explained the process, and began with basic questions. She sketched an outline of the guy's head, removing lines, clarifying, and redrawing. When Sherwanda was happy with that, she moved on to facial features. The room was warm, thought Matthew as he leaned back against the counter. If he were in a more comfortable seat, he might have fallen asleep sitting up while the conversation droned on.

After a few minutes, Mira quietly slipped back into the room.

"Is Joseph OK?" asked Matthew.

"Little cough. No hot," she replied.

"His cough is better and his temperature is gone?" clarified Matthew, happy to hear that update as Mira nodded.

"Yes," she said as she settled on the other end of the sofa from Sherwanda and leaned back into the cushions.

Matthew couldn't see what was happening with the sketch. As the process continued, his phone sounded. Seeing that it was Cici on FaceTime, he stood, excused himself, reassured Mira quickly, and slipped out of the room. Flipping the latch behind him to leave the door cracked, he answered the phone and continued down the hallway to a settee under a bay window in front of the elevators.

"Hi, Cees, good afternoon," he greeted her, quickly calculating the time in London.

"Hey Matthew. You're up and dressed and . . ." She hesitated. "Where are you?"

"I'm at the hotel where Mira is staying."

"Oh, the woman with the sick child you were telling me about?"

"That's the one. And there's another woman who's come forward now. She says she saw a guy we're interested in finding. A guy who left a stolen car behind."

"You mean the one that blew up?" she asked pointedly.

"I told you about that?"

"You did, yesterday morning. And I've been incredibly worried about you. I'm no less so now, you know. Wow, you really weren't cognizant first thing yesterday morning, were you?" she asked, laughing at him.

"Not when you catch me before coffee." He shrugged, grinning at her and wishing that he could get lost in her big golden-brown eyes in person. The indescribable ache returned, and he realized that the investigation was a blessing in disguise, as his mom often said of situations. He had been so incredibly busy with it that he hadn't had time to sit around and mope about how much he missed Cici. Not that he was much for moping, ordinarily, but this might be the exception.

Cici told him about her dinner with the London clients she was working with. Matthew had met them when he'd visited her the previous summer and seen them again recently when Cici brought them back with her for a brief stay over the Christmas holidays. He listened intently as she told him about their dinner conversations and the progress for moving operations to the US.

Matthew and Cici switched from FaceTime to a phone chat to wrap up their conversation in relative privacy. Nobody, so far, had ventured into the little foyer off the elevator. How thick the walls were or if there was anyone lingering in the hallway, though, Matthew couldn't know. When they'd said their goodbyes for his morning and her early afternoon, Matthew ambled back down to the hotel room and opened the door in time to see the sketch artist stuffing supplies back into her bag and standing.

"You're finished already?" asked Matthew, thinking that was a quick job.

"We are. Ms. Raynor is wonderfully observant."

"Ah," said Matthew. He agreed that the woman was smart. Some of it was what he'd define as "street smart." Wherever she'd been, she'd definitely graduated from the school of hard knocks to end up on the street and survive it. She seemed toughened and savvy. *Wily*, maybe was the right word to describe her.

"May I see?" he asked.

"Sure," she said, handing him a tablet, on which was a sketch of a guy's face. It was long, as Sherwanda had said, and the eyebrows weren't low by themselves, but they looked low beneath a high forehead and small eyes that peered furtively from beneath them. Matthew squinted at the picture, covered the forehead with one hand, and squinted more.

"Do you know him?"

"I'm trying to decide if he might be somebody I've met," Matthew said, thinking of Preston Priestly. He couldn't quite make the sketch fit Priestly's face in his mind, though there were similarities. Maybe the expression was the problem, he thought. Priestly's face appeared to be flatly devoid of intelligent thought. Whereas this guy's face seemed to be contemplatively surreptitious. "But no, I don't think so. Can I get a copy of this?"

"I suppose so. If Detective Danbury approves it."

"Here," said Matthew, handing her a business card. "My email address is on there. I'll get Danbury's approval in just a minute."

Turning to Mira, he asked, "Do you have everything you need?"

"Yes, everything," she replied.

"OK, I'll check on you later. I'm happy to hear that Joseph is better."

"Yes, better," she said, smiling up at him.

"Call me if you need me," he said. Then to Sherwanda, he added, "And thank you, Ms. Raynor, for coming forward with this information. Finding this guy is a top priority right now."

"'Cause he blew up a car?" she asked.

"That's one reason," said Matthew, refusing to satisfy her curiosity about the rest of it. "If we need to ask you any other questions, can we find you down at the camp?"

"Naw, you can find me right here," she said, stretching back into the sofa. "Mira says I can stay as long as she stays."

"I see," said Matthew, with one eyebrow raised. "I guess you can help with Joseph," he added.

"Oh, he don't like me much," admitted Sherwanda. Matthew pondered the idea that the child might have excellent people-reading skills. He had his reservations about leaving the woman in the hotel room with Mira. If Mira was truly comfortable with her there, then he wouldn't object for now. Searching Mira's face, he saw no concern. He would be watching them a bit more closely now, though, because it was his credit card on file for any damage or disruption.

"OK, have a good day, and I'll check in on you later," he said, closing the door behind himself.

"I'll walk you down," he added to the artist. "I want to airdrop this recording to Danbury and get his approval to send me that sketch," he added, hobbling back down the hallway with her.

Danbury was happy with the sketch and the report and said so with as much excitement as he ever displayed. After the artist emailed the sketch to both of them and left, Matthew airdropped the audio recording of Sherwanda to Danbury, explaining what she'd seen and from what vantage point.

"Good work, Doc," said Danbury, clapping Matthew on the shoulder and pulling up the sketch on a tablet he was carrying. "Doesn't look much like Priestly."

"You sound disappointed."

"More surprised. But this doesn't match. At least not completely. There are similarities."

They said their goodbyes, and Matthew left Danbury studying the picture and hobbled out to his Element. He fought the morning traffic, heading into the rising sun for once, all the way back to his office in Peak. When he parked and pulled his satchel and coat from the passenger seat, he felt like he'd already put in a full day's work, and he hadn't even gotten into the office yet.

As soon as he walked in the back door, he met up with Gladys, who had just come from the stairwell outside of Matthew's office door.

"Good morning, Doctor," she said, then, looking around to see nobody else out in the hallway, she whisper-hissed, "Matthew, what have you been doing? You look awful."

"Thanks, Gladys," he said sarcastically.

"I don't mean any offense," she said, but not apologetically. "I just meant that you look pale and like you might be coming down with something."

"Bite your tongue, Gladys. I don't have time to be sick right now. I just haven't slept well this week."

"Yeah, I can see that," she said, looking up at him after sipping her coffee. "You'd better make time for some rest. Or you will be fighting something. And by the looks of you, you'll be losing."

"I was just going to go get some coffee and prop my foot up for a few minutes before we start seeing patients this morning," said Matthew as he turned to unlock his office door.

"OK. I'll check in on exam room six to get vitals and see you when you get there," she said, then hastily retreated in the other direction.

"Huh," muttered Matthew under his breath as he hung his coat on the rack behind the door. "Interesting. All I really need to do is tell Gladys I'm taking care of myself, and she's happy." He mulled that thought over as he unpacked his satchel and climbed slowly, right foot first on each step, up the stairwell to the break room on the floor above.

As he rounded the corner into the break room, Matthew met Dr. Garner, who was on his way out.

"Matthew, I hear you've been caring for a child in need up in Durham." Matthew nodded and Steven Garner continued, "Good job. I knew you were the right fit for this office when we brought you in."

Steven Garner, the senior partner in the practice, was broad-shouldered, dark-skinned, and good-natured. He was always concerned about his family first and patient care right behind that. Dr. Garner was so well connected in the field that he could have gone anywhere and probably made a lot more money, Matthew had always thought.

Like Matthew, he had chosen a profession as a general practitioner to help the most people in the greatest need. He chose Peak to live and work in when he opened the practice many years before because he thought it was a nice town in which to raise his children, then young. He'd liked it and stayed, becoming an integral part of the community, even after his children were grown and pursuing their own education and careers.

Unlike Matthew, he was extremely athletic. He'd given up a football scholarship and star position in college, much to the chagrin of his university, to apply himself more fully to his studies when he decided that medical school was in his future. Nearly as tall as Matthew, he was also nearly twice as wide through the shoulders. At fifty-five years old, he worked out every morning before coming to the office, and he was still a powerhouse. Matthew had been jogging and lifting weights the year before. One look at Steven Garner told him he needed to get back to that.

"Yeah, a little two-year-old boy. His mom thinks that his dad was deported, and she's looking for her daughter, who lives in Durham somewhere. That reminds me that I need to ask Danbury what progress he's made on finding them. Thanks for sending the supplies the other day. That was a huge help."

"You're welcome," said Garner, clapping Matthew on the shoulder. "Keep up the good work."

"Yes, sir."

"Hey, speaking of good work," Dr. Garner said, turning back from the doorway. "I really like your friend Penn's new gym. She thought of everything when she designed it. Including the coffee bar. I just need to lay off the flavored lattes on the way out. It almost defeats the purpose of going." He chuckled heartily. "It's been so full this week that I've had to get in earlier in the morning to get the equipment in the order I want. Anyway, on to the patients."

Matthew could hear the click of Steven Garner's heels as he headed down the hallway to his office, which was on the second floor with the break room. As he piled the sugar and creamer into his coffee cup, Matthew thought momentarily about a workout routine and figured it would be at least another week before his ankle was willing to cooperate with even light exercise. He sighed as he poured his coffee and carefully limped back down the stairs with it to call Danbury and ask about finding Mira's family.

Something about Sherwanda's description of the guy she'd seen was niggling at the corners of the back of his mind. Whatever it was, it wouldn't present itself front and center in his brain, and Matthew was frustrated by that. But it was there. Something that should be revealing, helpful in finding the guy, if he could just figure out what it was. He struggled to put those thoughts aside to turn his focus to his patients for the day.

19 ~ Developments

After a full day in the office, Matthew was happy to be heading home and hoping for a quiet evening with his guitar, his favorite beer, and an early bedtime. He'd had a conversation with Cici at lunch, but he realized that he hadn't heard back from Danbury, whom he'd been unable to reach that morning.

He locked his office door behind him and was juggling his satchel and keys when his phone vibrated in his pocket. He pulled it out to see an incoming call from none other than Danbury. A sense of foreboding and trepidation came over him as he tapped to answer it.

"Hey, Doc," said Danbury as Matthew answered his phone on the way out of his office.

"Hey, Danbury, any progress on locating Mira's family?"

"Yeah, bad news. We finally got an answer. From ICE. That's the Immigration and Customs Enforcement Agency."

Matthew refrained from saying "I know" and instead waited patiently for the update.

"They've confirmed it. They have Joseph Velázquez. He's being held. For deportation."

"Do you know where? And can you intervene? Maybe on the grounds that his wife is a potential witness in a murder investigation."

"I'm trying. I filed the paperwork. To prevent deportation. Back to Cuba. I contacted a buddy of mine. From back in the Corp. He's with ICE now. I left him a message."

"Ah, they're Cuban. I didn't know that," said Matthew.

"Little Joseph is the key. He was born here. In Florida. His paperwork was in the bags. Mira left them when she fled. ICE has them. And they know the child is a citizen. By birth. But Mira's help is a selling point. You're right. Not that she saw anything. At least not directly. But she did get Ms. Raynor to come forward. She is helping with the case. At least indirectly."

"Yeah, do what you can and let me know if I can help. I don't have any direct governmental contacts, though."

"I'm working on it, Doc. I'll let you know. About that and everything else. Any new developments."

"What else is developing?" asked Matthew, and then wished that he hadn't voiced his curiosity.

"Not much that makes sense," said Danbury. "I read the whole autopsy report. You were right. About the hysterectomy. Whatever that means."

"Maybe nothing," said Matthew. "There could be any number of reasons why a young woman had a hysterectomy. Maybe it was cancer. It might have had nothing to do with sterilization. What else?"

"We've got the name. The last on the car title. Before Misty Blue. It is a woman. From Mississippi. We're tracking it down."

"What's the name?"

"Melanie Wimble."

"Does that mean anything to anyone you've asked so far?"

"I haven't asked yet. I just got the name. From DMV records. The car was in Mississippi. A little town north-east of Jackson. Before the name on the title changed. To Misty Blue. We've checked the last known addresses. Since Misty owned it. There are four of them. So far, nothing. Nobody can tell us anything about her. We're running background checks now. On Melanie Wimble. I'll let you know. When I know something."

"Oh," said Matthew. "OK, what else?"

"We have our profiler. The one we requested. She's willing to help."

"What about the officers injured in the blast? What's their status?"

"Both are improving. They have a long road ahead. But they'll recover."

"That's great news! That's because you reacted so fast to check on the guys and staunch the bleeding. Anything else?"

"That isn't enough?"

"OK." Matthew chuckled. "Thanks for the update. I'd really like to go check on Mira. I'm nervous about Sherwanda being there in the room with her. Not for Mira's sake or I'd have asked you to remove her. They seem to get along well enough. I just don't want her causing any trouble for the hotel. But I'm not going back over there tonight. I'm headed home to get a quick dinner and relax for the evening, with this ankle propped up and iced. Then I'll check in with them in the morning."

"I can check. If you want."

"No, you can't. They're terrified of you. Especially Sherwanda."

"Oh," was all Danbury said to that. "You're not up for the club tonight? I'm going by in a couple of hours. After they're all there. Before it gets too busy. To show the sketch. See if anyone there knows him. Or has seen him there."

"You're on your own for this one. I need to take care of my ankle, and I need a decent night's sleep."

"OK, Doc. I hear you. I'll let you know what I learn. If anything," said Danbury. "There's just one more thing."

Matthew didn't like the sound of that; neither did he bother to dignify the comment with an answer. He just waited, knowing that he didn't need to ask what that was for Danbury to continue.

"Misty's cat. She's clean. No fleas. No diseases. All vaccines are current. Can you take her? Just for a few days. If I bring her to you?"

Matthew took a deep breath, thinking of the cat's well-being before he answered, "Yeah, I guess so. Just bring all of her stuff. She can spend the night in my guest room. So that she isn't overwhelmed with meeting Max and being in yet another strange place all at once. And I have no idea how Max will react to her being there. He was around other cats when he was a kitten, but that's been several years ago now."

"Thanks, Doc. I'll bring her by. In, say, maybe an hour. Maybe a little more. Does that work?"

"Yeah, about as well as anything," said Matthew.

The drive home in the Friday evening traffic was slow. Matthew was happy to live only seven miles away. He maneuvered out Middle Street, by the city offices in the old train depot, and across the train tracks. The roadbed remained the same as he drove out of town, but the name changed to Highway 20. He could do the drive in his sleep, so his mind was wandering back to his early-morning discussion with Sherwanda and her description of the guy who'd left the car. He was still bothered by it. Something about it was familiar and unsettling, but Matthew was still drawing a blank as to what it was.

When he arrived home, Max appeared like an apparition from somewhere in the house and began to rub up against his legs. After dumping his satchel and coat on the end of the sofa, Matthew rinsed and refilled the food and water bowls for Max, then dug out some chicken cacciatore leftovers that he and Cici had made together the previous weekend from his freezer. While that defrosted in the microwave, he changed into his warm flannel sleep pants and a soft cotton T-shirt.

Inching his left foot gingerly into the men's Ugg slipper that Cici had given him for Christmas, he was thankful that those were one of several thoughtful gifts that she said he'd enjoy. In this moment, he thought the slipper was the best thing he'd had on his foot yet. He put on the right one and went back to the kitchen to change out the ice pack in his ankle brace.

He fixed his plate and a glass of wine, taking them into his living room and placing them carefully on the computer desk in the corner. After elevating his foot on the kitchen chair he'd pulled alongside the desk, he said a blessing over his meal and nibbled on it absently while he was working on patient charts at the computer.

Content to enjoy the relaxing evening at home, Matthew cleaned up from his dinner and sat down with his guitar. He was hoping to get a eureka effect and remember what it was that was bothering him about Sherwanda's description. Playing his guitar sometimes helped to free his mind and give him that insight, but it was still an elusive shadow this evening. Putting the guitar aside, he took a moment and replayed the recording of her description of the guy, what she'd seen and observed.

Whatever it was that was bothering him about it still wasn't coming to mind so he picked the guitar back up and played until Danbury arrived with Misty's cat. Or maybe the cat had belonged to Melanie, the mysterious woman from Mississippi, Matthew mused as he opened the front door to Danbury.

After seeing Danbury out and getting Fluffykins settled in his guest room for the night, Matthew's eyelids were drooping. He'd switched the ice pack one last time and taken a naproxen sodium before hobbling down the hallway for bed. The ankle had stiffened after having been propped up for the evening. The swelling, a byproduct of being on his feet all day, was down after having iced it for a couple of hours.

Getting situated in bed and propping the ankle on pillows, he felt Max wander up from the bottom of the bed, where he'd been crouched, to snuggle up beside him. Max had been curious about the new addition to the household, but he didn't seem to be disturbed by her presence. Thankful that the next day was Saturday and he wasn't on call this weekend, he drifted quickly into a deep sleep.

Filmy dreams flitted through Matthew's mind, of which he was not much aware until he suddenly sat upright with a jolt and exclaimed, "Klinefelter!"

20 ~ When Inspiration Strikes

Matthew was instantly awake as he realized what had been bothering him and tugging at the corners of his mind the day before. The description Sherwanda had provided. It sounded like the car bomber had Klinefelter syndrome. If he was right about that, the guy was in a tiny percentage of the population who had it and probably a smaller population who actually knew that they did. If he knew.

Max had been startled from around Matthew's head when he had bolted upright in bed. From where the big cat sat at the foot of the bed, Max was staring accusingly as Matthew rolled over and turned the bedside lamp on. Checking the time, Matthew saw that it was five a.m. It wasn't a time he'd normally have wanted to climb out of bed and begin his day on a Saturday. And maybe not a time that he actually would. Making his way stiffly and carefully to the kitchen, he swapped out the ice pack and picked up his tablet computer.

When he noticed that Max hadn't followed, he was curious until he saw the big gray tabby cat hunched in a playful posture in the hallway outside the guest room door. From under the door, he saw a mottled white paw protruding and batting around. Max reached over and tapped it and the paw retreated under the door, poking back out a few inches away, and the process repeated itself.

Maybe they could play later, but right now, Matthew was intent on climbing back into his bed and doing some research. Klinefelter syndrome, he knew, occurred only in men, and it involved an extra X chromosome. While women have XX chromosome pairs and men have XY chromosomes, men with Klinefelter have an extra X chromosome, or XXY. The result manifested differently across subjects who had been studied. Some had much more feminine attributes than others, though there were fairly common characteristics that most men with the syndrome shared.

If he was right about his diagnosis, it explained why the man had longer limbs, a shorter torso, and a more rounded abdomen. He might have wider hips and other more feminine bodily characteristics as well. Propping up in bed, Matthew put the tablet on his lap and began tapping it to look up the syndrome and what it could mean for a person who had it. Checking the clock again, he saw that it was five thirty and a fine time to contact a homicide detective who apparently needed little sleep.

Not wanting to disrupt what rest the guy did manage to get if this was one of the few hours he was sleeping, he texted Danbury, "Hey, I have new information. Can you talk?"

Within seconds, his phone chimed with the incoming call.

"Hey, Doc, what's up?"

Amused that Danbury arranged the question that way instead of the image that came instantly to mind of a tall cartoon rabbit munching on a carrot whenever Danbury said it, Matthew chuckled to himself. Then he explained, "There was something about Sherwanda's description of the guy who dropped the car off. It bothered me all day yesterday. I woke up a half hour ago finally knowing what it was."

"And?"

"The description is unique. A tall guy with longer-than-normal legs and arms who she thought, from a distance, could have been a woman if she hadn't already seen his face."

"Yeah?"

"Klinefelter syndrome. It affects a small percentage of men, and it's an abnormality in chromosomes. It's congenital, something they're born with, not something that can be altered. Men with the syndrome have an extra X chromosome on some of their genetic pairings. It affects them differently, but some of the characteristics are pretty common. Like long limbs, a short torso, broader hips, a more rounded abdomen, possibly increased breast tissue, little body hair. Sometimes these guys are also on the autism spectrum too. But it gets worse for them. They can be underdeveloped in other areas, sometimes drastically so, and they might not be able to produce sperm or father children."

"Wow!" said Danbury. "That's good work, Doc."

"Maybe it'll help your expert profiler."

"Likely so. The guy might be angry at women. He might have good reason to be. After that last bit of description. I can see that being a motive."

"Yeah, I thought of that too. It could well be a motive. Maybe he vacillates between understanding women and being angry with them for identifying so closely with them if he doesn't want to."

"Is it treatable? Would that show up? In a DNA sample?"

"It can be treated with hormone replacement, though that doesn't improve their ability to father children because they've often lost their capability to produce sperm. Patients can be administered testosterone to offset some of the breast tissue and lack of body hair. Breast reduction surgery is also an option to remove the extra breast tissue. As with anyone being administered testosterone, it would deepen the voice and increase the ability to build muscle mass. There's a whole spectrum of symptoms that men with Klinefelter might have many of, or very few. Men who have few manifestations might not even be aware of it," Matthew explained.

"This guy might not know?"

"That's a possibility, though his characteristics seem more pronounced on that spectrum. But he might not have sought treatment even if he knows. Either way, it would explain the body type that Sherwanda described."

"Is there a database anywhere?" asked Danbury.

"Of men with the syndrome? Probably, but that information would have been gathered for research. You won't be able to access it to find a particular person. That would fall under the regulations of HIPAA, the Health Insurance Portability and Accountability Act, which protects personal patient information and prohibits sharing it without their consent."

"Where does that leave us?"

"I'm not sure it helps with finding him directly. But it might help your profiler to build a more accurate picture of the guy we're looking for. If I'm right about this, it means he has a more difficult time than most people hiding in plain sight, blending in."

"Yeah, true," agreed Danbury.

"Was anyone at the club helpful last night? Had any of them seen him?"

"Nobody admitted it if they had. One woman hesitated. Before she answered. One of the strippers. We might ask her again later. And there was something off. With Charlene and Misty."

"What was off about them?" asked Matthew.

"Charlene didn't report Misty missing."

"Yeah, she said she thought Misty wasn't coming back."

"Misty had a contract. One that was almost over. But not quite. Cara told us Misty would make good on it. Then she told me Misty wasn't planning to renew it. Charlene seemed to know that too. Maybe she knew where Misty was. Maybe she was involved. In her murder."

"Or maybe she didn't care. Because she knew Misty wasn't going to renew her contract," postulated Matthew. "She'd be losing Misty soon anyway. She doesn't seem the type to give much away. I think she's had years of practice at cloaking her responses and probably skirting legal issues with the videos she's making, if not with the strip club itself."

"She spins her responses. No doubt," agreed Danbury.

"I wonder how she really felt about Misty's plan to leave? Was she really so ambivalent? Or was she really angry?"

"All good questions. Maybe you can get answers. She won't talk to me. Maybe her workers need medical care."

Matthew groaned. "And I'm supposed to offer medical services? Danbury, I want to help, but. . ." He left the sentence unfinished.

"But what? That's an underserved population. Right?"

"Yeah, I'd say so."

"So you'll consider it?" prodded Danbury.

"I'll consider it. What about the tire store?" asked Matthew, changing the subject completely. "The one that the receipt in Misty's box of belongings led you to. Any help there on where she was going, or would they maybe have seen this guy?"

"Not on where she was going. We'll ask about the sketch. Tracing her steps backwards. To try to follow her forward. We finally got the warrant last night. To search Kent's house. Misty's last boyfriend. The missing guy. Who might have been in the trunk."

"Oh, good. I hope you can learn something from that search. What about the security footage from the hotel?"

"Our guy didn't go that way. Not through the parking lot. We didn't see the car come in. And we didn't see him go out."

"Oh," said Matthew. "I guess it was a long shot."

"Where are you today?"

"I'm planning to get some work done around the house," said Matthew with a sigh, thinking that wasn't his favorite thing to do but it was necessary and past time that he did it. "Laundry and some cleaning. Nothing too exciting. Right now, though, I'm going to try to get back to sleep for a couple of hours. I've had very little of that this week."

"OK, Doc. Thanks for the update."

"Sure. Let me know if any of it pans out. Keep me posted."

"Will do," said Danbury.

Matthew pulled his pillows down and snuggled under the covers, allowing himself to fully relax after having followed up on his waking moment of inspiration.

*****

When he awoke again, it was due to an annoying noise coming from his phone.

"Hey, Cees," he said, pushing himself up in the bed as he realized that it was a FaceTime request.

"Hey, sleepyhead. I'm sorry I woke you."

"It's OK. What time is it?"

"Nearly ten your time."

"Oh! I haven't slept in this late in a long time."

"Sounds like you needed it."

"I guess I must have. How're things in London this evening?"

"Afternoon," she corrected. "I'm only five hours ahead of you. It's nearly three here. I did a little shopping, cleaned my flat, and was just about to go shower and wash my hair to get ready for the evening. I thought I'd FaceTime you first, though."

"I'm glad you did. What's going on this evening?"

"I'm going out to dinner with my clients who are taking out some of their clients. They want me to meet them. It's likely to be a late night and probably not very entertaining."

"Schmoozing the client's clients, huh?"

"Something like that. How's the ankle? Anything new on your investigation?"

"The ankle will be better since I can stay off it more today. We might have a lead on the guy who dropped off the car."

"And then blew it up?"

"Yeah, that guy. We have a witness who saw him, a sketch of his face, and a physical description. So that should make it easier to find him."

"And he's the murderer?"

"It's a strong possibility. Otherwise, why would he leave the car with a bomb in the trunk?"

"Unless he was just a guy someone paid off to do just that, to drop a car off without knowing about the murder or the bomb."

"Maybe," agreed Matthew. "It's possible, but I'm not sure how likely. Either way, we need to find him."

"Please be careful, Matthew. I know I say that a lot, but I really want to come home and be with you in four months. You have to be there and in one piece for me to be able to do that."

"I'm not directly involved in any of this. I was just there when the car blew up."

"How are the officers who were injured in that explosion?"

"Danbury says they're both improving. It'll be a long road, but they're both expected to recover."

"That's great!"

"It really is. We were lucky."

"But there was a delay, right?"

"Yes, and that's one thing we're not sure about. Why was there a timer at all? I mean, if you want to blow the evidence and the car up why not just leave it on a timer when you walk away? Or if you want to booby-trap the trunk for the bomb to go off when it's opened, why not have it go off immediately?"

"You're right. That doesn't make sense."

"It feels like this guy thinks he's a cat toying with a police force full of mice. Oh, and speaking of cats, I have a visitor I need to check on this morning."

"A feline visitor?"

"Yeah, she's a cat."

"Whose?"

"She's the victim's cat. Her name is Fluffykins, and she lives up to that name. She's a long-haired, blue-eyed, very pretty calico cat. She seems really sweet-natured."

"You're not keeping her," said Cici matter-of-factly. After a momentary pause, she asked, "I mean, are you?"

"No, I'm just cat-sitting. Until either Leo comes home from a week working at their business in Denver or the hostess from the club where Misty worked convinces her grandmother to let her have a cat."

"Ah, good. I love Max, but I'm not sure two cats would work so well."

"Work so well for what?" asked Matthew, raising an eyebrow at her.

"Work so well for us, silly man," she said, waggling her eyebrows back at him. "I'm not sure how I'd feel about having a second one."

"Fair enough." Matthew chuckled. "I'm not planning to keep her for more than a few days."

"I hear you," she said somewhat accusingly. "But that's really up to you," she quickly added. "I've got to run and start getting organized for tonight. It'll take me an eternity just to get my hair dry."

Matthew loved Cici's long, thick strawberry-blonde mane, and he'd watched her patiently blow dry it, layer by layer, on many occasions.

"Talk to you tomorrow morning? Your time?" she asked.

"Sounds great. Go knock 'em dead tonight, Cees. I love you."

"I love you more!" she said.

"That's not even possible," he replied.

After they'd said their goodbyes, Matthew felt the familiar ache of longing for her as he climbed out of bed and went to check on the cats. In an attempt to distract himself, he texted Danbury, "Did you find anything at Kent's place?"

21 ~ NEXT STEPS

As Matthew set about his morning routine, he saw the incoming call from Danbury.

"Hey, Doc," said Danbury. Without further preamble, he added, "We searched Kent's house. He hadn't lived there long. Boxes still stacked in a spare room. Looks like he stepped out. Like he'd be right back. But he hasn't been. There're no recent signs of him. Mail accumulated. Nothing is out of place. No signs of struggle. It looks undisturbed."

"That's strange," Matthew answered.

"It is. I've got to go. Just giving you the update."

"Thanks, Danbury. Keep me posted."

"Will do."

Pondering that exchange, Matthew started on his to-do list for the day, most of which entailed cleaning and organizing his condo after the holidays. It was something that he hadn't bothered to do while Cici was still there and that he hadn't had time to do since she'd been gone. He started on his laundry, emptying the overflowing basket in the back corner of his closet.

Deciding to test the cats' reaction to each other, he took up both food bowls and let Fluffykins out of the guest bedroom. He was relieved to see it go well. Max was the perfect host.

Max's litter box in his hall bathroom scooped itself, so Matthew just had to change the little bag in the front. He realized that he'd just inserted the last little bag. In addition to replacing those, he knew he needed staple grocery items. Picking up a few things for Mira and checking on Joseph were also on his list. After finishing his cleaning chores, he decided to prop his foot up for a few minutes, and then a trip to the grocery store was his next priority.

"What should I do with you?" he asked Fluffykins, who had snuggled on one side of him, with Max on the other, when he sat down on his soft leather buttercream sofa to elevate his foot. Both cats had taken advantage of that opportunity. They were getting along well so far, he was pleased to discover, but he wasn't sure he wanted to leave the house with Fluffykins out. Max had always had full run of the house, and Matthew wasn't sure how they'd interact with him gone.

He put Fluffykins back in his guest room while he was away, locked up, hobbled out, and drove to the Fresh Mart on the edge of Peak. He liked the store because it had mostly organic foods and stocked items that were difficult to find elsewhere.

As he perused the aisles, he had just added fresh local milk to his cart from the back of the store when his phone sounded.

"Hey, Mom," he said after seeing Jackie Paine's name on the display when he pulled it from his pocket and tapped to answer. "What's up?"

"Hi, son. I'm just checking in. I know your dad talked to you earlier this week, but I hadn't. I was wondering if you were coming to church with us in the morning and then out to lunch?"

"I usually do, Mom. Why wouldn't I?"

"I guess because I knew you were involved in another case with your detective friend."

"I am helping Danbury, yes. But that doesn't usually preclude me from my family time on Sundays."

"Not usually," she hesitantly agreed. "Sundays are usually a little hectic, though, and I don't always get to chat with you. How are you doing this week with Cici gone?"

"That's why I signed up to help Danbury. I really miss her, but I'm trying to stay busy."

"And everything is going well for you?"

"Well," he said, deciding to broach the subject. "It's been a lot busier than I thought. I sprained my ankle the other day."

"Is it serious?"

"No. It would be much better by now if Dr. Rob weren't away or if it weren't cold and flu season, which means heavy patient loads. Or if I had a job where I could stay off it for a few days. But I've been on it for both work and the investigation that I'm helping Danbury with."

"How did you sprain it, son?"

Matthew chose his words carefully. He knew his mother worried about him, but he also knew that she prayed at least as much as she worried, so he figured he'd fess up. "I was helping Danbury on this case. We were at the end of a road up near Durham, and I had to jump into a ditch."

"Why did you jump into a ditch?" she asked, suspiciously.

"Because a car blew up."

"Matthew, you were there? I saw that in the news. Nobody was killed, but two were seriously injured, right?"

Except whoever was in the trunk, he thought. Aloud, he said, "That's right. And they're recovering."

"Your ankle wasn't listed among the injuries, huh, son?" He could hear the smile in her voice as she asked the question. He knew that she was trying to make light of the situation but that underlying her words, there was motherly concern.

"No, that's not considered a significant injury, at least by police definition, and not at all compared to the two who were listed as injured. I was glad to be there to triage and help. Danbury had one situation mostly under control. And I moved back and forth between them until the ambulances arrived for transport. I'm grocery shopping right now," Matthew added, changing the subject. "Something I haven't done since before Cici left—I'm out of everything."

"I hope your ankle heals quickly, and I'm happy to hear that you weren't seriously injured," she said. "It'll be good to see you in the morning. It's nice just to hear your voice, Matthew. I love you."

"I love you, too, Mom. See you in the morning."

Shuffling slowly and stiffly through the store, he collected the supplies that he was out of. Seeing more items that he knew he was running low on, he tossed those in the cart too. As he finally approached the register with his cart full of groceries, Matthew's cell phone sounded again. He pulled his cart aside from the line and answered the incoming call.

"Hey Doc!" said Danbury. "Have you considered it, yet?"

"Considered what?" asked Matthew. "I'm in the grocery store about to check out."

"Considered treating the, ah, workers," said Danbury. "At the Silver Silhouette."

"Oh, that," said Matthew.

"Yeah, the underserved population."

"Don't they have health care?"

"They don't have benefits. Not through the club. I'd bet not at all."

"But they make decent money, right?"

"I'm not sure. Some strip clubs, maybe. Probably not this one. It's not a first rate club. More likely the starting point. Where performers get experience. Probably why Misty was leaving. Everybody says she had talent. She wasn't stuck there. Some might be. But it sounded like she wasn't."

"I'm going to go check out now, and I'll think about it."

"That's what you said before," protested Danbury.

"OK, OK," said Matthew. "How would this work? Would they come to my office?"

"Probably not," admitted Danbury. "You'd have to go to them."

"I see," said Matthew. "And do the consultations and exams where? At the strip club?"

"Yeah, I guess so."

"And Charlene is in agreement with this?"

"I don't know."

"Why not?"

"I haven't asked her."

"But you will."

"Or," said Danbury. "You could. You're less scary. And a health care professional."

"I'll think about it," said Matthew, reverting back to his initial comment, given that every time he agreed to do something to help Danbury lately, it seemed to escalate into multiple somethings more.

"OK, Doc. I'm going back over tonight. I want to talk to two more people. One woman and a man. Neither were there last night. You sure you don't want to come?"

"I'm positive that I don't want to come."

"OK, I get it. Just one more thing."

Matthew held his breath, as those were four words he didn't relish hearing from Danbury lately.

"I tried to talk to Priestly. To show him the picture. He refused. He said he was done talking. At least to me. Could you have a go at him?"

"You want me to show Priestly the artist's rendering?"

"Yeah. I wouldn't ask. If I hadn't already tried. I got nowhere. He wouldn't even look." Danbury hesitated, but when Matthew didn't immediately refuse, he plowed ahead with the request. "Gauge his reaction. When you show it to him. You hear responses. When you question people. But you also see their responses. You see beyond their words."

"Yeah, I guess I can do that."

"Thanks, Doc. I'll check in with you later. Or text if you learn anything."

*****

After stopping by Franco's Italian Restaurant, which wasn't exactly on his way home, to pick up the lasagna he'd called to order, Matthew arrived home. He seemed to be stuck in a rut where food was concerned lately – hung up on Italian. He began putting the groceries away, and after feeding both cats, he sat down to enjoy his dinner. Saying a blessing over his food, he realized how blessed he truly was.

Surrounded by a loving family and growing up in a nice neighborhood, he'd gone to great schools and gotten an advanced medical professional degree with certification. Pondering the backgrounds and upbringing that some of the women working at Silver Silhouette must have endured, he thought again about Danbury's request to treat them.

It wasn't an outrageous request.

It was completely in keeping with his reason for going to medical school to begin with. He was ashamed of himself for getting too comfortable in his privileged life and forgetting that momentarily.

Putting his fork down, he picked up his phone and texted Danbury, "I'm in on seeing the workers at Silver Silhouette. I can talk to Charlene. Or try to."

"Tonight?" Danbury texted back.

Matthew just groaned. Danbury never seemed to run out of energy. He ate a lot, slept little, and didn't run on a surplus of caffeine, from what Matthew had seen. The guy seemed to think that everyone around him could do the same. Matthew, admittedly, had functioned for long periods of time on very little sleep when he was in medical school, but he thought he'd paid his dues then.

Checking his watch, he saw that it was after six. Maybe he could be back in a couple of hours. His primary goal was to be in bed early enough to get up in the morning and meet his family in north Raleigh at the church he'd grown up in, their weekly ritual. It was one he'd resented when he was younger but that he'd come to depend on as he got older. It was a rock in the midst of life's storms, something he could always count on that was solid, for which he was now very thankful.

He needed to drop off the groceries that he'd bought for Mira and check on Joseph. Then, ask Priestly about the picture. If he could find the guy. He'd be heading toward Silver Silhouette anyway, and maybe he could talk to Charlene quickly and it wouldn't take him that long.

"Yeah, OK," he texted back. "I bought groceries for Mira. I'll drop those and check on her and Joseph. Then Priestly. Are you there now?"

"Not yet."

"OK, see you there."

"Thanks, Doc."

I was home one night and got some rest, thought Matthew. *Why would I think I could manage two in a row?* Still, he knew that it was the right decision as he finished what he wanted of the huge serving of lasagna and stashed the remains in the refrigerator to enjoy later.

Determining his next steps for the evening, he wondered what the next steps for the investigation would be. He could connect with the women and the few men who worked in the club by helping them with whatever medical issues they had and building their trust. But could they provide any new information? If Misty kept to herself and if none of them seemed to notice that she was even gone, maybe that was a dead end, at least as far as the investigation went. Dead ends. A poor choice of terminology, perhaps, but there seemed to be lots of them.

22 ~ A FEW MORE THINGS

After cleaning up the kitchen, Matthew switched the ice pack on his ankle brace, then scooped up Fluffykins and put her back in his guest room. Gathering the groceries for Mira, he left lots of lights on, locked up, and turned the alarm on.

In the car, he cranked up his playlist, selected a classic rock song, and set off pondering the best approach to convince people to do what he would ask of them. Preston Priestly needed to look at the sketch and talk to him. Charlene or Phillip O'Connell needed to allow him to provide medical care for their employees. After that, he'd want Dr. Garner's approval to use office supplies.

When he arrived at the hotel, he was happy to find Mira and Joseph both well. The small boy was sitting in the middle of the floor on a blanket in front of the television, and he turned to give Matthew a big toothy grin when he arrived. Matthew helped to unpack the groceries and take stock of what was left, which wasn't much. He was relieved not to find Sherwanda there but refrained from asking where she was because he assumed that Mira wouldn't be able to explain anything that complex.

On his way out, Matthew decided to call his older sister, Monica, and ask if she'd kept any of his niece Angel's toys from that age. Anything that she'd be willing to relinquish would give Joseph something to do besides watching television. His niece Angelina, who they called Angel most of the time, was nearly five and precocious. She had outgrown toys for a two-year-old long ago.

"Hey, Moni," he said, calling her by the childhood name that he rarely called her as an adult.

"Please tell me that you're not calling to beg off tomorrow," she said.

"Beg off? You mean from going to church and out to lunch? No. Why would I do that?"

"Because I hear you're working on another investigation with the homicide detective."

Word about the investigation had apparently traveled quickly through his family. And somehow they thought that would preclude him from keeping up with their family tradition this week.

"I'm not calling about that. The opposite, really. Do you still have any of Angel's toys or books or activities for two-year-olds that you'd be willing to part with? I'm working with a Hispanic woman and her son, who had a bad case of croup. They're searching for her daughter, and Danbury is trying to keep her husband from being deported back to Cuba. They literally have nothing."

"There are bins of toys up in the attic," said Monica. "I guess I could make a trek up tonight and see what I can find. I didn't save everything, but I know there are some things of Angel's from that age up there."

"Thanks, that'd be great! Can you bring whatever you find to church tomorrow?"

"Sure. I'm relieved to hear that you'll be there," she said. "Angel looks forward to seeing you, having you come get her from children's church, and doing your hide-and-seek game with her. She gets really upset if she thinks you're coming and then finds out that you're not."

"Yeah, I know. Thanks, Monica. I'll see you in the morning." They said their goodbyes, and Matthew headed for Durham to talk to Priestly.

Knocking on the door of Priestly's residence, Matthew was surprised when the door was yanked open immediately.

"Oh, it's you," said Priestly.

"You were expecting somebody else?" asked Matthew and immediately regretted having asked.

"Yeah, a photographer. She helps with my InstaFans app posts."

"InstaFans?" asked Matthew.

"Yeah, I'm a model," said Priestly.

Matthew was pretty sure he didn't want to know the details about what that entailed, so he changed the subject to get the answer he actually cared about.

"I see," said Matthew before diving in with his question. "Just one quick question. If I show you a sketch, can you tell me if you've seen this guy before?"

"Yeah, I guess so," said Priestly grudgingly. "If it's fast."

Matthew quickly pulled a printed copy of the artist's rendering from the folder he'd brought it in and stuck it under Priestly's nose before the guy had a chance to change his mind.

"Yeah, that's that weird guy who came asking about Misty's cat," said Priestly matter-of-factly.

"Her cat? When? Where?"

"Here. Yesterday."

"What did he say?"

"He told me to hand her over to him. He was serious about it too."

"What did you tell him?"

"I told him that Cara took the cat to the police, that Danbury dude. I told him I didn't have her anymore. He didn't believe me at first. Then, I told him no self-respecting man I knew of would keep a cat named Fluffykins and he could just . . ." Priestly trailed off. "Well, I told him what he could do if he didn't believe me."

"And did he? Believe you?"

"I reckon so. Either that or I scared him off. He left."

"You said he was a weird guy. You're sure it was this guy?" he asked, holding up the picture again.

"Yeah, he was ugly. He had messy brown hair, and he was skinny. He had skinny arms and legs."

Matthew suppressed a smile because Priestly had just perfectly described himself. "Have you ever seen him before?"

"That's the thing. I think I have. At the club."

"At Silver Silhouette?"

"Yeah."

"Do you know when?"

"Right before Misty left."

"The week between Christmas and New Year?" clarified Matthew.

"I reckon so. I ain't been back since Misty was gone."

"Was he with anybody? Talking to anyone in particular?"

"Mostly he was hanging out at the bar. But I think he was talking to Phillip, you know, O'Connell. Behind the bar."

"I've met Phillip O'Connell. Thank you, Mr. Priestly. That's helpful. If he comes back or you see him again, would you contact me?"

"Yeah, I can do that," Priestly agreed as Matthew pulled out a business card and handed it over.

As he left Priestly's house to head for the club, he saw an older Ford sedan pull up to the curb. The photographer must have arrived, and he was happy to be leaving.

*****

The parking lot wasn't full when he arrived at Silver Silhouette, but there were more cars in it than he thought he'd find before eight. But then, it was a Saturday night.

Entering, he found Danbury in what looked like a heated conversation with Charlene. That wasn't what he wanted to see when his job was convincing her to let him set up a medical clinic for her staff.

Curious, he stepped into the close circle of light where they were standing beside the bar. The lighting was already lowered for the evening, but there were no performers on stage yet. Patrons were scattered throughout the room, already imbibing. Background music played softly, which is why it was easy to overhear Charlene yelling as Matthew approached.

"No!" Charlene said. "That is not a reason for murder!"

"Then why didn't you?" asked Danbury.

"I told you—I thought she'd just left. Her contract was about to be up and it was no secret that I couldn't offer her more money. I thought she'd decided not to come back after I made her work New Year's Eve. That happens here a lot. They come in, cut their teeth on the trade, get some experience, and then the best performers move on to flashier clubs that can afford to pay them more. It's not like there was a lot I could do about it if she broke her contract. She knew that. I knew that. I wasn't really surprised."

"You know nothing about her murder? Who killed her?"

"I shouldn't even answer that!" she retorted hotly. "But I will. NO! I know nothing about it! Nothing!"

"I had to ask," said Danbury. "Hey Doc," he said, calmly turning to Matthew as if he hadn't just been yelled at.

"Everything OK?" asked Matthew.

"Charlene and I were just talking."

"Not about me, I hope?" said Matthew, trying for some levity, but Charlene turned on her heel and stalked away in a huff.

"I was asking about Misty. Why Charlene didn't report her missing. Or seem surprised. Or upset. When she didn't come back."

"Ah. I thought you'd already questioned her."

"I did. But not quite that directly."

"And now I'm supposed to sweet-talk her and convince her to let me set up a clinic here?"

"Yeah, bad timing. The woman I talked to tonight. She thought she'd seen the guy in the sketch. Talking to Charlene. But Charlene claims she doesn't know who he is. Just a casual customer. If she talked to him. But she doesn't remember him. So I was pushing a little harder. To see what happened when she got upset."

"And?"

"And she denies any involvement. And all knowledge. Of everything. Who this guy in the artist's rendering is. Where Misty went. Or why she didn't come back."

"The guy has been here," said Matthew. "Priestly said he'd seen him here, too, the week between Christmas and New Year's. Not that I'd normally trust his word much by itself, but if he wasn't the only one, that adds credibility to his statement. More importantly, he said the guy had come to his house yesterday demanding that he hand over Fluffykins."

"The guy in the sketch? He wants the cat?"

Matthew nodded.

"Tell me," said Danbury, and Matthew recounted the brief conversation he'd had with Priestly.

After a momentary pause, Matthew said, "Charlene isn't likely to agree to me treating her staff now. I'm wasting my time here tonight, aren't I?"

"Maybe not. Maybe you don't need Charlene's permission. Maybe you just hand out business cards."

"I suppose I could do that. But I would need Charlene's permission to go upstairs and backstage," said Matthew thoughtfully, eyebrow raised in concentration. Normally, his foot might have been tapping too. With the sprained ankle, he'd done less of that lately when he was concentrating.

"Maybe we revisit that idea. I'm sorry. To bring you all the way up here."

"No problem," stammered Matthew, in shock that he'd just gotten an apology from Danbury. "OK, I guess I'll just head back home now so that I can get up and meet my family at church and for lunch tomorrow. You know, the usual Sunday tradition. I checked in on Mira and Joseph and took them groceries on the way over. It's a good thing I did. They were nearly out of everything."

"Good man," said Danbury approvingly.

As he started to turn and make his way to the door, Matthew noticed that Danbury seemed rooted to the spot. "You're staying here?" he asked.

"I'm going to hang around," declared Danbury, thumbing the blond stubble on his chin. "Observe all of the coming and going. Maybe Charlene doesn't know. Where Misty went. Or why she didn't come back. But she's hiding something. Maybe it's about the sketch. Maybe it's something else entirely. But I'm going to hang around awhile. See if anybody interesting shows up."

"You mean the guy in the sketch?"

"Namely, yes. You said Priestly had seen him here. As had the woman I questioned earlier. She was pretty sure. She said he was talking to Charlene. When she saw him."

"OK, I'll check in with you tomorrow," said Matthew, wondering how Danbury managed to work the kind of hours he did or why Penn wouldn't be upset about him being in a strip club on a Saturday night. She seemed to be very understanding. But then, Danbury had said that she'd been putting in long hours too at her new business. There seemed to be a lot of that this new year, a lot of really long work hours.

As he drove home, Matthew wondered how many long hours it would take to catch a crazed killer—or if it would even be possible. Would they be able to catch the murderer with any number of hours invested?

23 ~ Got a line

Awaking to a warm Sunday morning, particularly for January, what Matthew most wanted to do was snuggle back under the covers and doze a bit longer. Pulling his phone from the bedside table, he realized that he hadn't gotten a FaceTime request from Cici.

Deciding to get his coffee and then crawl back into bed for a little longer, he figured he'd FaceTime Cici before beginning his morning routine. He cared for the cats and returned to his bedroom with his coffee, happily noticing that his ankle mobility had improved. Icing it constantly and propping it up more the day before must have helped.

"Good morning, sleepyhead," said Cici answering his FaceTime request and smiling brightly at him. "I see you haven't fixed your hair by Max yet. Or is that hair by two cats now?"

"No," answered Matthew, chuckling. "Fluffykins sleeps and eats in the guest bedroom. Max isn't being territorial at all, and Fluffykins isn't antagonistic. They're getting along well, so far, and I don't want to change that. I just let her out when I'm here and they're not eating. Speaking of eating, how was your dinner last night?"

"It was far more entertaining than I thought it would be," she replied. "I knew they were going to talk shop, and that's not terribly intriguing to me because it's totally devoid of any legal topics most of the time. I think it's the British sense of humor that makes their conversations fascinating, though. They're so clever with whatever they're saying. They rarely just say it outright. So even business topics that should make me snore are cloaked in humor to sound more interesting. And you know the British have a wicked wit. They can insult you so cleverly that you'd roll laughing instead of taking offense."

"And did they? Insult you?"

"Oh no, not me. Sometimes each other. And the waitstaff last night apparently wasn't on their A game, so they caught the brunt of the comments. Are you headed off to church with your family this morning?"

"I am. And then probably to take some toys to Mira for Joseph after lunch. I asked Monica to see what she could find of Angel's old toys from that age, and she agreed to check her attic last night. Right now, though, I'm having trouble getting out of bed."

"I see that. I was going to say that I wished I were there to go to church with you and out to lunch with your family. But really, I'd rather be there snuggled up in bed with you this morning."

Matthew sighed deeply. "I know, Cees. I miss you too. So much that it feels like a physical ache."

"I completely get it," agreed Cici. "Me too. Four months seems insufferably long when I'm away from you."

They chatted, catching up on every little thing in each other's lives. After they said their goodbyes, Matthew got up, made the bed, and refilled his coffee.

Letting Fluffykins out on his way by, he took her bowl up because she'd left a little of her food. There was no such issue with Max, who'd emptied his and would happily go eat hers, too, if Matthew hadn't put it up. Having two cats was a bit more work, but they were getting along well, and Max seemed to enjoy the feline companionship.

As he was turning the water all the way up to the hottest setting for his shower, his phone rang. Seeing that it was Danbury, he turned the water off and answered it instead.

"Hey, Doc," Matthew heard. "I've got updates."

"Wow, you don't waste any time, do you?"

"Not if I can help it," said Danbury solemnly. "I think I found the guy."

"The one Sherwanda saw?"

"He has a doppelgänger. If it's not him."

"Where? How?"

"At the club. Last night. I was giving up for the night. It was late. I was just about to leave. And the guy walked in."

"And?"

"And I watched him. He talked to Phillip. At the bar. He checked out the strippers. He followed Charlene around. And then he cornered her. She looked upset. So I stepped in."

"How'd that go?"

"She yelled at me."

"She yelled at *you*?" asked Matthew. "Again?"

"Yep. Told me it was none of my business. To butt out."

"What did you do?"

"I butted out. Then I followed the guy out. He turned around and confronted me. Told me I didn't want to do that. To follow him. I told him I did."

"What did he say to that?"

"His beady little eyes narrowed. They're like daggers. His stare is disturbing. Just like in the picture. But I think he means for it to be. So I introduced myself. And he visibly cringed. And then he got mad. Told me to leave him alone. Not quite that nicely. I told him I had some questions. That I wanted to talk to him. He started ranting at me. Police harassment. And brutality. And he'd sue."

"Then what?"

"I told him he could talk to me there. Or we could talk downtown. He said he had nothing to say. He'd done nothing wrong. He was adamant about that. He said I didn't have grounds. He's right. I didn't. Not really. And he knew it."

"He wouldn't go with you voluntarily?"

"Not at all. I couldn't force him. He just looks like the guy we're looking for. I can't prove that he is. I was going to follow him. He knew it. So he went back inside. I went in behind him. But he'd disappeared. So I waited in the parking lot. For over two hours. The bar emptied. He never came out."

"He wasn't inside the bar still?"

"No. I went back in. Asked around. Talked to the staff. And a few remaining customers. Nobody saw him. Charlene wouldn't talk to me. Phillip said he didn't see him come back in. Then he clammed up too."

"The guy got past you?"

Danbury took a deep breath and admitted, "He did. I'm not sure how. Or where he went. Or with whom. He knows I'm looking for him now. If he didn't already."

"I hope he doesn't run."

"Yeah, that's my concern. If I spooked him. We might have lost him. But why is he still around? That's the first question. Why isn't he long gone already? He should be. If he is the murderer."

"Maybe he has unfinished business."

"Or maybe he's just brazen. Thinks he can't get caught. He's not stupid. If he is the guy. That's for certain."

"Maybe you can ID him some other way and find out who he is."

"Maybe. No hits in any database. Not yet. Not based on the sketch. And it's pretty accurate. Your witness did a good job. She described him well. Looks just like him."

"Wow! Yeah, I think she's smart. *Wily*, maybe is a better word, but not at all stupid."

"She wouldn't misguide us. Would she?"

"You mean purposefully send us down some wrong path after a guy who was never there?"

"That's what I mean."

"I don't think so. She confirmed the physical appearance that Gerard gave you. If she did, what's the motive? She called the guy by name who stole the tires. And she saw that we had no interest in that guy or the tires. So why send us after another one?"

"Some personal vendetta, maybe?"

"Maybe. But she seemed honest enough in coming forward."

"Maybe you can ask her."

"Yeah, I'll double-check when I drop some toys off for Joseph later today. Can you get the feds to release Mira's bags to you, the ones she abandoned when she ran? She needs the clothes for both of them that are in those bags."

"Working on it. They're locked up in Raleigh. I've filed the request. To release them with Joseph. I've followed up. On his release. Before you ask."

"Any progress on finding Mira's daughter?"

"We found the last place they lived. No forwarding address. We're still looking." Returning to the original discussion, Danbury added, "And we're adding surveillance. On the strip club. And on Charlene O'Connell."

"Good. It sounds like she knows a lot more than she's admitting."

"No doubt. That was always my impression."

"Maybe that'll make her talk to you, just to get rid of the surveillance on her club, if nothing else. What about Phillip?"

"He's slick. If he's involved. Or if he knows anything. He doesn't react. Or give anything away. We'll be watching him too."

"Maybe that's why they act like they hate each other. Whatever they're into, he's the straight man."

"Maybe. And we have a lead. A line on Melanie Wimble."

"Really? That's great!"

"Yeah, we're checking it out. Might be Misty Blue. Thanks to your idea. About the previous car owner. And the VIN check."

"It sounds like things are moving in the right direction, at least."

"Slowly. But they're moving. Let me know what Raynor says. If she changes her story. In any way."

"Will do," said Matthew and cranked his shower back up to its hottest setting. Long, hot showers were one of what he considered to be his many vices.

24 ~ Solid things

After church, Matthew and his family went out to eat at their favorite French bistro. Monica, true to her word, brought a small box of toys for Joseph. His niece, Angel, seemed to enjoy handing off the box, pulling out each toy, showing it to Matthew, and telling him all about each one.

After lunch, Matthew took the box of toys to Mira.

He knocked softly, and Mira cracked and then opened the door, smiling up at him. "Dr. Matthew," she said. "Come in! Joseph sleeps."

Putting the box on the floor, he told her what he'd brought. Her face lit up. "Joseph love. . ." she began. "Like toys," she amended.

"How is he feeling? Still no fever?" She shook her head no. "And the cough is better?"

"Is better," she repeated, nodding her head.

"Detective Danbury is working to get your bags that you left at the train station. He's filed paperwork to have them transferred to him. He's also filed paperwork petitioning for your husband's release from custody. Your husband is still being held in Raleigh. And Danbury's team found the last address for your daughter in Durham. She's not there anymore," he added quickly, before she could get her hopes up. "But they're still trying to locate her."

"Thank you," she said with tears in her eyes. "Gracias!"

"Where's Ms. Raynor? Sherwanda?"

"*No sé*," she answered with a shrug.

"When was she here last?" asked Matthew.

"Sherwanda go." She hesitated, struggling to find the words. "Before today," she added.

"Yesterday?" prompted Matthew. "The day before today?"

"Yes. Yesterday," agreed Mira, nodding her head.

"She was only here one night? Just Friday night?"

"Yes. One night."

"Do you know where she went?"

"*No sé*. She go. Yes-ter-day?" Mira faltered, and Matthew nodded.

"Did she say if she was coming back?"

"No. No say," she said, looking confused.

"She didn't tell you," said Matthew for her. "Right?"

"Right," Mira answered, looking relieved to have communicated that much. Her huge, expressive eyes gave so much away that she was easy to read.

"Mira, you were with her when she saw the guy who left the car behind, right?"

This question seemed to frustrate her, and she began trying to pantomime, in between a few words, what Matthew thought meant that she was behind Sherwanda. He interpreted. "You were behind Sherwanda when she saw the guy?"

"Yes." She nodded her head vigorously.

"You didn't see the guy?"

"No. I see . . . I see Sherwanda," she answered, shaking her head.

"Could she have been able to see him clearly? From where she was standing? From where you were walking in the woods at the edge of the road?"

"*No sé*." She shrugged. "I am," she began and hesitated. Finally, she said triumphantly, "Sorry. I am sorry!"

"It's OK, Mira. Thank you for telling me what you know. I'm going to go look for her. Do you or Joseph need anything else?" asked Matthew.

"No." She shook her head.

"OK, I'll check on you again soon. If you need anything, call me," said Matthew, making the motion of holding a phone up to his ear.

"Yes. Call." She nodded.

Matthew left the hotel, climbed into his Element, and followed the road to its dead end. Passing the blackened spot where the car had erupted into flames from the blast, he thought it eerie now in the watery afternoon light, particularly under the tree cover where the branches from trees on both sides overhung the road. Parking off to the right beyond the scorched spot, he got out and followed the little pathway at the end of the road to the edge of the camp.

The guy they'd called Gerard was seated with his back to Matthew in front of a fire in the makeshift firepit. Without turning around, Gerard said, "Stop. Don't come any closer." Then, he added, "Hello, Doctor. What do you want?"

"I want to talk to Sherwanda."

"She isn't here. She's moved on."

"Moved on? Moved on where?"

"Does this look like permanent housing to you?" asked Gerard, waving his arm around but still not turning to face Matthew. "People come; people go. They don't leave forwarding addresses. It's the definition of vagrancy. What do you want with her?"

"I wanted to talk to her about the guy she saw leaving the car that blew up. You saw him, too, right? From a distance?"

"From a distance."

"Did you see Sherwanda when the guy dropped the car off? Or know that she could see him more clearly from where she was standing?"

"Why do you want to know?"

"Because she provided a pretty accurate description of the guy. Much more detailed than most witnesses can provide."

"What are you saying?"

"Nothing. I'm not saying anything. I was hoping to get her to show me where she was when she saw him. That's all."

"I can show you," said Gerard. "If you'll go away and not come back."

"Show me and I'll go away," agreed Matthew, but he wasn't agreeing not to come back.

Gerard rose slowly and turned to Matthew. The guy wasn't very old, not nearly as old as Matthew had thought him to be. He had a beard, likely of necessity because shaving out here wouldn't be an easy task. It would also serve as a barrier against the cold. Neatly trimmed, there were only a few strands of gray in it. Most of it was a golden brown. Close-cropped brown hair showed beneath the beret on Gerard's head; his face was tanned but not wrinkled.

The man was maybe forty but certainly not any older than that. Matthew wanted to ply him with questions about why he was out here and where he'd been that led him to this place in his life. If he were only going to get a few questions answered, though, he figured he needed to make those count.

He followed Gerard back down the pathway, but they didn't go out to the street. Instead, the pathway they followed veered off to the left and took them down beside the road. They were, as Sherwanda had said, partially obscured from the view of the road by new understory tree growth and some branches and brambles leftover from spring, now mostly devoid of leaves. In any other season, they'd have been entirely invisible from the street, though it was only maybe twenty feet away.

Gerard hesitated a couple of times, then moved farther along the path. Finally seeming to be satisfied with the location, he stopped and said, "Here. They would have had to have been here for Sherwanda to see clearly but not be easily seen."

"Thanks, Gerard," said Matthew. "If I give you a card with my phone number on it, would you call if Sherwanda comes back?"

"I don't have a phone," said Gerard. When Matthew looked quizzically at him, he said, "And I don't want a phone."

"Would you give her the card and ask her to call me, then?"

"I might," said Gerard, though he stuck his hand out and took it when Matthew pulled out a business card and held it out to him. "But she's not likely to come back."

"Thanks. And you can use the number on the back if you need anything. That's my cell number that's jotted back there."

"I won't need anything," said Gerard.

Matthew picked his way carefully through the brambles back to the road and his car. He turned once before he'd gone very far from the pathway, and Gerard was gone, vanished like a mist, noiselessly. At least it was noiseless in comparison to the racket Matthew knew he was making tramping through the dried leaves and brambles.

Back in his car, Matthew put his phone on the dash holder, tapped to put the audio on the car speaker, and called Danbury to report in. There wasn't much to report, except that Sherwanda had disappeared and that he'd seen the spot where she must have watched the guy leaving the car.

"We didn't get her to sign her statement before she left," Matthew added regretfully.

"True. Maybe we don't need to. We have the recording. Could she have seen him? As clearly as she described? From the spot by the road?"

"If she has perfect vision," Matthew answered, slowly considering. "If the windows of the car weren't tinted, and if he were going slowly enough, she could have gotten a good look at him as he went by."

"That's a lot of ifs," said Danbury.

"She might have disappeared because she was afraid he'd seen her too. She mentioned that. She wasn't positive that he hadn't. It's why she came forward to give us the description. Maybe it isn't collusion but simple fear that made her disappear."

"Maybe," said Danbury. "Do you want to go to Mississippi? Tomorrow morning."

"No," said Matthew definitively. "I have patients to see in the morning and all week long. You're going to follow up on the Misty-might-be-Melanie angle?"

"Yeah. Tracking her backward. Or trying to. Nobody knows

anything about her here. Or about Kent's whereabouts. Because he hadn't lived here long. Just a couple of months. We're hitting dead ends. On both of them. Without more forensic evidence. For him, particularly."

"I hope this trip helps, then. You're just going to ask around about her, anybody you can find from her last known address?"

"Yeah. I'm taking copies of pictures. From the album under her bed. A composite sketch of what she'd look like alive. And a summary of the DNA sample. For whatever that's worth. Somebody there might tell me something. Maybe she ran. And they can tell me from what or who."

"Or maybe it's *to* what or who. She might not have run from anything but to this area for some reason."

"It's possible. She changed her name, though. That would suggest otherwise."

"I guess you're right. Safe travels, and keep me updated on what you learn."

"Text me if you change your mind. If you want to come to Mississippi. I fly out in the morning. I should be back in a couple of days," said Danbury.

Ordinarily, Matthew admitted to himself, he might have wanted to fly to Mississippi to help learn about the deceased woman. He'd chosen to help with the investigation to take his mind off Cici leaving, but he'd had no idea how overwhelmed and exhausted he'd be as a result. It wasn't an option that he could even consider.

25 ~ Crazy Days

Winter days were always busy, with children indoors and people sharing germs like they were at a swap meet. Mondays were the worst, though, because many people waited until the Peak Family Practice office opened instead of going to an urgent care clinic over the weekend. Mondays in the winter months were predictably the craziest.

Matthew was working through his morning patients when Gladys approached him in the hallway.

"Good morning, Gladys. Are you headed to exam room six?"

She nodded. "As soon as I finish this cup of coffee," she responded, taking a sip.

"I'll be there in a minute. I'm going to get a coffee too," he called after her as he opened the door to the stairwell and climbed the steps to get to the break room. The travel mug of coffee from home had been mostly empty by the time he'd made the short drive into the office.

Sipping the coffee quickly, he went back down the stairwell, ready to start seeing patients.

Tossing the empty disposable coffee cup in the trash and washing his hands as he entered the exam room, Matthew met a young man in his early twenties who was experiencing constant nausea. A muscular guy, he reported feeling lethargic and that he hadn't been able to keep food down for several weeks. It was interfering with his workout routine, job, and life in general.

Gladys had already gotten all of his vitals, and Matthew poked and prodded, asking if anything in particular hurt as he palpated his stomach. "I'm ordering some bloodwork, just to check things out," he told the guy. "We'll get results back quickly for a couple of these tests, probably in fifteen or twenty minutes. Gladys will draw blood, and if you want to wait for the first results to come back, I'll come talk to you about them when they're ready."

"OK," said the guy. "Thank you, Doctor."

Matthew tapped the tablet he carried to order the tests and then went to see the next patient. Diane, the other nurse who frequently worked with Matthew, was waiting for him in exam room three, and she had done the preliminary work for a teenage girl with a fever and a chronically sore throat. Matthew examined her and ordered a throat culture. He'd bet his reputation on it being strep, but before prescribing antibiotics, he needed to be certain.

Leaving the teenage girl with Diane, Matthew paused in the hallway for Gladys, who was waddling quickly toward him and waving for him to wait.

"Dr. Paine," she called out breathlessly. Looking around to see nobody else in the hallway as she approached, she said, "I'm not questioning your judgment, honey, but did you really mean to run *all* of these tests for the guy in room six?" She pointed at the order on her tablet.

"Yes, all of them."

Gladys shook her head and said, "OK, if you say so. You're the doctor, but this is crazy." And she went off down the hallway, mumbling.

The next patient, a geriatric gentleman who had recently lost his wife and somehow become a hypochondriac in the process, frustrated Matthew. There was technically nothing wrong with the guy. He was just lonely, and that was something that couldn't be treated. At least not directly. There was no magic pill for loneliness, though he often wished that he could offer more help somehow. He'd recommended various programs to the guy, including exercise classes at the nearby senior center. It was as much for connecting with people as for getting actual exercise. The exercise was an added benefit to stimulate endorphins and improve the guy's mood.

As he made his way back to exam room six, where the guy with the fatigue and nausea waited for him, Gladys came waddling back up the hallway before he reached the door. They reconvened momentarily, and she showed him the rapid test results.

"How did you know?" she asked quietly. "And who's going to tell the patient?"

"There were a few signs I picked up on," Matthew said, running his fingers through his soft, wavy brown hair, his big brown eyes showing the concern he felt about the situation. "The symptoms could be myriad other things. This patient doesn't have a prominent Adam's apple, though, or one that I could see at all. It just fit."

Matthew hesitated before adding, "And I'll tell him. It's a part of my job that I don't relish, giving patients potentially upsetting news. But it is my job."

Knocking, he entered the exam room and steeled himself to give the waiting guy the test results, happy that the guy was sitting down.

"We have your rapid test results," said Matthew as he dropped onto the stool in front of the exam table. "And I can tell you what the issue is. The good news is that it's not life threatening. You don't have anything fatal, as far as I can tell. But it could be potentially life altering."

Perched on the examining table, the guy looked expectant. Matthew decided not to sugarcoat it and said, kindly but directly, "The test results indicate that you're pregnant."

Matthew prepared to reach for smelling salts or to catch the guy if he passed out and toppled over. Instead, a huge grin began at one corner of the guy's mouth and spread slowly across his whole face.

"I'm pregnant," the guy repeated softly in a deep voice. "That's, that's…well, it's surprising, but it's actually not so bad. I haven't had the surgery yet to fully transition from female to male, obviously. Just the hormones. This was one of the things that made me hesitate to have the surgery. I want a family. I want children. So does my partner. He wants children too. I guess I'll have to find a great way to tell him tonight."

After prescribing prenatal vitamins and providing a referral to a local obstetrician/gynecologist for follow-up, Matthew slipped from the room to see the results of the strep test for the teenage girl. Shaking his head in wonder because there were things he'd never considered when he started medical school. Telling a woman who was transitioning to a man that he was pregnant topped the list.

Having done his best to be empathetic and sensitive in breaking that news, he was relieved that it had gone so well.

*****

Matthew had gotten through the day and collapsed into the desk chair in his office, propping his foot on an adjacent chair. Looking at the pictures from Danbury, he first scrutinized the picture of Misty Blue and then the sketch of the guy who'd left the car.

Who was he? Matthew pondered the possibilities. He might have been just a guy who was hired to drop a car off in a specified location, maybe at a specific time. He might not have known why, who it belonged to, or what was in the trunk. Matthew realized that counting Preston Priestly, Charlene O'Connell, and Phillip O'Connell out was not keeping an open mind. He knew virtually nothing about the guy whose sketch he was studying closely on the computer screen. They really knew very little about any of them.

Intently staring at the sketch, as if willing information somehow to spring from it into his mind, Matthew hadn't noticed Steven Garner standing in his doorway. Dr. Garner filled any doorway he stood in with his broad shoulders. Matthew was so deep in thought that he was startled when Garner cleared his throat.

Looking up, Matthew greeted him, "Hi, Dr. Garner. I didn't realize you were there."

"Obviously." Steven Garner smiled, his white teeth perfect against his dark skin. "What are you studying so intently there?"

"It's an artist's rendering, and it seems to be a pretty accurate one, of a guy the police want to find," answered Matthew, spinning the computer screen around for Garner to see.

"I've seen that guy," said Garner.

"This guy?" asked Matthew incredulously.

"Yeah, he stands out in a crowd. You can't really miss him. He couldn't go much of anywhere incognito."

"When? Where did you see him?"

"This morning at your friend Penn's gym. He was watching her from a distance across the larger workout room. His gaze followed her as she made her way around the weight room. He was holding up his phone like he was reading something, but I think he was taking pictures of her. When she went back upstairs, he left pretty soon after. You say the police want him?"

"Yes, at least for questioning," said Matthew, alarmed that the guy had been at Penn's place of business. Rising, Matthew began to pack up, retrieving his satchel from under his desk and stuffing the tablet into it. "Did you need me for something?" he asked Dr. Garner.

"I was just stopping by to discuss the clinic you want to open. It's at a strip club?"

"Maybe," said Matthew. "But I wouldn't call it a clinic exactly. It would just be helping an underserved population occasionally."

"I see."

"But it's not looking like it's going to work out right now. One of the owners is really peeved with Detective Danbury, and she knows I've been working with him. She isn't all that likely to talk to me right now about anything, even if it's to benefit the people who work for her."

"That's a shame," said Dr. Garner. "I was going to talk about a budget for supplies and maybe overtime hours for Gladys. Or replacement hours, something like that. If she's willing. Have you mentioned it to her?"

"I haven't. I just sent the note about it to you as something I might volunteer to do. But right now, I really need to get to Penn," said Matthew, checking his watch.

"It's nearly seven," said Garner, mirroring Matthew's gesture and glancing down at his watch. "I'm sure she's still there. At least she has been the couple of evenings that I've been there after work when I didn't make it that morning."

"Her brother is in Denver, and Danbury flew out for Mississippi this morning. So she's going home alone. If this guy was lurking around Lingle Wellness today, I can't let her do that. Hers is an old historic home with secret entrances and passageways. I don't think she has adequate security at all."

"OK, I'll let you get to it," said Steven Garner. "Just let me know when you're ready to talk about your idea for the occasional clinic."

"Thank you. I really appreciate it. And I'm sorry to be rushing off like this, but I am worried about her."

"Think nothing of it," said Garner, stepping back out into the hallway. Matthew heard his heels clicking as he rounded the corner and headed up the stairs before the stairwell door closed behind him.

Snatching up the last of his things and swapping the lab coat for an outdoor coat, Matthew locked up and pulled out his phone, tapping it to call Penn. After several rings, it went to voice mail.

Out at the car, Matthew pondered what to do next. On the one hand, he'd love to get home and pull his guns out of their locked case on the top shelf of his closet before setting off to find Penn. If he could just reach her by phone and tell her to stay put until he got there, that was plan A. Plan B, if he couldn't get her at all, would be to drive straight there.

He tried again, but this time on the office number for the business. A woman's voice answered on the third ring, but it wasn't Penn. When he asked for her, the young female voice said she was teaching a yoga class and asked if she could take a message. Identifying himself, Matthew asked what time the class would end.

"Oh, it just started," said the cheery voice. "I'm sorry, but it'll be an hour before she's free."

"Great!" said Matthew, a little too enthusiastically. "Tell her to stay put until I get there. It's important. I know she's very independent, but tell her I'm on my way over and that I need to talk to her there, before she leaves."

"OK," said the young woman slowly and hesitantly. "I'll give her the message as soon as she's finished with the class."

"Thank you," said Matthew. "I should be there by then. But if I'm not, please stress the importance of my message."

Going by his condo, he fed the cats, grabbed a protein bar and a bottle of water, then loaded his Glock 19 with a magazine. Packing it in a shoulder holster, Matthew dashed from his house and quickly through a misting rain across Peak to Lingle Wellness.

Finding a spot near the front, Matthew noticed that the parking lot was only about a third full of cars, which were scattered around it. Light from tall pole lamps in the well-lit parking lot sparkled like thousands of diamonds on the wet cars and the pavement. Bolting through the front door, Matthew saw no one at the front desk. As he slid behind the desk in search of a phone or intercom system, a round, earnest, freckled female face appeared at the glass window behind him. She stood and then entered the front area from a door to the left of the window.

"May I help you?" she asked, not unkindly but uncertainly, as he had clearly invaded the staff space behind the front desk.

"Yes. I'm Matthew Paine—I called earlier about trying to catch Penn before she left."

"Oh yeah," said the young woman, obviously relieved. "She's down this hallway on the left. She should be just finishing up the yoga class, but she probably won't leave for another hour. We don't close until nine."

As Matthew rushed down the hallway, he wished the young woman had told him that last bit when he called. Not that it would have mattered. He'd still have rushed to ensure that Penn wasn't going home alone with a potential murderer prowling after her.

"Matthew?" said Penn, looking up in surprise as he rounded the corner and stopped short in the doorway of the exercise room. "If you came for yoga, we just finished," she added with a smirk. Matthew saw about a dozen people, mostly women, rolling up mats and retrieving bags, changing shoes, and chatting with each other.

"Great class," said one of the women on the way out the door.

"Thanks," said Penn. "Glad you enjoyed it."

Several other women were gathering around her, and Matthew said quietly, "I need to talk to you, Penn, but I'll wait. Take your time."

Looking past one of the women at Matthew, Penn's brows knit in concern. She turned back to her class attendees, answering questions and chatting with them until, finally, the last one left the room.

Matthew stepped forward and said, "Penn, when does Leo get back?"

"Not until Wednesday," she said. "Why?"

"Did Danbury fly out for Mississippi this morning?"

"As far as I know. That was his plan, at least. I don't have my phone in here. I haven't had it for several hours, actually, so if he's texted to tell me where he is, I haven't seen it yet. Why? Is he OK?"

"I'm sure he's fine. Penn, I don't want to scare you," began Matthew.

"You're not scaring me, Matthew. Right now you're annoying me with all the questions. Whatever it is, just tell me."

26 ~ Sightings

"OK," Matthew said, as Penn's annoyance with his intrusion seemed to be growing. "There's a man the police are looking for. They have a sketch, but Danbury has seen him in person. He's potentially dangerous."

"And?"

"And I was looking at a sketch of him in my office just now, and Steven Garner, our senior partner who works out here, said he saw him here this morning."

"Here?"

"That's what he said. He also said that this guy was watching you when you were making your rounds through the weight room, and he left right after you came back upstairs."

"Oh," she said. "You said he's potentially dangerous? What's he done?"

"Maybe nothing. But you know the car that blew up last Tuesday?"

"A car blew up?"

"It was all over the news."

"I haven't seen the news.

"Wow, Danbury really doesn't tell you anything, does he?" asked Matthew, realizing that an explanation was now required.

"Not about the job, no."

"A car blew up, and a guy who looked like this guy was seen leaving it there before it did. He's very distinctive. If you see him, you know it. Here," he added, pulling his phone from his pocket and tapping to open the picture of the sketch.

"Huh," said Penn. "Yeah, he does have a very distinctive look about him."

"It's even more distinctive if you see all of him," said Matthew. "He's tall and slender, with longer arms and legs and a shorter torso. He might have wider hips and a fuller abdomen, maybe even enlarged breasts."

"You're sure he's a he?"

"He is. Look at the face. It's elongated, and he has a little hair on his chin, but it's sparse."

Taking the phone from him, she looked closely at the artist's rendering.

"You don't recognize him?" asked Matthew.

"I don't."

"Let's see if anybody else who's still here saw him."

"You said it was this morning?"

"Yeah, Dr. Garner saw him before he came into the office, so it was probably early. How do your members get in?"

"They have badges that will get them in all of the facilities, the workout spaces, locker rooms, steam room, pool, and spa. We're planning to install biometrics. Either iris readers or fingerprint, but that's not in yet."

"Do the badges have their pictures on them?"

"They do."

"And you have these pictures stored somehow?"

"Yes. We have a file for each member with all of their information."

"And the members don't sign in?"

"No. Only visitors sign in."

"Have you had many?"

"Visitors? Oh yeah, people like to come in and try it all out before they commit to joining, so we've had lots of visitors. Tis the season for New Year's resolutions. It's a great time to have a gym."

"Do they provide identification?"

"Not if they're with members. If they're with a member, the member signs them in. If they're not, they provide contact information—a phone number and address."

"But that could be easily forged if you don't ask for ID."

"You're right. We should probably change that. They provide ID when they join. We should start requiring it when they visit."

"Could this guy be a member?"

"It's possible, I suppose. We're growing too fast for me to know them all, even by sight. But I haven't seen him before."

"Can I see the visitor sign-ins from this morning? Danbury will want a copy of it, too, so you might as well scan it for him."

"You sound a lot like him, sometimes, Matthew," she said, rolling her eyes. "OK, I can clean up and put all of this away later," she said, motioning to the mats and equipment stacked neatly along the far wall. "Let's go."

She led the way back down the hallway to the front desk. "Patrice," she said. "Would you please copy and scan the sign-in sheets from first thing this morning until about, what, eight?" she asked Matthew.

"Yeah, about then. What time do you open?"

"Six," she said. "But I wasn't in this morning until almost seven. Patrice wasn't in until lunchtime. None of the morning staff members are here. We don't do split shifts."

"Six until eight, then, to be thorough," Matthew confirmed.

"Sure," said Patrice. "It's only a page and a half. I can copy and scan just those pages, if you want?"

"Yes, please," said Matthew.

"We'll need to scan through your member information. Can you sort those by gender, at least?"

"Yes, and by age," said Penn. "And a few other things."

Matthew sent the artist's rendering to Patrice and began poring over the list of visitors from the morning. Patrice printed the picture, pulled up the membership files on the computer at the front desk, sorted them, and began comparing.

"We should be focusing on the male names, but there are a couple here that could go either way," Matthew told Penn. "There's a Chris and a Peyton. And here's a Carter. They could be men or women with those names, right?"

"I suppose," said Penn. "Patrice, could you hand me my phone, please? It's right there behind the desk."

"Sure," she said, handing over the phone and going back to the computer.

"OK, I pulled up the visitor list from the scan," said Penn after tapping her phone and then waiting a few minutes. "And I'm sending it to Warren. Are you explaining?"

"Yeah," said Matthew, tapping his phone to text, "Hey, Danbury. I'm at Penn's gym. Dr. Garner saw your suspect here this morning. Staring at Penn. I came to warn her. She doesn't recognize him. Likely not a member, but we're checking. She's sending the sign-in page of this morning's visitors. What do you want us to do?"

"I'm calling it in," said the text that immediately came back from Danbury. "Stay put. I'll send an officer. He'll want to see security footage. Tell Penn I'll call her."

"Danbury says he's calling it in and sending an officer over. They'll want to see your security footage. He'll call you after he calls it in."

Penn drew a deep breath and blew it out slowly. "OK, I'll go pull that up. We've got about eighteen cameras, I think. None in locker rooms or anywhere intrusive, but they're on all entrances, exits, on either end of the pool, hallways, and outside bathrooms and the spa."

Matthew could see her on the other side of the glass window in the little office behind the front desk. As she sat down and adjusted a monitor in front of her, she picked up her phone. She talked, nodding and knitting her eyebrows. As she was putting the phone down, two uniformed officers came through the front door and headed straight for Matthew without pausing.

"Matthew Paine?" one of them asked. Matthew just nodded. "We need to talk to Penn Lingle."

"Right there." Matthew motioned to the glass window. "She's pulling together the video footage from the security cameras this morning. Here's a copy of the sign-in sheet of visitors between six, when they open, and eight this morning. Patrice is going through member files, comparing pictures to a printout of an artist's rendering of the suspect."

As the mention of her name, Patrice looked up and nodded briefly before returning her attention to the computer screen.

"Thanks," said the officer, taking the pages from Matthew. "We can narrow down the list by male names first. If the security cameras caught him, then that will narrow down the window of time. Do you have one up here?" he asked Patrice.

Without comment, Patrice stepped back and pointed up. Behind a cornice board that wrapped lighting mounted atop the wall behind the front desk above the glass window, a tiny camera lens was barely visible. It was inarguably discreet.

"That's good," said the other officer. "And Ms. Lingle is compiling that footage now?"

"Right," said Matthew.

"OK, we'll talk to her when she's done. I'll go have a look around outside, just to see the entrances and exits from that angle."

An hour later, they had evaluated the only two potential member pictures that even remotely resembled the sketch and determined that neither matched. The security camera facing a back door near the pool had captured a tall, lanky, shadowy figure entering around seven thirty that morning. The camera was mounted a distance away from the door, and the footage wasn't at all useful. Attempting to zoom in on the image pixelated it beyond recognition.

The figure appeared to be male, and the body type fit the description Matthew had heard from Sherwanda Raynor, long and leggy. The guy seemed to be looking down and away from the camera, as if he knew it was there, so facial recognition would have been impossible even if they'd had a closer view.

"That's a service entrance," explained Penn. "It's primarily used for treating the pool, but we bring in larger supplies from there. It's a sort of loading dock, I guess. That door isn't opened often. There's nobody else around who could have let him in. How did the alarm not go off when the door opened?"

"He didn't come through the front to sign in. So this list won't help," said Matthew, plopping the visitor sign-in sheet on the counter.

"If he were here for any legitimate reason, he'd have signed in. Or at least he'd have come through the front entrance here," said Penn. "But he snuck in instead. Did he exit the same way?"

After a thorough review of the security tapes, they could see the guy in the weight room, where Steven Garner could also be seen putting almost everyone else around him to shame. As Garner had said, the guy was holding up a cell phone as if looking at it. Intently following a moving target with the phone, he paid no attention to the equipment in front of him. Keeping his own face diverted from the cameras in the room, he then slunk out and away from camera range entirely. What they couldn't see on any of the cameras was him in a hallway afterward or leaving the building through any of the exits.

This, Matthew remembered, was the same guy who had given Danbury the slip. But how? How was he leaving places, even one with security cameras all over it, without being seen?

"I'll call the security company," said Penn. "And have them check on it first thing in the morning."

"Is it OK with you if I leave now?" Patrice asked Penn before she could get on the phone.

"Sure, Patrice. Would you walk her out to her car?" Penn asked one of the officers, who nodded his consent. Penn thanked him and began tapping her phone.

Matthew and the remaining officer were quiet while she explained the situation. "So now I'm worried too," she told them.

When she'd completed the call and had begun locking up the office, Matthew asked, "Why don't I come home with you to get your things, and you can stay in my guest room? Until either Danbury gets home or this guy is caught. If the guy has associated you with Danbury somehow, he might know where both of you live. But he has no reason to know who I am. At least, I hope not."

"Fair point," said one of the officers. "And a good idea. I'm going to call Danbury back and report in. Can I tell him that's what you're doing?"

Penn gave the officer a hard stare before she said, "I know you're trying to help, but I'm a grown woman. I'll tell Warren what I'm doing, when, and where."

"Yes ma'am," said the officer sounding as if he'd been chastised.

Both officers accompanied Penn to check through the facility, ensuring that all doors were locked and bolted closed. They all walked out together, and the officers told them good night, then watched as she got in her car and Matthew began following her to her house in downtown Peak.

As they walked through the back kitchen door of the historic home, Maxine materialized and began rubbing up against their ankles, meowing up at Matthew.

"What are we going to do about Maxine?" asked Penn. "I could feed her now and lock her in the bathroom with water and her litter box for the night."

"She's lonely," said Mathew. "We can take her too. If you're OK with her in the guest room with you?"

"Really?" asked Penn.

"I already have two cats in my house—what's one more?" he asked Maxine as he scooped her up and scratched her under the chin. She purred happily in his arms.

"OK, give me just a few minutes to gather my things and hers," said Penn. "And thank you, Matthew. You're a good friend."

"I try. You are too. Danbury would do the same if the situation were reversed."

"He would," Penn agreed with a huge grin. "He's a pretty good guy too."

Matthew helped Penn load the kitten's supplies in her car. She locked up, and he followed her to his house. They got Maxine settled in the guest room with Penn for the night. Fluffykins, who was getting along well with Max but had hissed at the kitten, was allowed out into the house at large for the night. After they'd said their goodnights and retreated to their bedrooms, Penn closed her door, and Matthew left his ajar so that the cats could come and go during the night.

It didn't take him long to fall into a deep sleep, but he rose to the surface of consciousness once, aware of odd dreams of women and men morphing and changing in psychedelic-colored lights, like kaleidoscopes. He went back to sleep, but the oddity of the dream clung in the recesses of his mind.

27 ~ Saddest Story Ever

When Matthew awakened, it took him a moment to remember that he wasn't alone in his house. The delicious smell wasn't a dream; it was actually emanating from his kitchen. Before he could go to investigate, Cici FaceTimed, and they had their usual morning chat. Matthew told her that Penn was there, and he explained the situation.

"Good thing she's dating Danbury," said Cici jokingly. "He's one guy you're not going to cross."

"Never entered my mind," said Matthew with an eyebrow raised. It hadn't felt awkward bringing Penn home with him. She belonged with Danbury, and they both knew it. It was more like having his sister, Monica, staying with him than anything else.

When he and Cici had said their goodbyes, Matthew went to investigate the heavenly smell. Penn had constructed omelets from various supplies in the refrigerator. It was a very good thing he'd gotten to the grocery store over the weekend, he thought.

"Here you go," she said, handing him a plate. "It's healthy."

"Thanks," said Matthew, not doubting at all that the omelet was entirely so.

"Mind if I get a shower first?" she asked.

"First?" he inquired.

"I won't take all of the hot water, I promise," she said.

"Don't worry about that—you can't. I have a heat-on-demand system that's fueled by natural gas. It'll take a minute for the hot water to get there, but once it's there, it'll last as long as you want. That was my solution for my shower vice. I tend to take long hot showers," he confessed.

"Nice," she said, then headed back to retrieve her things from the guest bedroom before going to shower in the hall bath.

Perching on a stool at his kitchen bar, Matthew said a blessing and dug in. The omelet was delicious and the perfect start to what was certain to be a busy winter Tuesday.

*****

Matthew had gotten through lunch before he'd had a chance to check in with Penn. There had been no further sightings of the guy he had begun to call Klinefelter in his mind because they had no other identity for him.

After seeing the last patient of the day, Matthew was on the way to his office when Danbury called.

"Hey, Doc. Can you talk?"

"Yeah, I just finished for the day, at least with patients. What's up?"

"We have a match. And a lot more. Misty Blue is Melanie Wimble."

"Wow! Does that help at all with the investigation?"

"It might. If her murder is tied to her past. I haven't found the tie yet. If it is. Her story is sad. She was raised in a commune. Some sort of cult. She escaped. And was disowned by her parents. Because she left. She was in a girls' home. And then foster care. Until she was sixteen. She was raped and had a baby. There were complications. The baby died. On New Year's Eve. She comes back every year. To put flowers on the grave. And sing to her."

"That has got to be one of the saddest stories I've ever heard. And that's a long drive. Could she have gotten there and back between the time she was missing and when she was found?"

"It's a good twelve hours. Each way. And it gets worse," said Danbury.

"How could it possibly get worse?" asked Matthew.

"The complications from the birth. That's why she had the hysterectomy. She was sterile. But not by choice. She lost the only baby she could ever have. She was hospitalized afterward. For a long time."

"You figured all of this out in just two days? How do you know all of this?"

"Pure luck. A college application Melanie filled out. At a community college. It had references. One of them is now retired. But the address is the same. She was a nurse. She cared for Melanie at the hospital. After the baby was born. And then after she died. That wasn't immediate. Melanie had two weeks with her. Before she died. The nurse remembered it all. She said Melanie was her most precious patient. Her words. They stayed in touch for a while."

"When was the last time she saw her? Did she see Melanie every year when she came back? Has she seen her lately? Did you ask?"

"Whoa. Slow down, Doc," said Danbury. "I asked. It's been a couple of years. Since she saw Melanie. She saw her every year. For a few years. But hasn't seen her in the past three."

"Oh," said Matthew, who had let himself into his office and slumped in his chair. "How horrible. Did you tell the nurse you think Melanie is Misty and that she was murdered?"

"Yeah. I had to explain. Why I was searching for her. And asking so many questions," said Danbury sadly. "She said it might be for the best. That Melanie is with Cloe. That's what she named her daughter. Cloe. She said she's holding her in heaven now."

That news certainly cast a pall over the evening.

"Not sure that helps us," said Danbury. "I can't find the rapist. I've requested the records. They were sealed."

"As in, you've found nothing so far in her background that means she was running from someone who might have caught up to her and killed her?"

"Right."

"Maybe it'll help put the pieces together in some other way," said Matthew.

"Here's hoping."

"Is there still nothing on Kent?"

"Nothing. No banking or card activity. We've found family. His mother. And a sister. Neither has heard from him. Not since Christmas. Neither seemed surprised. Or concerned. He's not in regular touch with them. And he's moved around. A lot. That's all I learned from them. His car was at his house. It wasn't disturbed. Like the house. No sign of forced entry. Or of a struggle."

"This is all so weird," said Matthew. "The more questions you get answered, the more questions you discover that need answers."

"True," said Danbury. "I'm on my way to the hotel. I'll fly home tomorrow. I couldn't get a flight out tonight."

"OK, Penn can stay with me again tonight. And Leo is due back in tomorrow, too, right?"

"Last I heard."

When they'd ended the call, Matthew sat, fingers templed on the desk in front of him, deep in thought. How could one person's life be so horrible? And how could she have survived all of the heartbreak? Yet somehow, she seemed to have moved forward with her life, only to be murdered, thus ending it.

It was no wonder that she didn't readily let people get close to her. It explained why she held everyone at arm's length and nobody thought that they really knew her. Of course, the world she was working in wasn't exactly conducive to deep and meaningful relationships.

Nor was it any wonder that the one person Misty had let in was a young, innocent woman whom she'd defended against men—Cara—then taught how to defend herself against them. That, now, all made perfect sense. Cara was probably the closest to Misty of anyone they'd encountered so far. What else might Cara know that she didn't know she knew?

Contemplating the complexity of that thought, Matthew was startled by his phone sounding. Yanking it up off the desk and clicking to answer, he heard Danbury saying, "Hey, Doc. Better news this time. I just got word. Mira's husband is being released. Tomorrow morning. One of our officers is picking him up. And taking him to Mira. Along with their bags."

"That's great news! I guess we have to take the good with the bad, huh?"

"Yeah, I guess so. I figured you'd want to know."

"Thanks. I'll go check on them before I go home. I was about to do some charting and planning for tomorrow before heading out."

"OK, later, Doc."

"Safe travels."

There would be a lot of moving home on Wednesday. Danbury and Leo would return to Peak, and Mira's husband would be returned to her and little Joseph. Still, a sadness lingered about Melanie Wimble, who had become Misty Blue. Hers was one of the saddest stories he'd heard in a while, maybe ever.

Trying to shake off the sullen sadness that had washed over him, he left the office and went to tell Mira the great news about her husband. Whether or not they could easily find their daughter, at least they would have each other to continue the search. Matthew wasn't sure how Danbury had gotten the elder Joseph released or if it came with any perks, like a green card. Maybe it came with stipulations, like staying in the area in case Mira's testimony was ever needed. Either way, he was elated that baby Joseph was well and that the family would be reunited.

As he drove, his mind wandered back to Misty Blue. In this emotional roller-coaster ride, this was the downhill side. Could Klinefelter, the creepy guy, be somebody from her past who had been looking for her and finally found her under her new name? Due to his condition, if Matthew was right about that, he probably wasn't the rapist. Melanie wouldn't have been very likely to get pregnant if he had been.

Could he have randomly chosen her for some unknown reason? Matthew pondered the possibilities. Or had he not chosen her at all and had nothing to do with her disappearance and murder or that of her latest boyfriend? Any of those options were entirely possible at this point. How frustrating to know so much about a murdered person but so little about her murderer.

Maybe they should revisit Preston Priestly as a suspect. Was he the last to see her alive when she dropped Fluffykins off? Or had Cara seen her after that? And why would Klinefelter want Misty's cat? That made no sense at all, if Priestly was telling the truth. But why lie about something like that? Charlene O'Connell definitely had something to hide. She had lashed out at Danbury when he questioned what she knew about Misty Blue's disappearance. Or maybe Misty's murderer was someone else entirely, someone they had yet to encounter.

Pulling up in front of the Home Away Hotel, Matthew parked, walked briskly in, and crossed the lobby. Waving briefly at the front-desk clerk, he headed up in the elevator. Mira welcomed him warmly, as did little Joseph. Joseph was babbling about something that Matthew assumed he wouldn't understand because it was in Spanish. He just nodded, smiling at the toddler, and made all of the appropriate adult responses.

When he told her that her husband would be joining her in the morning, Mira literally jumped for joy, clapping her hands and hugging Matthew. That, he thought, was a nice antidote to the news about Misty Blue. At least there were still some happy endings, he thought as he left the hotel and called Penn.

There was no answer, so he headed for Penn's business in Peak. It was on the way home, and he wanted her agreement on sushi takeout for dinner. He was already hungry, his stomach rumbling in protest as he turned in and parked near the building. It would be even later when Penn finally got a chance to eat. Looking around observantly for any furtive figures, he walked the short distance to the door and entered Lingle Wellness.

28 ~ Restless for a Reason

Penn readily agreed to sushi and salads, which Matthew called to order and picked up on the way home. He ate his and spent a quiet evening working on patient charts, then settled in with an acoustic guitar. The cats had eaten and the kitchen was cleaned long before Penn arrived after nine.

Matthew perched on a bar stool at his kitchen counter while Penn ate, and they talked about their busy days. She had heard from Danbury, who had secured a flight home the following morning.

"I've been so busy with the new business that I wouldn't have had much time to spend with him anyway," she confessed. "But it'll be nice to have him home."

"I'm sure," said Matthew, fighting the now-familiar ache for Cici. "I'll feel better when he's protecting you, too, with Klinefelter watching you in your own gym."

"Klinefelter? You know who he is now?" asked Penn, her luminous blue eyes widening in surprise.

"Oh," Matthew said with a chuckle. "No, I don't know his name. I just suspect from the descriptions and now the video from your gym that he has that syndrome. It occurs only in men, and it's an extra X chromosome that causes certain specific physical attributes. There's a range, though. Some men have it and don't even know it. While others, like this guy, have it, and it's obvious to anyone who knows what to look for."

"And Warren knows about this?"

"He does. I'm not sure if it'll help with the investigation at all, but if there's any DNA to match, it could be useful."

"Yeah, I guess it's just getting that DNA, huh?"

Matthew nodded as Penn tried to stifle a yawn.

"It's OK, I'm tired too," said Matthew. "I'll set up the coffee maker and get things laid out for the morning, and then I'm going to bed. You go ahead if you want."

"Thanks. Rebranding Lingle Wellness in Denver and opening the duplicate here is exciting, and I love every bit of it. But it's also completely exhausting and a lot of hard work. I'm glad Leo will be back tomorrow. He's really stepped up since we opened this one here. I'm so proud of him. And I've also come to depend on him—a lot."

"I'm glad they'll both be back tomorrow," Matthew agreed as he rinsed her plate and put it and the glass in the dishwasher. Filling the coffee carafe with filtered water from the second spigot by his sink, he set the coffee maker to grind and brew fresh coffee in the morning.

"I'll go get organized without letting Maxine out," said Penn.

"I had her out earlier this evening. I think Fluffykins is adjusting to her."

"Figures. Since I'll take her home tomorrow. Is she OK here for the day tomorrow? Or do I need to take her home on my way to work?"

"She's fine. The other two cats are getting along well out here together, so don't worry about it."

"Thanks, Matthew. You're a prince."

They said goodnight, and Penn slipped into the hall bedroom. Matthew walked past to his bedroom and Max followed him in. Fluffykins was already perched on his bed, bathing. She had apparently made herself right at home, Matthew thought with a chuckle.

After laying out his clothes and washing up for the night, Matthew climbed into bed and picked up a book he'd been reading back before the holidays. It was a historical account from a pilot in World War II that he enjoyed reading at night when his eyes would stay open long enough. He'd been so busy lately that he was usually exhausted when he hit the bed at night.

Reading for a few minutes until his eyes grew heavy, he laid it aside and turned the light off. Falling into a deep sleep, oblivious to reality and unaware of space and time, he felt a quick and oppressive weight hit him. Fighting to the surface of consciousness, he ruled out the cats as culprits.

It was Penn who had burst into his bedroom, pushing down on his raised shoulder and shaking it as he slept on his side with his back to the bedroom door.

"Matthew!" she whispered fiercely. "Matthew, wake up! He's here! He's outside my window! Matthew, wake up!"

"Who?" he asked, rolling over. "Who's here?"

"The creepy guy!"

"How do you know? Did you see him?" asked Matthew, reaching for his phone. He saw that it was shortly after three in the morning.

"He's outside my window!" she said in a stage whisper. "And no, I didn't see him! I didn't open the blinds to look. I woke up to a screeching sound like fingernails on a chalkboard. I think he was scraping his on the window! And then he said, 'Penelope. Penelope.' The way he said my name was beyond disturbing, dragging it out. And then he said, 'I know she's there. And she's mine. Give her to me.'" She cringed visibly as she said it.

"He called you by name?" Matthew sat upright, suddenly fully awake. Turning on the lamp beside his bed, he tapped his phone to call 911.

"He did! He's stalking me!" she hissed in a hoarse and exaggerated stage whisper.

Sliding out of bed, Matthew went to his closet and pulled the locked gun case down, putting the phone on speaker and placing it on the shelf while he put in the code to open the storage box. He pulled out his Glock 19 and clicked in a magazine while talking to the emergency operator.

"Nine one one. What's your emergency?"

"I need a police officer," he told the professional voice. "I have a . . . I don't know, a stalker, at least. Or a potential intruder or murderer. I'm not sure."

"OK, sir, what's the address?" the voice asked calmly, as if he'd just told her he'd stubbed his big toe, or something equally benign.

Matthew provided the street address and heard, "Please stay on the line, sir. Stay in your house, and don't confront the person."

That, thought Matthew as he heard the radio static of the emergency operator calling the nearest police unit, was just common sense. He had no idea who was out there, and the last thing he wanted was a confrontation with him. "Right," he said in response, then explained what had happened to the emergency operator when she returned to talk to him. Penn, meanwhile, had climbed into the middle of his bed with Maxine in her arms.

She wore a soft, fuzzy robe that she'd had the wherewithal to grab on her way out of the guest bedroom. With her knees pulled up as close to her chest as she could get them, she hugged them with one arm while holding the kitten under her chin with the other. She snuggled into Matthew's comforter and sat, stunned and shaking, her vibrant blue eyes wide.

"What could he want with me? He said I'm his and to give me to him," she finally choked in a soft, scared voice that was uncharacteristic of the Penn Lingle he knew. Obviously, this had rattled her to the core. Penn was as tough as women got, from what he'd seen, and she wasn't afraid of much. She'd been married, cheated on, and divorced; she chose to stay in Denver alone and expand her business there afterward.

Then, her younger brother, Allan, was murdered and she went home to handle all of the family business that resulted from his demise. She'd gotten shot in the process. Afterward, she helped to get her youngest brother, Leo, back on track and moving forward with an MBA degree and a joint business venture. A good match for Danbury, she was another of the toughest people Matthew knew.

"I wish I knew," he confessed.

"Are you hearing anything else outside?" asked the voice on the phone.

"No, but what was heard earlier was at the back of the house. My bedroom, where we are now, faces the front of the house. There's only a set of glazed block windows in my bath at the back of the house, so I can't see out from here. The house is locked and has security alarms on the doors and windows, but I haven't walked through to be sure nobody has bypassed them. I am armed and will stay that way until the officers arrive."

"Yes, sir. I'll inform the officers," she said. "Hold just a moment."

He could hear radio static as she gave the responders an update on the situation.

"They should be there in three minutes," she said.

"OK, we're staying put until they get here," said Matthew.

A few minutes later, he could hear sirens approaching and then silence. They had turned off the sirens before turning onto Chester Road from Highway 20. Chester Road, only a mile long, dead-ended into his condominium community, which was mostly filled with older adults, mainly retirees. They were quiet, the perfect neighbors, and there were no loud parties or noises after about nine at night, even in the summer months.

When flashing blue lights appeared through the closed slats of his window blinds, Matthew went out into the hallway, turning on lights and looking around as he went. Making his way to the front door, he admitted the officers and identified himself while holding his hand with the Glock in it pointing ceilingward. The officer nodded and Matthew lowered his arm, carefully laying the weapon on the library table, with the muzzle facing the wall just inside his front door.

One officer came in and walked through the condo, then started asking questions while the other went back outside to circle the perimeter. Penn wandered cautiously to the edge of the open space of Matthew's living room, introduced herself, and began answering questions. When the outdoor officer returned, he asked Matthew to take him into the garage. Nothing there, Matthew was relieved to see, appeared to have been disturbed.

"The car in the driveway is locked up tight. It doesn't look like anyone had tampered with it," said the officer. "I see no damage, and I can't see any prints. Is that your car?"

"No, it's mine," said Penn from where she was hovering in the open area at the end of the hallway. She stepped forward and introduced herself to the second officer. Neither she nor Matthew explained their relationship.

"That's the golf course behind you there, right?"

"Right. That's the corner of the back nine behind me."

"And behind it, a wooded area? Like here at the end of your street?"

"Right. There are utility lines that run through there, so there's a clearing for that, but there's nothing else directly beyond the end of my street."

"What's on the other side?"

"Of the woods? It's industrial. Maybe about a half mile away. Maybe a little more."

"So this person likely came from the golf course."

"Probably so. I'd like to tell you that I've never even thought about that, but it's happened before."

"Oh?" asked the officer.

"Yeah, a disgruntled lawyer who thought I was too much into his business hired a thug to throw a Molotov cocktail through my bay window last spring."

As he said it, Matthew remembered the abject terror of the moment when he had to choose to reach for the fire extinguisher and put the resulting fire out before rescuing Max. His house would have been destroyed, likely along with the two others attached to his condominium unit, had he run for his bedroom and tried to escape with Max out of the window. He'd suffered some smoke inhalation but nothing too severe, and he was thankful to have gotten Max out safely.

The memory gave him a physical jolt. It also completely changed the way he was thinking about the current murder investigation. He had felt sorrow for the young woman who had been murdered and wanted to find and incarcerate the person responsible. Now, however, a dear friend and his home had been threatened again. It had just become personal, and he redoubled his determination to catch the killer.

"Oh!" said the officer. "Any chance this is connected?"

"No," Penn spoke up. "He's behind bars. Hopefully for the rest of his life. If he ever comes up for parole, I and a lot of other people in Peak will have something to say about that. He was responsible for my brother's death, and he shot me."

The officer looked a bit taken aback by this and scratched his head with the end of the pencil.

"This," said Matthew, "I think, has to do with another murder entirely."

"Another murder?" asked the other officer, looking incredulous and confused.

"Penn's boyfriend is homicide detective Warren Danbury," explained Matthew.

"Oh!" both officers said in unison.

"He's out of town, but a guy he's been watching was spotted at Penn's place of business yesterday, so she's spent the past two nights here until Danbury gets back. Her house isn't very secure." Looking meaningfully at Penn, Matthew added, "But it will be."

Penn just nodded her agreement.

"What can you tell me about the man who was at your business? And where is that, your place of business?"

Matthew showed them the artist's sketch, and Penn told them about her gym and spa, explaining that she had him on her security camera recording, which had already been sent to the police department. As the officer asked and they answered a string of questions, Matthew figured it was going to be another long night without much sleep because there was likely no chance of going back to bed.

29 ~ Fully Invested

The officers left around four-thirty with more information than they'd be able to plow through quickly. They promised to patrol Matthew's street, the golf course, Penn's house, and her business. Matthew and Penn had curled up on the sofa and overstuffed chair, respectively, as Penn hadn't wanted to go back to the guest room. She'd refused Matthew's offer of his bedroom and instead opted for the overstuffed leather chair and matching ottoman. Protectively, he'd covered her with an afghan and stretched out on the adjacent sofa.

Sleep for the next couple of hours was fitful, at best, and Matthew awoke to a FaceTime request from Cici and the smell of breakfast and coffee emanating from his kitchen. Removing Max from around his head on the sofa, he leaned up on one elbow and answered.

"Good morning!" said Cici a little too cheerfully, and Matthew winced. "Matthew, you've got the worst hair by Max I've ever seen. What's wrong?"

"It was a rough night," said Matthew, running his long, tapered fingers through his disheveled hair.

"What on earth?"

"Somebody is stalking Penn. Probably the Klinefelter guy," Matthew said and then told her about the events of the night before. After agreeing, repeatedly, to be careful, they said their goodbyes, and Matthew wandered into the kitchen to find a plate of breakfast waiting on the counter.

"That one's yours," said Penn. "I'm going to shower and get my things together. I'm staying at Warren's tonight and taking Leo with me. I've decided."

"That's a good idea. Thanks for breakfast, Penn. It smells wonderful."

"You're welcome,'" she said distractedly as she left the kitchen. "Oh, and Matthew." She turned back after she'd started down the hallway.

Matthew looked up from his breakfast, turning to her as she hesitated. "Could Maxine maybe hang out here a little longer? Would it be too much trouble?" she asked quietly.

"Sure, Penn," he said, swallowing the first bite of breakfast. "No problem."

"Thanks. You are a prince!"

"Too bad we can't teach them to bark," he said, realizing that he was punchy from lack of sleep when he said it. "They'd make great guard cats." He thought Penn groaned as she slipped into the guest bedroom, but he wasn't sure.

Matthew chuckled to himself. If Preston Priestly thought no self-respecting man would have a cat, what would the guy think of having three? Finishing his breakfast, Matthew cleaned up the kitchen, cared for the cats, and got dressed and ready for the day. He and Penn left simultaneously after Matthew had double-checked that all windows and doors were locked and the alarm system was engaged and functioning properly.

The short drive to work was uneventful, and Matthew began it with a full travel mug of coffee that was mostly empty by the time he arrived. The caffeine seemed to revive him—or something did—because he didn't feel as tired as he should have after the disrupted sleep.

The morning round of patients had mostly been seen and cared for when Matthew felt his cell phone vibrate in his pocket. Between the next two patients, he stepped into an alcove and checked it.

"Have news. Call when you can," was Danbury's text.

Quickly tapping to call Danbury, Matthew hadn't heard the phone ring before Danbury said, "Hey, Doc. Mira and Joseph wanted to thank you. They're together. We dropped them in Durham. They checked out of the hotel."

"Are they OK?"

"Yeah. Joseph had cash. He got it back. When he was released. They're in north Durham. At a cheap hotel. They're looking for their daughter. Joseph is looking for work. He says he can easily find it. He's a carpenter. And a builder. Those are in high demand. Green card or not."

"Ah," said Matthew. That made sense, and if Joseph had some cash to tide them over until he could find work, so much the better. "You're back in town?"

"Yeah. Got an early flight. First thing this morning."

"Oh good." Matthew breathed out a sigh of relief, knowing that Danbury would be protecting Penn.

"I'm near where the body was found. Just down from there. In that new neighborhood. Where the houses are going in. We found a suspicious freezer truck. Parked behind a house. One under construction. In a cul-de-sac."

"Nobody reported it being there where it didn't belong? How long has it been there?" asked Matthew.

"It's been here at least a week. Nobody reported it until now. Everybody thought it belonged to somebody else. So nobody thought it was odd. Construction crews thought it belonged to another crew. There are a few residents. Some thought it was a construction truck. Others thought another neighbor owned it. For their business."

"Why is that important?" asked Matthew, distracted, watching Gladys enter the exam room where the next patient waited.

"It might be the murder scene. There are meat hooks. It's been washed out. The black light shows blood spatters. It could be bovine. But it's odd that it's here. We're checking it out. Not sure where it came from. We're running the VIN."

"I hope it leads somewhere helpful," said Matthew. "It's about time we got a break on this. It's like they're taunting us, like it's all a game of cat and mouse to somebody. They leave weird clues on the first body, a diamond and bite marks, freezing and thawing it. Then they allow us to see the second body just before blowing it up. We see only what they want us to see, and we're constantly trying to play catch-up. It's past time to turn those tables and go on the offensive!"

"Happy to hear you say that. You're fully invested now."

"What?"

"You're a lot more effective," responded Danbury. "When you're fully invested."

"Oh," said Matthew, considering that statement for a moment. Something had shifted in his attitude the night before, though he hadn't stopped long enough to consider it. It was impressive, though, that Danbury had noticed it.

"I think I was invested when that car blew up in our faces. But yeah, I am fully invested. Right now, I've got to go get invested in my next patient. Let me know if you need my help later. I should finish up with patients today shortly after four."

"You got it. Oh, and Doc," Danbury began.

Matthew hesitated before disconnecting the call.

"Thanks for protecting Penn. I appreciate it."

Before Matthew could respond, Danbury was gone.

*****

Back in his office after a full afternoon of treating patients, Matthew saw a missed call and a voice message from his dad and several text messages from Danbury. He listened first to the message from his father, who was doing the weekly check-in. The text messages revealed that Danbury had a lead on the freezer truck and asked if Matthew wanted to meet him back in RTP.

Deciding to join Danbury, Matthew packed his satchel, swapped his lab coat for his jacket, and texted Danbury. "Drop a pin. On the way."

"Not there yet. Address 107 Defender Drive. Meet you there."

Defender Drive Matthew knew all too well. It was the street that looped the Home Away Hotel and then dead-ended where the car had been found and then blown up. There must be other businesses around the other side of the hotel on the loop part of the road that he hadn't seen.

Plugging the charging cord into his phone and mounting it on the dash, he put in the address and set out, calling his dad from the speaker on the way. Despite the heavy traffic, chatting with his father for most of the trip made it go by much faster, and Matthew arrived at Duncan Meat Packaging and Shipping, the business at the address Danbury had sent, just over thirty minutes later.

Pulling into the parking lot of the business, Matthew didn't see Danbury's big black SUV in the nearly empty front parking lot. He found a parking spot near the front door and texted Danbury, "Here."

A fleet of panel trucks with the Duncan logo on them were parked like sentinels in a lot off to the left behind a tall chain linked fence. Matthew sat there a mere minute, looking around, when Danbury pulled in and parked beside him.

"Hey Doc, thanks for coming," said Danbury as they met up on the sidewalk.

"Sure. The truck you found belongs here?" asked Matthew.

"It does," Danbury responded. "The VIN is registered to this business. They reported it missing two weeks ago. On the second. We need to get the details."

"OK, if there's anything in particular that you want me to do, just let me know."

Danbury nodded as he opened two sets of glass doors in turn and led the way into an industrial-looking office. A counter was immediately in front of them, with multiple sets of metal desks off to either side.

"How can I help you?" asked a woman, who Matthew guessed to be in her midforties, from behind the counter.

Danbury introduced himself, flipping his badge open, and then Matthew in turn. "We're here about the missing truck," said Danbury.

"Oh, good. I heard it's been found," said the woman. "Horatio? They're here," she said, pushing a button and leaning toward what looked like a speaker. A set of heavy metal doors swooshed open behind her, and a stout man who also looked to be in his forties stepped through. His dark hair was thinning, and he had a dark mustache that wasn't quite a handlebar but was approaching that status.

"Horatio Duncan," he said, extending a hand first to Danbury and then to Matthew as they introduced themselves. "You found our truck?"

"Yes," replied Danbury.

"When can we get it back?"

"Our tech team is going over it now," said Danbury. "It'll be soon if they find nothing. Longer if they find something."

"Find something?" Horatio Duncan repeated. "What are they looking for?"

"A crime scene," replied Danbury. "If it was used for a crime."

"Oh!" said the woman behind them, and her hand fluttered to cover her mouth.

"And where's that scoundrel Mick?" demanded Duncan.

"Mick?" asked Danbury.

"The guy who was driving that truck when it disappeared."

"One of your employees was driving it? When it was stolen? It wasn't stolen from here?"

"It left with Mick that morning and never came back. He had a full day of deliveries to make that Thursday, two weeks ago. I haven't seen him or the truck since. The morning deliveries were made, but not the afternoon round. And the GPS tracking device on the truck was disabled around lunchtime. So I assumed that he drove it off somewhere he didn't want us to see. What I don't know is where or why he didn't finish the route and bring it back."

"When did you know it was missing?"

"That evening, Thursday, the second of January. Around seven that evening. I tried to call Mick because he was usually always back by six. I got no answer, and my call went straight to his voice mail. And that was full."

"That's when you reported it missing?"

"Yeah, that's right."

"Tell me about Mick."

"He's worked for us for a couple of years. He was usually dependable, so I was surprised when he wasn't back and didn't answer my call."

"What's his last name?"

"Nichols."

Danbury tapped on the tablet he held before looking up and asking, "You reported him missing?"

"Yeah, when the truck went missing. I told the officers who came that he was gone, too, but I don't know if they thought he'd been gone long enough to be missing."

"Does he have family? Anyone to ask about him?"

"Yeah, but not here. He has family out in Wyoming, I think, and a kid with a woman who refused to marry him. She took off, took the baby with her, and left him here. Mick tried to find his son. Last I heard, he hadn't. That's about all I know. I want you to find him, and I really need that truck back."

"It looks like you have a whole fleet of them out there," said Matthew.

"Yeah, but not like this one. I only have two of this type, and now I'm down to one."

"What's different about it?" asked Danbury.

"Those out there," said Duncan, motioning through the plate-glass window to the lot of trucks that Matthew had noticed earlier. "They are mostly residential delivery and some restaurant."

"And this one isn't?"

"Not at all. Those you see out there have refrigerated and freezer compartments. Residential customers get their orders shrink-wrapped and frozen, so those compartments maintain a specific temperature. Local restaurants we deliver to get their orders shrink-wrapped but refrigerated, so those compartments are set to a different temperature."

"And the missing one?" persisted Danbury.

"That one is a freezer truck," said Duncan.

"Meaning all of the compartments are freezer compartments?" asked Matthew.

"No, meaning that the whole compartment, the whole thing, is one giant freezer. We ship whole sides of meat, frozen, to industrial customers all over the place. These trucks are specialized and expensive. You can fill it and drive it cross-country, and the beef stays frozen to an exact temperature."

That had their attention.

"So the missing truck," began Danbury. "Could you put unfrozen meat in it? And then freeze it on the way?"

The guy shifted the wire-rimmed glasses up his nose. "I guess you could. That's not what we do, though. The beef sides are frozen here and then transported in the truck. Why?"

Without answering his question, Danbury changed the subject. "Did Mick leave a car here? His private vehicle? If he was driving your truck?"

"Yeah, he rides a motorcycle, even in the worst weather. It's off to the left out there," he said, motioning toward the front doors. "Chained to the outside of the fence. It's not huge, so I doubt you'll find anything on it. I mean, there's no storage that I know of."

"OK," said Danbury, tapping his tablet. "I'm not finding a driver's license. For a Mick or Michael Nichols. Not in this area. I'll need an address."

"He has a Class C, I know, so I'm not sure why you aren't finding it. We've got that information and his current address. Diana," he said to the woman behind the counter. "Pull up Mick's address, would you, shug?"

"Sure," she said, clicking keys on the computer in front of her. "Here it is. You want me to just call it out?"

"Yeah, go ahead," said Danbury, and he tapped the tablet as she read out an address in Thorny Branch, which was slightly north and slightly west of them.

"OK, hang on." Danbury quickly got on the phone and relayed that information.

"I've sent officers to check it," he said, returning to the conversation. "I have a few more questions."

"I'll help if I can," said Horatio Duncan. "I'm happy you found my truck. Like I said, those things aren't cheap, with all of the special equipment to transport meat for longer distances at exact temperatures. And I hope you can find Mick," he added, almost as an afterthought. "If he didn't steal it."

"Let's start with a description," said Danbury. "Height, weight, hair color. What he was last seen wearing."

"Not too tall," said Horatio Duncan, looking over at the woman he'd called Diana. "What, maybe five foot nine or ten?"

"Something like that. And a slender build. He's not a big guy. He has brown hair. Probably about the color of yours," she added, indicating Matthew. "And green eyes. You notice that about him as soon as you meet him. Darker skin. Not *dark* dark, but tanned."

"He would've been wearing one of our brown delivery uniforms. They look a little like the UPS drivers, but we didn't do that on purpose," explained Horatio.

Danbury, meanwhile, was tapping his tablet. Then he asked, as he flipped the tablet around for their inspection, "Is this him?"

"That's a horrible picture, but yeah, I think that's Mick," answered Diana.

"It's from the DMV," said Danbury, as if that explained why it would be a bad picture.

"Oh," she said, making a disgusted face. "License pictures are the worst. When somebody asks for mine, I stick my thumb over the picture before I show it to them."

"I found his Class C license," said Danbury. "Listed address is a coastal town."

"Yeah, I don't know about that," said Horatio Duncan, shrugging.

"OK, I think that's it for now," said Danbury.

"You'll let me know when I can get my truck back?" asked Duncan.

"Will do," said Danbury. "Thanks for your help."

Matthew followed Danbury out into the evening sunset. The day had been exceptionally warm for January, but as the sun was sinking, so was the temperature. Danbury paused, tapping his tablet, and Matthew, shielding his eyes against the setting sun that hovered just above the tree line, nearly bumped into him.

"Well, that was informative," said Matthew. "The killer could easily have frozen a body, or bodies, in the back of one of those trucks. I wonder how long that process would take?"

"Right question to ask," said Danbury, turning and holding out the tablet. "What do you make of this?"

Peering down at it, Matthew was looking at two driver's license pictures captured side by side. One was Mick Nichols, the missing driver, and the other was Trent Kent, the last known boyfriend of Misty Blue. The faces didn't look much alike, Matthew noted, but the height was identical, as was the hair color. Both men were five foot ten inches with brown hair.

"Huh," said Matthew. "It could have been either one of them in the trunk of the car, couldn't it? I know it was just a quick impression before the explosion, but Ross Dresden did say the body had on brown or dirty clothing."

"He did. Which Mick was wearing. When last seen. Let's have a look at this bike. Just in case Duncan was wrong," said Danbury, leading the way off to the left. As they approached the fence, what they found wasn't a motorcycle but a locking mechanism, which had been cut and it dangled from the fence.

Danbury's cell phone chimed, and he glanced down at it. "The traces of blood we found. Earlier today in the freezer truck. A splatter on the wall of the truck. And in the slotted galley down the edge. This message says there's a match. The DNA in the galley matches Misty. The wall splatter wasn't hers. But it's human, not bovine. They're running it now."

"So she was in the freezer truck, then. Maybe that narrows down who was in the truck with her. If it's Trent Kent's DNA, that makes Mick Nichols a suspect."

"It does. We've put an APB out on Nichols. Let's go see about a motorcycle," said Danbury, leading the way back into the Duncans' business.

Diana Duncan looked up in surprise. "Do you need something else?"

"The motorcycle. You said it was on the fence. When did you last see it there?" asked Danbury.

"What?" she asked. "Isn't it there now?"

"There's a locked chain and bar hanging from the fence," said Matthew. "But it's been cut, and the motorcycle is gone."

"Oh, that can't be good," said Diana and pushed the button again for Horatio, who swooshed through the metal doors.

The conversation that followed yielded no new or helpful information. Neither of the Duncans knew when the bike had been removed or by whom, and there were no cameras on the outside of the fence or on that side of the lot. The security cameras were interior and on the fleet of trucks on the other side of the building.

How long it would take to freeze a side of beef in the stolen truck depended, Horatio Duncan informed them, on the temperature the freezer was set to. It would take more than a couple of hours, even at extremely low temperatures, to freeze a side of beef. It could easily be at least partially frozen within a day, though, if the freezer temperature were set low enough.

"No help with the timeline. We need connections," said Danbury as they walked out into the setting sun again. It was now beneath the tree line, but the sky above the trees made them look like they were on fire with vibrant red and orange hues.

"What is Mick's connection to either of them—or to Klinefelter?" Matthew asked. "And how does Klinefelter fit? He must, somehow."

"Klinefelter?"

"Oh, yeah." Matthew grinned at having said that aloud again. "That's just what I'm calling the guy who left Misty's car because we don't know his real name."

"Oh. I'm going to Mick's apartment. It'll be searched next. Want to tag along?"

"Yeah, I do," said Matthew, remembering the guy who'd tracked

Penn home with him the night before. "I want this guy caught sooner rather than later."

He was, indeed, invested in finding the murderer now that whoever the ambiguous "they" might be had found his home and apparently included it in their nefarious plans.

As much as Matthew was invested in finding the murderer, his stomach wasn't. It growled loudly. Danbury had given him the address in case they got separated, but Matthew was managing to track behind him along the backroads leaving RTP and heading in the general direction of the airport. Thorny Branch offered a plethora of shopping options, with restaurants galore to meet any taste or ethnicity. How long, Matthew wondered, before he could get to one of them? How long before his hunger for food or justice would be sated? If not one, then the other would suffice at the moment.

30 ~ Which Cat?

Thorny Branch was a suburb of both Raleigh and Durham, if that was possible, because both cities were expanding and nearly bumping into each other. In addition to the stores and restaurants galore, huge neighborhoods had also sprung up in the area. These were carefully designed to incorporate apartments, condominiums, and large single-family homes, along with parks, sidewalks, greenways, and clubhouses. They went to none of those.

As they were pulling in front of an older brick apartment complex, Matthew's cell phone sounded. Glancing down, he saw that it was the security company that monitored his house. He immediately answered the call.

"Matthew Paine."

"Mr. Paine," said a male voice on the other end of the phone line. "This is Secure Watch." The guy provided the identifying security phrase before asking, "Can you give me your security code, please?"

Matthew quickly spieled off the numeric form of Cici's October twentieth birthday.

"Are you locked out or trying to gain access to your home without your security code?"

"I am not," said Matthew in alarm. "I'm not there."

A second call was beeping into the conversation, that from Cordelia Drewer, the neighbor on the other end of his condominium unit, whom he'd befriended the spring before. For the moment, he ignored that one.

"One of your window alarms was set off on the back of your house. We're sending officers now."

"Tell them I'm on my way," said Matthew. "I'm about a half hour away, though."

"Would you like to receive updates on this incident, Mr. Paine?"

"Yes," Matthew responded definitively. He jumped out of his Element, motioned to Danbury, and quickly explained.

"I'd come with you," began Danbury. "But . . ." He left the thought hanging as he motioned to the two police cruisers and another unmarked vehicle that were assembled in the parking lot.

"It's OK," said Matthew, noticing two officers standing at the bottom of a flight of metal steps and pointing up. "But I need to go."

"Keep me posted," said Danbury. "If there's anything you need."

"Will do," replied Matthew, jumping back into his Element and spinning around out of the parking lot. Maneuvering out to I-540, he went south straight down to the toll road, the fastest route home.

The drive back to Peak was shorter than the trip up, though the traffic hadn't thinned much by shortly after six. Two text messages came in from the security company, and he had the phone read them. The first message said there was an officer on the scene at his house, and the second said that the house was secure, but the officer was awaiting his arrival.

A police car from Peak, not a car from his security company, was in front of the house when Matthew pulled into his driveway. The lights on the motion sensor lit his short driveway brightly.

The officer, who Matthew guessed to be close to his own age and clad in the Peak uniform with which he was well familiar, approached. After introducing himself, he asked, "Are you the owner?"

"I am. Matthew Paine," he added by way of introduction, and the officer shook his hand firmly. "I just had a call from the security company that the alarm on one of my back windows went off."

"I got that report," said the officer. "And one from your neighbor. A, ah"—he consulted his tablet—"a Cordelia Drewer. She reported a strange man down here at the end of your street asking about you. The window wasn't fully breached, and your house still looks to be secure. Do you want me to walk through with you to be sure?"

"That would be great," said Matthew, going back to the Element, reaching in, and pushing the button to open the garage door. Leading the way through the garage to the side door, he unlocked it and punched in the code. Turning on lights as he went, he made his way through the house with the officer in tow. Fluffykins came out to greet them, but Matthew knew he'd find Max in the back corner of his closet, where he habitually hid when he heard a strange voice or a commotion. Maxine was still happily ensconced in the guest bedroom, where the window alarm had sounded. From the inside, the window was intact and looked undisturbed.

"Looks like somebody tried to jimmy it from the outside," said the officer. "There are scuff marks at the locks."

"Scuff marks?" asked Matthew.

"Nothing too noticeable," the guy amended. "You wouldn't see them if you weren't looking for them." Then, changing the subject entirely, he asked, "The neighbor who reported the suspicious person, is she next door?"

"No, the next door down," said Matthew.

"I need to talk to her," said the officer.

"Me too," said Matthew. Having ignored the call from Mrs. Drewer, he fully intended to go thank her. She'd been a nosy neighbor and a thorn in his side initially, but she'd come to be a friend, and he appreciated her reporting the suspicious person. He also wanted a full account of that person.

"OK, lead the way, then," said the officer as Matthew locked the door, reset the alarm, and went back through the garage and down to Mrs. Drewer's front porch. Oscar began to bark before he rang the doorbell, and then he heard Mrs. Drewer shuffling about inside. When she answered the door, she was alone, but Oscar was still barking from somewhere behind her in the house.

"I thought that would be you," she said, pushing the door closed and removing the chain she was peeking out through before swinging it wide. The officer introduced himself, and she added, "Come on in."

"Thank you, Mrs. Drewer, for calling me earlier. I was on the phone with the security company, so I'm sorry I didn't click over to take your call," apologized Matthew.

"That's all right," she said. "We were probably calling you about the same thing."

"Can you tell us what you saw, ma'am?" asked the officer, tablet poised.

"Certainly. Have a seat if you'd like," she said as she settled into the far corner of her sofa. Matthew perched on the other end, and the officer took a seat on a wingback chair opposite her.

"I was out walking Oscar after his dinner," she said. "We were down at the other end of the neighborhood, near the entrance. I saw a silver SUV, a smallish one, drive in slowly. The driver seemed to be looking around. I didn't think anything of it at first. I figured it was just somebody's grandchild looking for them or perhaps a pharmacy or pizza delivery."

Matthew nodded, and the officer tapped his tablet as she continued, "Then I saw them come all the way to our end down here, turn around, and pause in front of your house, Matthew. The car stayed there while I was cleaning up after Oscar, and this tall, lanky guy got out and went up on your front porch. He was looking all around. Then he got back in the car and slowly made his way back toward me. I scooped up Oscar and stepped in front, flagging him down. The guy stopped, but I could tell he really didn't want to."

"What did he look like?" asked the officer. "Can you describe him for me?"

"He was a bit odd-looking," said Mrs. Drewer, and Matthew leaned forward, pulling his phone from his pocket.

"Did he look anything like this?" asked Matthew, tapping his phone to pull up the artist's rendering of the guy he'd begun calling Klinefelter.

"He looked just like that!" exclaimed Mrs. Drewer. "Who is he? Is he someone you know?"

"Not exactly," said Matthew. "But unfortunately, I guess he knows me."

"Who is that?" the officer asked as Matthew showed him the artist's rendering and partially explained. He wanted to provide enough information in front of Mrs. Drewer to keep her on the alert for the guy but not enough to scare her. That the guy was wanted for questioning about a missing car, he explained. That the car had belonged to a murdered woman and been blown up with a body in the trunk, he neglected to mention.

Mrs. Drewer cocked her head at him, and he figured she hadn't missed the connection at all. She already knew all about the car bombing. Word hadn't gotten out about the body in the trunk because that information had been carefully withheld by the police.

"What did he say when you stopped him?" asked Matthew before the officer could comment or continue the questioning.

"He said he was looking for a missing cat."

"A missing cat?" asked the officer dubiously.

"That's what he said. He said it was a long-haired, fluffy calico cat. Calico cats are usually female, right?"

Matthew nodded as she continued, "I told him the only cat that lived at that end of the street was a big male gray tabby cat but that he wasn't lost and he was indoors, so he wouldn't be out roaming around. I know I shouldn't have told him anything, Matthew, but I wanted him to go away and not come back. If you're here looking for him, it must be more serious than that, mustn't it?"

"It's complicated," said Matthew. "But yes, it's much more serious. I think he did come back, but probably from the golf course, and he tried to get in my back window."

"Oh!" she exclaimed. "But I told him there was no calico cat down there."

The officer looked over her head at Matthew, who admitted, "Yes, but there is. There are currently three cats in my house."

"Oh!" said Mrs. Drewer again, knitting her brow. "Did you find a calico cat that someone lost and is looking for?"

"No, she's not lost. I know who the owner is. I'm cat-sitting for a couple of people at the moment. Max has lots of company."

"I don't understand, then," she said.

"Neither do I, but I think I'm starting to. I'll explain when I can, Mrs. Drewer, but thank you. Thank you so much for keeping an eye on my house and calling the police about the suspicious person lurking around," Matthew responded as he stood to leave.

"I almost didn't. I mean, I didn't at first," she replied. "When I came back up the street here, I was thinking about it, and after I came in, I finally decided I should call and report it."

"You didn't happen to see the license plate, did you, ma'am?" asked the officer.

"I'm so sorry, but I didn't even think to look. I should have. I really should have."

"It's OK, ma'am," said the officer. "Most people miss those. You did the right thing to call it in."

"Mrs. Morgan next door said she saw blue lights down here in the middle of the night last night. I must have slept through that. Were they at your house?" she asked.

Matthew nodded. "Yes, ma'am."

She looked alarmed as she asked, "Is there something going on that I should be concerned about?"

"No ma'am. This guy shouldn't bother you. He'd have no reason to," answered Matthew honestly.

"If you see this man again, or anyone or anything else that looks suspicious or doesn't belong, please call us," said the police officer who had walked to the door.

"Of course," said Mrs. Drewer. "We have a neighborhood watch meeting tomorrow evening. I'll alert everyone to be on the lookout, especially for that car and that lanky guy."

"Thank you ma'am. You have a good evening now," said the officer, tipping his hat to her.

"Thank you, Mrs. Drewer," repeated Matthew. "I'll let you know what's going on when I can."

"Good night," she said, and they heard the chain rattle and the dead bolt drive home after she'd closed the door behind them. Oscar barked from just behind the door again as they stepped down the two steps of her porch and onto the sidewalk beyond her driveway.

"It's odd that somebody is looking for this cat," said Matthew. "There must have been something transported with her that I haven't found yet. Not that I was looking for it. Either that or maybe somebody thinks something was transported with her."

"I was just about to ask about that," said the officer. "What's the significance of the cat?"

"She belonged to a woman who was murdered up in Durham, probably about two weeks ago now. The body was found a week ago this past Sunday. But what I don't understand is why her cat is suddenly important to someone, maybe to the killer, for some reason."

"Is there anything unusual about this cat? Is this the one I saw in your house earlier?"

"Yeah, that's Fluffykins."

"Fluffykins?" the officer asked, stifling a laugh.

"Hey, I didn't name her. I'm just cat-sitting, remember?" asked Matthew.

"Right," said the officer.

"And no, I haven't noticed anything unusual about the cat. Or any of her belongings that came with her. But I was thinking that it all merits a second look now that we know somebody wants her so badly. Wait." Matthew stopped, considering.

"The guy said something last night about her being his and to hand her over," Matthew remembered aloud. "He called Penn's name. Penn is Detective Danbury's girlfriend. He's the homicide detective who's working the case of the murdered woman. Penn was staying with me while Danbury was away because this guy showed up at her business. Last night, it was to her window, the same one that was jimmied this evening, that the guy went. He called her by name, and she thought he was talking about her being his. Maybe he was talking about the cat."

After a momentary pause in which he turned it all over in his mind, Matthew added, "I'm going to call Danbury. He was at another site that could be involved in that case earlier this evening, but he'll want this update. And maybe to examine all of the cat's belongings himself."

"I'll leave you to that if you could just read and sign your statement about this incident?" asked the officer, holding his tablet out to Matthew as they entered his garage.

"Sure. Come in for a minute and let me read through it."

"OK," the guy answered, following. Matthew read through and signed the document on the tablet. After promising overnight patrols of both the neighborhood and the golf course behind Matthew's condo, the police officer left.

Matthew called Danbury.

"Hey, Doc. What's up?" asked Danbury, who answered after the first ring.

"Somebody tried to jimmy open my back window shortly after one of my neighbors saw Klinefelter at my house. She stopped him and asked if she could help him. He told her he was looking for a missing calico cat. She didn't know I had Fluffykins here, so she told him the only cat down here was Max. He must not have believed her and came back around from the golf course.

"If the guy was here last night, I'm surprised he didn't just start from there this evening. But the back nine has been lit at night this week because it's been so warm. Golfers have been out later. Maybe that's why he didn't come in the back way at first."

"He's looking for Misty's cat?" asked Danbury. "Interesting."

"It is. Last night when he said that 'she was his,' Penn thought he meant her because he was at her window, he'd been at her business, and he called her by name. But maybe he was talking about Fluffykins."

"I'll let Penn know. She'll be relieved. And we need a closer look. At all of the cat's things. There wasn't much. I didn't take the food bin. Just the food. There was nothing in her food. What else? A bed. A litter box. A couple of toys?"

"Yeah, one toy that Priestly could find and two bowls. That's it, other than Fluffykins herself."

"The cat wouldn't have, ah"—Danbury hesitated before adding—"been forced to ingest anything?"

"If she did, it's long gone by now," said Matthew. "If that were the case and the killer knew Fluffykins had ingested something, he'd have also known that it wouldn't still be around. I'll have another look. Are you finding anything up there at the apartment?"

"It's what we're not finding. That's what's telling. It's like Kent's place. Like he just stepped out. Expecting to be right back. Mail piled up. A couple of lights left on. I don't think it's been tossed. The guy wasn't a complete slob. But not neat. It's taking some time."

"I wonder if that's purposeful. On either of their parts."

"Meaning what?"

"That one or both of them wanted it to look like they were coming right back. Innocently."

"Good point. I'll keep that in mind. Speaking of Kent's place," continued Danbury. "The DNA test is back. From the blood splatter. The one on the wall of the truck."

"That was fast."

"It's faster if you have something to compare to. It's Kent's."

"Huh," said Matthew. "That could mean one of two things."

"It means he was there," offered Danbury.

"It does, but in what capacity? There are several possibilities."

"Name them."

"As the killer who got injured killing Misty. Or as the killer who put his blood there to make us think he's dead. Or as another victim, and maybe he was in the trunk of the car, not Mick Nichols. Surely, you thought of that?" asked Matthew.

"I did. But I wanted to hear your take."

"Ah. I'll go have another look at the things that came with Fluffykins," said Matthew. "I'll let you know if I find anything."

After the call with Danbury, Matthew went first to the hall bath where he and Penn had placed the litterbox that came with

Fluffykins—alongside the one already there for Max—when Maxine arrived. It made the hall bath a bit crowded. But he wanted all of the cats to have their own litter boxes to discourage feline accidents in the house. Max appeared, probably from the back of his closet, and was watching him with a steady gaze.

"I know, big guy," Matthew told Max, reaching to scratch him under his chin. "You're hungry. Me too. I'll feed you first. Just a minute." Max purred his approval.

Unlike the one he'd put there for Max, this litter box had no mechanical scooping mechanism, and he thought it was time for it to be cleaned out again anyway. As he carefully removed the clip-on top and raked, Matthew tapped the bottom of the plastic box with the scooping tool. There was no false bottom and nothing in the litter but, well, exactly what was supposed to be there. Nothing was written or etched in the plastic that he could find as he cleared it section by section, moving the litter around to look at the bottom of the box under it.

Before clipping it back in place, Matthew flipped the clip-on lid over to examine it more closely and pulled the charcoal filter from the little slots in the top. There was nothing unusual there either. Reassembling it all, he moved on to the fluffy cat's bed which had been relocated to his bedroom when Maxine came to stay. The fluffy cat hadn't bothered to get in it much and was watching contentedly from the bottom corner of his bed, the opposite side from where Max habitually perched.

There was a zippered compartment in the bed so that the cover could be removed to be laundered. Matthew disassembled the bed entirely, flipping the cover completely inside out. There was no writing on the inside, and nothing fell out or was attached. He scrunched the padding all around but felt nothing there either, no paper or anything else.

Reassembling the bed, he managed to find her cat toy, which had migrated out into the living room. It was a little mouse with a blue feather on it that crinkled when the cats carried it around. He could feel the crinkly plastic and padding inside, but short of disassembling it, he wasn't finding anything else. Could there be a slip of paper amid the crinkling plastic? The integrity of the toy hadn't been compromised, so he ruled that out.

There were no hidden messages, no locker keys, or any other hidden objects, and he chided himself for having read a few too many spy novels as a kid. Of course, it would help to know what it was that he was looking for.

As he went to feed all three cats, separating them to eat, Matthew checked the food and water bowls that came with Fluffykins. No messages were etched into them or attached to them. They were small, with no layers in the plastic where anything could be hidden. Maxine was relegated to eating in his guest room, Fluffykins in his bedroom, and Max under the desk in the kitchen, his usual spot. All three cats dove into their food.

After assembling, eating, and cleaning up a quick meal for himself, Matthew returned to the search. Danbury had gone through the cat food when he removed it from Misty's apartment. The only thing left was the cat herself. She had on a collar, so Matthew plopped her in his lap and scratched her behind the ears with one hand while pulling her fur away from the collar with the other.

Spinning it all the way around, he saw nothing unusual about the collar. It was pink and blue, the outer layer a blue faux leather with tiny rhinestones that were obviously glass attached at intervals along it. He ran his fingers under the collar and felt an inner layer of soft, fuzzy pink material. The clasp had a break-away stretchy band designed to snap if Fluffykins got it hung on anything. Attached on a tiny ring beneath the clasp were a rabies tag and one with her name and Misty's phone number on it that jingled slightly when Fluffykins moved. Both were devoid of any other information, with nothing else etched or attached.

Disappointed, Matthew texted Danbury that he'd found nothing unusual in any of the cat's belongings, and he started his evening routine, going through patient charts and then setting up for the next morning. Pulling clothes from his closet to lay out in his bathroom, he noticed that he'd uncharacteristically not locked his Glock 19 back in the box after having it out in the middle of the night. Instead, it and the magazine for it lay on the top shelf beside the lock box.

That might not be such a bad idea, anyway, he thought, so he pulled both down and tucked them into the top drawer of the nightstand. He'd be prepared to use it in the middle of the night if anyone attempted to enter his house again. That was the last thought he had after crawling into bed for the night and falling, exhausted, into a deep and dreamless sleep.

31 ~ On the Offensive

Thursday morning and half of the afternoon were gone before Matthew managed to catch his breath. He had paused only long enough to hurriedly eat the lunch-train meal between patients. Dr. Rob would be back next week, and for that, Matthew was exceedingly thankful.

The day had started normally enough with the morning FaceTime chat with Cici, and the ache for her was becoming more bearable. The thing that surprised him, as he slipped momentarily into his office for the first time since early that morning, was that he hadn't heard from Danbury at all.

Checking his phone to see that it was on and operational, he had about ten minutes before the next patient. Calling Danbury, he got an answer after multiple rings.

"Hey, Doc, what's up?"

"Just checking in. Any progress last night?"

"Not really. Long hours. No new leads. It's frustrating. I'm doing some surveillance tonight. Want to come to the club?"

"Silver Silhouette? Sure, why not? I got a decent night of sleep last night, so I'm game. What's the plan?"

"There was another sighting. Of the guy you call Klinefelter. Last night. The team called me. But he was gone. By the time I got there. Like before. He went in. But nobody saw him come out. We'll have a team on the inside. And the outside. I'll be outside. If you want to join."

"Sure. What time are you planning to go?"

"The team convenes at eight. That's when things start happening. From what we've seen so far. I'll get there at seven thirty."

"OK. I'll get dinner and take care of my growing herd of cats," Matthew said sardonically.

"I know. I'm sorry, Doc. I wouldn't ask Cara now. She wouldn't be safe. Not with somebody after the cat. Penn and Leo are with me. At least for a week. Until we can install security at their place. They're deciding what they want to do. They have the outside entrance to secure. The one into the passages behind the walls. They might close it off. Expand from inside. Lose the passages altogether. They're talking to contractors."

Matthew refrained from pointing out that neither was he safe. So far, the attempts to get to Penn, if indeed the guy had been after Penn, or Fluffykins, had been thwarted.

Instead, he said, "I'm sure that's not the norm, securing homes like the Lingle Plantation. The security company won't know what to do with the hidden passageways in the walls and the outside entrance to them," Matthew added, remembering how he'd discovered the secrets of the old historic home the spring before. It wasn't just that the place had no security to speak of, it was also that it would be difficult to secure.

Growing up in the house, Leo and his deceased brother Allan had known about the passageways. Penn had not. There was an entrance into the passageways behind the walls from the outside of the Lingles' house. That had been a major factor in Matthew's concern about Penn going home alone after Klinefelter had been at her gym.

He well remembered discovering the extra six feet of space that ran along the outside right wall of the two stories, the attic, and a cellar, with steep circular metal stairs that connected the floors. A panel opened onto each floor that was so well disguised as to be unnoticeable and completely concealed. The passageways had been constructed when the kitchen was added on at the back of the house.

"The security company already looked. At the Lingles' house. Yesterday. Now they're discussing solutions. Meet you at the club at eight?" asked Danbury.

It was time, no, way past time, Matthew amended his thought, to go on the offensive. He was ready to do whatever it took to put a stop to uninvited people showing up at his house, however secure he might think it to be. He needed to add security cameras on the outside himself, he thought. But that would have to wait.

"I'll see you at seven thirty," Matthew answered.

*****

Entering the Silver Silhouette parking lot, Matthew spotted a black SUV near the back door of the business and pulled alongside it. It wasn't, he realized belatedly, the right SUV. He looked up in time to watch a tall, slender woman with long legs in stiletto heels walk in gliding strides, as smooth as the silky dress that clung to her, up to the SUV and get in it.

Though she was exceptionally graceful in them, she didn't at all need the heels. She was probably nearly six feet tall in her bare feet. Why did women do that to themselves? Stiletto heels couldn't be comfortable. Cici, he knew, wore heels because she was five-foot-nothing and wanted the boost in height. This woman, though, would tower over most men in those heels, himself included.

Dismissing the thought, Matthew backed out and then found a spot farther away from the doors along the back row of the long, narrow parking lot to watch. After waiting a mere two minutes, he saw the right black SUV pull into the lot. Danbury backed it in beside Matthew's Element at an angle so that the driver's side had a full view of both the front and rear exits.

Locking his car, Matthew climbed out and into the passenger seat of Danbury's SUV.

"Hey, Doc," greeted Danbury. "We'll settle in here. I'll meet with the team. But only by com packs. Here," he said, tossing a headset to Matthew. "You can listen in. If you want."

"I want." He nodded. "I want to do whatever we have to do to get this guy and put him away. I'm tired of playing catch-up while he toys with us."

Matthew saw the grin that Danbury was trying to suppress as he nodded and donned his earwig listening device. After a few minutes, the parking lot started to fill up, and Matthew heard two other teams check in on his headset. Danbury gave instructions for who was going where. Two went in, one hung around the back exit, and the other monitored the periphery on foot.

The night would be exceptionally mild for January in North Carolina, Matthew knew, because he'd checked the weather forecast. The high had been over sixty during the day, and the overnight low wasn't supposed to go much lower. A cold front would move in the next day, but for the moment, a foot patrol around the building would be pleasant.

Everyone was in position. Danbury was watching the building and the cars coming and going with a small set of flip-down goggles. The minutes ticked by, and then an hour, with nothing exciting happening except some mild chatter on the com system that Matthew was listening to on the headset.

For a Thursday night, apparently, business was booming. One of the guys who was working inside reported that Thursday was ladies' night and they got free drinks. Matthew hadn't seen many women enter or exit. But maybe that was the point, to try to draw them in.

Lulled into a relaxed stupor, Matthew suddenly jerked up in his seat, startled by a loud thumping on the window beside him. Through the tinted window, he saw Charlene O'Connell glaring back. She was pointing for the window to be lowered, and Danbury, who seemed less surprised by her appearance, dropped the window.

"What are you doing here again?" she demanded. "And why are there two more of you inside? You're bad for business!" she yelled without waiting for any sort of answer.

"You're scaring the customers away! They can tell you're cops! I want you all to clear out and leave, or I will call my lawyer! This is police harassment! Stop following me, and get away from my business! Or I'll file harassment charges!" She continued to yell until Danbury held a hand up.

"Ms. McConnell," he said so quietly that she had to lean in to hear him. "We're not breaking any laws. Or rules. We're searching for someone. A guy who has been seen here. More than once. We'll be happy to leave. If you help us find him."

"This again?" She rolled her eyes angrily, though that did seem to set her back. "This guy you're looking for, what's he done? Why are you so dead set on finding him?"

Matthew winced at her choice of words, but Danbury calmly responded, "He's wanted for questioning. Initially about an incident in Durham. And now for several others."

"Well, he's not here! And if you don't leave, I will call my lawyer."

"Ma'am, that's your prerogative," replied Danbury, politely calling her bluff.

Her face reddened, and in a huff, Charlene marched back into the building.

"Did you know she was there?" asked Matthew.

"Saw her coming," said Danbury.

"You could have given me a heads-up."

"What's the fun in that?" asked the big detective with a mischievous grin. Matthew figured he'd just gotten a glimpse of what Warren Danbury was like as a child.

Then Danbury added, before flipping his goggles back down to make another visual sweep of the premises, "I thought you'd seen her too."

Settling back into his seat, Matthew determined to be more aware of his surroundings, all of them. After what seemed like hours but was probably only minutes, Danbury said, "Huh," and then into the com system, "Check the silver SUV. Just drove into the lot."

"On it," said one of the guys in Matthew's ear as he saw the vehicle in question. "Affirmative," said the voice in his ear. "Do you want to approach?"

"No. Hang back," said Danbury, directing the others to be on guard as a lanky guy got out of the SUV. His head darted around, checking his surroundings, and then he ambled toward the front door of the Silver Silhouette. He was hunched over as if trying to be incognito, but his body gave him away. There wasn't much he could do to disguise it.

Chatter on the communication devices increased as the team inside picked him up and reported his whereabouts. He approached Charlene, who shook her head and said something to him. Then he disappeared into the doorway to the right, the one leading backstage and up to the dressing rooms. There was only one way out from there without coming back through the bar and out through the front door. Both of the guys monitoring the outside got in position to watch the back door.

All was mostly quiet for the next forty minutes, but Matthew could tell from their chatter that the guys inside were poised for action and frustrated by the lack of it. The back door opened, and two women walked out. A short, plump redhead, too thick to be Ruby, emerged with a tall, lanky blond woman.

"Evening, ma'am," one of the guys near the back door murmured. The shorter woman went back inside, and the lanky woman headed for the back corner of the parking lot, aiming for a car a few down from where Matthew and Danbury were parked.

As she drew closer, Matthew watched the already-long legs that looked longer in the stiletto heels confidently striding across the gravel toward the back of the lot. The movements weren't as fluid and silky smooth as those of the woman he'd watched earlier. This woman moved more awkwardly, loping along, heels and all. His mind wandered back to Monday, when he'd had to tell a woman becoming a man that he was pregnant. Suddenly, it all made sense. The epiphany was so strong that if he'd been a cartoon character, a light bulb would have come on over his head, flashing blindingly.

"That's him!" Matthew hissed softly but vehemently in the closed car. "And that's how he's been getting by you!" he added as the realization fully formed and flooded his mind.

Danbury quickly conveyed the information across the com system without bothering to ask Matthew if he was sure. He jumped out of the SUV and converged quickly with the two officers from the back door on the striding figure, announcing that they were police officers and telling her to halt. She turned, initially in surprise. Matthew was close enough to see the look of fleeting panic cross her face before she made a fatal mistake and took a swing at Danbury.

Ducking aside and catching the fist firmly, Danbury wrenched it behind her back. As Danbury was spinning her to pin her onto the hood of the car she had been walking toward, Matthew saw an expression of resignation on the long face with the high forehead that had been mostly obscured by a blonde wig. They had their guy at long last, thought Matthew, triumphantly as the two officers from inside ran across the parking lot toward them.

The coms were still active, and Matthew heard Danbury say, "Thanks for that. You just made my job easier." He proceeded to tell her not to move and that she was under arrest for assaulting a police officer. Even better. This guy wasn't merely under suspicion of anything anymore. Attempted assault on a police officer was an arrestable offense.

Danbury Mirandized her, and they were just about to lead her off to one of the police cars when she started yelling, in an oddly high-pitched voice, "Charlene! Charlene! Get me out of this mess!"

Looking to see where she was yelling, Matthew saw that Charlene had come out of the bar from the front door, and there was already a group of onlookers assembled by the back door. Marching toward them, Charlene had lost most of her fire from earlier. It seemed that she was trying to regain it, but her indignation was falling flat.

"How dare you arrest her!" yelled Charlene. "You have no grounds! Let him go! Right now!"

Matthew noticed the mixed pronouns immediately, but he didn't need that validation to know that they had the right person, regardless of gender preference at the moment.

One of the officers stepped into Charlene's path and said quietly, "She took a swing at a police officer, ma'am. We have grounds."

"Where are you taking her?" she demanded. Before anyone could answer, Charlene yelled across the parking lot to the tall, lanky figure who was being stuffed carefully into the back of one of the unmarked police cruisers, "I'll follow you! I'll be right there. Don't say anything! We'll call a lawyer."

"Why do you care?" asked the officer.

"Because she's my brother!" she retorted hotly. "Now where are you taking him?"

32 ~ Black Ice

When Danbury returned to the SUV, he looked a bit disheveled but as triumphant as Matthew felt. Finally, they had the bomber, the stalker, and probably the killer.

"Interesting," was all that Danbury said as he slid in behind the wheel. "You coming downtown?"

"Yeah, if I'm invited." Danbury nodded, and Matthew added, "But not with you. I'll drive my own car. I'm not coming back up here for it later."

"Makes sense," said Danbury.

"I want to know how this plays out, but I also need to get some sleep tonight. And I know that you won't." Matthew checked his watch and saw that it was half past nine. "You're headed downtown—the precinct on Cabarrus Street?"

"That's the one," said Danbury.

"See you there," Matthew replied, sliding out and moving over to his own car.

Had he been tired, the events of the evening so far would have rejuvenated him. The drive back into downtown Raleigh was quicker than he'd expected, and Matthew was elated as he pulled into the parking deck behind the police precinct and walked briskly down the sidewalk. He smiled at the shimmer wall across the street. The massive oak tree on the wall on the side of the Raleigh Convention Center was designed to look like it was swaying in the breeze, and he usually appreciated the grandeur of it. This evening, though, it seemed a particularly impressive feat of engineering as he rounded the corner of the downtown district police building.

Danbury was pacing back and forth under a well-lit awning in front of the entrance and talking on his phone.

"Yeah, it's him. But don't go home." After a pause Danbury added. "No, not yet. He might not be working alone." After another pause, he said, "Would you just listen to me?" And then, "I know, I know. But please stay there. Until we know more."

Matthew was trying not to eavesdrop as he approached and paused momentarily, turning back to admire the swaying oak as Danbury said, "Be sure it's armed. The whole alarm system." After another pause, he added, "OK, good. I love you too."

"Hey, Doc," said Danbury. "Women!"

"Everything OK?" asked Matthew.

"Yeah, I guess. Penn's ready to go home. I don't know why the rush. Leo tried to talk her out of it. Good man. They settled on a security company. She and Leo. It's the one I liked. So that's good. They have a construction team. They'll close off the cellar to the house. But the secret passageways. Those they can't agree on. What to do with them."

"Leo wants to leave them. Penn wants to remove the walls inside. And the stairs between floors. Open the rooms up. Include the passageways in the interior."

"Ah," said Matthew. "So they're ready to do the work if they can agree on what to do?"

"Yeah. That's the size of it."

"Until we know whether Klinefelter was working alone and if he was after Penn herself or using her to find the cat, I can see why you want her to stay at your place."

"Right," said Danbury, opening the door and holding it for Matthew.

After registering at the front desk and getting a temporary badge, which was expedited considerably because Danbury was with him, Matthew followed the big detective through more doors and down the main hallway within. The building wasn't huge, but it was a labyrinth of short hallways and doors everywhere. Danbury opened one and motioned Matthew inside.

"They've just processed him in," said Danbury. "So I can question him. You can watch from here."

The room was one that Matthew had been in before—either that or he'd been in an identical one in that same building. He was betting they all looked alike. A two-way mirror took up the entire side wall of the small room. Through it, he could see the guy he'd been calling Klinefelter. He was sitting in a chair, minus the blonde wig, slumped over the table, head in his hands, his long arms making a triangle with his body and the table.

In front of the window, a slender guy with auburn hair was already seated. Another guy was seated at the audiovisual controls on the wall directly in front of the door.

"Hey, what's his…" began Matthew, but Danbury was already gone.

"Detective Dale Conover," said the guy seated in front of the window, without turning around. He was leaning on the sill, carefully studying the suspect on the other side of the glass.

"Matthew Paine."

"Have a seat. Make yourself comfortable. It could be a while. But maybe not. I don't think the perp has lawyered up or said anything at all yet. So it's a good opportunity to try to get him to talk."

"OK, thanks," replied Matthew, sliding a stool closer to the large window, plopping down beside Conover, and leaning on the sill to study the guy too.

It was a few minutes before anything happened, but then Danbury entered the room and sat, with his back to the glass, across from the long, lanky guy.

"Mr. Kincaid," said Danbury, immediately answering part of the question Matthew had been about to ask when Danbury had abruptly left. He'd wanted to know the guy's real name. It stood to reason that his last name wasn't O'Connell because that was Charlene's married name. *Kincaid* was somewhat close to *Klinefelter*, mused Matthew, as Danbury settled in.

"This conversation is being recorded," Danbury said as he plopped a fat file folder down on the table between them. "I have some questions for you. You've been read your rights. This is serious. More serious than swinging at me. There are multiple other offenses. You've been busy," he added, flipping the folder open and looking down at it as if he needed it to remind himself, though Matthew knew he didn't.

"Breaking and entering. Attempted breaking and entering. Car theft. Car bombing. And murder."

"Murder?" the guy said in his oddly high-pitched voice as his long face snapped up from his hands and he stared at Danbury for the first time, abject terror clear in his eyes. "I didn't kill anybody! I didn't even hurt anybody!"

"Let's back up, then," said Danbury. "Are there other offenses? Any you'd like to plead guilty to? It would save us a lot of time. And you a lot of grief. If you just tell me what you did. And how. And why."

"I don't have to tell you anything!" the guy shot back, his face contorted in a mixture of fear and anger, all of which was enhanced, almost comically, by the smudges of makeup that had been rearranged on his face when he'd held it in his hands.

"That's true. You don't. But I'll find out. It'll be worse for you. When I do. Let's start with Friday. That's January third. Did you drop a car off? On a dead-end road. In Research Triangle Park."

"What if I did?" The guy looked pointedly at Danbury and asked, "What would happen if I did?"

"That depends," said Danbury patiently. "Did you put a bomb in it? Before you dropped it off?"

"A bomb? What bomb?"

"How about a body? In the trunk?"

"What body?" the guy asked, looking truly shaken and like he might be sick. "I don't know anything about a bomb or a body!"

"But you did drop the car off?" Danbury persisted.

Dropping his head into his hands again, he moaned and cringed visibly. "There wasn't a bomb really, right? And no body in the trunk? You're just yanking me around now."

"No yanking. I need to know what you know. About that car. Where did you get it? Why did you leave it there?"

"I don't think I know anything about that," said the guy, looking up suddenly like he was trying to be sly. His face was readable. Even from where Matthew sat, and through the smudges of makeup, there was fear. Was it possible that the guy didn't know about the bomb or the body? Was this guy that they'd been chasing for a week really not the murderer? Or was he more psychotic than they had imagined? Matthew wasn't sure.

"OK," said Danbury, gathering the folder as if to stand. "If that's your story. But I'll prove that you did. That's my job. I take it very seriously. And I'm good at it. It'll be worse for you that way."

"Wait," said the guy softly. Then he vehemently insisted, "I didn't kill anybody! You're not pinning a murder on me that I didn't commit! I've never killed anybody!"

"OK, then let's talk about it," said Danbury, leaning forward again. "What you did do. And what you do know."

Matthew listened for over an hour while Danbury wheedled information out of the guy. He admitted to being paid to pick up the car and drop it off. He also admitted to badgering Preston Priestly about the cat; to tracking Penn as a means of getting to the cat, or so he assumed; and to trying to break into Matthew's house. That was all to get the cat. He said he'd been paid in cryptocurrency online, and he didn't know by whom. He'd been hired in an online gaming chat room. But that was it. And then he said something that made everything seem to slow down.

"They didn't want the cat," he asserted. "Just the collar."

"You weren't told to get the cat?"

"Well, yeah, if I had to so that I could get the collar. The message said I could ditch the cat anywhere and in any way I wanted to. They just wanted the collar."

Matthew jumped to his feet.

"Is anybody else looking for it?" demanded Danbury.

"No clue," said the guy, hands spread.

"That's it for me," said Danbury, abruptly jumping to his feet.

"Settle in. We'll have more questions."

"But ... wait! What is this, like, solitary confinement? I'm cooperating!" the guy started to object, but Danbury was already out of the room.

A little solitude might be good for him, thought Matthew as he ran out of the room behind Detective Conover and they met Danbury in the hallway. They were both talking at once, Danbury asking Matthew, "Didn't you check the collar?" while Matthew was saying, "I didn't see anything odd about it. I don't know what it is that I'm looking for!"

"Let's go," said Danbury, and Matthew didn't have to ask where. "Conover, take over. Get the details. On the hires. The specific instructions. The payment method. You know the drill."

"Got it," Conover answered, poised outside of the interrogation room while Danbury bolted into the lobby with Matthew on his heels. Matthew hurriedly handed over his temporary badge and noticed three of the officers who'd been on the scene at the strip club talking with Charlene O'Connell. Charlene, however, wasn't talking. She was yelling.

"Where did you take him? Where is my brother?" she demanded. "You can't keep him here! I want to see him right now!"

"Garrison, you're with me," Danbury called to the group. "Mason, Dubois, search again. The residence of Nichols. And Kent's places, too. Specifically for electronics. And get a search warrant. For Kincaid. I want all electronics. From all three locations. Computers. Gaming systems. The works. Bring it all in. If it looks electronic, get it."

"On it," said the two, looking immensely relieved to be leaving the shouting Charlene for the assignments.

"On your six," said Garrison, turning away from the boisterous scene that Charlene was creating to follow Danbury out. They went for Danbury's SUV while Matthew jogged up the ramp of the parking deck to retrieve his car.

"Stay with me," Danbury yelled from his car window as Matthew pulled alongside and just before he flipped on the blue lights and took off. Through the downtown streets, which were mostly void of vehicles at eleven at night, they raced. Out to I-40 and heading for Peak, Matthew followed in Danbury's wake. Permission to speed had been not only granted but demanded, thought Matthew, wishing he were driving the Corvette. The Element handled well most of the time, but it was top-heavy, and he couldn't take corners terribly fast.

Danbury had been running without sirens, and he cut the blue lights as they pulled onto the other end of Chester Road. Matthew clicked the garage door opener, and Danbury and the officer he'd called Garrison got out, weapons drawn, and began looking around.

"Garrison, check the perimeter," said Danbury. As Garrison disappeared around the corner of the house, Danbury escorted Matthew inside.

"Clear," said Garrison, returning. Only when the alarm system was disarmed and the door locked behind them did both officers holster their weapons.

"Don't scare her," said Matthew. "Let me get her to come to me, and then I'll give you the collar." He need not have worried because Fluffykins came sauntering down the hallway curiously, sashaying her fluffy tail behind her, to greet the visitors. She rubbed up against Matthew's leg, and he scooped her up. Talking softly to her, he gently removed the collar and handed it to Danbury.

Taking it to the small kitchen table in the eating nook, Danbury laid it out to examine the faux leather with the cut glass line of "diamonds" mounted at close intervals along it. Flipping it over to inspect the inside layer, Danbury said, "It's been glued. Here on this end. Got a knife, Doc? A sharp one?"

"Sure," said Matthew, setting the cat back on her feet, then retrieving a knife from his kitchen and handing it over.

Danbury carefully slit the stitching down the outer edge of the collar, starting at the end where the two layers had been glued back together. As he wriggled the knife slowly down the collar, splitting the layers apart, they all caught their collective breath. Small black diamonds tumbled out, one after another, until the collar was flayed open and there was a pile of them on Matthew's kitchen table.

33 ~ Wake up, Doc

What was left of Thursday night was a blur for Matthew. Both Danbury and Garrison got on their phones almost immediately. Garrison, from what Matthew could hear, was reporting in with their superior, and Danbury was requesting secure transport for the diamonds.

While they were otherwise occupied, Matthew sat down at his table and picked up the knife that Danbury had used to split open the collar. Leaning over, he began to prod the diamonds with the knife, examining each in turn. Nineteen, he counted, forming a line of them. The one in Misty's tooth would make twenty. They were all black diamonds, and they looked to be the same size to his untrained eye.

How, Matthew wondered, had they gotten into the cat's collar? And why? When Danbury got off the phone after extended periods of being put repeatedly on hold, Matthew posed those questions.

"Priestly might have known more than he told us. He did say that he volunteered to take the cat at first," pondered Matthew aloud. "But he couldn't have put the diamonds there or known they were there. If he had, he wouldn't have been so eager to get rid of her. Fluffykins was at the vet overnight before she came here. But given the diamond in her tooth, Misty is the most likely person to have put them there. How did she get them, and why put them in the cat collar?"

"We'll catch a killer," replied Danbury. "When we answer that."

Danbury perched on the stool at the bar in Matthew's kitchen and began tapping his tablet.

"I'll start writing up the report," said Garrison. "At least the preliminary one."

"Good. I'm requesting the gemologist. And filling out the transport information. They still require the forms for both," said Danbury in annoyance. His task was interrupted by his phone, and he reached to answer it.

Privy only to Danbury's side of the conversation, Matthew heard a few affirmations and some grunts before Danbury said, "Good. Get that gaming system. And computer equipment. And whatever else looks electronic."

After a pause, Danbury added, "Yeah, comprehensive. You don't need a specific warrant." A few moments later, Danbury said, "I don't care. Wake him up! OK. Yeah. Thanks for the update."

When Garrison looked quizzically over at him, Danbury just muttered, "They're collecting electronic equipment. From both places. Nichols and Kent. And getting the search warrant. For Kincaid's place. He was hired online. In a gaming chat room. Paid in cryptocurrency. That's a new one. Hard to trace, maybe. But we have to try."

"Oh," said Garrison, going back to the report on his tablet.

Danbury had finished tapping his tablet, and Matthew assumed they were just awaiting the arrival of the people Danbury had requested when the front doorbell sounded.

"It's not the gemologist. We had to get her out of bed," said Danbury, looking up. He checked his watch as he added, "Or the transport yet. They had to assemble a team. And then get the transport truck. After the request was approved."

Garrison looked askance at Matthew, who nodded his consent, and then answered the door. Garrison admitted two guys in dark coats who flipped badges and seemed to expect immediate kowtowing. Garrison, however, looked unimpressed. Danbury was even less so when they started barking orders about taking custody of the diamonds.

When one of the guys, who'd identified himself as an FBI special agent, whatever that meant, said the words "Local yokel," Matthew thought he saw smoke come out of Danbury's ears. Nobody had apparently contacted them, and Matthew wasn't sure how they had known to show up. Danbury was standing his ground. *It's my ground, actually*, Matthew thought to himself ironically as he slipped back into his living area and out of the fray in the kitchen.

These guys were nothing like the agents he'd worked with several times in the past. The previous FBI agents he'd worked with had been much more helpful and far less aggrandized. Humility, apparently, wasn't a strong suit for these two.

"They're part of an ongoing murder investigation," Danbury insisted angrily. Seething, he added, "An important part. As such, they're being transported. Momentarily. A gemologist is on the way. As is the transport truck. We're maintaining chain of custody."

"Chain of custody comes to us now," said one of the guys, the one who Matthew had overheard announcing himself as a special agent. Nobody had bothered to introduce themselves to him as he sat on the end of the sofa with his notebook computer in his lap. What he was most curious about in that moment was how they had arrived so quickly after the diamonds had been found. How did they know about them? That was worrying, Matthew thought with an eyebrow raised and foot tapping in concentration.

"They're part of an ongoing smuggling operation investigation that we've been working on for eighteen months. We've got way too many hours and funds invested in this thing to have it blow up now. It's federal. That trumps a local investigation."

"An investigation, yes," retorted Danbury. "But this is a murder investigation. At least two victims. Maybe more. Chain of custody goes through our office."

A brief stare-down in which neither side was backing down ensued, and then all four of them got on their respective phones, ostensibly with superiors, and all started talking at once.

Matthew couldn't believe that his house had so quickly transitioned from the scene of an attempted break-in to being invaded by a host of government officials arguing over the proper chain of command for possession of black diamonds.

Possession of diamonds must be a pretty big deal, though these didn't look all that impressive to Matthew's untrained eye. They weren't huge, but apparently they were otherwise perfect. At least, that was the story he was overhearing from the FBI agents.

It wasn't as if his home were a crime scene, he thought. Nothing of note had happened here. Except that a small handful of black diamonds had been discovered in a cat's collar. Why they couldn't take the gems elsewhere and argue over them there, Matthew wasn't sure. The issue seemed to be who would take them and to what secure location.

The importance of a local murder investigation, multiple murders, in fact, was apparently being weighed heavily against that of a federal investigation of a smuggling operation. Ordinarily, Matthew figured from overhearing the initial confrontation, the FBI showing up trumped all else. National interest won out over any local one. But nothing about this murder investigation could be considered ordinary.

Before any of them were off their respective phones, there was another knock at the door. When nobody else made a move to answer it, so involved were they all in posturing and presenting and restating their positions on their phones, Matthew laid his computer aside and got up to answer it himself. It was, after all, his door. On the front porch stood an attractive woman, probably slightly older than him, who looked uncertain about her whereabouts.

"Hi," she said, then introduced herself. "I'm a gemologist and I'm looking for homicide detective Warren Danbury."

"Matthew Paine," he said, introducing himself and holding the door open for her. "Come on in and join the party. They're currently all arguing with superiors, or so I gather, about who gets possession of the diamonds. The big guy there is Danbury, but I guess you've met him before."

"No, not yet, though I've spoken with him at length on the phone."

"Ah. I knew somebody had been talking to him because he's given me a pretty thorough education on black diamonds."

She chuckled and then asked, "You found the diamonds where?"

"Between the layers of a cat's collar," he responded.

"Wow," she said. "That's not a place I'd think to look."

"I guess that was the point," answered Matthew. "Can I take your coat?" he asked, remembering his southern manners.

"Sure, thanks," she said, switching hands with a case she was carrying and pulling off her coat.

"I'll hang it right here in this closet," he said, showing her the coat closet around the corner in the hallway leading to the bedrooms.

"OK, can I just start evaluating the diamonds?" she asked.

"Beats me. I just live here," Matthew quipped. "They're on the kitchen table in there. If you can get to them, I guess they're all yours to look at," he added, pointing past the collection of men pacing around his kitchen and eating nook.

"Thanks, Mr. Paine," she answered. As usual, Matthew had neglected to provide his title preceding his name when he'd introduced himself, and he refrained from doing so after the fact. What was the point, really, in correcting anyone? He sunk back down on the sofa as she entered the fray.

Eventually, things started to calm down, and Matthew perched on the arm of the sofa and peered around the corner to see what was happening. Nobody looked happy, but they were all off their phones.

"That's the most ridiculous thing I've heard," said one of the FBI agents. Matthew smirked, noting that it was the guy who'd called Danbury a "local yokel," as the guy added, "There's no such thing as joint custody of evidence—or a joint investigation—when there's federal interest involved."

"Apparently there is," answered Danbury. "We're stuck with each other. Let's see what we can learn. About these diamonds. Then we can brief each other. On the cases we're working."

The FBI agent balked, blanching visibly at that comment, but he gathered with the others around the small table. The gemologist was busily studying the diamonds, each in turn, under a large microscope that she'd pulled from the heavy case she'd been carrying. It had a light on it, and she was turning the stones carefully underneath it with a forceps.

"I usually just magnify to ten power," Matthew overheard her say. "But I'm checking them at thirty."

"And?" asked one of the FBI agents impatiently.

"They match the one I evaluated initially in size and that one odd attribute with the cut. That first one is still at the GIA lab for further analysis, but I remember all of its attributes."

"That there's an extra facet," said Matthew.

"Right," she said, looking up.

"And you are?" asked one of the FBI agents, seeming to see Matthew for the first time and sounding alarmed by his knowledge of the diamonds.

"Dr. Matthew Paine," he said, using his title for full effect because he figured this guy would no doubt think he was a yokel too. Deciding he could care less one way or the other and going for some levity, he added, "Owner of this fine establishment where you're all currently gathered. Initial examiner of the body, finder of the first diamond, and co-finder of this batch."

"Oh," said the agent, looking less than impressed. "We can talk about the body later." Turning back to the gemologist, he said, "I saw your report on the first diamond. Why the extra facet? What's the significance?"

"There could be any number of reasons," she answered.

"In your professional opinion, then," the agent prodded.

"It might be as simple as someone's preference. Or maybe it's a signature of some sort. Identifying it as coming from a specific place or being cut by a certain gemologist."

"And you thought the first one was from the CAR?"

"It's just a guess, but yes. The GIA lab can either confirm or exclude Sam Ouandja in the CAR as the origin. We don't have their report back yet."

"I see," said the FBI agent. "Continue, please. Check them all. Thoroughly."

Matthew leaned back into his soft butter-cream leather sofa as she went back to her task with the diamonds and the voices droned on behind him. The sounds were fading softly into the background as Matthew drifted into the shadow world. He jolted upright momentarily as a new and distributing thought struck him. "He's still out there," Matthew muttered to himself before drifting off again.

*****

"Doc," Matthew heard through the haze of his mind. "Hey, Doc, wake up."

Somebody was shaking his shoulder again. It wasn't Penn this time, Matthew realized as he swam to the surface of consciousness.

Opening one sleepy eye, Matthew looked up to see Danbury standing over him. "We're done here. You can lock up behind us."

"What?" Matthew realized he was sprawled on his sofa and began to recall the events of the evening before, diamonds and FBI agents and a pretty gemologist. As he glanced around him, he saw none of them. There was no light coming through the blinds on his front window, and he was confused.

"What time is it?" asked Matthew.

"Four thirty. Everybody's gone. Garrison is waiting for me. Out in the car. I can't set the alarm. If I go through the garage. I can't close the garage door."

"Oh. OK, I'm . . ." Matthew began as he tried to lean forward and get up. "I'm coming. What did I miss?"

Danbury laughed. "Not too much. Call me when you wake up again. I'll fill you in."

After locking up, Matthew set the alarm and left a few lights on before staggering down the hallway to his bed. He sincerely wished that he had more than a couple of hours left to sleep. Probably less than that, he thought, because Cici usually contacted him on FaceTime before his alarm actually went off.

Groaning, he fell into bed between Max and Fluffykins, clothes and all, and into a fitful sleep.

34 ~ Connections

Startled awake by his phone, Matthew tried to remember where he was in the space-time continuum. The last thing he could remember was Danbury shaking him and telling him to wake up. But that seemed like days ago. Danbury, and everyone else who had filled his house the night before, was gone.

His mouth was dry, and his head hurt as he rolled over to pick up his phone and clicked to connect to FaceTime.

"Matthew!" he heard Cici exclaim. "What on earth?"

"Is it that bad?" he croaked. "I need water. I didn't set up the coffee maker last night either," he added as he tried to pull himself from bed to make his way to the kitchen. Taking the phone with him, he first swigged down a glass of filtered water from the tap beside his sink, and then he used it to add water to the coffee maker and set it to brew.

"Don't take this the wrong way, but you look awful. Are you OK?" Cici asked in concern.

Matthew wasn't sure how many ways he could possibly take that comment. Regaining himself after the coffee beans had ground while waiting impatiently for the coffee to begin to drip, he responded, "I could tell you, but then I'd have to shoot you."

"I'm on the other side of an ocean," Cici protested.

"You communicate with a whole group of people in Raleigh. Regularly. And lawyers, at that."

"Suit yourself," she said, blowing out a breath in frustration.

"I'm just kidding. Last night is kind of a blur, but I'll tell you. I will swear you to secrecy, though. I wasn't kidding about that part." He then summarized the events of the previous evening.

"Wow, so you found the guy you were looking for, but he's not the killer?"

"He's pretty convincing when he says he isn't, but I don't know yet. I'm no expert on reading criminals."

"And then you found a bunch of black diamonds? And had a house full of federal agents? Matthew, please be careful!" The alarm in her voice and the concern on her pretty face were genuine.

"Yes, ma'am," he said with an eyebrow raised as he put the requisite scoops of sugar and cream in his mug, tapping his foot and awaiting the coffee maker to finish brewing. "I'll do my best."

This was all pretty new, Matthew thought, that Cici would be the one telling him to be careful. Historically, he'd been the more careful and reserved of the two, and Cici had called him an old soul; it was Cici who had wanted to be right in the middle of things. Social gatherings were more her style, but still, it was a relatively new phenomenon that she should be the one admonishing him.

Max, during their conversation, had been rubbing up against Matthew's legs, so after saying his goodbyes to Cici, he set about feeding and caring for the cats. As he went through his morning routine, Matthew's mind was entirely occupied by the investigation. He missed Cici, but his preoccupation with the murder and all of the things that had happened afterward were, as he'd hoped, consuming and usurping the longing ache for her. At least momentarily.

What bothered him most was that Kincaid, the guy he'd been calling Klinefelter, possibly wasn't the murderer. Or was he? Where did he fit in the puzzle? What was his connection to Misty Blue or to either of the missing men, Trent Kent and Mick Nichols? And how was Mick Nichols connected if he wasn't the killer? It made more sense to Matthew that he was a victim whose truck somebody needed. Somebody who had planned elaborately to murder and then cover it up.

But if that were true and Nichols was merely a victim, where was he? Where was his motorcycle? The one he always drove in any weather. Why was Kent's blood found in the back of the truck? And what about the guys that Misty had rebuffed? There were several, from what Cara had said, in the past few months. Had any of them gotten angry enough to want revenge? Had Danbury checked them all out?

It was as if each piece of information, each thing he'd learned so far about the investigation, blazed to the forefront of Matthew's mind, only to blur into the background behind the next thing. None of it was coming together into any sort of reasonable pattern or workable theory. It was entirely frustrating. He liked order and predictability, but there was neither in this case so far.

Matthew mulled it over from every angle, turning it repeatedly in his mind, all the way to his office. When he arrived and slid out of the Element, he was surprised that the morning was chilly. Garages would do that to you. It felt like it was above freezing, but the warmth of the past few days seemed to be just that, in the past.

Pulling his coat on, he grabbed his satchel, snatched up his nearly empty travel coffee mug, and went in through the back side door. As he prepared to see patients, Matthew was still pondering what they knew and what they still needed to know to understand what had happened to Misty Blue—or Melanie Wimble.

Connections were what they needed, and that was what was mostly missing. Danbury would be the first to say that motive is often the last thing to know, but Matthew would prefer it the other way around, to understand the why that led to the what of the matter. And why, while he was wondering about this case, had so many people changed their names? If anyone might want to do that, he himself had a reason, but it had never occurred to him to do so.

Throughout one of the busiest Fridays Matthew remembered having had in a while, the facts of the investigation were never far from the corners of his mind. After a crazy morning and full afternoon of back-to-back patients, including a few walk-ins—who chose to preempt a potential weekend of sickness or a trip to an urgent care clinic—Matthew was settled at his desk.

As he was working on his patient records at the end of the day, his phone vibrated in his pocket. Pulling it out, he saw that it was Danbury, so he tapped to answer the call. He had a vague memory of the middle of the night, in which he thought maybe Danbury had said to call him. He hadn't.

"Hey, Doc," said the familiar voice. "Are you recovered yet?"

"From last night? Sort of," answered Matthew. "Enough coffee and I'm at least functional. What's up?"

"Some new information."

"From comparing notes with the FBI agents last night?"

"Not much from the feds. They don't share. But with our investigation. We're having second looks. Now that we know what we're looking for. They searched homes last night. And they're still MIA. Both Nichols and Kent. A team is heading to Misty's now. And I need to talk to Priestly again."

"Hey, how much did you look into Misty's past boyfriends? Would any of them have gotten ticked off enough with her for dumping them that they'd have been vindictive about it?"

"We're building files. On four past boyfriends. The three who proposed to her. And Kent. Names are the hard part. Identifying them. Cara came up with one more. And Ruby did too. If you can believe that. Why?"

"Just trying to connect the dots. We have a lot of information, but the connections don't seem to be there, at least not in my mind. I can't make them come together. But it all has to make sense somehow, right? We must be missing something still. I've been thinking a lot today about how to get to those connections, and I think you're holding the connection card."

"Come again?" asked Danbury.

"Klinefel . . . I mean, Kincaid. What's his first name?"

"Jonas."

"Jonas Kincaid might be your key to finding the connections. You're getting the gaming systems and the computer equipment from Nichols, right? From his place?"

"Yeah, we got that. Why?"

"And Kent? Does he have that sort of equipment too?"

"Yeah. We got that too. Why?"

"Did you get anything else out of Kincaid?"

"Doc!"

"I am going somewhere with this—just give me a minute."

Taking a deep breath, Danbury replied, "He's still claiming ignorance. That he doesn't know anything. Not about the car bombing. Not about the body. Or why he was tracking Penn. At least not at first. And then it was about the cat. Or so he says. Priestly told him that I had the cat. Not sure how Priestly knew that. Unless Cara told him. I wasn't there."

"I think I let that slip."

"Oh. Then he heard that you had her. Kincaid's last instructions were to find the cat. And get the collar."

"Do you believe him?"

There was silence for a moment before Danbury answered, "I don't want to. But our profiler does. She studied him thoroughly. She thinks it all fits. She says he's telling the truth. That he's a hired hand. Not the mastermind behind it all."

"He said yesterday that he was hired through a gaming chat session and paid in cryptocurrency, right?"

"That's what he claims. He told us all about it. The gaming system. The game. Something called DOD."

"Like Department of Defense?"

"*Directive of Duty*. They call it DOD. And there's an online chat. The guy's gaming tag. Get this. It's HavocWreaker13."

"That fits."

"Yeah, it was all foreign to me. Until we got to the voice."

"It was a voice chat?"

"Just once. The others were text. Kincaid described the voice. Soft and quiet. Never raised. Medium pitch. That doesn't help much. Not without a recording."

"It can be disguised anyway, right? Run through some sort of electronic device to digitally alter the sound of the voice?"

"It could be. But we could work on it. Our tech guys. To restore it to the original quality. If we had a recording of it."

"Maybe we can get a recording. What if you get Kincaid back on the game and see if he can reconnect? If they don't know he's been taken into custody, it could work. Unless Charlene has made a big deal about him being arrested, maybe word hasn't gotten back to whoever is behind this."

The line was quiet, and then Danbury said slowly, "That might work, Doc. It's worth a shot. We'll need to move him. To the North Raleigh Police Department. That's where all the tech is. And where his gaming system was taken. And his computer. Our tech team is searching through it. We've set up the other two. Whatever electronics Nichols and Kent had. We're having a look at those too."

"Good plan. And Priestly. He has gaming equipment too."

"How do you know?"

"I saw it when Cara and I picked up Fluffykins. There was a gaming system in his living room. It's in a low cabinet under his TV. The doors of the cabinet were open, and I saw it. If Kincaid can reconnect, could he tell the guy that he has the collar? He could offer to hand it off."

"Yeah, I guess so. You want to come watch this?"

"This is the precinct where we were last spring, up on Six Forks Road?"

"That's the one."

Matthew remembered the North Raleigh Police Department well. It was housed in an oddly shaped three-story brick building with a rounded corner. Much newer than the downtown branch building that Danbury mainly worked out of, it also provided lots of parking. Outside of the downtown area, parking wasn't at such a premium, and parking decks were fewer.

With a chuckle, Matthew said, "Sure, why not? I need to go take care of my herd of cats. What is a group of cats called? A pride? Or is that just lions?"

"No idea, Doc."

"Anyway, after I take care of the cats and grab a bite, I can head up. You said you wanted to talk to Priestly again. You want to meet at his place first?"

"Yeah, that's good. I have a couple more questions. He talks to you better."

"OK, I'll text when I'm on the way."

*****

After feeding the cats, Matthew quickly constructed and ate two sandwiches. He then texted Danbury and headed out. He was relieved that the drive wasn't bad on a Friday evening; most of the traffic heading home or out of town for the weekend was already through the RTP area on I-40 when Matthew got there. Pulling up in front of Priestly's duplex, he thought it was a good sign when he saw lights blazing inside.

Danbury's black SUV was already parked at the curb, so Matthew slid out and met him on the sidewalk. Neither of them spoke as they stepped up to the front door. Matthew really didn't like Priestly after his earlier comments about the women in the films he made, neither knowing nor caring about their ages or how or why they were there. Trying to force that memory from his mind, Matthew took a deep breath as Danbury knocked loudly to be heard over the racket within.

When Priestly opened the door, he was at least better clothed than the last time Matthew had shown up on his doorstep. Clad in an old gray sweat suit, the pants of which were obviously too long, as he was walking on the bottoms of them, Priestly said, "What do you want this time?"

"Just a couple of questions for you," said Danbury.

"Yeah, yeah, and then a couple more," complained Priestly.

"Really, there are only a couple, and the faster you answer them, the faster we leave you alone," said Matthew, wanting to help the process along.

"OK, I reckon I got time for a couple. C'mon in," he responded. As he stepped aside to admit them, he asked, "So what is it this time? No, I still didn't kill Misty, and I still don't know who did," he added sarcastically.

"It's about the cat," said Matthew, trying to sound calm, as Danbury nodded to him. "Do you know how anyone knew that you had her?"

"Lots of people knew that I had her. That skinny guy said he heard Cara say that I had the cat. I told that guy that you took him but that the police probably had her, like this guy here," he said, indicating Danbury without making eye contact with him.

"Why did you think the police had her?"

"Well, didn't they?"

Touché, Matthew thought, to that response. But he changed his line of questioning and said instead, "Did Misty tell you anything specific about caring for her cat? Did she leave any specific instructions?"

"She told me to give her a scoop of food twice a day and to keep the litter box cleaned out. Under no circumstances was she to go outside. That's what she said," he added with a chuckle. "Or pretty close to it. And she said to guard her with my life."

"Why didn't you tell us that before?" asked Matthew.

"Because you didn't ask. And anyway, isn't that just something people say?"

"Did Misty ever ask you to guard anything with your life before?"

"Well, no, but what's the big deal?"

"Then wasn't this different?"

"Yeah, I reckon so," said Priestly. "But this was her cat. And she loved that cat. So I didn't think nothin' of it. She gave me her vet's number and told me to call them if anything happened."

"That would have been very good information to have shared earlier," said Matthew, glaring at the guy. He had tried to calm his disdain of Priestly earlier, but it wasn't working now.

"He's all yours, Danbury," said Matthew. "Oh, and the gaming equipment is under that cabinet." Matthew motioned. "I saw it last time when it was open."

"Yeah, I got old gaming systems. So what?" Priestly asked as Matthew stepped outside in annoyance, taking a few deep breaths.

"You said, 'If anything happened.' Like what?" Matthew heard Danbury ask as the beat-up storm door was closing, none too gently, behind him.

35 ~ Professional Assessment

Preston Priestly had provided no new information except the contact for the veterinarian, which was closed at this hour on a Friday night. Matthew called anyway to see if there was an emergency after-hours service. The recorded message provided a number for another clinic to call, which wasn't at all helpful.

When they arrived at the North Raleigh Police Department, Matthew turned down Westbrook to park behind the building and chose a spot behind the closest rows where the blue and white cruisers were parked. Some of the spaces between the police vehicles were unoccupied, but he didn't want to risk parking in any of them.

"Did you take Priestly's gaming system?" asked Matthew as he donned his coat against the cool January night air and approached Danbury from across the parking lot.

"No."

"Why not?"

"Didn't see the need. It was covered in dust. He hasn't touched it. Not lately. Unless there's another one. I'd need a warrant to look. No probable cause to get one."

"Oh," said Matthew as they entered the building. "It sounds like Misty knew that Fluffykins was carrying the diamonds. Unless she was habitually dramatic. From what Cara has told us about her, I doubt that. I think she knew the diamonds were there. Maybe she put them there, and that's just one more reason that she was reluctant to leave the cat with Priestly."

"I agree," replied Danbury as they approached the reception desk off to the right.

As they checked Matthew in, Danbury asked where Kincaid was being held. "He's where?" Danbury asked in alarm, leaning forward on the counter when he heard the answer.

"In the second-floor lounge," repeated the receptionist, shrinking back from him in surprise.

"Why did they set him up there?"

The receptionist just shrugged.

"Great," muttered Danbury as he climbed the stairs two at a time and strode purposefully down the hallway. Outside the room where they were told to find Kincaid, Danbury asked the officer posted by the door, "He's in here?"

The guy nodded, and Danbury groused, "We're making him cozy. Letting him game. That's the way we treat criminals."

"It's the background, Detective," answered the officer. "If the contact we're trying to find requests him to go on camera, the perp has to believe he's at home. Or at least he's at somebody's home. The background can't look like a holding cell."

"Yeah," said Danbury. "I get it. Is the other guy on camera? If Kincaid is?"

"I don't know, Detective," replied the officer as Danbury slowly opened the door and peered in. He slipped through and motioned for Matthew to follow, closing the door quietly behind them. The wall immediately to their left was lined with chairs, in which several technical guys sat behind two end-to-end tables of makeshift controls.

Two police officers, one in uniform and Conover, the other detective that Matthew had met the night before, were seated there. Leaning against the wall was one of the FBI agents Matthew remembered being at his house the night before.

To their right and facing all of that was Kincaid, sprawled on a sofa. In front of him on a low table was a monitor, the back of which was to the onlookers. Clad in jeans and a jacket, with a headset on, he was talking loudly to someone while holding a gaming control, clicking and yanking on buttons and a joystick rambunctiously.

"Yeah, I got 'em!" he said loudly. "Hey, look out behind you!"

The FBI agent motioned Danbury out into the hallway, and Matthew followed.

"We're getting our own recording of that," said the agent. "Both the sound and video. I've got some other business to attend to, but if Kincaid connects with the guy who can lead us to the diamonds, let me know. I'll be back."

"Yeah, me too," said Danbury unhelpfully. Turning, he stalked down the hallway, and Matthew had no choice but to follow in his wake. Matthew wasn't any more excited about further conversation with the FBI agent than Danbury seemed to have been.

"Where are we headed?" asked Matthew.

"It's too crowded in there. No observation booth. I want to see if they've found anything. On the electronics of the other two guys. Nichols or Kent. We can watch from the tech room."

"OK," said Matthew as they rounded a corner and Danbury badged into another room. Matthew recognized the room as one he'd been in before. It was a darkened room, loaded with more electronic control boards and display monitors than he cared to count.

After greeting and checking with the tech guys who were apparently recording everything going on in the lounge down the hallway, including angles from cameras that Matthew hadn't noticed behind Kincaid, Danbury questioned them about the equipment from Kent and Nichols. There wasn't any update yet, he was told.

"You can watch what's going on down the hallway on those monitors," one of the techs said, motioning, and then he helpfully explained the gaming world. First-person shooters versus third-person games, teamwork, and online gaming chats all sounded foreign to Matthew, though he listened intently to understand what was happening. Then the tech handed them headsets so that Matthew and Danbury could listen in on the gaming conversations. They settled in to watch, hanging their coats on the backs of their chairs.

"You know, Doc," began Danbury, pulling one side of his headset away from his ear. "This might be like paint peeling. It could be hours of nothing. It might be days of nothing."

"I know," said Matthew. "But I think it's worth a shot."

"Me too. Obviously," said Danbury, pushing the headphone back into place.

After watching for nearly an hour, Matthew turned as he noticed light from the hallway streaming into the darkened room behind them.

"Detective Warren Danbury?" said a tall, broad woman. At first glance, Matthew thought she looked like a female version of Danbury. Her blonde hair was pulled back severely in a no-nonsense bun at the nape of her neck.

"I'm Danbury," he said, turning and pulling his headphones off as Matthew followed suit.

"I've completed my assessment. Of your subject. Jonas Kincaid," she said by way of introduction.

"Ah, our esteemed profiler. Dr. Hillary Allman. Good to meet you in person." Danbury stood, reached out, and shook her hand. Then he introduced her to Matthew.

"Anything new to report?" asked Danbury.

"Would I be here if there weren't?" she replied matter-of-factly.

There was no edge to her comment at all. It was just stated factually, and Matthew stifled a grin and a snicker at it. She sounded like Danbury.

"Tell me," Danbury answered.

"I'll spare you the background. And provide the core information. I do not believe him to be your killer. He is rather simple. Chalk his actions up to ignorance. Not ill intent. He isn't aggressive. Unless he feels cornered. Or threatened. His motives are immature."

"OK. What about our killer?"

"He's far more complex. His motivations are complicated. As are his thought processes. He's driven by multiple factors."

"Which are?" prodded Danbury.

"Gain. Personal, as he sees it. And likely revenge. A need for control. Total control. Probably as compensation. For some past slight. It could be actual. Or perhaps perceived. He's smart. Extremely so," she added.

"Why leave the black diamond? If he's smuggling diamonds. These not-quite blood diamonds. That doesn't make sense."

"Because he's a narcissistic, psychopathic killer who thinks that he's smarter than everybody else and that he can't be caught," said Matthew.

"Precisely," she said, turning to him as if she'd forgotten he was standing there. "That's exactly right."

"He's toying with us," added Matthew. "He's showing just enough of his hand to be completely confusing while having cards up his sleeve and hidden away everywhere else."

"That's entirely possible," she replied, studying Matthew more closely. "Are you a psychiatrist?"

"No, I'm a general practitioner at a family practice," said Matthew.

"Ah," she said. "I guess you GPs see it all."

"Every time I think so, something else happens that makes me realize I haven't seen anything yet," Matthew answered, remembering his pregnant patient. That experience, though, had helped him understand how Kincaid had disappeared multiple times in plain sight. Sometimes things weren't at all what they appeared to be. Quite often, neither were people.

"Anyway, how can I help?" Dr. Allman asked Danbury. "What else do you need?"

"Details. On this killer. His motivation. His thought patterns. Tell me what he ate for lunch."

She nearly cracked a smile, Matthew thought, at that last quip. Instead she said, "OK, let's find a table. We'll go through my notes."

"Done," replied Danbury. Gesturing to Matthew to leave their jackets, he leaned over and said something to the tech, who nodded. Then Danbury led them out of the room and down the hallway past a few doors.

"It's quieter in here. And lighter," said Danbury, opening another door and switching on the light.

They convened around a table that looked like it was on the wrong side of an interrogation suite. Putting her satchel on the table, she began to pull file folders from it, placing them in a neat arc around her. That was a rather old-fashioned way to go about it, thought Matthew, but he leaned in closer as she began opening them.

"You understand that this is speculation," she hedged. "It's based on research. But it can't be conclusive. Not without finding this guy. And studying him directly."

"Understood," said Danbury. "Tell us what you can."

"Your killer is a loner," she began. "Though he doesn't appear to be. He tries to blend in. To relate. But he can't stand people. He has a superiority complex. Nobody measures up to his ideal. No male friends. And certainly no females. He likely has a problem with women. A need to dominate them. He probably bullies and badgers them into submission. If they don't comply with his wishes immediately. He was likely abused as a child. Or severely bullied. Or both. There was some substantial trauma in his childhood. The size of the chip on his shoulder is exceeded only by his ego.

"You wouldn't know any of that," she continued, opening and closing file folders as she went. "If you were to meet him. He can be gregarious. He likely has a wicked sense of humor. He'd seem like a regular guy. You would think you're friends. That you've built a rapport. That he relates to you. Maybe that he understands you, even. But it's all an act. He's incapable of empathy. Of understanding another's point of view. He's manipulative. Anything you tell him, he'll remember. But only for his own use. For whatever he might need later."

"Wow, sounds like a real stand-up guy," Matthew chimed in.

"What might he look like?" asked Danbury. "Any idea?"

"He likely doesn't stand out. Not in any way. He's able to blend in. So probably average height. Average build. Not somebody you'd notice. Not somebody who calls attention to himself. He doesn't think he has to. He thinks the world revolves around him. That he's above it all."

"Huh," said Danbury. "Unlike Kincaid."

"Precisely," she said. "He wouldn't like Kincaid. He's likely never seen him. If he had, he wouldn't work with him. Kincaid stands out. He's anything but normal. And your killer would despise him for it."

"For something he can't control?" asked Matthew. "Kincaid didn't give himself Klinefelter syndrome. He was born with it."

"Your killer doesn't care," she replied. "He'd see it as a weakness. Why the weakness exists is irrelevant. At least in his mind."

"So why kill Misty?" asked Matthew, getting to the point.

"There's a range of possible reasons," she responded. "Maybe she did something he didn't like. Or said something he didn't like. It wouldn't have to be anything serious. To cause a personal vendetta. Perhaps it was simply a means to an end. Whatever he's fixated on. That's his primary goal. He'll do anything to achieve it. He thinks he's justified. Totally justified. Maybe she got in his way. Nobody has a right to question his authority. Or his desires. Ever."

"Wow," said Matthew, blowing out a breath he only then realized he'd been holding.

"Have you reviewed the other files?" asked Danbury.

"The ones you compiled on the boyfriends? Just Trent Kent. And the truck driver. Mick Nichols. And Preston Priestly. Kent's a possible. The other two look less likely. Are there more now?"

"There are. Three previous boyfriends. All of whom proposed. All of whom she broke up with when they did. Would that be reason enough? For the vendetta you mentioned?"

"Possibly. Let's have a look."

"You want the paper, right?"

"I do. I'm a visual thinker. All of these pages"—she indicated the file folders—"they were all tacked on my wall. Where I can move them around. Reconnecting them. Making new patterns. Trying alternate theories."

"Thought so," said Danbury, standing. "Be right back."

After he'd left the room, Matthew queried, "You don't think Preston Priestly or Mick Nichols could be our guy? You said they were less likely."

"Not from what I've seen. Neither has the mental capacity. Unless they've hidden it well. Your killer probably wouldn't boast. But neither would he hide it. He'd think his superiority obvious. And that it should be so. To everyone around him."

When Danbury returned, he held the door wide and said, "Come with me."

"Sure," she said, gathering her file folders, stacking them neatly, and sliding them back into her satchel without asking where they were going.

Up a floor, Danbury led them into a conference room with a long wooden table, a white board, and much to her apparent delight, a whole tack board wall. She completely ignored the stack of display screens on the wall facing it.

"Here you go," said Danbury, sliding the stack of folders he carried onto the table and stepping back. "I thought you might want the wall."

"That's perfect," she said. "Can I have this room? For a couple of hours, at least."

"If you're up for it tonight," said Danbury, checking his watch. "It's all yours."

"Definitely," she said, retrieving the folders from her satchel and adding them to the stack. Matthew soon realized that their presence was superfluous as Dr. Allman began pulling papers, rearranging them on the table, and then pinning them to the wall. It was as if she'd already forgotten that they were still there.

"You have my number," said Danbury. "Text if you need anything. Or when you're done."

"Will do. Oh, and one caution," she said, turning to look at them in concern. "He's brilliant at calculation. His mind is better than a computer. If he's playing chess, he's not just one move ahead. He's already on the next game. Don't underestimate him. Ever," she cautioned before turning back to her work with the files.

"Noted," said Danbury over his shoulder as he and Matthew left the room and headed back downstairs. Matthew thought her advice was entirely sound from what they'd learned of the killer so far. They certainly shouldn't underestimate him.

"Hey, Detective," said the guy Matthew had seen in the tech room as they approached. "I was just coming to find you. We need you in here."

Matthew dutifully followed Danbury, who was following the tech guy, back into the dark room with all of the monitors and equipment.

"OK, he's here," the guy said as he slid into his seat and picked up his headset. "I'll patch you in."

After a moment, the large monitor to the left showed a uniformed officer standing under what appeared to be a streetlight. He was obviously holding his phone out in front of him as if he were taking a selfie. The background was blurry, so he could have been anywhere.

"Detective Danbury," he began. "We've got something up here you'll be interested in seeing."

"Tell me," said Danbury.

"Behind the house where the freezer truck was parked, there was a backhoe sitting on a mound of dirt."

"Yeah, I remember it," said Danbury.

"It wasn't supposed to be there. It was missing from another home site down the street and around a corner. The construction crews on the site thought kids had been joyriding on it and moved it. One of the crews working at the house it was behind thought it was to put a pool in. The other crew thought it had buried a septic tank. Until they talked to each other. Then they discovered that there is no pool going in, and sewer and water services are provided by the city. So there are no septic tanks out here either."

Things must get confusing with so many people working on job sites throughout a neighborhood, thought Matthew. Right after the holidays, with multiple crews working on multiple home sites, miscommunication and misconception could easily occur.

"What's under the backhoe?" asked Danbury.

"That's what we're about to find out," said the officer. "Because it's the site where the freezer truck was found, as in possibly a murder site, we thought you might want to be here."

Before Danbury could answer, Hillary Allman burst into the room behind them.

"There you are!" she said. "I found an anomaly. It might be an important one. So I wanted to explain in person."

"Just a minute, Officer," said Danbury to the screen. Turning to Dr. Allman, he said, "Tell me."

Before she could, the tech guy said, "Detective, we have contact!"

Matthew had never seen Danbury ruffled, and this was no exception, though Matthew was at a loss as to which way to turn. Things were happening faster in that moment than most people would be able to follow.

"Contact with the killer?" Danbury asked the tech guy.

"We think so. Kincaid has been asked about the cat. As instructed, he told them he doesn't have her, but he said he knows where she is and can get the collar."

Matthew shuddered with this news, but Danbury calmly responded, "Good. See if he can keep him talking. I'll be right there."

Turning back to the screen to the left, he said, "Either I or Conover will be there. Just as soon as we can."

"Do we have permission to dig?" asked the officer.

"You have my permission. If the developer is in agreement."

"He is."

"OK, go ahead. Contact me. If you find anything. Before Conover or I get there."

"Thanks, Detective," said the guy, and the screen went black.

Turning to Dr. Allman, Danbury simply said, "What anomaly?"

"In your interview with Cara Mason. The initial one. Your notes say she told you Misty broke up with Adam Wilson. Back before the holidays. Because he wanted to take her to meet his parents at Christmas, engaged. She refused. He was pushy. And she broke it off with him."

"That's right," said Danbury.

"But Adam Wilson doesn't have parents. They were brutally

murdered. When he was a child. And he was in the house at the time."

"Wow. That's serious childhood trauma," said Matthew.

"Precisely," replied Allman.

"Is there any other explanation?" asked Danbury. "Foster parents? Close relatives who raised him, maybe? Somebody he'd consider parents?"

"Not that I can find," she responded.

"I'll check that with Cara. Unless it's too late to call," Danbury added, looking at his watch.

"It's not too late to text," offered Allman. "You should start there anyway."

"What? Why?"

"She's twenty, right? Gen Z. You always text Gen Zers before you call them."

"You do?" asked Danbury. "Since when? I call you. Whenever I need to talk to you," he said to Matthew. "And it's OK with you, right?"

"Well, yeah, but we're millennials," chuckled Matthew. "And I've heard what she's telling you before. Gen Z is all about texting before calling."

"I hate texting." Danbury sighed, pulling out his phone. His big fingers trying to type on the tiny key spots did seem arduous. Matthew was surprised that Danbury ever texted anyone, the effort seemed so great. But he'd gotten texts from Danbury many times, and some of them lengthy. The guy seemed to be managing it.

"OK," said Danbury. "I asked if I could call. Told her I needed a clarification. A quick one."

After a moment, they heard a ding, and Danbury tapped to call Cara. "Hi, Ms. Mason," he began. "OK, Cara," he amended.

"I need a clarification. About Misty's ex-boyfriend. Adam Wilson." Danbury hesitated. "Yeah, that one. Misty told you he wanted her to meet his family. At Christmas, right? Did he say his parents, specifically? Or his family, in general?"

He looked up from the phone, nodding at Allman. "Yeah, he wanted to be engaged. And take her home for the holidays. Did she mention where that was? His home? Where he wanted to take her?"

Danbury shook his head at Allman to let her know that he didn't have a location.

"That's what I needed. Anything else you can remember about him? Anything Misty might have said? His profession? Or background?"

After a moment, Danbury added, "If you think of anything, let me know. Just send me a text," he said with a grin. "Thanks, Cara."

Putting his phone back in his pocket, he clarified to Dr. Allman, "Cara doesn't remember. If Misty mentioned a location. She can't tell me where. But she definitely said parents. Misty seemed to have a had a thing about parents. Cara is certain of that."

"That he said parents is enough to keep digging," replied Allman. "I'll dig deeper on relatives. And potential foster parents. Anybody he could have called his parents."

"Good plan," said Danbury. "I've got to go. Are you sticking around?"

"Yeah. I'm like a dog with a bone," she said, almost smiling at him. "Or so I've been told. I can't let it go."

"OK, you know how to reach me," he said, grabbing his coat. Matthew followed suit, and they went back to the room where Kincaid was gaming. Cracking the door, Danbury motioned to Detective Conover, who joined them in the hallway.

"I need to go to the murder scene," Danbury said and briefly explained the situation. "Is there camera footage? Of the ask?"

"No, this guy isn't giving that much away. It was all over a text message on the gaming system. Kincaid answered back that he knew where the cat was and could get the collar."

"Any response?" asked Danbury.

"The guy asked why he didn't already have it. Kincaid told him he hadn't risked it yet, but he would. The guy said he'd get back to Kincaid."

"Disdainful," said Danbury. "Of what he sees as failure. That fits with what Allman says about him. Extremely smart. And thinks everyone else is beneath him. Stay on it. If the guy comes back, set up a location. Or a drop of the collar. We've put it back together. Just in case the guy knows what it looks like. Use it if Kincaid agrees to get it. If the guy asks for pictures or verification."

"OK, will do."

"You with me?" asked Danbury, turning to Matthew as he strode quickly down the hallway and took the rounded staircase down, two steps at a time.

Checking his watch and thankful for long legs to keep up, Matthew followed Danbury and answered, "Yeah, I'll drive myself home from there unless you need me for anything else tonight. It's been a long week, and I'm tired."

"Tell me about it," said Danbury as they handed over Matthew's badge to the receptionist and headed out of the building, pulling on their coats as they went. "I'll send the exact address."

36 ~ THAT'S A NEW ONE

As he followed Danbury to Durham, where they had already been earlier that evening, Matthew felt the fatigue set in. All he really wanted was a good night's sleep. Relieved that his house should be out of the picture as a target for stealing the cat and collar, he cranked up his playlist and cracked his window to blow cold air on his face. That should do it to keep him awake. It always had.

As they pulled in front of the newly constructed house, the exterior looked to be complete. The driveway, however, was still red mud under a thin layer of gravel. It and the front yard were already full of cars, police and what Matthew assumed were the cars of the construction crew members. Pulling up along the curb, he parked and slid out to follow Danbury up the driveway on foot. The dark night sky was brightly illuminated behind the house.

After greeting the officer they'd seen on camera in the tech room and completing introductions, they followed him behind the house. The backhoe was already at work, scooping up loads of dirt and then emptying them to one side, sifting them slowly. Danbury joined a clump of men, including another uniformed officer, who looked on from beside the hole. Matthew hung back, watching from a distance.

Following several mesmerizing rounds of scooping and dumping, a heavy-set guy standing over the hole and shining a bright spotlight down into it held up his hand. To the backhoe driver, he yelled, "Hold up!"

The hydraulic arm of the backhoe jerked to a stop and then froze in midair, the shovel poised for the next scoop. "Pull back!" The guy motioned. "I see something down there."

Several other guys, including the police officers, rushed to the edge of the hole. They were shining lights down, discussing, pointing, and gesturing.

"What's going on?" asked Matthew as Danbury approached.

"We can see something down there. It looks metallic. Discussion is about the walls of the hole. How well they're shored up. And if they can dig a ramp. To provide access. The hole is deep. But it's also wide. So they think that'll work. To do some more delicate digging."

The backhoe shifted positions and backed up, beginning to pull dirt from one end of the hole and turn to pile it, not as carefully, beside the hole. Over multiple back-and-forth trips, up and down the in-progress ramp, the backhoe jolted repeatedly, the bucket folding under as it tamped down the earth. Then it halted entirely, backing up the ramp. Two guys donned headlamps and began to walk slowly down the ramp created by the backhoe. After a few minutes, Matthew could hear yelling from the hole. Several others, including Danbury, took up shovels and headlamps, disappearing down the ramp and into the hole.

One of the bright lights was shifted into place from above. Matthew waited patiently until Danbury reappeared, followed by four others. They were all spattered with mud and looked concerned.

"What is it?" asked Matthew.

"We think we found the missing motorcycle. The one that belonged to Nichols," said Danbury.

"Why would anybody bury a motorcycle?"

"Because we found Nichols. We think. Buried with it."

"Oh! Is your ME on the way?" asked Matthew.

"She's about to be," Danbury responded, wiping his hands on his pants and pulling his phone from his pocket, tapping it to request the medical examiner.

Matthew stood by while Danbury made that call and two others, one to Hillary Allman to check on her progress and another to report in and check on the status with Kincaid and the gaming situation.

"Do we need to call the Forensic Entomology Department?" one of the officers in uniform asked Danbury as he approached.

After considering for a moment, Danbury answered, "No. We have a window. Beginning Thursday, the second. The truck was reported missing. And Nichols with it. Ending Wednesday the fifteenth. When the truck was found. This mound was here then. It just had no significance. Yet. I'm not sure it would help. Having a tighter time frame. The ME's on the way. She might consult the forensic entomologist. If she finds bugs." After a pause, Danbury added, That's a deep hole."

"Was there any other progress to report?" asked Matthew when the officer walked away to return to the hole.

"Allman is running a deeper background check. On Adam Wilson. But that's slow going. She's hitting walls. Businesses aren't open. Not on Friday nights. She's still working on it. No further word from the gaming. They're going to shut down for the night. In another hour or so."

"It's past time to turn the tables on this killer, and I have an idea about how to do that. But you're not going to like it."

"What's that?" Danbury asked cautiously.

"He doesn't know we've found the diamonds, right?"

"We assume he doesn't. But remember what Allman said."

"Yeah, never underestimate him. We won't."

"What are you thinking?"

"Kincaid was told to go after Penn earlier. We think it's because the killer thought she had Fluffykins or that she could lead him to her. Maybe he thinks Penn had her while you were away. That's our current operating assumption, right?"

"Yeah."

"We don't really know why Kincaid was sent after Penn, though. What if it was about Penn herself? She has the same vibrant blue eyes that Misty had. It's something about her that you notice immediately. What if that was about her and not the cat? Or both?"

"It's possible," said Danbury, rubbing the blond stubble that was barely visible on his chin with his thumb.

"Maybe we tackle both at once," said Matthew. "By leading the killer to believe that Penn has Fluffykins."

"Using Penn as bait?" asked Danbury, concerned.

Matthew winced at the bluntness of the question. "I wouldn't put it like that exactly. She'd be well protected, of course."

Danbury seemed to consider this for a moment. "It might work," he said. "If she's willing. I'll need approval. To use the resources. To stage the operation. But I'll ask Penn first. We'll start there."

After another hour of careful digging with shovels by one of the excavation crew and two police officers, they unearthed a motorcycle and a corpse. They loaded the body carefully onto a tarp, then pulled the tarp up the ramp from the hole. It was difficult to tell what the person had looked like, except that he was definitely male, Matthew thought, noting a prominent Adam's apple. The victim looked to be of a medium build and height.

Danbury began tapping his phone, pacing, and talking after he reappeared from the hole and brushed his hands off on his pants. Matthew wasn't close enough to hear what he was saying or to whom he was speaking, but he was catching other snatches of conversation from the team assembled around and working in the hole.

"Buried with a bike," said one of the officers as two of them pushed and pulled the motorcycle out of the hole behind the body. "That's a first. Why bury a motorcycle?"

"Maybe because it belonged to the victim, and the killer didn't want either one found," the other, older officer hypothesized. "But that is a new one. I've never seen anything like this before."

Matthew assumed there'd be no use evaluating the body on the scene because, having been buried, it was caked in mud. His assumption proved correct when Danbury motioned to a transport van from the medical examiner's office as it backed into place beside the hole. "Load him up. Wrap him carefully. Secure the tarp around him."

The medical examiner, whom Matthew had met earlier, greeted him and Danbury. Then she looked on, giving directions, as the body was wrapped in the tarp and carefully loaded into the back of the van.

She handed Danbury a tablet for his signature and promised to let him know what she found as soon as she could. "It'll be sometime tomorrow, though," she said. "Before I'll be able to start examining him."

"Thanks for the Saturday shift," said Danbury.

"No problem," she replied. "There are lots of things I'd rather be doing on a Saturday, but I want this killer apprehended as quickly as possible before the trail goes cold. If working a Saturday helps to accomplish that, I'm happy to help."

She slid into the passenger seat of the van, and the driver carefully navigated back across the slick red mud that was piled around the hole, around the house, and out onto the street. Matthew saw one last flash of brake lights, and then it was gone.

"Now what?" he asked Danbury, who seemed to be lost in thought.

"Your plan. We put it in motion."

"How?"

"We're setting up twenty-four seven. At the Lingle Plantation. Penn will be seen coming and going. We'll stage it overnight. So that she's not actually there. Get the word to the killer. Through Kincaid."

"Ah," said Matthew. "So she agreed?"

"She did. She wants this guy caught. She agreed to help. With one stipulation. She's not there overnight."

"How are you going to manage to get her out?"

"The passages are still there. They might be useful now."

"Could the killer possibly find out about them?"

Danbury considered this for a moment before he responded, "Allman said not to underestimate him. So it's possible. Penn grew up in that house. And she didn't know about the passages. Not until last spring. There are no blueprints dating back that far. So you'd have to know. Or have been told. Or have been in the house. And be paying close attention."

The original portion of the historic Lingle Plantation was built along the railroad tracks as they were being constructed, and it dated back to the eighteen hundreds before what Matthew habitually called the Uncivil War. The kitchen addition and the passageways were added at a later time, though when was uncertain.

"True," said Matthew. "You'd have to have been inside the house to even consider that there is extra space from the outside. Most people would never notice the additional six feet along the right end. But then, word got out somewhat after Allan Lingle was killed. I mean, I know about it. And I don't think we're dealing with 'most people,' are we?"

"No, you're right. We have to consider the possibility. This guy might know. Or he might find out. If he looks for the best way in."

After considering for a moment, Matthew slowly added, "Maybe the best way to get Penn out is the simplest way. In plain sight."

"How so?"

"If you and an officer go into the house, ostensibly to do one last walk-through to ensure Penn's safety before leaving for the night, and then they switch places."

"That could work. It's logical. One last sweep of the house. Each night."

"Exactly. You and the officer go in, and you and Penn come out, with Penn dressed as the officer. She keeps her head down, and if the guy is watching, he won't see anyone sneaking around the house. He'll just see something logical that he might expect to see."

Checking his watch, Danbury said, "Tomorrow night. If Kincaid can make contact again."

"Yeah, maybe Kincaid tells the guy that the cat is at the Lingle Plantation and that he overheard that the owner has decided she's not going to be scared out of her own home. She'll be there."

"What about Leo?"

"Maybe he's back in Denver for a few days. Or maybe that's what Kincaid says if he can get back in touch with the guy online."

"It's worth a shot," said Danbury thoughtfully. "I'm going to finish up here. Then go back to north Raleigh. I'll make the calls from that office. Fill out the requests. Put all of it in motion."

"I'm going home to get some sleep tonight. If you can put the word out that the cat is at the Lingles' house, that's great. Then I won't sleep with my Glock."

"Doc," began Danbury. "You know that's not a good idea."

"Neither is having some psychopath outside my window in the middle of the night or finding a small fortune in black diamonds in my possession. Or yet another murder victim. Nobody is coming into my house again. I can promise you that! I'm going to beef up my security system with cameras and all of that as soon as I get the chance."

"Yeah, I get it," conceded Danbury. "Just turn on the security system. What you do have in place."

"It's always on. But then, so was Penn's at Lingle Wellness. That didn't stop Kincaid from getting in. I would like to know how he did that, while you're asking him things."

"He didn't. We already asked."

"What do you mean he didn't?"

"I mean, it was done remotely. Somehow. He was told the specific time. And the exact door. The alarm was disabled. On that door. At that time."

"Oh," said Matthew pensively. "It wasn't physically disabled at the door itself?"

"Right."

"Great," said Matthew sarcastically. "That's not comforting."

"Somebody has an in."

"Or a back door in," said Matthew with a chuckle, momentarily shirking the seriousness of the conversation. "Sorry, I'm tired and punchy. So you think somebody was able to tap in online? Like into the computer system of the security company? Or that somebody has an in with the security company and could manipulate it from the inside?"

"We don't know yet. But we're checking," said Danbury. "I'll let you know. When I know."

"OK," said Matthew, now hesitant to go home. That sentiment, though, just made him mad. His home was supposed to be his safe haven, one carefully chosen for peace and tranquility. It was not going to be someplace he waited for the next psychotic killer to show up. As he turned resolutely on his heel to make his way carefully back through the mud to his Element, one of the FBI agents from the night before approached.

Curtly, the guy nodded his head at Matthew in acknowledgment.

Equally as curtly, Matthew nodded back before adding over his shoulder to Danbury, "See you tomorrow."

"G'night, Doc," Danbury mumbled before turning his attention to his phone, and Matthew heard him placing the call to the North Raleigh Police Department office and beginning to explain the proposed operation.

37 ~ STINGING

It seemed to be a foregone conclusion, Matthew realized as he sat listening to Danbury, that he would participate fully in this investigation. Danbury was updating his team on the developments, explaining the evening's objectives, and leading a planning session from one end of the boardroom table at the police station in Peak. At the other end of the table, Matthew yawned. Not that the conversation was boring at all. Far from it. Setting up a sting operation at the Lingle Plantation was the primary topic of discussion and debate.

The large room felt overly warm and overcrowded. Five uniformed officers were around the table, three of them from Peak and two from Raleigh. Four plainclothes detectives were interspersed, including Detective Conover, whom Matthew recognized from the North Raleigh Police Department office. The two FBI agents who had invaded Matthew's home two nights before were quietly scowling on one side of the table, without contributing to the conversation. Dr. Hillary Allman sat quietly beside Danbury and seemed to be taking it all in. Danbury had assembled quite a team for this operation, thought Matthew.

The Peak police officers reported that they had been making regular rounds at the Lingles' house and property. They were patrolling the area every two hours during the overnight time frame.

"I hope the perp is paying attention," said Danbury. "It'll help us. If he knows the times of those rounds." Continuing, he explained that the person they suspected of being the killer had been told by Kincaid that the cat, the collar, and Penn Lingle would all be in the Lingle house, ongoing. The night before, Kincaid had managed to relay that information to HavocWreaker13 through the gaming chat.

"As Dr. Allman and I thought," Danbury explained, "HavocWreaker13 told Kincaid to stand down. Abruptly. He said he'd be back in touch. But he'd handle the cat himself."

That news surprised nobody who had seen Allman's report on the killer's superiority complex.

The body unearthed the night before had been quickly identified by matching DNA from the apartment of Mick Nichols. Nichols, the delivery guy who was last seen driving the freezer truck for Duncan Meat Packaging and Shipping, had apparently been inseparable from his motorcycle both in life and in death. His was the motorcycle that was buried with him. It had been identified, after carefully removing layers of mud, by the VIN that was stamped on the right side of the steering head.

Still unknown was when the bike was removed from the Duncans' business and specifically when Nichols had been killed. The cause of his death was also as-yet undetermined, though the medical examiner had reported that she was working on a couple of theories for both the time and the cause.

That left Trent Kent and Adam Wilson, both past boyfriends of Misty's, on their list of suspects. Either one could be the killer or have been in the trunk of Misty's car when it blew up. It was equally possible, Matthew considered, that somebody else, somebody they didn't even know about yet, could be either the killer or the body in the trunk. Maybe that was even more plausible than Kent or Wilson.

Priestly had been ruled out by Allman because he didn't exhibit the intelligence or other characteristics required to have orchestrated all of the events that had transpired. And because he'd had the cat but hadn't removed the diamonds or the collar before handing her over. Matthew still wondered if the sleazy guy was a better actor than they thought even if he wasn't behind all of it. He was hiding something—that was certain.

Despite managing a decent night's sleep after the lateness of the hour at which he'd fallen into the bed the night before, Matthew caught himself yawning again. Having slept in that morning, he thought he shouldn't be yawning. Thinking about his late morning reminded him of his FaceTime chat with Cici. Then, realizing that his mind had begun to wander to Cici, he consciously snapped his attention back to the plans for the evening that were being discussed.

"The local team will help. The Peak officers, here," Danbury said pointing to a map that was projected onto the wall beside him. "They'll continue patrolling regularly. Through the night hours. Their ongoing presence is crucial. To look like nothing has changed. No heightened presence. No new knowledge to alter that."

Danbury paused, looking around the room as the officers nodded their understanding and approval.

"We've moved our command center here," Danbury continued. "This station in Peak is close. We're only a couple of blocks away," he said, and he seemed to be talking mostly to the FBI agents. "The Lingle Plantation is just down the street. We'll use Peak Family Practice. For night surveillance. We've been granted access. It's close to the Lingle property. Here," he said, pointing to Matthew's office on the projected map on the wall.

"The Peak officers patrol. Starting here," Danbury added, pointing to the long driveway approaching the house from Chapel Street. Chapel Street was oddly shaped. It came in as a one-way street from Winston Avenue. Then it curved sharply to the left behind the parking lot for the cultural arts center and in front of Matthew's medical practice. To the right of the sharp curve, the Lingles' private driveway connected.

"Every two hours all night. Starting at six. When the sun goes down. They circle the property. And exit here," continued Danbury, pointing to the gravel driveway that exited from the rear of the house and onto the street behind the Lingles' property. Historically, it had been a servants' entrance at the rear of the house, only recently restored from an overgrown mass of underbrush.

"This area around the house. It's heavily wooded. There's an old tree house here." Danbury pointed. "It's just on the edge of the woods. There's now a clear sightline to the house. We have a volunteer for that location."

A thickset officer with a completely bald head nodded his acknowledgment. There was probably no fat on the guy at all, Matthew thought, but his shirt was taut across his shoulders and chest.

Being posted in his own office building would put him out of any potential action, which suited Matthew just fine. He'd seen plenty of action since befriending Danbury, more than he'd ever wanted to. He was needed mostly to provide access to his building for the officers who would be coming and going. Intending to spend the evening there, Matthew had no plan to spend all night with them.

From that vantage point, they would be watching the street and driveway into the Lingle Plantation. The French doors leading onto the balcony off the upstairs break room provided an excellent view over the hedge, down the street, and up the Lingles' driveway. It would be mostly unobstructed. If the guy parked elsewhere and came in on foot farther down the hedge that lined the sidewalk along the street, they could potentially miss his approach.

As Danbury continued discussing strategy, another officer volunteered to be in the tree line on the right front corner of the house. Two other officers offered to be posted in the woods on the left side of the house, providing a complete view around the outside of it. Danbury rubbed his chin with his thumb pensively as he seemed to consider the suggestions from these volunteers.

Two officers, a woman who would switch places with Penn when she checked in at eight that evening and an FBI agent, would be stationed inside the house overnight.

The female officer would remain in the Penn disguise as she moved about the house, turning lights on and off, before proceeding to Penn's room for the night. She would not, however, be sleeping after she turned Penn's bedroom light out. If the first night was uneventful, the officer would leave the house at Penn's usual time and drive around to ensure she wasn't being followed before dropping the car at Danbury's for Penn and catching a ride with Danbury back to the Peak office.

After the whole plan had been discussed and debated, Allman spoke up. "Are you sure?" she asked.

"About?" asked Danbury calmly, though Matthew guessed he was annoyed beneath the impenetrable surface because she had waited until they'd discussed the plan in detail before she objected.

"All of that police presence. This guy is smart. Probably on the genius scale. He'll be careful and observant. He won't fall into that trap. He won't likely come straight at the house."

"What would you suggest?" Danbury asked, some of the annoyance visible to anyone who knew the man well.

"Police presence in the house. Maybe in the tree house. And from the doctor's distant office. But not around the perimeter of the house. This guy will watch. And wait. He'll spot them."

"I agree," Danbury conceded, scratching the stubble on his chin again thoughtfully. "We need to scale back. Reserve resources. For later. If he doesn't show up tonight. Let's regroup."

"You could put officers in the passageways in the house easily enough," Matthew spoke up hesitantly.

"The passageways?" asked Allman.

Danbury nodded his approval, though he didn't directly answer Dr. Allman's question. "I was thinking that too. It is a better plan."

In the final plan, two officers maintained their positions, the one in the tree house and the female officer posing as Penn. One of the officers was moved from the tree line to the passageways in the walls of the house. He looked intrigued at the assignment after it was explained to him. There were few secrets about the mysterious Lingle Plantation left, and this had become one less. The other two officers would rotate in the following night if another night was needed.

After everything was planned and everyone, including Allman, was happy with the plan, the room began to empty, and the officers dispersed. Checking his watch, Matthew saw that it was just four in the afternoon. The officers to be posted in the house were going into place immediately, but there was an hour and a half before the rest of the operation would commence. It would be done in stages, with the last to be when Penn and the female officer posing as Penn switched places at nine that night.

At five thirty, Matthew was to drive Detective Conover and one of the FBI agents to the parking lot of his medical practice to enter with him through the back side door. From there, they'd get set up in the break room on the second floor above his office.

Penn would arrive home just as the first police cruiser circled the house at six. The officers would stop and chat with her for a moment to show anyone who might be watching that she was home.

"You hungry?" asked Danbury as he and Matthew left the room.

"Eat when you can?" asked Matthew, quoting part of Danbury's creed back to him.

"Right."

"Sure," said Matthew, chuckling to himself because Danbury could always eat.

"Peak Eats?" asked Danbury. "Proximity."

"Yeah, that sounds good. Then I've got to go by my house and take care of the cats. I'll be back here just before five thirty to get your detective and the agent."

"OK," said Danbury as they handed Matthew's guest badge to the receptionist and stepped out of the Peak police station and into the waning afternoon light. Matthew had parked at his office and walked over to the station, which was just down the street on the block behind Winston Avenue, the main street through the historic little town. Peak Eats was a block farther down on Winston Avenue, just a short walk in the brisk afternoon air.

A dimpled Mallory was happy to greet and seat them as they walked in, cutting the younger server, Evie, off in the process. Expertly, she descended on them before any of the other servers could manage to intervene and steered them to their favorite booth in the back corner.

Matthew was beginning to feel sorry for her because she seemed so desperate for male attention. Initially, he hadn't noticed it until Penn had pointed it out the spring before. *How did I not see it?* he wondered now. As always, he was kind to her, thanking her for the excellent service, but careful not to do anything that could be construed as flirting back.

*****

After a quick trip home, Matthew pulled up alongside the Peak police building on the farthest side from his office, which was also the farthest side from the Lingle Plantation. Detective Conover and one of the FBI agents, who had both been in the meeting earlier, stepped from the building, carrying what looked to be heavy canvas bags.

The two men were polar opposites in appearance. The agent had a compact build, dark hair, a wizened look about his eyes, and an intense expression. Detective Conover appeared to be younger. He was taller, with auburn hair and a light complexion that looked like it would burn if the guy spent more than a minute in direct sunlight. The agent opened the clamshell doors of the Element; they shoved their equipment in, then climbed in after it.

"Dr. Paine, right?" asked Detective Conover, without any further acknowledgment of the irony of the name.

That was unusual, thought Matthew. He'd come to expect some sort of comment, a snicker at least. "That's right. But Matthew is fine."

"Just trying to remember your real name. Danbury always calls you Doc."

"He does." Matthew chuckled, as he pulled through the parking lot and wound around to Chapel Street, then into the parking lot of his office. Locking the Element as they got out, Matthew unlocked the back side door and led the officers up the stairs to the break room. They lit it initially only with dim penlights as they moved around in the darkened room.

The FBI agent unzipped a bag and began rolling some sort of clingy black plastic, which stuck as he went, down the French doors. After that was accomplished, he placed the end of a long lens against the black plastic, tracing it with a small knife and removing the center panel. He attached the lens to a long device with a base and strategically placed the whole contraption on a stand in front of the hole he'd made in the black plastic. It looked to Matthew to be a mix of a high-powered camera and a telescope. Then, they turned the lights on in the room.

"Coffee?" asked Matthew, running his fingers through his hair and realizing that he'd never actually made coffee in the break room before. *How hard can it be?* he thought, as the officers accepted the offer and he set about figuring it out.

After they were settled in, Matthew slipped down to his office momentarily and turned the desk lamp on. It needed to look, from the outside through the slatted blinds, like he was in his office, hard at work. Back upstairs, he settled in with the detective and agent to wait.

"You know, this could be hours of boredom followed by moments of sheer adrenaline," said Detective Conover.

"Or it could be just hours of boredom," responded the agent. "You don't have to stay. Unless you need to babysit us in your building," he added sarcastically to Matthew.

Matthew bit back the snide response that was forming in his mind. Instead, he just chuckled at the notion of babysitting detectives and federal agents and answered, "I'll stay for a while. I'm not hanging out all night. I have standing plans with my family to go to church and out to lunch afterward on Sundays. My little niece would be very disappointed if I didn't make it in the morning because I'd been up all night."

His niece, Matthew realized, wasn't the only one who would be disappointed. He needed the weekly ritual himself, the normalcy in the craziness of the past couple of weeks.

They chatted amicably, detective and agent taking turns behind the telescopic lens device, as they settled in for the night. The device was mounted so that they could sit in a chair behind it and watch the entrance to the Lingle Plantation through the glass French doors.

Perking up momentarily, the agent at the window reported Penn's arrival. Then they settled back in to wait and watch. At eight, the police cruiser made the next round, and in between, all was quiet. At nine, Danbury's big black SUV drove up to the house, and he and the uniformed female officer got out and went to the door. Matthew couldn't see any of that happening, but he was getting a blow-by-blow description from the agent whose turn it was to watch.

"The officer is in place, and her wire is working fine," reported Conover, who was sitting at the break room table with some sort of computerized device, apparently listening through a headset to the conversation in the house. "We've got more ears inside now."

The officer in the hidden passageways in the walls of the house was connected to the conversation with a tiny microphone and earwig listening device, as was the other FBI agent who was in the downstairs study for the night. After a few more minutes, Danbury's SUV left the house. The swap had been made, and Penn was safely out of the house for the night. That was mostly what Matthew cared about. He'd still love to have the killer caught and incarcerated, though, he thought, as he pondered his plans for the evening.

"I guess it's OK that my car is still in the parking lot?" he queried.

"Are you normally in the office this late?" asked the agent without turning from his seat at the window.

"Never on a Saturday night," Matthew answered. "I can do everything I need to do remotely, even when I'm on call. I can check on patients, update records, submit prescriptions, all of that. All of our patient records are in an EMR system online that I can access from anywhere."

"EMR?" asked Detective Conover from his seat at the break room table.

"Electronic medical records," said Matthew. "We use a software system called EPIC to securely update and access our patients' medical records, either here in the office or remotely. So no, I'm not ever here on a Saturday night."

"Oh," said Conover. "I think we're far enough removed from the house that it'll be OK. Townsfolk who are attending the ballet at the cultural arts center tonight and parked in that lot behind it would be the only ones who could easily see back here anyway." He obviously knew the small town well, though Matthew had initially met him at the North Raleigh Police Department office.

Foot tapping and mind racing, Matthew had been seated near the break room table. Every few minutes, the tension and the waiting got to be too much, and he got up and paced around the upstairs, where both Dr. Garner's and Dr. Rob's offices were located. Both had large offices up here on the second floor behind locked doors.

Matthew had declined the opportunity to move upstairs earlier, deciding that he was already happily ensconced in his smaller office downstairs. The upstairs space, he thought, was put to better use now anyway. Megan Sims, the physician's assistant who had joined the practice back in June, and Sadie Peterson, the resident she'd brought with her, needed the bigger office on the second floor because they shared the space between the two of them.

Matthew had just finished a lap through the upstairs hallway when Danbury texted.

"Let me in. Back door downstairs."

Matthew hurried down the stairs and opened the door to Danbury.

"Hey, Doc," he said. "All is quiet so far."

"Penn and Leo are safely at your place for the night?" asked Matthew as he led the way back up the stairwell.

"They are," responded Danbury. "I've got a patrol circling my place. Every hour. Just to be cautious."

"Caution is merited, from what Dr. Allman says. Keeping Penn and Leo safe is the top priority."

"Yeah, we really want this guy," said Danbury. "But you're right. They are the top priority."

No more able to sit still than Matthew had been, Danbury, too, was pacing the upstairs while listening to the chatter in his earpiece and occasionally talking on his phone. Matthew heard Danbury's phone ding twice and saw him stop in his tracks.

"No!" said Danbury, loudly enough to make them all jump.

38 ~ Stung

"What? What is it?" asked Matthew of Danbury's sudden outburst.

"We've been made," was all that Danbury said, though he said it through gritted teeth.

"What?"

"How?"

"Says who?"

The three other men asked their questions all at once.

"Hang on," said Danbury, tapping his phone. Then, into it, he said, "Danbury. Tell me."

After a few pauses between staccato questions, Danbury said, "OK, I'm calling it off."

Stepping into the break room, outside of which Danbury had halted his pacing up and down the hallway, he said, "The perp just connected. HavocWreaker13. On the gaming chat. He knows we're here. He's not coming."

A quiet pall fell over the room. After a moment's contemplation, Matthew asked the question that was most important to him, personally, and seemed an important detail in general: "Does he know that the cat isn't there?"

"That, I don't know," admitted Danbury.

"If he knows she isn't there, does he know where she actually is?" asked Matthew aloud, though it was a rhetorical question that he knew likely couldn't be answered yet.

Nobody bothered to respond, and all three men seemed to be momentarily frozen, as if in a trance. Danbury was rubbing the stubble on his chin in deep contemplation.

"What did he say, exactly?" asked the FBI agent, interrupting Danbury's thought process.

"The text message," began Danbury, tapping his phone. "It came in over the gaming system. Said he knew we were here. And we might as well go home. Because he wasn't dancing at our party."

"It said the Lingles' house specifically?" the agent asked for clarification.

"It did," said Danbury.

"Did he say anything about swapping out your girlfriend? Does he know that's not her?" the guy asked pointedly.

"He didn't say," said Danbury. "He knows Kincaid's in custody now. That he's talking to us. And refused to answer questions."

"OK," the agent all but snarled as he reached over, detached the end of the lens, and began disassembling the device in front of the door. Detective Conover followed suit, beginning to disconnect and pack the audio equipment until Danbury halted him.

"Let me tell the team," Danbury said. "Then you can tear it down."

Conover nodded, handing Danbury a microphone. "This spans the whole team."

"Attention, everybody," said Danbury into the microphone. "We've been made. Tear it down." Excluding the female officer posing as Penn and one of the officers in the walls, he called them all back to the Peak command center. The officer posing as Penn would remain in place until Danbury could come and pick her up, he explained. Just in case the killer was watching because the guy would expect that.

"An officer is remaining in the walls?" asked the agent.

"Right," answered Danbury. "He was in place early. And Penn's double. We don't know what the perp knows. He'd expect me to move her. If he thinks that's Penn. What about your agent?"

"He'll stay," said the guy over his shoulder, as he pulled the plastic sheet from the door and began rolling it up.

"Hey, Doc," said Danbury. "How would you transport a cat? What would you use?"

"A cat carrier," answered Matthew. "Misty apparently didn't have one of those because Preston Priestly said she'd carried Fluffykins in her lap when she brought her to him. The same way you transported her to the vet for that first overnight stay and to get her checked out. I'm surprised they didn't complain about that."

"I told them why. When I dropped her off," said Danbury. "I introduced myself. As a homicide detective. Told them her owner had died. They were sympathetic. And happy to help."

"Fluffykins?" asked Conover in apparent amusement. He hadn't commented on Matthew's last name and title, but that, he was amused by, thought Matthew. He mentally gave the guy a tick mark of credit.

"Yeah, the cat's name is Fluffykins," answered Matthew. Turning to Danbury, he asked, "Why were you asking about transporting her?"

"Could our officer carry a bundle? Like blankets? Would you carry a cat in blankets?"

"I guess you could," said Matthew. "You might if the cat were scared, if you were worried about her getting away from you, or if it's cold out."

"Then let's assume all of that," said Danbury. Pulling the microphone back out, he explained to the officer that she was to meet him at the door with a bag that looked to be packed and a blanket bundle. He told her where to find a bag in Penn's closet and to wrap blankets up to make them look like they contained a cat.

"How could he know this time?" asked Matthew, pacing again. "How is he always at least one step ahead of us in all of this? How?" he demanded.

"Doc, if I knew that," answered Danbury despondently, "he wouldn't be."

The FBI agent had disassembled the observation equipment and packed it into slotted sections of thick foam board made for the shape of each piece. After packing it and the rolls of clingy black plastic into the big canvas bag, he just said, "I'll see myself out, and I'll walk back." His hostility had been palpable, and Matthew was relieved when he was gone.

"OK, to pack up now?" asked Conover of Danbury.

"Yeah, pack it up," he answered glumly. "We'll regroup. Again."

After turning off the lights and locking up his office, Matthew drove Conover, with the heavy bag of audio equipment, back to the Peak station. Like the FBI agent, Danbury had opted to walk. There was a quick discussion happening when Matthew and the officer returned, and then Danbury left to go pick up the substituted Penn. How they were switching cars and getting Penn's back to her, Matthew wasn't sure, but he was certain that he was tired and ready to call it a night.

*****

Sleep had come easily to Matthew after he'd done a walk-through of his house, leaving lights on strategically outside, locking up everything, and setting the alarm. Exhausted, he was dreaming happily when something startled him awake. At first, he had to remind himself where he was and what was happening in his life.

Once he had those bearings, he heard a slight noise again. It wasn't loud, and it wasn't long. It was just a soft click, then nothing more. Reaching into the top drawer of his bedside table, he retrieved the Glock 19 that he had been keeping nearby, softly clicked in the magazine, and slid stealthily from his bed.

Is it just one of the cats in the litter box or in the kitchen? he wondered. He wanted to be very careful not to shoot an innocent cat. The last thing he wanted was to fire his weapon at all. But he was tired of his home, his peaceful haven, being invaded, and he knew that to wield a weapon meant to be ready to fire one.

Both Fluffykins and Max stared between him and the bedroom doorway from the bottom of his bed. Max hadn't been curled around his head, Matthew realized. He was already on the alert. Maybe Max's movement had been what woke him up. Carefully, Matthew crept to his bedroom door, which was cracked open. He pulled it silently open, thankful, in that moment, that he'd kept his door hinges oiled and cleaned.

Peering quickly from around the door frame down the hallway, he saw that it was shadowy, with the outside lights he'd left on filtering through the blinds in the main part of his house. But he saw nothing unusual. The door to his guest bedroom, where Maxine was housed, was still closed, as was the door to the hall coat closet. As it should have been to allow the cats access to their litter boxes, the hall bathroom door was ajar.

With his Glock raised in a ready position in front of him, Matthew slowly made his way down the hallway, noiselessly on his bare feet. He stopped when he reached the hall bath, uncertain as to whether to turn his attention away from the hallway that opened into the main part of his house to check the bathroom first.

That quickly became a moot point as a shadowy figure emerged from around the corner of his living room at the end of the hallway. They were a mere ten feet apart, the two men, and both were staring down the muzzle of the other's handgun.

Startled, Matthew managed to hold the Glock firmly and steadily in his hand. He heard a voice, as if from a distance, demand, "Who are you, and what do you want?" He realized that the voice was his own, and it sounded far calmer than he felt in that moment. Adrenaline was coursing through him, all vestiges of sleep chased from every corner of his mind and body.

"I want you to put that gun down," answered the shadowy figure. The guy was shorter, Matthew noticed as he looked down at him, but the muzzle of his handgun was aimed dead center at Matthew's chest. "And then get me the cat."

"That's not going to happen," Matthew heard his voice say, sounding steady and purposeful. He caught glimpses of his life in that moment, saw his parents; his little niece, Angelina; his sister, Monica; and her husband, Stephano. His mind raced through images of his friends and family, but then it stopped, caught on the image of Cici, as if she were standing right in front of him. The image was so vividly clear that he felt as if he could reach out and touch her. It almost made him hesitate, but he sensed that would not end well for him. Hesitation or loss of focus wasn't an option, not even for a second.

God help me if I put this Glock down, he thought to himself, and then he understood the calm that had washed over him. God was indeed helping him. They were in a standoff, he realized, eyes locked and guns poised in the dimness of the hallway.

"Just give me the cat." He heard the derision in the guy's voice. "You don't have to die tonight for a cat."

"Neither do you," Matthew heard himself say. "Just back up and get out of my house."

"That's not going to happen," the guy said, repeating Matthew's words back to him.

"Then we have a problem," said Matthew, feeling the anger roiling up inside. Fighting for control against that anger, he prayed silently and again felt an indescribable, surreal calm wash over him. He couldn't flinch, and he couldn't put further pressure on the trigger because as soon as he did, so would the other guy. He knew that in the deepest part of his being. But he also knew that if the other guy shot first, his reaction would be the same. Neither of them would come out alive.

Unless. A plan started to formulate in Matthew's mind. *This guy is smart*, he remembered. *On the genius scale. Never underestimate him.* Trickery wouldn't work. But maybe the truth would.

"They're not here," he said.

"Who's not here?" the guy asked. "The cat? I know there are cats here. I only want one of them. Just put the gun down and hand her over."

Without flinching at all, standing immovable and ramrod straight, with a strength that he didn't know he had and would later swear wasn't his own, Matthew simply told him the truth. "The cats are here. But the black diamonds are not here. You could shoot me to be sure. But you won't walk out of here if you do."

This seemed to take the guy off guard, but only for a split second did Matthew see him hesitate before he demanded, "How do I know they're not here?"

"The fact that I know about them should tell you that they're not here. The cat is here. The cat's collar is not here. Neither are the black diamonds that were hidden in it."

From outdoor lighting that was filtering through the front window, Matthew watched a dark anger rise in the guy's face. His brown hair, cropped short, caught flickers of light that crept through the cracks of the blinds in the front window behind him. He was neither tall nor short, a medium build, easily hiding, as Dr. Allman had said, in plain sight.

It was just a slight movement, but Matthew didn't miss it. The guy seemed to be losing control of his steeled reserve, and he'd flinched, ever so slightly. Then, everything happened, first in slow motion and then at such warp speed that Matthew later had trouble remembering the exact sequence of events. There was a second slight movement, this time from behind the guy. From Matthew's kitchen, another shadowy figure had emerged, and this one was the most welcome shadow Matthew ever remembered seeing.

A familiar voice spoke from behind the guy, and as he startled from the voice, Matthew dropped to the floor, rolling, not away from the guy, where a shot could more easily hit him, but right into the guy's feet, knocking him off guard. A shot rang out in the quiet night. Matthew felt the guy topple over him as the shadow tackled him from behind, knocking him to the floor in front of Matthew and pinning him there.

Raising himself to a sitting position on the hall floor and sliding over to prop himself against the wall, Matthew took stock of himself. Arms, legs, torso, shoulders, head. He felt no pain points from a bullet, so that was good, he thought. More shadowy figures emerged, wearing night goggles, through the kitchen door. They fanned out behind him, and someone had the wherewithal to flip a light switch as they all lifted their night-vision aids.

On the hallway floor in front of him, Matthew saw Danbury sitting astride the guy. The guy had been relieved of the gun, which was placed carefully behind Danbury, in front of Matthew but well out of the guy's reach. One of the other officers stepped around Matthew and retrieved the weapon from the floor, ejected the magazine, and pulled the slide back, clearing the chamber and palming the bullet in a gloved hand.

Matthew had managed to place his own weapon, the Glock 19, on the floor beside him, with the muzzle facing the wall, when he dove into the guy's feet. A second officer retrieved it and, more quickly than Matthew had ever managed, dropped the magazine and ejected the bullet from the chamber.

"This yours?" the officer asked Matthew, whose ears were still ringing a bit from the shot.

"Yes, but it hasn't been fired," he answered, realizing how thankful he was to be able to make that statement.

Danbury had wrenched both of the guy's arms behind his back, and he was barking out orders not to move. "You have the right to remain silent," Danbury began as he quickly cuffed the guy's hands behind his back and hauled him easily to his feet, as if the guy weighed nothing at all.

After he'd fully Mirandized the intruder, Danbury turned to Matthew and nonchalantly said, "Hey, Doc. Meet Adam Wilson."

Rarely was Matthew at a total loss for words, but this was one of those occasions. He didn't know where to start. Had Danbury known the guy would show up here? Had he been used as bait? Or was he to be thankful that Danbury and some of his team had figured it out and shown up in time? Confusion reigned in Matthew's brain in that moment.

Finally, Matthew muttered, "We've met," as he, too, stood, shakily at first.

Regaining his balance and his sense of himself in time and space, Matthew turned back to his bedroom. Fluffykins was happily bathing on the foot of his bed, as if nothing had happened, and Max was nowhere to be seen. He was probably hiding in the back corner of the bedroom closet, as he usually did when there were strange voices or noises in the house. If he hadn't been before the shot was fired, he surely was now. Matthew had to be certain that Max had not been in the line of fire.

Flipping on the closet light, he leaned over and slid the clothes on their hangers away from the back corner. Max regarded him with huge luminous eyes as Matthew talked soothingly to him and reached in, pulling the big cat out. Snuggling him to his chest and scratching him behind the ears, Matthew checked Max over, one end to the other, turning him around to ensure that he wasn't injured.

"OK, big guy," he said as he put Max gently back on the floor in the corner of the closet and pulled his clothes back in front of him. "As long as you're OK, you can hide as long as you like. I don't blame you. I might hide, too, if I could."

On the way back out of his bedroom, Matthew quickly checked the fluffy calico cat, retrieved his cell phone from the charger on his bedside table, and saw that it was four thirty in the morning. Well, he'd gotten a few hours of sound sleep, he thought, tucking the phone into the pocket of his flannel sleep pants and making his way back out to the crime scene that his house had become.

Back in his living room, the chaos that was ensuing must have been organized. Neither Danbury nor the guy he'd called Adam Wilson was in sight. Instead, his kitchen and living room were filled with police officers in full gear. They'd apparently called in the infantry, he thought as he wandered through, looking for Danbury.

"Matthew Paine?" asked one of the officers. Matthew recognized him as the bald, barrel-shaped guy from the planning session at the Peak precinct the previous afternoon. That seemed like an eternity ago, and he searched his memory for the guy's name. He was the guy in the tree house, Matthew remembered.

"Yes, I'm Matthew."

"We're going to need to get a statement from you."

"Sure," said Matthew, dropping into the big buttercream leather chair in his living room. "It's pretty simple, really. I went to bed and was awakened by a noise. I'm not sure what the noise was. It wasn't loud or long. Just soft and subtle. But it woke me from a deep sleep. When I heard it again, I got my Glock and slipped out of bed to listen at my bedroom door. I didn't hear anything, so I peered around the doorway into the hall. I didn't see or hear anything, so I stepped out, and I was moving slowly down the hall when suddenly, this guy appeared right in front of me. He was holding a gun aimed at my chest. Likewise, mine was aimed at his."

"Did he say anything?" asked the officer.

Struggling to remember the chain of events, Matthew answered slowly, "I think I asked him who he was and what he wanted. And then I think he told me to put my gun down. I figured if I did that, I was dead, so I told him I wasn't going to do that. We were in a standoff. So I decided to tell him the truth to see if that would motivate him to leave."

"The truth?"

"That the cat was here, but the collar and the diamonds were not. He didn't seem to believe me at first. Until I pointed out that if I knew about them, the black diamonds wouldn't still be here. That stopped him up short, and he seemed to be undecided as to what to do with me when Danbury came in behind him. I tucked and rolled into the guy's feet as Danbury tackled him from behind."

"Wow," said the officer. "That was some nice teamwork. Like you'd planned that ahead of time."

Matthew hadn't thought of that, but now that the guy pointed it out, he realized the truth of the statement. He and Danbury had planned nothing in advance, and that sort of coordination certainly couldn't have been conveyed in the moment, yet it had been perfectly synchronized.

"The guy was trigger-happy, and he fired off a shot. I don't know where it went," said Matthew. "But he fired his weapon."

"OK, good," said the officer, calling over a second officer and relaying that information.

Pulling out of his protective gear, the second officer said, "I'll go get the kit and find it," before he disappeared from the room.

"Good?" Matthew mumbled, thinking that shot was meant for him, and clearly it had missed, but that might not have been the case.

"He fired a shot at you. Until we can pull the rest of the case against him together, we can hold him on more than B&E. We've got him for attempted murder."

"B&E?" asked Matthew, thinking that he should know what that was, but his brain was understandably fuzzy at this hour of the morning and after the trauma he'd just experienced.

"Breaking and entering," the officer answered as Matthew nodded, knowing that he should have remembered that. "Wilson could get out on bail for a B&E easily enough, but now it's a lot more complicated because he fired the shot."

"I see," said Matthew.

39 ~ Blinding blur

The rest of the night until the dawn crept over the windowsills of his house was blurry in Matthew's mind later on. He'd given his statement twice, having it recorded as an audio file the second time. After signing a copy of it that had been printed out, he gave his permission for the sheetrock at the end of his hallway to be cut away from the bullet hole to retrieve the bullet.

A forensics team removed a section of the drywall and found the bullet lodged in the back of Matthew's shower casing. His master bath was on the other side of the wall at the end of the hallway. Nothing, he'd been reassured, except the square hole cut out of his wall to retrieve the bullet, had been damaged.

After the bullet was bagged and tagged along with the gun, the magazine, and the bullet removed from the chamber, all of it was transported to the police station. Had the guy worn gloves, Matthew wondered, trying to re-create the scene in his mind, or would there be fingerprints? It was such a blur in his mind. It was as if he'd been blinded to it all after the fact. Probably a self-preservation mechanism, he thought.

Another of the officers helped him to clean up the mess from where the section of the wall was removed, and he was told that he could file a claim for the damage to be fixed. That, he thought, would not be the first thing he'd do on Monday morning when businesses were open again. The first thing he'd do would be to contact the security company that Danbury and Penn had chosen for the Lingle Plantation. His primary goal would be to get to the front of the company's line to upgrade his security system as soon as humanly possible.

The intruder, Adam Wilson, had easily bypassed his security

system, and locally this time. The sounds Matthew had heard that woke him, he was told, were probably Wilson entering the house through the kitchen door from the garage and disarming the alarm.

This time around, he'd add all of the security that Cici had at her house—and then some. She had a keypad entry on each door of her house and a second alarm with a keypad inside each of the doors. There were cameras covering all angles of her tall, deep, narrow house in her upscale neighborhood in Quarry. Her house was set neatly close to the street on a main road, and the sidewalk with constant foot traffic was much too close to her front door to suit Matthew's taste.

Still, her security system had not been bypassed twice. Nobody had threatened her there, and certainly, nobody had thrown a Molotov cocktail through her back window because nobody could easily get to her back window. Matthew regretted that he was unable to say the same. Cici had houses close behind her, separated only by a privacy fence. There was not much room between Cici's house and the ones on either side of her, but maybe living in the middle of everything wasn't so bad after all. It had its advantages. Nothing was secluded; everything was in plain sight. The paradox annoyed him.

All but one of the officers and Danbury had cleared out by the time Matthew went back for another cup of coffee from the pot he'd made in the early-morning hours—and found none. Wilson had been transported to the downtown Raleigh police precinct, where he was wanted for questioning involving three murders and was being held there for attempting a fourth.

Pulling his sounding cell phone from his pocket, Matthew saw that it was eight in the morning, and Cici was requesting to FaceTime with him. He had no desire, yet, to talk about the events of the previous night. "Hey, Danbury. It's Cici calling—can you keep it down out here? I'm not telling her about this yet."

"Sure, Doc," said Danbury, who was packing gear.

Matthew took the phone back to his bedroom and, closing the door, sat down on his bed. Leaning on pillows up against the headboard, he answered the call and couldn't remember being happier to see Cici.

"You look, I don't know, different somehow," said Cici after they'd exchanged all of the usual greetings.

Realizing that the conversation wouldn't get any easier the longer he waited to tell her, he decided to explain. "Yeah, my sleep was disrupted sometime after four this morning."

"Oh. By the cats?"

"No, by a killer," he said, going for the dramatic and getting straight to the point.

"What? Matthew, what's going on there? Are you OK?"

Deciding to leave out the worst of the details, Matthew said, "I'm fine. Danbury showed up in time."

"In time for what?"

"In time for me to be talking to you right now."

"Matthew Landon Paine, this is not being careful!"

Matthew could hear the panic rising in her voice and see it clearly in her face, but still, he answered defensively, "It's not like I invited the guy over for drinks at four in the morning."

"Did you call Danbury?"

"No, I didn't have time."

"How did he know you were in danger?"

"That's a question I haven't asked yet. I think I was afraid of the answer," Matthew explained and then briefly outlined the events of the evening. Leaving out the standoff at gunpoint between him and Wilson, he told her that Danbury had tackled the guy in his hallway.

There was silence on the line as she took all of this in, and her face looked ashen. Then, she began to pour out what was in her heart and in her mind to him.

"Matthew, one of the things that I always loved about you was how safe you made me feel. It's like the rest of the world could crumble and fall around us, but you felt so safe, this wall of protection around us. You never had a God complex as a physician. You never seemed to think that you were immortal or could conquer the world single-handedly, even when I first met you in college. You were safe and sane. But lately, just since we started seeing each other again last spring, I don't know, it's like you're another person entirely. One who seems drawn to danger suddenly."

"I'm not drawn to it. It seems to be following me. Just last month, the danger came from a man who wanted to possess you, and he wanted me out of the way, remember?"

"I do," she said, looking down. "I guess that one was my fault. You'd resigned as a medical consultant for the police department, and that just dragged you back in, didn't it?"

"Yes, but that's not your fault, Cees. None of that was your fault. I didn't mean to sound like I was blaming you. I wasn't. I was just pointing out that I didn't go looking for trouble. It found us. The guy was after you. You didn't do anything to encourage him. He knew you were back with me, and that didn't dissuade him at all."

"That's true. He did know. I made that very clear."

"I'm sorry if I'm worrying you or if I scared you. The good news, though, is that this guy is now behind bars. He's wanted for questioning for multiple murders."

"Just for questioning? They can't hold him forever unless you have an airtight case against him," the lawyer in Cici said. "Please tell me that you have an airtight case."

"Yes and no," said Matthew.

"Well, which is it?" Cici demanded.

"There's not an airtight case against him for the three murders that we know about yet. They're working to tie him to those. But there's an attempted murder that he can be held for."

"Oh, good," she said. "That should do it."

Matthew was relieved when her inquiring mind didn't ask who the intended victim was.

After they'd finished with their conversation and exchanged all the sentiments of love and adoration, Matthew puttered back out into his living room. He decided it was bullhorn-grabbing time.

"Tell me something," he said to Danbury, who was just returning from hauling equipment out to his SUV.

"What's that, Doc?"

"How did you know to get here last night? Was I bait? Or did you just figure it out in time?"

"Not intentional bait. If that's what you're asking."

"Then how did you get here when you did, just in time?"

"You can thank Allman for that. We were going back through everything. She and I reviewed the whole case. All of the notes. All of the information. Start to finish. We were up half the night. Still at the Peak offices. Then I just mentioned your questions."

"Which questions?"

"About whether he knew. That you had the cat. That she wasn't at the Lingles'. And never had been."

"Oh, that."

"Allman jumped up. She said, 'He's going to find the cat!'"

"And we both knew. She said it would be exactly what he would do. Let us set a trap. Show off his superior skill. In knowing that it was a trap. And telling us he knew. Then go after the diamonds himself."

"So you came to catch him here."

"We reassembled the team. Got most of them out of bed. I grabbed gear. We made assignments in transit. There was no sign of him. When we got here. But Allman was sure. And so was I. We circled the house. The team was checking the woods. And the golf course. I came to the garage door. He'd closed it behind him. But it opened. It wasn't locked. And I knew it should be. So I told the team. But I didn't wait for them. I came straight in. And you saw the rest."

"Yeah, up close and personal, I saw it all," said Matthew with a shudder. He owed Danbury, then, and Hillary Allman, he thought. Relieved, he realized that he hadn't been set up as bait. They'd just gotten inside the mind of a killer and come to assist in time.

"Thanks, Danbury," said Matthew. "I owe you a few."

"I'm not sure for what. I should have seen it. And I did give you the cat."

"What do you mean? What should you have seen?"

"Earlier, when Kincaid told Wilson the cat was at the Lingles'.

Wilson told him to stand down. Wilson didn't let on that he knew. Not yet. But maybe he did. Maybe he already knew that Kincaid was in custody. He knew the Lingle house was a trap. It's logical he also knew the cat wasn't there. Maybe he knew she never had been. He must not have known about the diamonds. That we already had them. Not just the cat and the collar. Or maybe he suspected. But he had to try."

"That's logical. So what happens now?"

"Now we get him processed. And we question him. He hasn't asked for a lawyer. Probably thinks he's too smart. Smarter than any lawyer. Maybe we can get something out of him. If he doesn't lawyer up. That's the plan anyway. You coming?"

"For his questioning?"

Danbury nodded.

"Maybe," said Matthew. "I don't know how I feel about watching this process, honestly. I know that I'm going to church with my family first and out to lunch afterward. After that, maybe."

"OK, Doc. *Maybe* is good."

Matthew locked up behind Danbury and the officer, for what little good that did, he thought, and went to take a shower. Max had come out of hiding and was sitting on the shower sill, as he often did, when Matthew emerged in the steamy bathroom that he'd fogged up entirely with the long hot shower.

After he'd shaved, fed the cats, eaten, and gone through his usual morning routine, he chose the Corvette and set off to meet his family at the church he'd grown up in. That was a comfortable known, a safe place, a most welcome place after the events of the night before.

As he drove out of his neighborhood, he was happy not to see Mrs. Drewer out with Oscar. Not that he dreaded talking to her anymore because she'd transformed from a pushy busybody into an exceptionally helpful neighbor when she'd become his friend. There was no way, however, that she'd slept through the police presence the night and early morning before, and he didn't want to have to explain it all to her.

He wasn't finished processing it all in his own mind yet. The events of the night before and everything leading up to them were still very raw and confusing. It wasn't up for discussion yet.

He knew that he wanted to be in his church this morning. That much, he knew for certain. It's not that he ever thought he could meet with God solely at church, or even more fully at church than anywhere else. He knew better. He'd had a meeting with God in his own house at shortly after four this morning. For that, he was entirely thankful.

Maybe it was to thank God that he wanted to be at church this morning. Whatever the reason, he knew he had to be there, and lack of sleep was no reason not to be. As he pulled into his habitual parking spot beside his parents, he realized that he must be early because they were just getting out of their car. Usually, he met them inside because they were there first.

Jackie Paine was a master at reading her son, as she had always been. She worried a lot about her two children, but Matthew knew that she prayed more than she worried, so it worked out for their benefit. She took one look at him as he climbed out of the Corvette and walked quickly to him. As Joc Paine looked on in apparent confusion, Jackie flung her arms around Matthew, hugging him tightly, and said, "Sweetheart, what's wrong?"

40 ~ Coming to Terms

As he hugged his mother back tightly, he remembered the images of her and his father that had flitted through his mind in the predawn hours when he'd been standing in front of a killer who was pointing a gun at his chest. For a mere moment, the grown man melted into the small boy who ran to her after being stung by a bee or scraping elbows and knees in a tumble from his bike. Then, as now, he had felt safe, loved, and cared for in the arms of his mother. He was surprised by the childhood memories that flooded freshly to the forefront of his mind, as if they'd happened mere moments ago.

"I'm OK, Mom," said the grown version of Matthew as he pulled back, still holding her loosely, and looked down at her. "I had a rough night, but I'm OK."

"Rough how, son? Is there anything you need?" asked Joc Paine, who had retrieved their coats from the car, locked it, and joined them between the two vehicles.

"Thanks, Dad, but there isn't. I just got closer than I wanted to be in this investigation that I've been helping Danbury with. That's all."

"The murder investigation? Doesn't it involve more than one murder?" asked Joc.

"There are at least three that we think are related," said Matthew. "As of last night, we think the killer is in custody. But there's still a lot of unraveling to do to figure it all out and tie him to all three murders."

"I'm happy to hear there's a suspect in custody. I hope it's the right one," added Jackie, looking concerned.

"Me too, Mom. I believe it is. So things should calm down now, I hope."

"I hope so, too, son," she replied, looping her arm through his as they made their way across the distant parking lot toward the big new addition to the church building.

Matthew had no sooner made it in the door than he was ambushed by his precocious little niece, Angel. She was always excited to see him. It was heartwarming, he realized, to be so adored by a child.

"Uncle Matt! Uncle Matt! Guess what?" yelled Angel as she jumped for him to scoop her up.

"What?" he asked, lifting her into his arms.

"We're having sp'sgetti for lunch! It's my favorite!"

"We are? How do you know?"

"Because it's right here at church!"

"There's a fundraiser for the youth to go on a mission trip this summer," supplied Monica, reaching over to give her brother a hug, child and all.

"What's the youth?" Angel wanted to know.

"That's what they call the teenagers in the church, the youth group," answered Matthew, realizing for the first time that it seemed an odd thing to call them.

"Oh," said Angel. "Will you take me to my class?"

"Sure," said Matthew as he turned, still holding her, and headed down the hallway to the children's area to check her in. He wasn't sure exactly what that process was because Angel was usually already in the children's area when he got there. Normally, his job was picking her up afterward and going through their ritual game of hide-and-seek to find her. *How hard can it be?* he thought. He had this.

Joining the adults in their usual spot, Matthew settled in for the teaching from one of the pastors on staff. What he heard wasn't what he'd have wanted to hear had he been able to choose the topic. It was about not harboring anger and how those who harbored grudges and anger were affected far worse than the people they wouldn't forgive.

Matthew had to pause and think about the anger he harbored against some of the people he'd helped Danbury to find and put away. Rage had risen up in him like a tsunami, threatening to overwhelm him sometimes, when he had dealt with the worst of society that he'd encountered. It was why he'd stopped working with Danbury the previous summer. He didn't like who he became when he dealt with people who purposefully harmed others. His anger, he realized, made him not much better than the targets of that rage.

That was a tough pill to swallow, and he wasn't enjoying the process. It was a revelation that he wished he hadn't had. As if on cue, his watch showed an incoming text from Danbury. His phone was on silent, but his watch alerted him that Wilson would begin to be questioned around two that afternoon, which was as soon as Dr. Allman could get there, if Matthew wanted to be present. Some people did require sleep, thought Matthew as he tried not to yawn and to refocus his attention on the teaching.

On the one hand, he was pretty sure he didn't want to see the guy who had killed at least three innocent people, which likely would have become four last night had Danbury not shown up when he did. On the other hand, he wanted to see justice done. He wanted to face his demons. If he'd had a third hand, it would have had something to do with what he was hearing in the teaching that morning. Matthew wasn't entirely sure that he would be able to let go of that anger and rage, though. It sounded far too simple in theory and much more difficult in practice.

In her great wisdom, Jackie didn't press Matthew to talk about what was bothering him all through lunch. Instead, she hugged him tightly when they were leaving the church after lunch and just whispered, "I love you, and I'm praying for you."

"Thanks, Mom. I love you, too, and I appreciate it," he said, hugging her back. He said his goodbyes to his family, slid into the Corvette, and headed for the downtown Raleigh police department. He was going to come to terms with the object of his anger head-on, he'd decided, and be part of the process instead of running from it.

*****

Parking in the deck behind the police station, Matthew trudged down the sidewalk and into the building. He went through the usual process of obtaining a badge and was ushered to one of the observation rooms, which was already crowded. Assembled in the small room, he saw the technical guy on the audiovisual board in the corner, Detective Conover, both FBI agents and Danbury.

"Hey, Doc. We're waiting on Allman. We'll get started. When she gets here," said Danbury, shielding his eyes against the blaze of light from the hallway when Matthew entered the darkened room. As his eyes adjusted to the low lighting, Matthew slid onto the one remaining stool in the far corner of the small room. The room felt overly warm and stuffy as they waited. He stood to pull off his jacket, folding it over and placing it on the only surface available nearby, the stool he was sitting on. Sitting back down atop the stool, jacket and all, he thought a little padding on the hard wooden seat wasn't a bad thing.

The FBI agents were standing, jackets open, white shirts rumpled, looking annoyed with waiting. Detective Conover was talking quietly to Danbury about something to do with the pending charges against the perp. Through the window, Matthew could see the top of Wilson's head. His face was buried in his arms on the table in front of him. Could he possibly be sleeping at a time like this? He appeared to be.

The small room got quiet before the door opened once again and Hillary Allman stepped in. Her silhouette was backlit from the bright hallway lighting, which was momentarily blinding until the door closed behind her. With barely a nod in acknowledgment of the greetings she received, she pulled her coat off and flipped it over the only empty surface in the room, a small chair that was against the back wall. She slid between the FBI agents and Detective Conover to lean into the glass and peer through at the slumped figure in front of her.

"Have you talked to him?" she asked Danbury.

"Not yet. I was waiting for you."

"I'm here now," she said nonchalantly, stating the obvious.

Matthew could almost feel the agitation from Danbury, though he said nothing as he rose and vacated the stool beside Matthew, motioning for her take it. Quickly opening and closing the door behind him, Danbury slipped from the room. It was several minutes before anything happened in the interrogation room. Then the lights came up and the door opened, as if a stage in a theater had just been set for the next scene.

All eyes were on the room, and Allman leaned forward in concentrated anticipation.

"Where am I? And why am I here?" the guy seated at the table asked quietly as he looked up and leaned back in his seat when Danbury entered. There was no rancor, no animosity, just simple questions. The bitter snarl Matthew had witnessed on this same face in the wee hours of the morning was completely absent.

"You're at the police department. In downtown Raleigh. You're here for questioning. Regarding three murders. One attempted murder. And breaking and entering. I'm homicide detective Warren Danbury, Mr. Wilson," Danbury told him.

"But I didn't do any of that," the guy said.

The tension and confusion that permeated the observation room were palpable as they all held their collective breath. Allman was transfixed on the next room, as if evaluating every nuance, every expression, every change in intonation, every minute detail.

"We picked you up at the scene," said Danbury. "After breaking and entering. Holding the homeowner at gunpoint."

"But I didn't. I wouldn't. That can't have been me. I have no memory of it." The guy looked back at Danbury in apparent confusion and concern.

Dr. Allman might bore holes in the thick glass of the two-way mirror as this conversation unfolds, Matthew thought, with the intensity of her stare. Having glanced over at her, he returned to watching intently too. The guy sitting placidly behind the table on the other side of the glass didn't look like the demon he'd encountered the night before, invading his home and threatening him at gunpoint. It was as if the guy had morphed, somehow, into another person entirely.

"Mr. Wilson, you were there," replied Danbury. "You broke into a home. You were holding a gun on the owner. Just confess. This will all be much easier."

"You must have made a mistake. I would never do something like that. I wasn't there. I have no recollection of any of this."

"No? Where were you last night?" asked Danbury authoritatively.

"I was at home in bed by about eleven or so," the guy answered.

"And this morning? How did you come to be here?" Danbury persisted.

"I don't know." The guy looked genuinely dazed. "I woke up here. And I don't know how I got here or why I'm here. I was hoping you could tell me."

Taking a deep breath, Danbury tried another tack. "Do you know Misty Blue?"

"Well, yes. She was my girlfriend. I wanted to marry her. But she turned me down, flat."

"How did you handle that?"

"Excuse me?"

"Were you angry?"

"I was sad. I really wanted her to come home with me for the holidays and meet my family. I really wanted her to marry me. I thought we had something special."

"Your family? In Oregon?" Danbury asked, checking the records he had in front of him.

"Yeah, that's right. I'm originally from Oregon. Most of my family is still there."

"But your parents aren't, are they?"

"No." The guy looked down at his hands and wouldn't respond to any further questions about them.

"You weren't angry with Misty? You didn't kill her?" asked Danbury, shifting back to the current murders.

"What?" Wilson asked, recoiling visibly. "No, of course not. I tried to talk her out of breaking it off with me, but I'd never have hurt her. I wanted to marry her, protect her, spend the rest of my life making her happy. Or trying my best to."

"You had nothing to do with it? Killing her?"

"No, absolutely not."

"And you know nothing about it?"

"I don't."

"Tell me what you know!" demanded Danbury, and Matthew watched Wilson draw back, as if fearfully.

"But I don't know anything," Wilson protested, spreading his hands helplessly.

Matthew saw Danbury glance over his shoulder at them, he assumed at Allman, behind the glass.

"OK, Mr. Wilson, let's talk about Trent Kent. Did you kill him?"

"Who?"

"Trent Kent. The guy Misty started dating. After she broke it off with you."

"Oh," said Wilson sadly. "I didn't know she was dating anybody else. I haven't dated anyone since we broke up. I didn't know she was."

"How about Mick Nichols?"

"Who?" Wilson repeated.

"He drove a specialized freezer truck. For a meat packaging and shipping company. He was murdered. And buried. Or maybe buried alive. We're not sure yet."

Wilson visibly cringed. "That's horrible. Where would I know him from? Why would I know him?"

"Because you murdered him," said Danbury.

"Officer," the guy began.

"Detective," Danbury corrected.

"Detective, I haven't murdered anyone. Or harmed anyone. And I don't know these two men you're asking me about. I've never heard of them."

"This is getting us nowhere," said Danbury as he rose from his chair, taking the tablet with him. "I'll be back later. If you don't want to talk now."

"But we are talking," protested Adam Wilson. "I'm answering your questions the best I know how."

"Give me a minute," said Danbury as he slipped from the

interrogation room and returned to the observation room.

"Allman, any ideas here?" Danbury asked without preamble as the door closed behind him with a decisive click. "This is not the same guy. Not the one we picked up last night. We could put him on a lie detector. I think he'd pass. I think he believes it. Everything he's telling me."

"That's ridiculous!" said one of the FBI agents angrily. "This guy's playing you! You're not pushing him nearly hard enough!"

"You know," said Allman to Danbury. "He's right. I have a theory. You might not believe it. And you definitely won't like it. Can Agent Shedrick here go in?"

"Yeah," said Danbury. "He can. Tell me."

"Not yet," she said. "I'm not sure I'm right. But Shedrick pushing him. And pushing hard. That might be the right trigger if I am."

41 ~ Pulling Threads

"Who are you?" Wilson asked curiously, though not at all aggressively, as the agent entered the interrogation room.

"I'm Special Agent Shedrick, with the Federal Bureau of Investigation," he answered, producing and flipping open a badge.

"Why does the FBI want to talk to me?" asked Wilson calmly.

"Come off it, Wilson! This innocent act of yours isn't convincing anybody!"

"What act?"

"Like you don't know anything about these murders! You've killed at least three people."

"I haven't," replied Wilson, looking entirely sincere.

"You were arrested this morning while holding a gun on a man whose home you'd broken into! He's here. He can testify as to exactly what happened. And he will. There are at least three others you've murdered!" the agent exploded at him, slamming the palm of his hand loudly down on the table. The noise sounded like a clap of thunder directly overhead, reverberating through the observation booth.

Wilson jumped, and then he leaned forward, studying the FBI agent closely, as if scrutinizing everything about him. His expression was changing from the benign look of innocence into more of a scowl.

"Adam Wilson," said the agent. "Why did you kill Misty Blue?"

"Don't call me that!" Wilson yelled at the agent.

"Call you what? Your name?"

"That is not my name," the guy said, evenly but between clenched teeth, the sneer deepening around his mouth, his facial features hardening.

"You're Adam Wilson."

"I am *not* Adam Wilson!" the guy responded vehemently.

"OK," said the agent. Then he asked patronizingly, "What's your name, then?"

"My name is Charlie Katz, you imbecile," the guy snarled at him.

"Why did you kill Misty Blue?" the agent repeated more quietly.

Wilson stared at him menacingly from his side of the table. "Misty wasn't cooperative."

"What wouldn't she cooperate with, Mr. Wilson?"

"Stop calling me that!" the guy yelled. "I am Charlie Katz! And it doesn't go well for anyone who calls me anything else!"

"Are you threatening me?" asked the agent, more calmly than he'd said anything else so far. "Why did you kill Misty Blue?" he asked again, without calling the guy by name.

"I never said that I did. I just said she wasn't cooperative."

"You knew Misty Blue," the agent stated as an established fact, not a question. When Katz was silent, he continued, "In what way would she not cooperate with you?"

"In every way."

"Give me an example."

"I'm giving you nothing!" spat back Katz, and the room grew quiet.

Sometimes silence worked in an interrogation or interview, Matthew knew. He was betting it wouldn't this time. If this guy was as intelligent as Allman asserted, then he wouldn't be at all intimidated or uncomfortable with silence, and he'd feel no need to fill it. This guy was either truly brilliant, or there was a much deeper issue here—and likely both. With his feet on the rungs of the tall stool, Matthew couldn't tap his foot in concentration, but his knee bounced as he thought through what this could mean.

Allman was leaning so far into the glass of the two-way mirror that her nose was nearly touching it. "I should have seen it," she said slowly and quietly. "I can't believe I missed it."

"Missed what?" asked Danbury.

"Don't say it!" said Matthew. "If you're about to say what I think you are, it might have legal ramifications. It could make a huge difference in how this guy gets processed, whether he goes to the prison cell that he deserves or ends up in a psych unit! If he's as intelligent as you've said, it might all be a ruse anyway, a smoke screen."

"DID?" she all but whispered to Matthew.

"Yeah, that's the thing we're not saying out loud yet." He nodded his agreement.

"What's DID?" Danbury wanted to know.

"You would probably know it by another name," said Matthew. Then, he said softly, "Multiple personality disorder, or maybe split personality. It's now called dissociative identify disorder, or DID."

"Exactly," said Allman.

"Huh," was all that Danbury said as he scratched the stubble on his chin with his thumb.

Matthew added, "We need to check the legal ramifications of this assessment. He might be faking it to try to get assigned to a mental health unit, from which he could later be released. Instead of a prison, serving life without parole. You said he was smart, on the genius scale," he added to Dr. Allman, trying to drive home his point.

"I did," she agreed. "And you might be right. OK, we're not labeling. At least not yet."

As they turned their attention back to the interrogation room, there seemed to be a stare-down in progress. They could see only the back of the FBI agent who was seated across from the accused. Neither spoke, and Katz, the guy who didn't want to be called Wilson, was staring evenly and without blinking at the agent.

Finally, the silent standoff was broken by Shedrick. "Why don't you tell me about murdering Misty Blue."

"Because I don't have to tell you anything," the guy replied, smiling with a demonic glint in his eye that Matthew found entirely unsettling.

"What about Trent Kent, then?"

"What about him?"

"What can you tell me about him?"

"Didn't you tell that little weasel Adam Wilson that Trent Kent was the guy Misty started dating after they broke up?"

"No, I told you that," said Agent Shedrick.

"You told me nothing!" the guy roared back.

Allman and Matthew looked at each other. "Interesting. He's aware of Adam Wilson," was all Allman said, and Matthew nodded because he'd been intrigued by that very thing.

"How about Mick Nichols?" Agent Shedrick asked.

"Who's that?" Katz shot back.

"The guy who drove the freezer truck for the meat packaging company."

The information was met by Wilson, or Katz, or whoever the guy was with a sneer. It was a mixture of a smile and something far more menacing. It looked evil. Matthew envisioned him twirling a black mustache like the antagonist from an old black-and-white film. He was just hoping for the "Curses, foiled again" line to follow, but it didn't seem imminent.

"You know who that is, right? The guy you killed. Likely to get the truck to freeze Misty's body in—and maybe Kent's too."

"You have a very active imagination," Katz replied smugly. The guy wasn't giving up anything. He had nothing to lose by clamming up, from what Matthew could tell. He seemed willing and able to play their game all day long.

Dr. Allman, apparently, thought something similar as she spoke up and said, "Here's how to play this. Exhaust him. Make him angry. Repeatedly. Then leave the room. We need Wilson back. That transition happened after he napped, right? Maybe that's the trigger. If this is not an act. Or even if it is. He'll be consistent."

"Huh," said Danbury. "I want a go first. At this version of him. Watch him closely, will you?" he asked Allman as he left the room. She nodded her agreement.

As if she'd been doing anything else so far, Matthew thought. He knew from past experience that Danbury played "bad cop" very well and could break most people. Of course, he also knew that they weren't dealing with "most people" with this guy, whatever name he chose to call himself.

Agent Shedrick reluctantly switched places with Danbury, and Allman explained the new plan to the agent when he returned to the observation room. Shedrick grunted in response but said nothing further.

"Ah, the detective with the hot girlfriend," Katz taunted as Danbury walked in and before he'd introduced himself, if that was even necessary. Matthew wasn't sure about that, but he was sure that goading Danbury about Penn was the one thing that might get a severe reaction. Apparently, Katz thought so too.

Instead, Danbury ignored the comment, merely flipping his badge open and identifying himself, "Homicide detective Warren Danbury."

"Warren. Nice name. It's not as nice as Penelope," Katz said, drawing out each syllable in a way that sounded calculated, like something out of a horror B-movie. After a pause while he seemed to be gauging Danbury's reaction, Katz continued, "But you don't call her that, do you? You call her Penn. She has the most strikingly beautiful blue eyes that I've ever seen. Well, almost ever seen. But that's not all, is it? She's tremendously hot. I'm sorry we didn't have the chance to get better acquainted." He looked lasciviously but evenly across the table at Danbury.

Matthew wasn't sure how Danbury was keeping it in check at that moment. If Katz had said similar things about Cici, he wasn't sure he could have managed not to deck the guy.

"You must have finished searching my residence by now," Katz continued, taunting Danbury, smirking at him as he settled at the table. "And you found nothing incriminating. How frustrating that must be for you."

Danbury seemed to be waiting him out patiently, to see if he'd say something convicting, anything that he could use against him. It was as if the guy knew that. Katz was tap dancing just at the edge of incrimination, but he seemed to know precisely where that line lay. Because he was incredibly smart, as Allman had reinforced repeatedly, he liked to play games.

"Did you search his house?" Matthew asked Detective Conover.

"We did. They did too." He indicated the FBI agents. "But with very different goals."

"And you found nothing? Nothing to tie him to the murders? Or the diamonds?" Tracing the trail of the diamonds, not finding a murderer, was the predominant goal of the FBI. Though Agent Shedrick had begun questioning him about the murders, Matthew knew it was information about the diamonds that they were seeking. The agent must have been frustrated switching places with Danbury before he'd gotten to question Katz about them.

"Nothing at all," answered Conover as the two agents just shook their heads. "Not even a gaming system to tie him to hiring Kincaid. But their guys are still tearing the place apart," he added, motioning to the FBI agents again.

"Huh," said Matthew.

"What?" asked Allman.

"Is that the house of Katz or Wilson? I bet they're different," said Matthew.

"Wilson's house," answered Detective Conover.

"We haven't found a listing for Charlie Katz yet," the tech guy said without turning around from the audiovisual boards. "But our team is on it. As soon as the guy gave that name, they started digging."

"I'd place my bet that you're right," said Conover. "Katz must have a separate residence from Wilson."

"Very likely so," said Allman without turning away from the glass. "They'd want very different things. Different décor and surroundings. Just as a starting point."

Danbury, on the other side of the glass, began poking the bear.

"How about some pictures? If names don't mean much," said

Danbury, as he tapped on his tablet and then flipped it for Katz to see.

"Who's that?" Katz asked nonchalantly, as if he really couldn't care less.

"That's Mick Nichols," answered Danbury. "Or it's what's left of him. After having been buried. For nearly two weeks. What do you know about him? Or how he got buried?"

Danbury must have shown the guy the picture of Nichols from the morgue, though Katz didn't flinch. Instead, he eyed Danbury carefully, as if sizing up his opponent. "What if I did? It's not like I'd tell you," he said sneering. "But it just so happens that I don't know him. Alive or dead, it doesn't matter much to me."

Danbury flipped the tablet back around, tapped it again, then turned it back to Katz. "What about this guy?"

"He looks more alive than the last one," responded Katz flippantly.

"He was. In this picture. Do you know him? Trent Kent?"

"Name doesn't ring any bells," said Katz. "But then, why should it? I don't know the guy, and again, alive or dead makes no difference to me."

Danbury was apparently giving the suspect one of his stares. Katz was glaring back, calmly but defiantly.

"We got a hit," said the tech guy, breaking the silence in the observation room. "On Charlie Katz. Charles Katz, actually. It's not much, just an online account, a login with that name associated. We'll keep searching for records, digging deeper to find the user of the account. And to see if we can tie it to HavocWreaker13."

After what seemed like an eternity later, Danbury was winding down his questioning, which had yielded no new information. He told Katz he'd see him later.

"Yeah, good luck with that," said Katz with a curt nod, looking bored by the whole process.

FBI Special Agent Shedrick returned to the interrogation room with the sole intention of wearing Katz down, though he wasn't missing another opportunity to ask about the diamonds. The diamonds seemed to pique the suspect's interest momentarily, and then Katz went back to looking bored. After an hour of questions and banal or snide answers or angry refusals to answer questions, they all left him alone.

"Hey, Doc," said Danbury, rising from the stool and looking around the room. "You up for an early dinner?"

"Sure," said Matthew. "How quick? We can go to Derrick's restaurant if we have time. It's not that far away. But that's a sit-down meal, not takeout."

"That's the guy you grew up with? The one who owns the pub and brewery?"

"Yeah, it's called Sonny's Place."

"I remember it. Good food. Let's go. Allman, you want to join?"

"Sure. We won't get anything more. Not until we get Wilson back."

They piled in Danbury's SUV for the short trek to Sonny's Place. Derrick wasn't there that Sunday evening, the waiter told Matthew, but the guy assured him that they'd take great care of him. Not that he'd been worried about that.

After placing their orders, Matthew looked around to be sure they were out of earshot of the other patrons before he asked, "Danbury, where is Kincaid? Is he still at the North Raleigh Police Department office?"

"Yeah, he's been charged. With several offenses. He's being held. Awaiting a bail hearing. Probably in the morning. Charlene could bail him out. If the judge sets a low enough bond. So he might be back on the street. It's likely. He's not a flight risk. The judge could decide he's not a danger to the community."

"Huh," was all Matthew said to that. Then, turning to Allman, he asked quietly, "It's interesting that Katz is aware of Wilson, isn't it?"

"I thought the same," said Allman. "It's one reason I want Wilson back. He might give us something. If he's aware of Katz. Unless this really is one big scam."

"That's what I was thinking too," said Matthew, with one eyebrow raised. "If it's not a scam, and if Wilson is as aware of Katz as Katz is of Wilson, maybe Wilson will tell us something useful about Katz. If Wilson 'confesses' that Katz is guilty, does that hold up as a confession?"

"Great question, Doc," said Danbury. "It does in my book."

"Legally, I guess we need to know the answer to that question, though. I'm not an expert on the disorder or any legal ramifications," Matthew said, turning to Dr. Allman.

"I can tell you about the disorder," she replied. "But not much about the legality. This disorder has been studied for many years. Findings show that the personalities are distinct."

Danbury held up a hand while the server came and brought them steaming freshly baked bread, butter, and their drinks.

"OK, what were you saying?" he asked.

"That the personalities of DID patients are distinctly different. As if there really are multiple people in one body. Their handwriting can differ. They perform differently on IQ tests. Definitely on personality tests. The patients' perception of their personalities can differ in age. They can even differ in race and gender identity."

"So you're telling me," began Danbury, "that a fifty-year-old woman, let's say. She could share a body. Maybe with a twenty-year-old man? In one of these DID patients. How is that possible?"

"They could, absolutely," affirmed Allman. "It's the patient's perception of individual personalities, remember. Their age, gender, and race. Not a physical reality. The patient could fully believe themselves to be a fifty-year-old Asian woman one minute. And a twenty-year-old Black man the next. Research has proven that. Only the name of the disorder is new. The disorder has been studied for hundreds of years. The separate personalities are not always aware of each other. In many cases, they're not. That's why Dr. Paine and I were so enthralled with this case. We didn't ask Charlie Katz about his age. He is definitely male."

"I have contacts within the legal profession," said Matthew, checking his watch and realizing that it was nearly six in the evening and too late to call Cici, who was five hours ahead in London. He did, however, have the number for one of her colleagues whom he'd helped the month before. The guy was still recovering from some serious injuries he'd sustained in a car accident that was meant to injure or kill

Matthew, but the last report Matthew had heard was that he was improving well.

"I can call one of Cici's colleagues from her law firm and see what he can tell us."

"Good plan, Doc," said Danbury.

"Should I take this outside?" asked Matthew.

Looking around, Danbury said, "No. Just switch places. You can see anyone coming."

Matthew was shocked by this solution to the problem. They were in the rear right of the restaurant, Danbury's favorite place. Danbury was seated in the back corner of the booth facing out so that he could see everything happening around him, also his favorite place, which he was about to willingly give up.

"OK," said Matthew, tapping his phone to make the call while standing to switch places.

"Hi, Kennedy, this is Matthew Paine. How are you? Still healing well, I hope?" Danbury was watching impatiently, but Matthew was not inclined to rush this conversation.

Hearing that all was going well in the recuperation process, Matthew launched into the discussion that he'd called to have. "Hey, I could use some legal advice. It's too late to call Cici in London, so I was hoping maybe you could answer a couple of questions for me."

"Did you get into trouble again?" Kennedy Reynolds joked.

"No, nothing like that." Matthew chuckled, happy to hear that the guy had found his sense of humor. "It's a case I'm working on with Danbury involving a suspect with DID—that's dissociative identity disorder."

"Ah. That's a tough one. There have been more and more cases over the years in which defendants claimed to have multiple personalities, some male, female, bisexual, or gender-fluid. There have been various ages and educational levels, sometimes differences in the ethnicity of the personalities as well. That's hard to prove, though, expert testimony helps and is taken into consideration. It makes for a media circus, too, so be prepared."

"An expert assessment, we have. Or at least we're in the process of assessing," Matthew amended, eyebrow raised and foot tapping under the table as he looked over at Dr. Allman. "But what happens when the personalities are aware of each other? Can one testify against the other? Does that hold up in court? Is there a chance of the person being declared incompetent to stand trial and moved to a psych ward instead of a prison?"

"There's no precedent for the psychiatric ward over the prison. There's not a great deal of consensus within the legal community and court system about holding DID patients responsible for their actions. I can tell you that the courts usually deny insanity claims for these patients, though. They're usually deemed competent to stand trial."

"If a psychiatrist labels a suspect as having the disorder, that doesn't jeopardize the chance of going to trial? Or of the outcome?"

"Not that I've seen, no. Unless the person is diagnosed with additional disorders that prevent them from being deemed competent."

"None that we know of," replied Matthew.

"I assume you want the defendant to stand trial and answer for the crimes?"

"Exactly," said Matthew.

"Then you should be OK with the diagnosis. Just a word of caution, though. There are cases where people have made such claims in an attempt to befuddle the legal realm. It probably doesn't make a difference if they have the disorder or not, but it has been used to attempt to escape harsh sentencing. That's just something to keep in mind. I would guess that the disorder is difficult to definitively diagnose, one way or the other."

"Thanks. That's a huge help."

"You're most welcome. Let me know if you need assistance with this when you get ready to try it. And if you don't need my help, let me know when it comes to trial anyway. I'd be interested in following this case."

"I'll let you know. Thanks," said Matthew, and they said their goodbyes.

Matthew relayed the information to Danbury, who immediately

stood to switch places again, and Dr. Allman, who just screwed up her face in contemplation.

"We need a lighter touch," said Allman after a moment. "With Wilson. If he's willing to cooperate. And if he's aware of Katz. We need an understanding person. Who can draw him out."

"Are you volunteering?" asked Danbury. "It'll be tricky. If you are. There's a fine line you have to walk."

"I know. To make it admissible in court. It can't be coerced."

"Right," said Danbury. "Are you up for it?"

"I suppose so. Or maybe my colleague here can help," she said slowly, including Matthew in her glance.

"I'll help if I can," answered Matthew. "I'm not sure that I have anything to offer, though. I'm neither a psychiatrist nor a lawyer. Nor trained in law enforcement, for that matter."

"You read people. Connect with them. Meet them where they are. Not where you think they should be," said Danbury in a moment of what Matthew could only call clarity.

"Just tell me what you want me to do," said Matthew.

"Maybe nothing," said Danbury. "We'll see how Dr. Allman does with him. Wilson doesn't seem to have a problem with women."

"Let's hold off. At least at first. On introducing him to Matthew," said Allman haltingly, as if reasoning her way through it all aloud. "That might trigger Katz. If Wilson recognizes Matthew from last night. At some point, we might want Katz or recognition of Dr. Paine. But not at first. First, I'll see what I can get out of Wilson. And evaluate him at the same time."

"Sounds like a plan," said Danbury.

"OK, I'll be on standby. You know I'll help if I can, but I don't want to make anything worse. It's like we've been pulling threads this whole time," said Matthew in frustration. "And it just keeps getting more complex. We either find more threads like Priestly, Kent, Nichols, Kincaid, and finally Wilson, or entire knots like Wilson and Katz. If you count them separately."

"Oh, I do," answered Allman pensively. "I definitely do. And we're not finished pulling those threads. We'll unravel him yet. I'm sure of it."

Matthew sincerely wished he were as confident of that.

42 ~ Knot Unraveling

After a steak and baked potato dinner that, as Dr. Allman had said, melted in their mouths, Danbury, Allman, and Matthew returned to the police station. From the observation booth, they saw that the FBI agent had done his job and worn Katz out. The guy's head was, again, on his arms on the table in the dimly lit room, and he appeared to be sleeping.

Absent from the observation room were both FBI agents and Detective Conover. Aside from the guy at the audiovisual controls, they had the room to themselves. It was a bit cooler and far less stuffy as a result. Matthew felt like he could breathe, and the oppressive atmosphere from earlier had cleared.

"We don't want to startle him awake," said Allman as she studied the interrogation room through the mirrored window. "Or we might end up with Katz back again. How long has he been asleep?"

"A little over an hour, best guess," said the tech guy over his shoulder.

Checking her watch, Allman said, "OK, let's give him another fifteen minutes. Then start to bring the lighting up. Slowly. We want him to wake naturally. We don't want to startle him."

They talked strategy in those fifteen minutes, Danbury prompting Allman for specific information. They needed Wilson to provide a detail about the murders that only the murderer would know. They hadn't, for example, made known the information about the body in the trunk of Misty's car when it exploded to anyone except Kincaid. He'd been in custody at the time, and every conversation he'd had since had been monitored.

Neither had they let slip that there had been a black diamond in Misty's back molar. Those were details that Allman needed to try to get Wilson to offer up. Admitting something simpler, like his gaming name being HavocWreaker13, could also be helpful.

As the lighting came up in the interrogation room, Danbury fitted Allman with an earwig listening device so that he could prompt her from the observation room.

"I'm really not wild about this," she said, accepting the device reluctantly and placing it in her ear as instructed. "I don't want you in my ear. So don't be constantly. Only if you need something very specific."

"Agreed," said Danbury. "It'll be muted to this room. Unless I need you to press a point. Or ask for a specific detail. You've been read in. On all of the details. The information withheld. That only the killer would know. I trust your judgment."

"Good to know," she said in a tone that surprised Matthew when she didn't roll her eyes as she said it.

As she slipped out of the observation booth, Matthew saw her pull her shoulders back and take a deep breath before the door into the brightly lit hallway clicked closed behind her. Maybe even renowned psychiatrists needed a moment to steel their nerves sometimes.

When the door opened into the next room, Allman was smiling pleasantly down at the man who was slowly waking, shifting his weight around in his chair. As she took the chair opposite him with her back to the glass, he finally looked up and around the room. His expression appeared dazed and disoriented, as if he was trying to figure out where he was all over again. Matthew took that as a good sign, one that perhaps meant Wilson was back. Unless there were others lurking within that they hadn't encountered yet.

"Good evening," said Allman pleasantly and introduced herself, minus her title.

"Where am I?"

"You're at the downtown Raleigh police precinct."

"Why am I here?"

"Because we hope you can help us. With an investigation we're working on."

"I was here before, wasn't I?" he asked.

"I believe you were, yes," she responded pleasantly.

"And they accused me of crimes."

"I'm not here to accuse you of anything," said Allman. "In fact, I need your help."

"You want my help?" he said, sitting up straighter in his chair.

"I do. First, would you please state your name? Just for the record. This conversation is, of course, being recorded."

"Sure," the guy said, and Matthew leaned forward. This was the first obstacle. Obviously, they weren't talking to Katz, but there might be others. He was relieved when he heard the guy say, "I'm Adam Wilson."

"Mr. Wilson, we're investigating the death of Misty Blue. You dated her back in November of last year, correct?"

"Yes, I did. I really loved Misty. I thought we had a future together. But she broke it off abruptly. I have never known why, exactly. And then I heard that she had died."

"How did you hear that?"

"It was on the news. Then I went by the club where Misty worked to see if it was true. I just couldn't believe it. I was glad that awful man wasn't there, but I found Charlene O'Connell."

"What awful man?"

While Wilson hesitated in the interrogation room, the two FBI agents slipped quietly back into the observation room. The hall lights blazed and then subsided around them as the door opened and closed noiselessly. Matthew was waiting for the guy to say Preston Priestley or Jonas Kincaid—or maybe even Charlie Katz if he was aware of him. What he did hear surprised him, his eyebrow rising and his knee bouncing as he perched on a stool in front of the mirrored window.

"Phillip O'Connell," Wilson answered clearly.

"Oh," she answered. "What did Charlene O'Connell tell you?"

"Not much. Just that it was true that Misty had been killed."

"I'm sorry for your loss," said Allman softly. Then she asked, "Mr. Wilson, do you know a man named Charles or Charlie Katz?"

Wilson leaned back in his chair as everyone else in the observation booth leaned forward. Wilson's face clouded over, and he didn't answer immediately. Allman waited patiently for a response.

"I don't really know him," Wilson finally said. "But I know of him."

Interesting, Matthew thought, blowing out the breath he hadn't realized that he'd been holding in anticipation of that answer. Both of the personalities who were living within this one person knew about each other. Maybe Wilson could tell them something useful, as they'd hoped. If he did, that pointed to the legitimacy of the disorder. If it were a scam, the guy was too smart to testify against himself.

"What can you tell me about him?" Allman asked quietly.

"He's worse than O'Connell. Much worse. I don't want to talk about him."

"Why not?"

"He's beyond scary. He's evil," responded Wilson with a shudder.

"I wouldn't ask you to talk about him. But it's important, Mr. Wilson. It's very important. I need to know all you can tell me about him. Please, will you help me?" Allman asked sweetly and quietly.

"OK." He hesitated. "I'll try."

Danbury pressed a button and said softly to Allman, "Ask for something easy. Something nonthreatening. Ask about HavocWreaker13."

"Is Katz a gamer?"

"A gamer?"

"You know, on online gaming systems."

"Oh. I think so. I'm not, so I'm not positive."

"Did you ever hear him mention a handle? An online gaming name?"

"Maybe," said Wilson, scrunching his face in concentration.

"If you heard it, would you recognize it?"

"Yeah, if he said it and I heard it again, I would."

"Was it HavocWreaker13?"

"Yeah," he said slowly and paused. "I do remember now. That's it. He uses that to game. He brags about how good he is at this game he plays."

"What game? Do you know?"

"Something about Duty."

"*Directive of Duty*," Danbury said into Allman's ear. "They call it DOD."

When she repeated that information, Wilson nodded and said, "Yeah, that's it."

"Now you can dive in," said Danbury into Allman's ear.

"Mr. Wilson, did he know Misty? Had he ever met her?"

"You can call me Adam."

"OK, Adam, did Charlie Katz know Misty Blue?"

"He met her once, at least once," said Wilson, leaning forward earnestly, as if he was sharing a great tragedy. "Whatever it was that he said to her is what made her break up with me. I don't know why he interfered. I loved her, and he doesn't even know me. He wouldn't want to know me. We're nothing alike."

That was an interesting assertion, Matthew thought, and Allman must have agreed as she leaned forward and asked softly, "What else can you tell me about him? We really need to know. Has he done anything illegal?"

"Plenty," said Wilson. "I'm sure I don't know the half of it. But he's done plenty of illegal things."

"Such as?" she asked.

"He's a swindler, a drug runner, a merchant of illegal goods, and a money launderer. He has some dangerous friends. I would advise you not to go near him. People who have gotten too close to him have disappeared. I'm not saying he killed them, but they never came back."

"Did Misty get too close to him?"

"You think he killed her?"

"Maybe," she said noncommittally. "Do you think so?"

Sliding back in his chair, the guy didn't respond immediately. Matthew could feel the tension in the room like electricity sparking all around him. Both the interrogation and the observation rooms were completely quiet.

"Yes," Wilson finally said softly. "I think he might have."

"Why would he do that? And how?"

"He said she disappointed him. I think he lured her into doing something illegal. I'm sure she didn't know about it. She wouldn't have agreed to do it. Misty was a good person. But I think she found out. And maybe that's why he killed her."

"What illegal thing did she find out about?" Allman prompted.

Wilson started to twitch in his seat, and Matthew was afraid that the reappearance of Katz was imminent. Allman must have had a similar thought because she said, soothingly, "It's OK. Just take your time. If this is painful for you to talk about, that's OK. You're safe here."

Wilson stopped twitching, and Allman reiterated, "You're safe. It's OK. Just breathe. Take a deep breath."

The effect was similar to soothing a dog that had gotten its hackles up. Wilson appeared to calm as he took a deep breath, like he'd been instructed to do.

"That's it," coaxed Allman. "Take another deep breath and relax. It's safe for you to tell me what you know. Misty would want you to tell me."

"She would," Wilson agreed. "She didn't deserve this. Not any of it. She was such a good person. She could have been a great person. She was so talented."

"I've heard that she was. It's no wonder you loved her. And why her death upset you. I understand."

Looking up, Wilson said suddenly, "You know, he's used at least half of them."

"Half of what?"

"Not what, who. The women at that club."

"The club where Misty worked?" asked Allman.

Wilson nodded, and Allman had the wherewithal to summarize the gesture that wouldn't be picked up on the audio recording. "Katz used the women at the Silver Silhouette where Misty worked?"

"Oh yeah, he's a user."

"For what, exactly? What does he use them to do?"

"He didn't use them directly. He used that awful man to manage them. But he selected the women, from a distance."

"What awful man?"

"O'Connell."

"Phillip O'Connell?"

Again, Wilson nodded. "O'Connell got the women to carry drugs and"—he paused uncertainly—"and other things."

"They're carrying drugs for Katz through O'Connell? Do they know they're carrying the drugs?"

"Most do. They get a cut."

Danbury leaned forward in the seat, pushing a button on the cord that dangled from his earpiece. "Ask him which ones. Ask him if Ruby is one of them."

"Is Ruby one of the women who has carried drugs for them?"

"Oh yeah, Ruby is a regular. She's hooked herself. Getting her to transport them was easy once Katz authorized O'Connell to offer her a small cut of the drugs."

"We'll notify the DEA," muttered one of the FBI agents. "But this isn't all that useful to us."

Danbury held a hand up to silence him.

"What else do these women transport?"

"Other illegal goods," said Wilson elusively.

"Do they know they're transporting them?"

"Not always. Misty didn't."

"What was she transporting that she didn't know about?"

"I think she did know, though. I mean, I think she found out. And that's why he killed her. Because she was going to turn them in."

"Turn who in? Katz and O'Connell?"

"Not who, what. She was going to turn over the goods she found to the authorities. I think he tried to stop her, but she refused. I think that's why he killed her."

"What did she find?" asked Allman.

The room was silent again as they held their collective breath, awaiting the answer.

"Diamonds," Wilson finally said. "Misty was carrying black diamonds."

"Now we're getting somewhere," muttered Agent Shedrick. "That's it. Tell us all about it," he encouraged from behind the glass, as if he were talking to Wilson himself.

"How was she transporting them? And how did she find out?"

"They were between the layers of her cat's collar. I don't know how she found them. Maybe they were lumpy and she felt them."

Matthew could attest to that. They were indeed lumpy between the layers of the collar. He was chagrined that he'd dismissed them. The back side of the collar was fluffy, and he'd thought the lumps were attachment mechanisms for the little glass studs on the outside of the top layer of the collar. Then again, he didn't know what he was looking for when he first examined the collar. He'd been looking for a note or writing or something, not black diamonds.

"Did Katz leave a diamond on Misty's body?"

"On her body? I don't think so. Where on her body?"

Changing her focus, Allman prodded, "Where did the diamonds come from?"

"Katz got them. Regularly."

"Where did he get them from?"

"I don't know."

"What did he do with them?"

"Gave them to O'Connell."

"Katz regularly gave O'Connell diamonds?"

Wilson nodded his head, the movement sharp and quick.

Allman summarized, "You're confirming that Charlie Katz gave Phillip O'Connell diamonds. For what purpose?"

"Transport," said Wilson.

Matthew had noticed that his answers were getting shorter and his speech more clipped. He leaned forward, watching Wilson's face as Allman asked him, "And Misty was transporting them in the cat's collar? To help Katz get them to O'Connell to be transported for sale?"

"Yes," said Wilson, his face clouding over darkly.

"Where did she get the cat's collar?" asked Allman.

This time, the jerking and twitching came on far too suddenly for Allman to be able to soothe him.

"From me! I gave it to her!" he bellowed and stood so abruptly that he knocked over the chair behind him, and it crashed to the floor.

As Matthew was still processing what was happening in the next room, Danbury bolted from the observation room so suddenly that he knocked over the stool he'd been perched on in the process. Danbury was pulling Allman from the interrogation room and closing the door squarely behind him just as the chair that Wilson had been sitting in was thrown at it in a rage with a great crashing force by Katz.

Hillary Allman looked a little shaken as Matthew and the two FBI agents met them outside the room.

"That's all we needed," said one of the FBI agents as they started down the hallway.

"Good work in there," said Agent Shedrick over his shoulder to Allman as they walked briskly away. "That's exactly what we needed. Now we can go after O'Connell."

"Hey!" said Danbury, jogging after them. "If you find anything else. Anything related to my murder investigation. I expect a notification."

When they ignored him, Danbury stepped in front of Agent Shedrick, cutting him off.

"I'm serious," said Danbury forcefully. "This is a joint investigation. Agreed on at the highest levels. In both our organizations. Don't make me force information out of you. I will if I have to."

"OK, Detective, I hear you. I'll let you know if we find anything," Matthew heard Agent Shedrick say before disappearing through the door to the lobby at the end of the hallway.

Because the FBI agents he had encountered earlier had been much more cooperative, friendlier, and easier to work with, Matthew didn't know what to make of these two. They had said little and contributed even less. He didn't even know the name of the other agent, just Shedrick. They were odd birds, lone wolves, Matthew thought before running out of animal cliches.

Danbury returned to the observation booth with Allman, and all three of them stepped back inside. Matthew realized how soundproofed the building must be. The volume was lowered significantly from the soundboard, but still, they could hear the shouts and screams, threats, and accusations of Katz from the next room. Mostly, Katz seemed to be yelling abuse at Wilson, threatening him for what he'd told the authorities.

Matthew had seen angry. He had been angry. But this was a whole new level of rage that he was thankful never to have witnessed before. He could, however, relate to the feeling of having rage uncontrollably welling up and threatening to come pouring out. If this was the result of failing to stuff it back down, he'd been right to be worried about his own anger issues.

That thought worried him exceedingly, and he felt a shiver down his spine as he wondered how disparate they really were, he and Katz. It was the most unsettling thought he could recall having had.

43 ~ Golden bow

"Thank you, Dr. Allman," said Danbury. "You did what I couldn't have done. Wilson needed your calming touch. And your reassurance. To draw him out. To feel comfortable. With telling us about Katz."

"You're welcome," answered Allman. "But I'm exhausted. Do you need me for anything else?"

"Not tonight," said Danbury. "We'll need you tomorrow. We have more questions for Wilson. About the other two murders. We might also need evals. On O'Connell. And whoever else we dig up."

"OK, no problem," said Allman, pulling her coat from the stack folded across the low chair that had sat, unoccupied, against the back wall of the room.

Matthew grabbed his coat and was surprised to see Danbury reach for his.

"I'll walk you out," Danbury said to Allman.

"No need. I'm a grown woman. Besides which," she said, motioning through the glass at Katz, who hadn't yet burned out on his tirade. "You caught the monster."

"One of them," Danbury muttered. "OK. I have a few loose ends. Paperwork to finish here anyway."

As Allman slipped out of the observation room, Danbury turned to Matthew. "You out, too, Doc?"

"Yeah, unless you need me for anything else tonight, I hope to go home and sleep well," he answered, trying but failing to stifle a yawn. It was incredible to him that they could be so nonchalant when there was another human being in the next room raging at the top of his voice. Katz was throwing the chairs, which apparently were the only things not bolted down, around the room, slamming them into the window and walls. All of that must have been heavily reinforced because nobody seemed concerned about it.

As they stepped from the darkened observation room and back into the brightly lit hallway, Matthew squinted at the silhouette of a familiar figure ambling toward them. He recognized the detective who'd been on the sting operation the night before and in the room earlier.

"Conover," said Danbury, checking his watch. "I didn't know you were still here."

"Yeah, just getting the paperwork finished up for all of this."

"Thanks for that," said Danbury as Matthew marveled. "I appreciate it. I was going to do that next."

"Sure thing. Did I miss anything?"

Danbury looked at Matthew and they both laughed. That question was akin to walking into a room just as the Super Bowl ended after a close game in which the underdog had finally prevailed and asking how the game had gone. There was no effective short answer.

"You missed Wilson confessing," said Danbury.

"I missed *what*?" exclaimed Conover. "I missed all the excitement!"

"He was more pointing a finger at Katz than actually confessing," said Matthew. "But apparently, that's close enough in a court of law. And you didn't miss all of the excitement. Katz is back now, if you want to see what true rage looks like."

"I missed tying things up," said Detective Conover.

"Mostly," admitted Danbury. "Big shiny package. Huge gold bow."

"It's not every day you get that handed to you," replied Conover, looking deflated.

"Katz is still railing against it," offered Danbury. "Testing the soundproofing. And the integrity of the room structure. At least he was a minute ago. If you want to watch. He's putting on a show."

"Anything else you need me to do tonight?"

"Just one more thing," said Danbury.

"Yeah, what's that?" Conover asked hopefully.

"Wilson also pointed to O'Connell."

"Charlene O'Connell?"

"No, Phillip. The feds are on their way now. To question him. They're getting a search warrant. I need to be close behind. Or they'll conveniently forget to include us. To share whatever they find. Would you move Katz to a holding cell?" Danbury asked, indicating the interrogation room. "When he calms down?"

"Yeah, I got it."

"Thanks, Conover," said Danbury as he and Matthew turned to walk out together. They handed in Matthew's badge, donned their coats, and stepped out of the building and into the chilly night air.

"Hey, Danbury, tell me something."

"What's that, Doc?"

"That rage that we saw in there. Do you ever feel that way about some of the people you question or arrest?"

"Sometimes," said Danbury, looking at Matthew quizzically.

"Like when Katz was talking about Penn, goading you, really. You deal with the dregs of society. How do you cope with that?"

"The people? Or the anger?"

"Both, I guess," said Matthew, trying to define it more precisely himself.

"Penn has helped. To burn off a lot of steam." When Matthew stared oddly back at him, Danbury laughed, blushing slightly, and clarified, "I mean at her gym. She enrolled me in kickboxing. And I do some work on my own. I lift more now too."

"Oh," said Matthew. "Got it."

"Where was your mind, Doc?" asked Danbury with a smirk.

"At the gym, dealing with rage," he answered promptly, chuckling.

"You should join," said Danbury.

"I should," responded Matthew. "I really should."

"G'night, Doc," said Danbury.

"Keep me posted tomorrow," reminded Matthew. "Update me on whatever you find out tonight."

"Sure, Doc. How does lunch sound? Assuming I'm free by then."

Matthew pondered that a moment, thinking about how busy Mondays usually were during the cold and flu season, but then he remembered that Dr. Rob should have flown back in from his trip with Ariel the day before, and he'd be back in the office in the morning.

"OK. I'll text you after I get home. I need to look through my schedule to see my patient load for the morning."

"Sounds good," said Danbury as he climbed into the big black SUV parked at the curb and Matthew continued up to the parking deck to retrieve his Corvette.

The drive across town wasn't bad at all at this time on a Sunday night, and Matthew was relieved to find his home well lit and looking undisturbed. He was annoyed, though, at the feeling of foreboding, like he'd been violated, the sensation of needing to look over his shoulder. His haven had been invaded, and he was wondering if he would have to move to get past the uneasy feeling when he approached his home these days.

It wasn't his place of peaceful solitude anymore; it was no longer the tranquil escape from the rest of the world that he had so carefully chosen. His world had been invaded. Again.

The first thing he knew he needed to do was feed and care for the cats, two out of the three of whom were waiting for him at the door. He felt bad for Maxine, who had been cloistered alone in the spare bedroom. After the cats had all had their meals and he'd taken the dishes up, he let her out. She and Fluffykins would just have to work it out.

Sitting down at the little desk in his living room long enough to check his schedule for the next day, he looked through the records of the patients he'd be seeing. Then, he texted Danbury to say that he could do a late lunch at one, and he began going through his usual evening routine. After locking up, turning on strategic outdoor lights, and setting everything up for the morning, Matthew fell into bed, exhausted.

Sleep came in fits and starts. When he awoke, Matthew knew that he'd dreamed of aggressive, shadowy figures. He'd still been groggy when FaceTiming with Cici. She was elated to learn they had finally caught their killer, and she was happy to hear that her colleague, Kennedy Reynolds, had been able to help Matthew with the legal ramifications of that situation in her absence.

Planning the day in his mind, Matthew went through his usual morning routine and then drove the short distance into Peak. Contacting the security company to convince them to place his job request at the top of their queue was his first task of the morning. Explaining his recent home invasion, despite the security he currently had in place, during which he was held at gunpoint, made the company more amenable to his request.

After they'd promised to arrive on Wednesday, he hesitated about making the next call he was contemplating. He knew he needed to do something, so he placed the call to make the appointment before starting on his morning roster of patients.

The morning flew by, and Matthew switched his lab coat for his bomber jacket at one to go meet Danbury. Walking the short distance to Peak Eats, he heard the bell jingle overhead as he entered, and Danbury nodded to him from the back corner, his usual spot.

One of the younger waitresses, Evie, bounced up to the table before Matthew could hang his coat and get settled in. She had apparently won the lottery to see which of them would get to serve him and Danbury. That was all such a foreign concept to Matthew still. After Penn had pointed it out, though, he'd seen it repeatedly himself, the waitresses vying for his attention and Danbury's. Mallory, who usually seemed to win the right to serve them, was nowhere in sight. That explained Evie's quick approach.

Taking the seat across from Danbury, Matthew slid into the booth as Evie quickly placed water glasses and cutlery in front of both men.

"Hey, Doc," greeted Danbury. "Did you sleep better last night?"

Matthew shrugged. "I slept last night, so I guess that's something.

Did you?"

"I got a couple of hours," said Danbury.

They paused as Evie returned to take their orders. "I don't mean to rush you," she apologized, grinning widely at them, "but you do usually seem to know what you want."

"No problem," said Matthew. It was Monday in the winter, so he already knew that the specials were beef stew and chili. "I'd like the special today, the beef stew, with a Caesar salad."

"Double that. But skip the salad," said Danbury as Evie turned to him, smiling sweetly.

"Would you like anything else to drink? Other than your water?"

"No thanks," said Matthew. "I'll get a coffee before we leave."

"Hot tea," said Danbury. "And sugar."

"Got it," she said. "Any lemon for your tea?"

"Sounds good," said Danbury.

When she'd sashayed back out of hearing range, Matthew asked, "What happened last night with O'Connell? Did you get anywhere?"

"Yes, and no," said Danbury. "He said he had hurt no one. Not physically anyway. He vehemently insisted. He pointed the finger at Katz. When we pressed him. Except that he called him Wilson. We asked leading questions. To see if he knew about Katz. He didn't give it away. If he knew."

"Interesting. From what we saw, calling Katz 'Wilson' got an explosive response. Maybe O'Connell just never called him by name."

"Probably not out loud," said Danbury. "They probably never called each other by name. In any conversation. Neither would want paths back to themselves. Not from each other."

"That makes sense," Matthew answered. "Did he give you anything specific on Wilson?"

"Just that it was Wilson. If anybody was physically harmed. Not him. He'd never hurt anyone."

"Well, at least not directly. Giving the women drugs isn't exactly helping them. What happened when you asked him about the diamonds?"

"That's the no. Of the yes and no. He clammed up. And then lawyered up. We can't get anything else out of him. Not on that topic. But that's OK. He's given us what we need. Pointing the finger at Wilson. And that he did. It's the feds' job now. To process him for the diamonds. That was their goal all along. They were using the murders. To find him. To pick him up for questioning. And to hold Wilson or Katz. That whole thing is confusing."

"It is to me too," agreed Matthew. "Watching Allman question him last night just made it more confusing. It was like Wilson knew the information about Katz, but he didn't remember it or wouldn't offer it up until she asked about it specifically."

"He did remember. We got more this morning. From Wilson. On Kent and Nichols. Wilson said Katz bragged about it. How nobody ever got in his way. Not for long."

"Got in his way how?" asked Matthew.

"Wilson said Kent tried to come to Misty's rescue. So Katz silenced him. Permanently. Then Nichols tried to stop him. When Katz was 'borrowing' the freezer truck. That was his word. He was going to 'borrow' it. Nichols had to be silenced too."

"Oh! You have a confession for all three murders now? That's tying it up nicely." After a momentary pause in which Matthew's eyebrow raised and his foot was tapping under the table in concentration, he added, "I wonder, though, if Wilson shouldn't be asked some of the same questions again. He readily agreed with everything Dr. Allman asked last night. Maybe he should be asked again and presented with some options so that nobody could ever accuse you of leading him with those answers."

"What do you mean?"

"I know from Cici that there's such an objection as 'leading the witness' in the courtroom, and I wonder if that applies here. For example, instead of asking Wilson if Katz was using the HavocWreaker13 handle, you could ask again and present him with three different options. HavocWreaker13 is one among several, and you ask him to choose from them. It's like Wilson knows, in the recesses of his mind, all of the information about Katz. But the way you pull it out might be important to the legal proceedings against him."

Danbury leaned back and chuckled. "You want this tied up tightly, don't you?"

"I do."

"Yeah, me too."

"What was that you told Detective Conover last night? Shiny package, big gold bow?"

"That was it. And that's a good plan," said Danbury. "I like it. I'll talk to Allman about it."

"So what happens next?" asked Matthew.

Danbury hesitated as Evie brought his tea and the lemons and then said, "We're formally charging him. Getting advised on how to do that. If we need charges against both. Katz and Wilson. Or just Wilson. That's the guy's legal name. Looks like it's Wilson or both. I'd go for both. Just to cover my bases. But we're waiting on legal to get back to us. The state lawyers."

"There's no chance for that guy, whatever name or persona he's going by at the moment, to get out of there, right?"

"No chance. The recordings are airtight. From last night and this morning. It's plenty to hold him on. And to charge him with. Allman got what we needed. She's coming back later today. We'll ask for the confessions again. Without leading the witness. As you said, we'll just watch closely. Like we did this morning. To keep from triggering Katz. She blames that on me. Says she'd have seen the transition. If I weren't talking in her ear."

"But you weren't. Not when that happened."

"Yeah," said Danbury with a chuckle. "I know. But didn't argue. Because she got Kent and Nichols out of him. Signed, sealed, and delivered."

"You know," said Matthew after pondering a moment, "this guy Katz isn't that brilliant."

"Come again?"

"Either he's not that brilliant or he let his hyperfixation on his ultimate goal get in the way of his common sense."

"How so?"

"Katz knew you had Kincaid in custody when he didn't come to the Lingle Plantation."

"Yeah."

"And Kincaid knew Katz wanted the cat's collar. Logically, he could assume that Kincaid would have told us that."

"Right."

"So why would I still have the cat's collar with the cat at my house? Why come after me?"

"Huh. You're right. There was a flaw in his logic."

"A pretty big one."

Evie arrived with their meals, and Matthew said a blessing.

As they dug in, Danbury said, between bites, "I have other updates. Some good news you'll like."

44 ~ Hope reigns

"What's the good news?" asked Matthew.

"Several things. Leo can pick up Maxine this evening. If that works for you?"

"I should be home by about seven thirty. If he can come then, I'll be there. I can text him when I get home."

"I'll relay the message."

"Thanks," answered Matthew.

"Cara got her grandmother to agree. To take Fluffykins. I can bring her over later. Unless you want to."

"That's great! I know Cara really wanted her. And Misty would want Cara to care for her. I can take Fluffykins to her, but I'm going to get her a cat carrier first. They'll need one for regular vet visits later anyway." Max had been a perfect host, and the cats had managed to get along well, but Matthew would be happy to be back to just the two of them again.

The table grew quiet as Danbury inhaled his food until Matthew prodded, "What else? You said several things."

Swallowing hard, Danbury asked, "Remember Gerard?"

"The guy running the homeless camp in the woods behind the hotel?"

"That's the one. He's going to do it officially."

"How's that?"

"At the homeless shelter in downtown Raleigh. They need a live-in manager. Gerard speaks Spanish. And he connects with homeless vets. He's the right guy for the job. The director at the shelter agreed to talk to him."

"Good luck convincing him to talk to them, though," said Matthew between bites. "He seemed to value his seclusion and being undisturbed in it."

"True. He likes being off the grid. But he likes helping people more. He talked to them on Friday. And starts later this week."

"That's great news too!" said Matthew, looking at Danbury in amazement. "You orchestrated that?"

"Mostly," said Danbury, ducking his head for another bite of his lunch.

"I wish we had such great news for Mira and Joseph," said Matthew slowly. "Do you know where they ended up?"

"I wasn't finished yet," said Danbury, swallowing. "Mira and Joseph are getting green cards."

"How did they manage that?" asked Matthew in surprise.

"A buddy of mine in ICE. He has connections. He's the one who got Joseph released. From being deported. I got the call from him this morning. Their applications are going through," said Danbury. "I told him Joseph was a structural engineer. Back in Cuba. It's a valued profession here."

"He was?" asked Matthew. "That's why he was working construction jobs. That all makes sense now."

"He can keep working them," said Danbury. "And do it legally soon."

"Did they find their daughter?"

"They did. They're all renting a house together. All five and a half of them."

"A half?"

"Their daughter, Maria, is pregnant. The guy she married has a green card."

"So they're going to be OK," said Matthew, happily taking it all in.

"That's really great news!"

Looking up, he realized that Danbury had finished eating, and his plate was being whisked away by Evie. "Any dessert, gentlemen?" she asked sweetly as Matthew continued to work on his lunch.

"None for me," said Matthew. "But that cup of coffee would be great now."

"Lots of cream and lots of sugar, coming right up." She smiled at him. Turning to Danbury, she asked, "Any dessert for you, sir?"

"What sort of pie do you have today?"

"Blueberry, banana cream, and chocolate chess," she answered.

"A slice of chocolate chess," said Danbury.

"Yeah, make that two. That does sound good," Matthew said, grinning.

"Perfect. That'll go great with the coffee," Evie cheerfully agreed. "I'll get it right out for you."

After Matthew had finished the final bite of his lunch, he asked, "Did Sherwanda ever resurface anywhere?"

"Not yet. We're on the lookout. We'll take her to Gerard. At the homeless shelter. If she does. She could be several states away by now."

"I don't think so," said Matthew pensively. "I think you'll find her. Just keep an eye on the street corners at the bigger intersections. She was teaching Mira to panhandle, and I think she's a pro at it."

"Maybe so," responded Danbury thoughtfully. "Anything is possible. Just one more thing, Doc."

Matthew wasn't sure what to expect, so he just leaned back into the upholstered booth seat and waited to hear what that could be.

"You agreed to see the women. The ones at the club, right?"

"You mean medically?" Matthew asked, eyebrow raised.

Danbury laughed. "Yeah, medically."

"I did, but then you ticked off Charlene before I could ask her about it."

"Yeah, well. I did ask her, though. Last night. And she agreed. If you're still up for it."

Matthew sat staring at Danbury in disbelief. "I am. Steven Garner, our senior partner, was very supportive of the idea. Maybe it could be a regular thing."

"Charlene suggested once a month. A couple of hours. One afternoon each month."

"That should work. We can plan the dates ahead," said Matthew. "I can set a monthly date with her and then ask for the staff to accompany me. I'll need one of the female nurses or Megan Sims, our PA, for that population. I don't want anything misconstrued, so I'll have to be careful."

"I'm just the messenger. You can work out the details," said Danbury dismissively, picking up his fork in anticipation as his eyes followed the slices of chocolate pie that Evie was bringing them. She slid the plates in front of them and set Matthew's coffee carefully on the table with cream, sugar, and pleasantries about enjoying them.

"Speaking of Charlene, what happens to her? I guess they hauled Phillip off last night?"

"Yeah, he's out of her hair," said Danbury between bites of pie. "At least for now."

"And she's innocent of everything? She wasn't involved with the drugs, diamonds, and whatever else he was running out of their club?"

"She wasn't aware of any of it," replied Danbury, finishing his final bite of pie before Matthew had begun eating his. "They both said that. She was furious. When she learned about the money laundering. And the drug running. Both out of her club. She yelled at Phillip. She said he wasn't helping. Her goal was to save the business. He was jeopardizing it all. Everything she'd worked so hard to build. He seemed happy to leave after that. Even under FBI escort. And in handcuffs."

"Yeah, I wouldn't want to be under her wrath. I think she can hold her own."

"No doubt. She'll be fine without Phillip. She's shut down the porn film business. All aboveboard for her now."

"I wonder what Preston Priestly will do for work now?" asked Matthew rhetorically. It wasn't that he cared at all. He really didn't like the guy, and that hadn't changed.

"Just one last question," said Matthew, thinking back through the information they'd gleaned the evening before from Wilson about Katz. "Do you know how the diamond got in Misty's tooth?"

"Not conclusively. Best guess? Misty put it there herself. She knew she wasn't going to walk away. Not from Katz. She likely hid it there. Bit down on it to embed it. For whoever found her. For us, basically. And she stuck it to Katz in the process. He was down one more diamond. Even if he got the cat's collar. And even if she'd never been found."

"Huh," said Matthew. "Smart thinking, and probably fast thinking too. It's sad, though, that she never met her full potential."

"It is sad. She's being shipped. Back to Mississippi. She'll be buried beside her daughter. Early next week."

"That sounds perfect. Like exactly what she'd want if you could have asked her."

"That's what we thought."

"How is that possible, though? I mean, financially. Her car was destroyed, and she didn't own anything else, did she?"

"Not that we've found. We took up a collection. Last week. Most of the precinct contributed. Penn contributed. So did Agent Shedrick. Believe it or not."

"Really? Is it too late for one more?"

"You don't have to do that, Doc. You've done plenty," said Danbury, sliding his plate to the edge of the table.

"I want to do it. Just tell me how."

"There's a fund. I'll text you the information."

"Great," said Matthew, regarding Danbury with new respect. It was one thing that a detective still had such a heart for people, but a homicide detective must see the worst in the worst of people. *Danbury meets the world with a hardened exterior, but Penn is right that he is a really good guy underneath*, Matthew thought.

*****

After a busy Monday, Matthew managed to leave the office at a decent time. He had one last appointment that evening, an important one. As he navigated around the city of Raleigh to reach the northern sector, he was contemplating how the conversation might go. He'd made the call just that morning and was surprised to get a quick response and a meeting that same day.

"Matthew, come on in," said Pastor Mark. "Or should I call you Dr. Paine now?"

"You've known me since I was born," said Matthew, shaking the senior pastor's outstretched hand. "You can always call me Matthew, Pastor Mark."

"And you can just call me Mark. Have a seat and tell me what's going on with you."

"I really appreciate you taking the time to talk to me," began Matthew. Though lately the senior pastor, Mark Kushner, had handed a good deal of the teaching over to one of the younger pastors, Matthew knew that he was still a very busy man.

"Sure, you know I'm always here for you and your family. What's on your mind?"

Matthew tried to explain the anger he'd been feeling as he'd dealt with the worst of society—thieves, rapists, murderers—and how sometimes he felt as if he were barely keeping a lid on the rage that welled up inside of him, threatening to burst out. It wasn't a part of himself that he knew existed until he'd started dealing with that population.

"I haven't really acted on the rage," said Matthew thoughtfully. Remembering that he'd punched a guy in Miami before Danbury had intervened and that he'd stood on the neck of another one who had broken into his house the spring before, when his best friend from childhood had stopped him, he paused. Then, he amended, "Well, at least I haven't acted on it much. I just don't like it when I feel like it's about to overpower me and I might explode. It's like I'm about to lose control."

"The fact that you're concerned about the possibility of acting on it is a good sign," said Pastor Mark.

Mark began to ask questions to help Matthew assess his thoughts and reactions. They discussed the triggers, coping strategies, and scripture to provide insight. Matthew, in that moment, felt more hopeful than he had in months, and he was entirely thankful for his senior pastor's wisdom and willingness to share it with him.

After Mark prayed with him, Matthew left the church office feeling a lightness that he hadn't felt in a while. He hadn't wanted to give up working alongside Danbury, but he'd been willing to do exactly that if it was the only way to avoid the rage.

Maybe there was hope, though, that he could continue his side job, as he'd come to think of it, and not lose himself in the process. Hope was a good thing, he thought. Actually, hope was a great thing. He smiled to himself and was humming one of the songs he'd heard in church on Sunday as he slid into the Corvette and headed for home.

Epilogue ~ A week later

As Matthew stepped out into the late-afternoon sun that was perched on the top of the tree line across the parking lot, Danbury looked over at him and asked, "Feel better, Doc?"

"Oh yeah, it's always a great feeling to beat the stuffing out of an innocent bag," answered Matthew with a grin.

They were leaving Penn's gym, where they'd just showered after working out.

"Hey, you asked me what I did. To work off the frustration from the job. Dealing with the criminals I catch. And the ones I don't. That was it."

"Yeah, and it's a good workout," admitted Matthew. "It's not that I don't need that these days. I get too sedentary during the winter months."

"You want to grab something to eat?"

"I would, but I've got an appointment. I'm meeting with my pastor again. He's helping me to work through this anger issue. It's bothered me a lot, and he's giving me some great perspective and management help."

"Yeah?" said Danbury, and then he hesitated. "I might want to talk to him too."

"About anger management?"

"No," said Danbury, hesitating longer. "About marriage."

"What?" asked Matthew, both excited and surprised. "You and Penn haven't been together a year yet."

"Nearly a year," said Danbury. "And who else would put up with me? My crazy schedule doesn't bother her. When you know it's right, sometimes it doesn't take you seven or eight years to seal the deal, you know?"

Matthew wasn't sure what to respond to first. There was the fact that he'd probably just heard the longest sentence Danbury had uttered all at once. And the fact that Danbury was clearly poking at Matthew and Cici's long dating history. The overriding fact, though, was that the guy was thinking about getting married.

"You're serious?" asked Matthew, incredulous.

"Completely."

"And you want to talk to my pastor?"

"Serious about that too."

"OK," said Matthew, pulling out his phone and tapping it to share Pastor Mark's contact information. "There's how to reach him. His name is Mark Kushner, and he's the senior pastor. I can tell him you're going to call if you want?"

"Yeah, an introduction is good. I haven't been in a church in a while. Not since I was a kid. There was too much hypocrisy. I saw it when I was a teenager. And I just quit going."

"Mark would be the first person to tell you that there are no perfect churches. Because they're filled with imperfect people. But I can say that mine is pretty open and honest about that, and they don't waste time fighting over stupid traditions like the type of music, any sort of dress code, or the color of the carpet."

"That's refreshing. Hey, Doc, while we're doing this heart-to-heart stuff," began Danbury, but then he hesitated.

"Yeah?"

"Would you consider being my best man?"

Matthew was seriously surprised by this. "Me? You want me to do that? I mean, I'd be happy to, but what about Leo?"

"I want Leo in the wedding. I know Penn will too. But I can rely on you. You're solid."

Matthew wasn't sure what to make of that remark, but they parted with the understanding that Matthew would stand up for Danbury when he and Penn got married. They wanted a small wedding, which made sense, given their general lack of families, and they wanted to do it outdoors at a park in Peak in the spring.

All of that made Matthew think about Cici returning in the spring. Maybe part of what he'd been holding back from wasn't Cici at all. Maybe it was the part of himself that scared him, the anger that threatened to overtake him. Maybe he was more ready to buy that ring and propose to the woman he loved than he'd thought.

Those thoughts carried him all the way to the other side of Raleigh, and it was with a goofy grin on his face that he walked into the church building, ready to meet with his pastor. What he heard when he got there wasn't at all what he was expecting, though.

First, they discussed a book that Mark had recommended and Matthew had read. After Matthew shared the insights he'd gained from it and Mark added a few additional words of wisdom, the conversation turned to Danbury's upcoming proposal to Penn. Pastor Mark agreed to meet with Danbury first, but he explained that it was his policy to meet with the couple together for a few months before he married them.

"Marriage counseling prior to making the commitment, fully understanding what that means, that's the best way I've seen to prevent divorce," said Pastor Mark. "They'll go into it eyes wide open when I'm finished counseling with them."

"That makes sense," said Matthew. "That makes really good sense. I might be next."

He watched the grin spread across the face of the man who'd been his pastor his whole life, the guy who'd baptized him, watched him grow up, and cheered him on as he'd gone off to college and then to medical school. "You mean that pretty redhead who was here with your family through the holiday season?"

"That's the one. That's Cici. Just don't call her a redhead. She'll quickly tell anyone, even you, that she's a strawberry blonde. I think maybe when she gets back from London in the spring, it might be time to pop that question," said Matthew, matching Pastor Mark's grin with his own.

"Oh, I remember Cici," said Pastor Mark, nodding his head. "She's an attorney, right?"

Matthew nodded, and Pastor Mark joked, "I won't hold that against her. Your sister introduced us while you were picking up your niece from the children's area one Sunday. Monica seemed pleased to do that introduction. And I saw the two of you together. This isn't the huge surprise you might think it is."

"Oh," said Matthew. He knew he'd never had a poker face, but it was probably even easier to read by people who had known him his whole life.

"You know I'll be happy to meet with the two of you, as well. In fact, I'd be delighted. It's always wonderful to watch you kids grow up and then send you on to create families of your own. It's one of the things I get excited about in this profession."

"Thank you, Pastor Mark. I appreciate that."

"Now, I do have something else that I need to talk to you about, Matthew. I wanted to talk to you about a situation that I need your help with. Yours and your friend Danbury's, if you're both willing. We can certainly talk and pray about all of it before you agree to get involved. And we will."

"I can always ask. Do you want to talk to him about it right now?"

"The sooner, the better," answered Pastor Mark, so Matthew pulled his phone from his pocket and tapped to place the call.

"Hey, Doc. What's up?" he heard Danbury's voice answer promptly. Ironically, the usual roles were reversed, flipping Matthew's universe on its axis. Instead of being summoned by Danbury to help, Matthew was doing the summoning this time.

Connect with us!

Join the author group to get all the latest updates on new releases—line the next book in the Matthew Paine Mystery series—events, giveaways, and more!

https://cypressrivermedia.com/connect-with-us

Start at the beginning

Want to start from the beginning of the Matthew Paine Mystery series?

- Get the prequel, *Pre Kill*, for free!

    https://dl.bookfunnel.com/k3xwi6l5f4

- Get Dead Spots, first in the series, from your local bookstore or all major online retailers:

    https://buy.bookfunnel.com/bgb7d97qo9

About the Author

Lee Clark is a coffeeholic and a dark chocoholic who resides in North Carolina with spouse, two mostly grown children who are in and out, and a diminishing petting zoo of geriatric dog and cats.

A North Carolina native, Clark is originally from Raleigh, with family roots in Virginia. Clark attended Campbell University, obtained a degree in Journalism from East Carolina University, and then a Master's in Technical Communication from North Carolina State University. After working in the software technology industry for over 20 years, creating and building highly technical user information for software developers, Clark decided it was time to pursue a true passion: fictional writing.

The Matthew Paine character is a fictional character, though inspired by two very important men in the author's life, brother Sean and son Will. Both will see characteristics of themselves in the character and identify with some of Matthew's struggles.

Made in the USA
Middletown, DE
22 May 2023

31106121R00225